"Those who prefer a leisurely pace, a touch of screwball comedy, and gentle puzzles in their mysteries will enjoy this paean to small-town nosiness and steadfast loyalties." —*Publishers Weekly*

Miss Julia Paints the Town

"Miss Julia's feisty attitude has won the hearts of so many fans."
—*BookPage*

"A fun confection where Miss Julia, in letting go of some of her own hidebound ideas and social prejudices, learns that her worst enemy may well be the guy she helped elect . . . and her best ally may be one she's always thought beneath her contempt. Yes, Miss Julia is back, and I, for one, am one happy camper." —J. A. Jance

PENGUIN BOOKS

MISS JULIA STIRS UP TROUBLE

Ann B. Ross holds a doctorate in English from the University of North Carolina, Chapel Hill, and has taught literature at the University of North Carolina at Asheville. She is the author of thirteen previous novels featuring the popular Southern heroine Miss Julia. She lives in Hendersonville, North Carolina.

Miss Julia Stirs Up Trouble

ANN B. ROSS

PENGUIN BOOKS

PENGUIN BOOKS
Published by the Penguin Group
Penguin Group (USA) LLC
375 Hudson Street
New York, New York 10014

USA | Canada | UK | Ireland | Australia | New Zealand | India | South Africa | China
penguin.com
A Penguin Random House Company

First published in the United States of America by Viking Penguin,
a member of Penguin Group (USA) Inc., 2013
Published in Penguin Books 2014

THE LIBRARY OF CONGRESS HAS CATALOGED THE HARDCOVER EDITION AS FOLLOWS:
Ross, Ann B.
Miss Julia stirs up trouble / Ann B. Ross.
pages   cm
ISBN 978-0-670-02610-4 (hc.)
ISBN 978-0-14-312489-4 (pbk.)
1. Springer, Julia (Fictitious character)—Fiction.   2. Women—North Carolina—Fiction.
3. Cooking—Fiction.   4. North Carolina—Fiction.   5. Domestic fiction.   I. Title.
PS3568.O84198M5725 2013
813'.54—dc23
2012039880

Set in Fairfield LT Std
Designed by Alissa Amell

146119709

This book is for Pamela Brown Silvers and for Patricia Toner, computer experts extraordinaire. Each of them has, at various times and for various reasons (mostly because of errors on my part), rescued me from the clutches of my wayward computer: For Pat who has the patience of Job and for Pam who always has the answers. Thank you.

The recipes collected by Miss Julia for Hazel Marie's edification can be found within the text. Lillian's recipes for side dishes and the like are listed at the end. A complete list of the recipes with page numbers is in the back of the book. Enjoy!

Chapter 1

Stepping carefully onto the newly sodded patches of grass at the side of the house, I stood by a hydrangea bush for a few minutes, admiring the graceful lines of my new Williamsburg chimney. Reassured that it was worth what it had cost to have it, I strolled across the lawn to the arbor near the back fence. After brushing dried leaves from the bench, I sat down to revel in the glorious October day. I marveled at the clear, blue sky—Carolina blue, as Lloyd called it—and the molten gold leaves of the gingko tree on the edge of Mildred's lawn next door. A light breeze ruffled through the almost leafless wisteria vine overhead, as a feeling of peace and gratitude for our blessings filled my soul. All the carpenters, painters, paperhangers, plumbers, and brick masons were long gone, leaving us with a remodeled and redecorated house. Well, not the whole house, but three rooms had been re-modeled and redecorated. Even better, extra furnishings, like the bedroom rug, which had been rolled into a stumbling block in the hall, were out of the house and the mattress was off the dining room table and back on our bed where it belonged. My house had been returned to its ordered self, and at least for these few minutes, all seemed right with the world.

Sam, my darling husband—acquired late in life, but all the more precious because of it—was home from his travels, working now in his new office in the old sunroom upstairs and loving it. "The best and most efficient office I've ever had, Julia," he'd told me, but I think that was because I'd had the foresight to put in the semblance of a tiny kitchen in a closet—a coffeepot and an under-the-counter refrigerator so he didn't have to tromp downstairs every time he wanted something to drink. The hall bathroom was right next door, too.

And Lloyd. My heart lifted as I thought of the boy foisted on me by my deceased first husband by way of a long-term adulterous situation, the boy who had become the center of my life. In spite of the fact that his mother was now well and truly married to Mr. Pickens—an event I'd almost despaired of ever happening— Lloyd didn't seem eager to leave my house for theirs. He was still in and out, spending the school week with Sam and me and most weekends with his mother and Mr. Pickens four blocks away in Sam's old house. I worried a little that the odd arrangement would warp his character but, on the other hand, having two homes with two helpings of being loved and wanted couldn't be harmful. Both apprehensive and excited, he'd started his first year of high school and now, after a couple of months, he was finding that a quick intelligence and a sunny disposition were making a place for him. I couldn't help but notice that he was still smaller and, in spite of his usual serious demeanor, younger-seeming than his classmates, many of whom were on the verge of manhood with their husky physiques and voices. And, actually, he *was* younger, for Hazel Marie had let him skip a grade before they came to live with me. Yet I had no worries about Lloyd fitting in. He was making new friends and meeting the new challenges set by his teachers. He was the joy of my life and, as I thought of him, I knew that at least for this moment in time, all was right with him and with the world.

Hazel Marie had her challenges as well, and to my constant amazement, considering the fact that she'd had such a disreputable background to overcome, she was meeting them head on. Who would have ever thought that the overpainted woman who'd flounced up to my door, bastard son by her side, announcing to me and the world what Wesley Lloyd Springer had been doing before he passed over, would turn out to be a sweet and valued friend, as well as an accepted member of Abbotsville society, such as it was?

Those twin baby girls—born, I am happy to say, firmly within wedlock—took almost all her time, but she would have it no other way. I had made the mistake of suggesting within Latisha's hearing that she employ a nanny or, at least, an au pair to give her a rest from the constant demands. Hazel Marie rejected the suggestion— she couldn't turn her babies over to anyone else—but Latisha decided that when she grew up she wanted to be either an au pair, once she learned what an au pair was, or a rock star. Lillian just rolled her eyes at her little great-grand.

Mr. J. D. Pickens, an erstwhile rambling man, seemed as contented as I'd ever known him to be, or as a freelance private investigator can be. I'd fretted a little about Hazel Marie's devotion to those babies, fearful that he'd feel left out, which I understand can occur when a wife is too busy or too tired to address her marital duties. When I carefully broached the subject to Hazel Marie, she assured me that Mr. Pickens lacked nothing in that department, and from what I can tell by the smug look on his face, she wasn't wrong. James, who'd looked after Sam for years before our marriage disrupted their cozy nest, is still with the Pickens family and, though he and I have a prickly relationship, I'm grateful that their kitchen is in good hands, which means that no one is going hungry. James rarely turns his hands in the rest of the house, but with playpens and toys and strollers and high chairs strewn everywhere, there's not much he can do in the way of keeping a neat house.

I leaned my head back against the bench, thinking with deep pleasure about my loved ones, safe and thriving and prospering— all was, indeed, right with my world.

"Miss Julia!" I looked up to see Lillian waving a dishrag at me from the back stoop. *"Miss Hazel Marie wants you!"*

I came to my feet and hurried to the house. It wasn't like Lillian to yell across the yard, so one drastic image after another flashed through my mind.

"What is it?" I gasped, my heart pounding by the time I reached her. "Is it Lloyd? The babies?"

"Neither one," Lillian said, her eyes big. "They jus' take James to the hospital."

"Oh, my word." I flew to the telephone and picked it up. "Hazel Marie? What happened?"

"He fell, Miss Julia!" Hazel Marie's voice was filled with panic. "Down the stairs on the side of the garage, you know, coming down from his apartment. I was so scared I didn't know what to do, but thank goodness J.D. was here. He called the EMTs, and he just called me from the emergency room. James's right wrist or hand or something is broken so he has to have a cast. And he sprained his ankle, too, but they just wrapped it up." She stopped and took a deep breath with a catch of fear beneath it. "I thought he'd killed himself."

"But he's all right?" I asked. "I mean, other than that?"

"J.D.'s bringing him home, so I guess so. I'm putting him in the back bedroom because he can't go up and down the stairs anytime soon, and I'll feel better having him close by. He can't even walk by himself, Miss Julia."

"Oh, my. But they'll give him some crutches, won't they?"

"J.D. said he can't use them because the cast practically covers his hand. Oh, the poor thing—we're all so upset over it."

They were going to be upset over more than that, I thought, when Hazel Marie, the world's most inept cook, had to take James's place in the kitchen.

It just goes to show that when you have a few minutes to glory in everything being right with the world, you'd better enjoy them while you can. It's never long before something comes along to turn your world inside out and upside down again.

"We better take supper to 'em," Lillian said, opening the freezer door. "Sound like nobody fit to do any cookin' over there, so good thing I got enough pork chops to go 'round."

"Yes, thank you, Lillian. I'll run up and tell Sam about James."

"He already know," Lillian said, just as I heard Sam's footsteps on the stairs. "He pick up the phone same time I did."

I went to meet him in the hall, knowing that he'd be concerned. James had been with Sam for years before we married and Sam thought the world of him, even though James got a little more averse to work every year that passed. Still, they'd gotten along well until Sam had brought me into the mix. There was no way in the world I would've put up with James's languid attitude toward getting things done. I'd once heard him tell Lillian that he enjoyed work, so much so that he could sit and look at it all day long. So it had been arranged for James to stay with the Pickens family when they took up residence in Sam's house. I didn't want him underfoot at my house and James didn't want me pointing out work to him.

"Hazel Marie said they're bringing him home," I said as I met Sam at the foot of the stairs, "so he must not be too bad off. Are you going over?"

"Yes, I better see about him. I'll tell you the truth, Julia—James is not an easy patient. The year he had the flu—a really bad case of it, too—I was up and down the stairs all day and half the night taking care of him." Sam smiled as he remembered. "I made the mistake of rigging up a bell that would ring in the house when he needed something. They're going to have their hands full with him."

"I doubt Mr. Pickens will be as compliant as you, and I expect James will find that out soon enough. Anyway, tell Hazel Marie that we're bringing supper so she doesn't have to worry about that." I walked to the door with Sam. "How long do you think he'll be in a cast?"

"I don't know. Five or six weeks, maybe, depending on how severe the break is."

Good Lord, I thought. In five or six weeks the Pickens family would be either poisoned from Hazel Marie's cooking or starved half to death.

Chapter 2

❧

Lillian and I began wrapping foil around bowls and bagging other ingredients for the supper she planned to cook in the Pickens kitchen.

"Oh," I said, putting a plastic tie on the last bag, "I better let Lloyd know where we'll be. I don't want him coming home to an empty house."

Pleased with my new knowledge of up-to-date messaging systems, I began to text to his cell phone. He had shown me how to do it, but I was not as dexterous as he and his friends were, their little thumbs flying over the keyboards. Still, with time and thought, I could send a message which I knew he wouldn't get until the final bell rang. Checking his messages would be the first thing he did when students were allowed to access their cell phones, so I typed in:

GO TO UR MOTHERS AFTER SCHOOL. XOXO.

"There," I said as I pressed OK to send it. "Quick, easy, and understandable. I hope. Although every time I type a message, I worry about the next generation's spelling skills. Or lack of."

As Lillian and I took bags and pots to my car, she said, "I forget to tell you, but somebody called Miss Hazel Marie right before she called."

"Who was it?"

"He didn't say. Jus' ast for her an' when I say she not here, he kinda grunt an' hang up."

"Somebody selling something, probably, or wanting her to donate to some cause or another. He'll call back if it was important."

When we arrived at the Pickens house and walked up onto the front porch laden with our half-cooked supper, we could hear James moaning. Well, not moaning, exactly—it was more like the steady, rumbling buzz of a thousand bees issuing from his throat. Hazel Marie had left the door open for us, so we walked into the hall where we heard the humming run up and down the scale. It never reached to a scream, just a rippling drone that let everyone know how miserable the hummer was.

"I hope he stop that pretty soon," Lillian mumbled as we made our way to the kitchen.

"I expect he will," I said, although the sound was putting my nerves on edge. "He's still getting over the fright of falling and breaking a bone. You know how it is—he's probably still in shock from it all. You want this pot on the stove?"

"Yes'm, jus' put it on a back eye and turn it on low. You think we oughta go in an' see him?"

"Yes, let's do and get it over with. He'll appreciate our concern, but, I declare, I never know what to say to someone who's bedridden."

So we walked back to the bedroom, the humming sound getting louder as we approached. Sam caught my eye as I walked in and smiled as he lifted James's foot and pushed another pillow underneath, then carefully lowered the Ace-bandaged limb. Hazel Marie, looking more disheveled than usual, stood by the bed wringing her hands, while Mr. Pickens stacked more pillows for James to rest his arm on.

"You have to keep your foot and your hand elevated, James," Mr. Pickens said, arranging the cast-clad arm and hand on the pillows. Only the ends of James's fingers extended beyond the cast. "Look," Mr. Pickens went on, "Lillian and Miss Julia have come to see about you. Come on in, ladies—visiting hours just started."

Hazel Marie's face lit up as we moved toward the bed. "Oh, I'm so glad to see you both. Can you believe this? Poor James, he feels so bad."

And to prove it, James started humming again. His eyes were half closed and a look of strain wrinkled his face. He was pitiful in his misery.

"I'm so sorry this happened," I said to him. Then, in an attempt to encourage him, I went on. "But look at it this way: It could've been so much worse. You could've broken your ankle instead of just spraining it. I mean, we have to look on the bright side, don't we?"

"Can't be no worse, Miss Julia," he said through gritted teeth. "I'm about stove up for good." He turned his head away and began to hum again.

Then suddenly his eyes popped open and his head came up off the pillow. "My forms! My forms!" he cried, then fell back, giving up the effort.

"What's he talking about?" I asked.

"No telling," Mr. Pickens said with an indulgent smile. "He's so full of pain medication, I doubt he knows."

"Maybe he needs more of it," I said, moved by his pathetic situation.

"He's loaded," Mr. Pickens assured me. "But he can have more later if he needs it."

James looked up at him, frowning, his good left arm waving limply in the air. "I gonna need it real soon," he whispered.

Sam patted James's foot and said, "You ought to try to rest now. Take a little nap if you can. We'll all be here if you need anything."

James's eyelids fluttered as he spoke in a voice so weak that Sam had to lean over to hear him. "A TV might he'p take my mind off the hurtin'."

Sam smiled and smoothed the sheet. "Well, we'll see, James, but you won't get good reception. There's no cable connection in this room."

James moaned, whether in pain or disappointment, I couldn't tell.

Lillian turned on her heel and headed out of the room. "I got to get supper on."

Lloyd arrived before long, coming straight to the kitchen wanting to know the reason we'd all gathered for a meal on a weeknight. "Is it somebody's birthday? If it is, I sure forgot it."

"No, honey," Lillian said. "We over here 'cause that sorry James tripped over his big feet and fell down the stairs."

"*Fell down the stairs!*" Lloyd was aghast. "Is he all right?"

"He pro'bly better'n he actin' like," Lillian pronounced. She had little use for James.

"Oh, Lillian," I said, thinking to temper her words, although I was inclined to agree with her. "He'll calm down after a while. He's still getting over the fright of falling."

"Mark my words," she said as she stirred the gravy, "I been knowin' James for years an' he gonna milk that cask for all it's worth. He gonna have everybody high-steppin' to his tune."

"Well, one good thing—he's Mr. Pickens's problem, not ours." I caught her eye and we smiled at each other.

"Can I go in and see him?" Lloyd asked.

"Yes," I said, "go on in and tell him that we'll have supper ready soon."

And by the time supper was ready, we were all frazzled. The babies had to be fed, and with two high chairs and Hazel Marie in the kitchen, Lillian and I hardly had room to move. Mr. Pickens came in twice to refill James's water glass, and just as we were ready to sit down at the table, James needed help to go to the bathroom. That took the combined efforts of Sam and Mr. Pickens, with Mr. Pickens declaring that he thought a sprained ankle would heal quicker if it had a little excercise. Then James discovered that he wasn't at all adept at feeding himself with his left hand, so Sam sat beside the bed and hand-fed him while his own supper grew cold.

"We need to think about this," I said as we sat around the table after eating. "James is going to need more help than we can give him, at least for the next few days."

"Oh, we don't mind," Hazel Marie said. "He's such a good old thing, we can look after him. Can't we, J.D.?"

Mr. Pickens frowned, but before he could say anything, Sam chimed in. "It'll be too much for you, Hazel Marie. You have enough to do already, and with Pickens gone, you won't be able to handle it all."

Hazel Marie's eyes widened as she looked across the table at her husband. "Gone? You're going somewhere?"

"To Birmingham," he told her. "You remember, I've got that insurance case down there."

"I thought that was next week." Hazel Marie's face had a stricken look. "Oh, my goodness, J.D., you can't go off now."

"Have to, honey. But don't worry, we'll figure out something. I'm not going to leave it all on you."

Hazel Marie obviously was not comforted by that promise. She never liked having her husband away in the best of times, and this was far from the best. He, however, was on retainer with a big insurance firm as an investigator of possible fraud cases and had to go when they called.

"What about this," Sam said, and I knew before he said it what it would be. "I'll stay with him until he can put his weight on that ankle, which shouldn't be but a day or so. Didn't you say the sprain is not that bad?"

Mr. Pickens nodded. "That's what they told me."

"Okay, so when he can walk, he won't need anybody. He can go back to his apartment and be pretty much on his own. Except for meals. He won't be doing much in the kitchen until that cast comes off."

"Wait, Sam," I said. "I'm not sure your staying over is a good idea. Let's call Etta Mae Wiggins. She'll know how to care for him." And, I thought, with her expertise as a home-health-care visiting semi-nurse, know how to keep him straight, too.

"Oh, I wish we could ask her," Hazel Marie said, looking distressed. "She'd be perfect, but we talked on the phone yesterday and she told me her boss is on a rampage about so many of her nurses wanting extra time off. Etta Mae thinks it was really aimed at her for staying so long with me when the babies were born. So," Hazel Marie went on, looking apologetic for having required so much help, "I don't think she can do it. And keep her job, too, I mean."

"Well," I said, resigned to turning elsewhere, "we can't expect her to lose her job for us. So, Sam, maybe it'll have to be you at least for a while."

Sam reached over and put his hand on mine. "It'll just be a couple of nights, and after that, James shouldn't need any help getting around. It'll be all right, honey. I'll sleep on a cot in his room."

"No need for that," Mr. Pickens said. "I'll be here tonight and tomorrow night."

Sam laughed in his good-natured way. "You don't know James. Somebody's going to be up with him every thirty minutes or so. Believe me, it'll be easier for me to stay with him than for you to be up and down the stairs all night. Besides, James would do it for me."

"I'll stay with you, Mr. Sam," Lloyd said. "I can sleep on the sofa in the den and you can call me when James needs to go to the bathroom."

After a few more minutes of arguing back and forth, Mr. Pickens subsided, knowing that he and Hazel Marie would be up with the babies at least once during the night and for good by 5 A.M., when the babies thought the day started.

"I'll check on you when I have to be up anyway," Mr. Pickens said.

So it was decided, at least for the next day or so, but I knew the arrangement had to be temporary. Sam would be worn to a nub if he had to do twenty-four-hour nursing duty for long.

Chapter 3

⁂

"Law me," Lillian sighed as she unloaded an armful of pans on the kitchen counter at my house. I put the leftovers in the refrigerator, then looked at her. We'd both been silent on the way over from Hazel Marie's, thinking, I suppose, about the problems that one little slip on the stairs now posed for us all. I shuddered to think what we'd have faced if James had toppled headfirst instead of tripping halfway down, to say nothing of how much more banged up he would've been.

"Miss Julia," Lillian said, turning, as she put the last pan in a cabinet, "this not gonna work. Miss Hazel Marie can't tend to them babies an' James, too. He gonna run her ragged and she too sweet to tell him no. An' Mr. Sam, he got no bus'ness liftin' an' pullin' on him, gettin' him in an' out of bed. It jus' too much."

"You're absolutely right," I said. "And it's too much for you to be going back and forth, cooking for two families."

"No'm, I don't mind. It kinda like havin' a ox in a ditch, just so long it don't *stay* in the ditch."

"No, Lillian, we've got to come up with a better solution. Neither of us is getting any younger and we don't need a double helping of work. To tell the truth, I'd been counting on having Etta Mae, but with her out of the question, I'm at a loss. Can you think of *any*body who'd come in and cook a couple of meals a day and help a little with James?"

"I been rackin' my brain, but I can't think of a soul I'd want in a kitchen. Everybody any good already got jobs. But here something to think about. What if I cook enough for all us, maybe two or three days a week, an' Miss Hazel Marie fix samiches or hot dogs or open a can of soup or something like that the other days? Lloyd can eat with us like he most always do anyway, an' the babies got their own food, so it won't be like anybody goin' hungry." She stopped and thought for a minute. " 'Sides," she went on, "if James get hungry enough, he'll get well faster."

We looked at each other and started laughing. "Oh, Lillian," I said, "that's low. But you may just be right."

After Lillian left, more than an hour later than she usually did, I locked the doors and went up to our newly refurbished bedroom. I wasn't quite ready to retire for the night, but with an empty house and no one to talk to, there wasn't much else to do. So I prepared for bed, crawled in, and propped myself up to study the situation in which we found ourselves.

It was a revelation to ponder the importance of each member of our family, such as it was. Oh, of course if it had been Sam who was laid up in bed, broken and sprained, or, heaven forbid, Hazel Marie—what with those babies—there would've been untold consequences, disturbing and distressing the balance of us. But James, whom I would ordinarily consider the one of least value to our overall well-being, had completely upset our little apple cart.

A sudden thought jolted me upright. It wasn't James who was of least value to the serenity of our days. It was me. If I were bedridden, the only disruption to our daily activities would be the bringing of trays upstairs three times a day. Everything else would stay the same. That was an eye-opener to say the least, and put me firmly in my place. James immediately rose in my estimation.

But now, with him laid up in bed, what in the world were we to do? My deepest concern was the preparation of meals for the Pickens family. I assumed that in a few days James would be able to be up and about, maybe needing a little help with buttons and the like, but with only the stubs of his fingers free of the cast, he certainly would not be able to cook. And even if Hazel Marie were the best cook in the world, she couldn't fix three meals a day, take care of two babies, and wait on James, too. And, believe me, she wasn't the best cook in the world. The last time she decided to cook a meal, she'd burned the bottom out of a saucepan and started a fire on the stove. The truth of the matter was, she wasn't safe in a kitchen.

Lillian, bless her heart, would willingly cook for two families for weeks on end if I asked her to, but I couldn't do that. Like me, she was getting slower and needed to sit down more often to rest her feet. Her corns had gotten so bad that she'd sliced up her shoes until they looked like homemade flip-flops. So it was too much to ask her to double her work, even with double the pay.

I mulled over the possibilities, even to the point of getting out the phone book from the bedside table to look up catering services. There weren't any.

I thought of arranging food deliveries from various restaurants in town, but who could eat pizza or hamburgers every other day? Well, Lloyd probably could, but not while I was around.

Gradually, though, another idea began to form in my mind, so I thought about it and looked at it from one angle to another, and decided that it just might work. It would entail talking Hazel Marie into using a babysitter for a couple of hours maybe once or twice a week, but she wouldn't actually be leaving the babies. She'd still be right there with them, just not having to drop everything to tend to them.

It could work, I thought, as I turned off the lamp and slid down in bed, and if it did, it would kill two birds with one stone—teach her some cooking skills and put some decent food on the table at the same time.

◦～◦

By the time I got downstairs the next morning, Lillian was already there and so was Sam. I stopped in my tracks when I saw how tired he looked. He was sitting at the table, nursing a cup of coffee, his face drawn and pale from his long night of nursing.

"Oh, Sam," I said, going to him, "did you get any sleep at all?"

"Very little," he said, smiling, "but I knew I wouldn't, so that's no surprise. Pickens relieved me a little while ago, told me to come home and go to bed, which is just what I'm about to do."

"Not 'fore you get some breakfast," Lillian said, setting a plate of eggs and bacon at his place. "You didn't hardly get to eat a thing last night, an' you can't go to bed on a empty stomack. That James kept you up all night, didn't he?"

"Just about," Sam admitted, picking up his fork and digging in. "I think that pain medication perked him up instead of putting him to sleep. He dozed off and on, but mostly he wanted to talk." Sam laughed. "And talk and talk. I heard all about his mama, his sisters, his first job, and on and on. And every time he nodded off, he'd start mumbling about his *forms,* then couldn't remember a thing about them when he was awake. I expect he'll sleep all day, just like I will. Oh, and by the way," Sam said, looking up from his plate, "remind me to take James a couple of pairs of my pajamas. I don't know what he usually sleeps in, but he needs more of whatever it is."

"They's no tellin'," Lillian muttered.

"What about Lloyd, Sam?" I asked. "Why didn't he come with you? He could've had breakfast here before school."

"Pickens is cooking, which is why I came home." In spite of his fatigue, Sam's eyes sparkled with his usual good humor, or maybe at the thought of Mr. Pickens in an apron. "Might be a good idea to get some cold cereal for them, Julia, after Pickens leaves. I guess I never realized how hectic it is in a house full of wet and hungry babies. There's no way Hazel Marie can fix a hot breakfast when they need to be changed and fed."

As Lillian set a plate before me, I got up to get a pad and pencil. "You better eat," she said.

"I will, but I want to start a grocery list. What kind of cereal do you think they'd like? Maybe get a couple of different ones. And milk, they'll need that. And maybe a coffee cake and bread.

There's no reason in the world why James can't put a slice of bread in the toaster with his left hand." Sitting down at the table, I turned to Sam. "He'll be able to get out of bed today, won't he?"

"Probably," Sam said, nodding, "but I wouldn't count on him moving around much. Maybe get him up to sit in a chair and watch television. That ankle is about twice its normal size, so he won't be walking on it. Well," he went on as he laid his napkin beside his plate, "I'm going to have a shower and hit the hay. But that was just what I needed, Lillian. Thank you."

I walked with him to the foot of the stairs, where he put his arms around me and kissed me. "It's going to work out all right, honey," he said. "Don't worry so much."

"I can't help but worry," I said, running my hand across his shoulder. "I know James means a lot to you, but I don't want you to wear yourself out taking care of him. Why don't I stay with him tonight?"

Sam laughed and tightened his hold around me. "That's the worst idea I've ever heard, sweetheart. You two would kill each other. But," he said, holding my face with his hands, "if James begins to malinger, I'll tell him you're coming. If that doesn't get him on his feet, I don't know what will."

We laughed together, then I watched as he trudged upstairs to bed. Sighing, I turned back to the kitchen, wondering if the idea I'd had during the night would help matters or make them worse.

"Lillian," I said, taking my cup to the counter for a refill, "what're we going to do? Sam can't keep this up for long. He'll make himself sick—then where would we be?"

"It worry me to death, Miss Julia. I called some friends las' night when I got home, see if they knowed anybody could he'p us out. But nobody know a soul. 'Specially to he'p out James. They all like Miss Hazel Marie, but they say nobody put up with James."

"My goodness," I said, sinking down at the table, "that's a terrible commentary. Of course, I don't get along with him, but I didn't know others felt the same way."

"Oh, they don't, really. I mean, he a lot of fun 'round church an' get-togethers, an' folks like him pretty good. It jus' they know nothin' ever good enough for him. Nobody be able to please him with they cookin' or cleanin' or anything."

"Well, that's ironic," I said, laughing, "because he can't please me with *his* cooking and cleaning and so forth. Still, we have to come up with something to help Hazel Marie—she's the one I'm concerned about. I expect James to be able to take care of him self in a day or so. It just has to be before Sam tires himself out."

"Mr. Sam don't need to be waitin' on James hand an' foot like he doin'," Lillian said as she joined me at the table.

"I know it, but maybe one more night and James will be able to go back to his apartment and be on his own. It could be weeks, though, before he's able to work in the kitchen, so that's what hangs heavy over my head. By the way," I went on, "Sam said that James is still mumbling about his *forms,* as if he's really worried about them. Do you know what he's talking about?"

"Huh," Lillian said. "Wouldn't surprise me if they was some of them men's corset forms. You know, the kind what holds men's stomacks in. James likes to look good for the ladies."

We sat without speaking for a few minutes, studying the situation, while an image of James pulling a corset on around his middle floated in and out of my mind.

Then Lillian, who was apparently not having the same vision, offered again to cook enough for two families. "We can have 'em over here, or we can take meals over there, whichever be easiest."

"No, Lillian, no. If it were only for a few days, even a week, I'd take you up on it. But for weeks on end, it's too much. We might have them over, say, once a week and maybe take supper to them another night, but to put all their meals on you with no end in sight is too much." I got up and brought the coffeepot to the table. While I refilled her cup, I went on, "Besides, I have an idea that's been swirling around in the back of my mind for a while now, and this may be the time to put it to work. Tell me what you think of this." And I started telling her.

Chapter 4

"See, Lillian," I began, "I came up with this about the time Hazel Marie and Mr. Pickens moved into Sam's house, which, as you know, gave Hazel Marie her own household. Now we both know that she is no hand in the kitchen and with two babies, well, let's just say that James taking over the cooking was an answer to prayer. But sooner or later, even if James hadn't put himself out of commission, Hazel Marie has to learn something about planning and preparing meals for her family.

"So my idea was to compile a cookbook with easy recipes and helpful household tips from each of our friends. I thought it would be personal enough to encourage her to try the recipes since she's probably tasted them at one time or another and knows how they're supposed to turn out. I planned to have recipes from Mildred and LuAnne and Emma Sue and you, of course, and from Etta Mae and Binkie and who all else I can think of. So, even if she never managed to make anything from it, it would be a keepsake she would treasure."

"That sound like a good idea to me," Lillian said. "Why didn't you go ahead an' do it?"

"Because of the summer we've had. With the house torn up and workmen underfoot all day, I just didn't have the energy or the space to do it. But now that the dust has settled, I can give it my full attention."

"Yes'm," Lillian agreed, "but one thing I don't see is how another cookbook gonna do her any good. She got all kinda cookbooks already an' they jus' settin' there on a shelf."

"That's where my new idea comes in," I said, hitching forward on my chair. "Think about this. What if I ask each person to contribute an easy recipe? *Then* ask them to go to Hazel Marie's house and show her how to make it? That way, she'd learn how to do it and have something for her family to eat that day."

Lillian looked at me from under her eyebrows, her mouth twisted in thought. "You think Miss Mildred Allen gonna cook in somebody else's kitchen when she don't in her own?"

"Well, no, but Ida Lee would. And I'd be there, too."

She looked even more skeptical at that thought, but she said, "I guess it could work, if everybody know when they s'posed to be there." She gave it a little more thought, then said, "She might not learn much cookin', but I 'spect she have a real good time tryin' to. I'd like to see what Miss Binkie teach her. I bet it be open two cans an' heat it up.

"One other thing, though," Lillian went on. "What if somebody want to he'p her fix choc'late balls or pecan pie or cole slaw or something like that? None of that make much of a supper for Mr. Pickens. Or Lloyd, either, 'cept I feed him over here, anyway."

That would be a problem, so I gave it some thought. "Well, what about this. What if I tell everybody they have to give her a main dish recipe—that would be the one they'd prepare—but they can also contribute another recipe for anything they want, but they wouldn't have to prepare that. That way, each person would have at least two recipes in the cookbook."

"Maybe, 'cept I don't know how you gonna tell 'em they *have* to do anything."

"Oh, well, I wouldn't put it that way. It's all in the way it's presented, Lillian. For instance, if I can get Mildred with Ida Lee onboard, and of course LuAnne, who'll talk it up all over town, then everybody else will rush in to volunteer. Hazel Marie could have a couple of meals prepared every week for as long as James is in a cast. You know how people are—as soon as they hear a family's having a hard time, they start bringing in casseroles or hams or cakes, anyway. Or in Emma Sue's case, a dump cake."

"Well," Lillian said, rising from the table, "I guess you better start linin' up them ringleaders, an' I better get some supper started. I'm gonna make that chicken dish what Mr. Sam like, an' send some to Miss Hazel Marie. He spendin' the night over there again?"

"He's planning to, I guess, unless James has had a remarkable recovery. Which I doubt."

"Uh-uh-uh," Lillian said, shaking her head. "It better be the las' night Mr. Sam spend over there, else we be nursin' him 'fore long."

I went into our new library and sat in a wing chair by the fireplace; giving the logistics of putting a cookbook together some deep study. The big problem wouldn't be collecting recipes—most people were happy to share them unless they considered one a secret family recipe. And nine times out of ten, you could find that secret recipe in *Joy of Cooking* or *Southern Living* magazine. I recalled the time when the recipe for red velvet cake was such a big secret until all of a sudden recipes for it popped up everywhere you looked. Which just goes to show that when you tell one person a secret, it won't be long until the whole country knows it.

But be that as it may, I knew that collecting recipes wouldn't be a problem. The problem would be getting hands-on cooks in Hazel Marie's kitchen.

I realized that our friends might look askance at my taking on such a project. They know I don't cook, never have, never wanted to, never intend to. I have Lillian, who can prepare any recipe handed to her, but who can also set out a fine meal without a guideline in sight.

But Hazel Marie, as sweet as she was, simply could not get the hang of it. When she finally married Mr. Pickens and was growing daily with expected twins, she'd suddenly turned domestic us. Every time I turned around, there she was, hanging around the kitchen, watching Lillian, questioning Lillian, wanting to help but mostly getting in the way. Lillian is a patient woman, but she said to me, "Miss Julia, Miss Hazel Marie gonna need a cook real bad. And real soon, too." So James's willingness to cook for her had been a godsend.

The problem for Hazel Marie when she'd been trying to learn everyday cooking, which is what she was most interested in for the sake of her new husband, was that Lillian hardly ever uses a recipe. Lillian cooks like she's always done—a little of this and a little of that, never measuring, never tasting, and never failing. She just knows how it's done. It drove Hazel Marie to distraction. She'd lean on the kitchen counter, pen in hand, ready to write down whatever Lillian did, which she couldn't do because half the time Lillian herself didn't know exactly what she did. Hazel Marie would ask, "Is that *half* a teaspoon of salt or a whole one?" And Lillian would look up in surprise and say, "Why, I don't know. Just however much my fingers pick up."

Take biscuits. Lillian can make them in her sleep. She began making biscuits before she was five years old, standing on a stool beside her granny, who taught her everything except how to measure. I think she cooks by ear. Some people can, you know. So, of course, biscuits were one of the first things that Hazel Marie wanted to learn to make.

So Lillian started telling her, and while Hazel Marie was poised to jot down the directions, I listened in.

"They's nothin' to it," Lillian began. "Just take some flour an' some short'nin' an' some milk, an' knead all that together. Then you roll it out and cut it with a biscuit cutter or a jelly glass, or you can pinch off some dough an' roll it in your hand an' pat it out flat, an' put 'em all on a bakin' sheet. Then you put the pan in a hot oven till they good 'n' brown, an' that's it."

Lillian glanced over at Hazel Marie, who was bent over her pad. "Well," she went on, "that's if you usin' self-risin' flour. But if you usin' reg'lar, you got to put in some bakin' powder an' some salt. An' that's if you usin' sweet milk, 'cause if you usin' buttermilk, you got to add some Arm an' Hammer, too."

"What?" Hazel Marie asked, frowning. "Wait a minute. How much flour did you say?"

So Lillian went through it again, and I have to say that I couldn't have made a batch of biscuits from her directions if my life depended on it. Too many *ifs* to keep up with. But Lillian did go on for a while about the merits of thin, crispy biscuits as opposed to the thick, doughy kind, coming down on the side of thin and crispy.

"That kind's 'pecially good with jelly," she said. Then she said, "Now, Miss Hazel Marie, what you do when you make biscuits for supper is you make enough for breakfast the next mornin'. So when you get up, you take an' split 'em in two, put a dab of butter on each side, and run 'em under the broiler till they nice an' toasted. That's good eatin', an' you won't have no trouble with your folks leavin' home on a empty stomack."

By that time, Hazel Marie had given up in despair. I think it was the Arm & Hammer that did it. "I guess I'll just use the Pillsbury frozen kind," she said, sighing, "and try to hide the package."

But being defeated by biscuits hadn't stopped Hazel Marie from continuing to ask everybody she knew for their recipes. We couldn't go to a circle meeting or to the book club or the garden club without her bringing up recipes. Just let her taste something she liked, and out would come a pad and pen to write down how it was made. Why, one Sunday Helen Stroud didn't get all the way through the lesson at the Lila Mae Harding Sunday school class because Hazel Marie asked what we reckoned manna was made of. That disrupted the whole class because everybody started guessing what the ingredients might have been. Miss Mattie Freeman said she'd always figured that manna was something like matzo balls, and that created a furor because half the class didn't know what matzo balls were. So that led to another discussion of kosher cooking, which led in turn to the question of the difference between kosher salt and regular salt—which then moved Adele Harrison to remind us all to use Morton's iodized salt so we wouldn't develop a goiter. And all this while Hazel Marie was trying to write down everything anybody said.

I finally leaned over and said, "Hazel Marie, forget about making manna. There's no way in the world you'll find the ingredients in this town."

And, my land, just let that white-haired Georgia woman with the big diamonds fix a dish on television, and up Hazel Marie jumps to print it out from Lloyd's computer. I won't even talk about when she tried to replicate those dishes, but we had to make a few changes in the kitchen. Since Lillian doesn't always come in on the weekends, I handed over Saturday and Sunday night suppers to Hazel Marie—this was while she and Mr. Pickens were still living with us before the babies came. She had the kitchen to herself, and we were the worse for it. Every weekend, Lloyd would sidle up to Mr. Pickens and carefully suggest that his mother needed to be taken out to dinner.

I declare, I don't know how that boy survived for nine years before coming to live with Lillian and me.

Well, I was long past worrying about that. Lloyd gets three good meals a day now, and he is thriving in spite of the fact that he's still skinny and probably always will be. But I'll tell you the truth, there must be a lot of nutrition in peanut butter, frozen macaroni and cheese, and hot dogs, which may satisfy a child, but may not go down so well with a new husband. From the way I've seen Mr. Pickens eat, though, he won't be a hard man to please. Except I've just seen him eat Lillian's cooking, so he might have to go through what might be called an adjustment period before Hazel Marie gets her act together.

Actually, the mistress of a house should know her way around a kitchen—whether she ever uses it or not—and she should know how to plan the week's menus, and she should be able to oversee whatever goes on her table. So it was to that end that I had at first set myself to the task of putting together a collection of recipes. And now, with all the commotion and disruption in her house, to also talk our friends into putting on aprons and personal demonstrations.

I must, however, issue one major caveat in case there are some litigious would-be cooks who happen to come across Hazel Marie's book: I cannot guarantee the success of any recipe written therein, so don't come to me. Either Lillian or a friend will have used each one, which means that I've eaten at one time or another the dish prepared from each recipe. But that's the extent of my involvement. I do not run a test kitchen, nor am I an accomplished cook, of which Hazel Marie is well aware. If she runs into trouble with any of them, she can call on Lillian. I myself can offer no help to anyone. When I get the recipes collected and written down, and arrange for the contributors to become instructors in the preparation thereof, I figure my job is done.

Chapter 5

"Lillian," I said, walking through the kitchen with a folder under my arm, "I'm going over to Mildred's. I'm taking a pad and pen and a calendar to start a schedule, and I'm counting on her being the first one on it."

"She know why you comin'?"

"Well, no, I just called and asked if I could visit a few minutes. I thought it'd be better to present it in person. That way it'll be harder to turn me down."

"Miz Allen, she a real nice lady, but she not too active." Which was Lillian's backhanded way of cautioning me not to expect too much enthusiasm from Mildred.

I had to laugh because Mildred was the least active person I knew. An unkind person might call her lazy, but Mildred's attitude was why should she do anything when she could hire it done. And, of course, her weight slowed her down considerably, although I would never mention that. Still and all, Mildred was a generous and thoughtful person and a very good friend, so I had high hopes of scheduling Ida Lee for the first cooking demonstration in Hazel Marie's kitchen.

"If Sam gets up before I'm back," I said as I went out the door, "ask him to wait for me."

"Yes'm, I'm gonna see he stay an' eat supper here. Might as well cut down on his long night much as we can."

"Oh, Mildred," I said as we sank into the cushioned chairs on her side porch, "it is so nice and balmy out here. It won't be long, though, before cold weather sets in."

"Yes," Mildred agreed amiably, as her large diamond flashed in the sunlight, "there's already a little nip in the air now and then. So if you get chilly, we'll go in. I thought we'd have coffee instead of something cold. And, see, Ida Lee has made some shortbread cookies."

Mildred is a heavyset woman, as I may have occasionally mentioned, the result, as she tells it, of a combination of inherited genes and glandular difficulties. "I have thyroid problems, Julia," she's said a million times, although I've never said a word to her about her size and wouldn't for the world.

But Mildred had Ida Lee to look after her, and I knew for a fact that Ida Lee worried about Mildred's weight. She had tried to get her to cut back, but it was a losing battle because Mildred was accustomed to getting her way. Ida Lee was not only a knowledgeable cook, she was an excellent one, as well. I knew because I'd eaten many a meal at Mildred's table at luncheons and dinner parties, and I knew that Ida Lee could serve Mildred healthy, low-calorie, but tasty meals, if Mildred would only be satisfied with them.

In fact, just as I brought up Hazel Marie's interest in recipes, Mildred started complaining about what Ida Lee had served her for lunch.

"I tell you, Julia," she said as she stirred sugar into her coffee, "Ida Lee's trying to starve me to death. But come to think of it, here's something that would be good for Hazel Marie to know. I expect she has some weight to lose, now that those babies have come, but since she doesn't have glands to worry about, a fruit salad will probably work fine for her. Would you believe that Ida Lee's served it to me twice this week? Of course, I'll have to say that it's tasty, but it's not enough for *my* taste. My blood sugar gets so low, I have to have a snack an hour or so later. I admit, though, that a fruit salad makes a nice lunch for a busy woman, but I wouldn't serve it to Horace or to Mr. Pickens, either. And I told Ida Lee that once a week is enough for me, and only on the days I'm having a late breakfast and an early dinner."

"I declare," I said, not wanting to comment on Mildred's eating habits. "At least no cooking is required, so It would be easy for Hazel Marie."

"Well, you know," Mildred confided, leaning close, "I am on a diet. Dr. Hargrove was quite firm about it, so I'm trying. But, Julia, Ida Lee has a wonderful chef's salad that I'm sure Hazel Marie will love. Here's what you do. Write it down. First, you put some shredded lettuce to make a bed on a plate, then you layer chopped fresh tomatoes, slivered carrots, sliced cucumbers, chopped celery, a few broccoli florets, and chopped onions. That takes care of your vegetables. Then you shred or chop up a couple of slices of smoked turkey and Virginia ham, slice a couple of boiled eggs, and crumble a few slices of bacon over that. Then grate Cheddar cheese on top, and there's your protein. Now, on the sides of the plate, put a heaping spoonful of cottage cheese, several slices of pickled beets, and some corn relish. Oh, and some olives, both black and green, and a bowl of Ida Lee's homemade blue-cheese dressing on the side. I like a few slices of buttered and toasted French bread with it."

"My word," I murmured, "that must make a plateful."

"Oh, it does. But Dr. Hargrove told me to eat lots of salads, so that's what I'm doing, but I have to watch Ida Lee like a hawk or she'll leave something out. Now, Julia, getting down to real eating, Hazel Marie has to have my boeuf bourguignon recipe. It's perfect for when she entertains."

"Well, I don't know, Mildred. It's delicious, but I doubt Hazel Marie will be entertaining anytime soon. Besides, something so hard to spell and pronounce might be too hard for her to make."

"You may be right. Let's see what Ida Lee thinks." Mildred picked up the little silver bell that was on the table beside her and gave it a tinkle. That bell was never far from her hand wherever she was in the house, and never long out of use.

In just a few minutes, Ida Lee walked out onto the porch. "Yes, ma'am?" she said to Mildred, then with a smile turned to me. "Good afternoon, Mrs. Murdoch."

I responded, thinking to myself what a perfectly mannered and highly capable woman she was. She was small in size and stature, with a lovely complexion that looked tanned all year round. She had been trained at one of those housekeeping schools in New York, so she was a professional in every sense of the word. I sometimes wondered how she put up with Mildred—and Abbotsville itself—when she could work anywhere and for almost anyone she wanted to.

When Mildred explained what I was doing, Ida Lee was most pleasant and cooperative, going back into the kitchen to get her recipe box.

"Look for my boeuf bourguignon first," Mildred said, as Ida Lee sat on an ottoman and began to look through the cards. "That's my favorite company dish."

Ida Lee nodded in agreement, even though I figured that the recipe was hers, and not Mildred's at all. Pulling out the card, she handed it to me. "It's a little complicated to make," she said, "so Mrs. Pickens might have trouble with it. Tell her to call me if she does, because it's worth the effort."

"Hmm," I said thoughtfully, glancing over the recipe as if I understood the first thing about the directions. "Maybe we should start with something simpler. But, listen," I said, girding—so to speak—my loins. "I have to admit that I'm here to ask for a little more than your recipes." And I went on to tell them of James's mishap and Mr. Pickens's call to duty, and to remind them of how much baby-tending Hazel Marie had to do, as well as of her ineptness in a kitchen. They were both dismayed to hear about James and both expressed commiseration for Hazel Marie.

"I'm glad you feel that way," I said, "because I have a huge favor to ask. Would you—both of you—consider spending a couple of hours this week showing Hazel Marie how to fix one of your main dish recipes? Now, I know," I went on quickly, "that it'll be mostly on Ida Lee to show her how to do it, but, Mildred, I thought that you and I could watch from the sidelines and offer encouragement." I trailed off as I watched their faces to see how they were taking the suggestion. "Or something."

"Why, I'd be glad to," Ida Lee said, her face brightening at the thought. "If it's all right with Mrs. Allen, of course."

"Oh, I think it'd be fun," Mildred said. "Except, Julia, for one thing, and I know you won't approve. But if you want me to do any cooking, I'm taking a bottle of wine. Somebody told me once that no woman should go into a kitchen without a glass of wine in hand."

Far be it from me to criticize Mildred for having a glass of wine. I was much more disturbed at the thought of Mildred demonstrating her cooking skills, of which she had fewer than Hazel Marie.

So I said, "I expect you and I will just be in the way if we try to help. Why don't we take some handwork to do while we watch? I have a needlepoint piece I've been trying to finish for ages. We'll sit at the kitchen table and supervise, and maybe offer a little entertainment."

"What, Julia?" Mildred asked, laughing. "You mean sing or something?"

"No, I mean entertaining talk. Like, for instance, what's going on with Thurlow and Helen Stroud? Have you heard anything lately?"

"Have I ever! Just wait till you hear."

"No, don't tell me now. Save it for, well, when? What's a good day to do this?"

We discussed that for a while, and finally decided on the Saturday coming. That would give Hazel Marie a few days to find a babysitter and also give James time to be on his feet, hopefully. It occurred to me that Mildred and I could possibly be the babies' caretakers, but I decided I'd already pushed my luck with Mildred about as far as it was likely to go.

Ida Lee held out another index card to me. "Here's a recipe for beef stroganoff. It's a lovely dish and easier than the boeuf bourguignon."

"That does look good," I said, scanning the ingredients. "I think you served this at your dinner party at Thanksgiving last year, didn't you, Mildred?"

"Yes, I believe I did," Mildred said. "I think people get enough turkey at home over the holidays, so I like to serve something different."

Ida Lee was still looking through her recipe box. "Do you think she'd like one for deviled crab? I have a simple one that makes an attractive entrée."

"If it's simple, I'll take it."

After looking over the directions for the deviled crab, I said, "Well, this would be simple enough for Lillian, but I don't know about Hazel Marie. She might get stuck on the white sauce."

I began writing them down, though, carefully checking each one to be sure I hadn't overlooked an ingredient. Hazel Marie was going to have a hard enough time replicating the dishes without using a flawed recipe.

Mildred bestirred herself. "Give her a salad one, too, Ida Lee. I like the one you make with cottage cheese, and cottage cheese is good for anybody who's dieting."

As Ida Lee began looking for that card, Mildred went on, "Oh, I know! Hazel Marie has to have the recipe for biscuit tortoni. That may be my favorite dessert. Well, maybe black-bottom rum pie is my most favorite, but biscuit tortoni is a close second."

"This sounds wonderful," I said, reading the card Ida Lee handed to me. "I really appreciate this, Ida Lee, and I know Mr. Pickens and Lloyd will, too."

"I'll be thinking about some others she might like," Ida Lee said.

By this time I had more recipes than Hazel Marie could manage and not enough actual plans. "We need to make a decision here. Ida Lee, if it's all right with you, I think the beef stroganoff would be the best one to start with. So if you'll write out a grocery list—and include everything you'll need, because I don't know how equipped her kitchen is—I'll buy the ingredients and have them at her house."

"Absolutely not," Mildred said. "We'll do the shopping and bring everything we need with us. We would've sent a dish anyway, once we heard of James's injury, so the only difference is the change of venue."

I thanked her with heartfelt gratitude, although I knew that all those *we*s she'd mentioned really meant Ida Lee.

I finished copying the recipes, confirmed Saturday morning for the lesson, and, thanking them both again, prepared to leave. Ida Lee walked me to the door, but on the way, she said in a low voice, "Forgive me, but I couldn't help but hear what Mrs. Allen was saying earlier, because I was dusting in the living room. I just want you to know that I serve her low-fat salad dressing and try to cut down on her calories any other way I can. Just please don't tell her."

"Of course I won't. And, Ida Lee, I know that you look after her as much as she'll let you. And in this case, what she doesn't know not only won't hurt her, it'll help her."

(Hazel Marie, these are Ida Lee's recipes, but we're pretending they're Mildred's.)

Mildred's Beef Stroganoff

2 tablespoons butter or margarine
1 garlic clove, peeled and split
1 bay leaf
2 pounds round steak, chuck, or sirloin, cut into cubes
2 medium onions, sliced
1 teaspoon salt
1 teaspoon paprika
1½ cups water
⅓ cup tomato juice
2½ tablespoons flour
2 cups sour cream
1 teaspoon Worcestershire sauce
1 cup canned mushrooms, drained (or ½ pound fresh, sautéed in butter)

In a Dutch oven, heat the butter and add the garlic and bay leaf. Add the meat and onions and brown. Add the salt, paprika, and water. Cover the Dutch oven and simmer until the meat is tender (about 1 hour).

Mix the tomato juice, flour, sour cream, and Worcestershire sauce in a bowl and add to the meat mixture. Add the mushrooms. Heat until hot, remove the bay leaf, and serve over noodles or rice.

Serves 6.

(You won't go wrong with this next one, Hazel Marie. It's one of Sam's favorites.)

Mildred's Biscuit Tortoni

1 cup sugar
3 tablespoons water
3 eggs
1 pint whipping cream, whipped
1 teaspoon vanilla
1 tablespoon sweet sherry
2 dozen stale macaroons, finely crumbled

Cook the sugar and water in a small saucepan until the sugar is dissolved and a syrup forms. Separate the eggs and beat the yolks and whites in separate bowls. Then beat the syrup into the whipped egg whites. Fold in the beaten egg yolks and the whipped cream. Season with the vanilla and sherry.

In a loaf pan, layer the mixture with the macaroon crumbs, starting and ending with macaroons. Freeze overnight. When ready to serve, run a sharp knife along the edges and dip the pan quickly in hot water. Turn out and slice. This is a lovely, light dessert for a ladies' luncheon, but men like it, too.

Serves 8.

Chapter 6

"Well, that's one day filled," I announced as I stepped into the kitchen at home. "Lillian, both Mildred and Ida Lee are excited about this. They're even looking forward to it. Can you believe it?"

"Believe what?" Sam asked, as I turned and saw him sitting at the table.

"Oh, you're up. Did you get enough sleep?" I put my folder on the table and sat beside him.

"I'm feeling a whole lot better," he said, putting his hand on mine. He looked a whole lot better, too. "I'm hoping the twins kept James awake today so he'll sleep tonight. But tell me what've you been up to."

So I told him, and he thought it was an inspired idea. "You know what it reminds me of?" he asked, his eyes sparkling. "The way Tom Sawyer got his fence painted, remember? And your timing is perfect. Pickens is leaving this afternoon instead of tomorrow, so he can be back here Saturday for the weekend. Won't he be surprised to have Ida Lee's fancy beef dish for supper?"

I beamed at the thought, then immediately began to worry about who I could get to be the next cook in Hazel Marie's kitchen.

"I'm going on over," Sam said, rising from the table. "Lillian, if you're sending something, I'll take it with me."

"It's awfully early, Sam," I said, having hoped to have a few more minutes with him before he left for the night.

"I know, but with Pickens leaving, Hazel Marie will need the help. I just spoke to her on the phone and both babies were screaming and James was clanging his bell." Sam laughed. "I told her a bell wasn't a good idea, but she was afraid he'd need something. Anyway," he went on as he picked up the foil-wrapped Pyrex dish that Lillian had prepared, "this just needs heating up?"

"Yessir," Lillian said, handing him a full sack. "They's some rolls in here and a can of peas. They need to be heated, too."

Just as Sam kissed me and headed out, with me vacillating over whether or not to go with him, the front doorbell rang.

"Who could be calling this near suppertime?" I mumbled as I hurried through the dining room to the front door.

"Julia!" LuAnne Conover cried as she rushed in. "I just heard about James. How bad is it? What's Hazel Marie going to do? I heard he broke both arms and a foot! My goodness, he'll be laid up for months." She didn't break stride until she reached the Duncan Phyfe sofa in the living room where she immediately sat, expecting me to follow.

"No, no, LuAnne. Where did you hear that? He only broke his wrist and sprained an ankle." I sat down beside her.

"Well, it's all over town that he's lucky not to have broken his neck. I mean, going headfirst over that little landing at the top of his stairs—it's a wonder he didn't kill himself."

"Wait, LuAnne, wait. He didn't go headfirst over anything. He tripped over his feet on his way down the stairs. I declare, I don't know how such rumors get started."

"I heard it at Velma's when I was getting color and then again in the drugstore. But it's just a wrist and an ankle? That's not so bad, then."

"Well, it's bad enough. It's his right wrist and he has a cast that covers most of his fingers. LuAnne," I said, leaning toward her with a pitiful note in my voice, "the poor thing can't use that hand at all, and you know he's right-handed. I don't know what in the world Hazel Marie's going to do. She's taking care of him, and with two babies in diapers and beginning to teethe . . ." I sighed.

"Oh," LuAnne said, her eyes widening as she realized Hazel Marie's critical situation. "He's not able to cook, is he?"

I lowered my eyes and shook my head. Sorrowfully. "We're doing all we can to help. Lillian is so generous with her time, but she can't be on her feet that much. Corns, you know. But," I said, lifting my head with a hopeful look, "Mildred and Ida Lee are going over Saturday morning, and Ida Lee is going to give Hazel Marie a cooking lesson. They're going to make beef stroganoff, so she'll learn how to do it and have something for supper that evening, too."

"Why, what a good idea!" LuAnne exclaimed. "I was going to take a dish myself. Like I always do, you know. But to show her how to make it herself, why, it's like what they say: Teaching a man how to fish is better than giving him a fish." She eagerly reached toward me. "Why don't I teach her one of my recipes? Not on the same day, of course, but another day, when she'll need another meal. What do you think, Julia? Which one of my dishes would she like?"

"Something easy, LuAnne," I quickly said. "I'm hoping that fancy beef dish of Ida Lee's won't discourage her. Think of something that will give her some confidence. And, listen, I've come up with an idea that I've been thinking about for some time. I want to collect recipes from all her friends and put them in a book for her to have. So, if you would show her how to make one main dish, I'd like to include that in the book along with any others you want to share. But you won't need to demonstrate those—unless you just want to. What do you think?"

"I think," she said, rising from the sofa, "I'm going to run home and get my recipe book. I'll be right back so we can decide on my main dish. You don't eat supper this early anyway, do you? Put me down for a day before they're all taken up. How about Monday? I'll be back in fifteen or twenty minutes."

And off she went.

"Lillian," I said, going back to the kitchen with a big smile on my face, "this is going to be easier than I thought."

When LuAnne returned bearing several books, we sat again on the sofa and she began leafing through the pages.

"Now tell me what you already have," she said briskly. "I don't want to go to the trouble of looking up mine if you already have them. I mean, who wants half a dozen apple pie recipes? And, besides, there are a few things Hazel Marie needs to know other than just plain old recipes."

I didn't know why it all had to be done at my house and not hers, for I had offered to drive up the mountain to her condo. But I hadn't insisted, because I figured she wanted an excuse to get out of the house, Leonard being ensconced in front of the television set all day, every day, without a word of conversation except, "What's for supper?"

So we sat there in my living room, LuAnne with a pad on her knee and a pen in her hand. "I'm also going to be writing down some little household hints that might come in handy—not right now, but over time, as I think of them. All you have to do is help me remember because, as you know, we've been doing these things so long that it's second nature and we don't even consciously think of them anymore." She paused, tapped her pen against the pad, then went on. "Well, maybe not you, since you have Lillian."

And right there was LuAnne's problem—she was resentful of the good fortune of her friends. It had taken me a long while to figure out that it wasn't envy, exactly, because she didn't want Helen Stroud or Mildred Allen or me to lose what we had. Although Helen, bless her heart, no longer qualified as an enviable subject due to the follies of her now-deceased husband.

No, LuAnne didn't want ours, she just wanted some of her own. So the resentment was not toward us, but toward Leonard, who seemed to have moseyed or slept through his entire working life and was now doing the same in his retirement.

"The first thing Hazel Marie needs to learn," LuAnne said

briskly, "is how to make her own mayonnaise. That's the sign of a good cook and a careful housekeeper."

"Oh, LuAnne, surely not. All that dribbling in and whipping—she'd never get the hang of it. There's good mayonnaise on the shelves and hardly anybody knows the difference anymore."

"Well, but there're so many choices. Some people say that you have to have Duke's for tomato sandwiches, which I like myself. Then others swear by salad dressing."

"Too sweet for me."

"Me, too. But, see, Julia, I know Lillian makes yours because you wouldn't have anything else in your house."

"That's where you're wrong, LuAnne. Lillian makes it only when she's in the mood and usually only for party sandwiches. Otherwise, we use Hellmann's."

"You do? Well, my goodness." LuAnne was momentarily stopped by the thought.

And that was the result of the problem I just mentioned. She wanted to live on the grand scale that she assumed her friends did, except they didn't. At least, this friend didn't. Why, one time she and I were co-hosting a circle meeting at my house and I found her in the kitchen hand-squeezing lemons into a pitcher of tea. I said, "For goodness sakes, LuAnne, don't waste your time. There's a bottle of ReaLemon in the refrigerator. Just pour some in and be done with it." She looked shocked for a minute, then said, "Well, that's what I use, but I didn't think you did."

It's my firm conviction that whatever convenience the Lord makes available, it's incumbent on us to be grateful for it and use it. I see no virtue in doing things the hard way merely for the sake of doing them the hard way. Just get on with it, is my attitude.

"If that's the case, then," LuAnne said in response to learning that Hellmann's mayonnaise took pride of place in my kitchen, "I guess I can give Hazel Marie some of my quick and easy recipes. But I promise you, Julia, I serve them only to Leonard. I'd never serve them to guests."

"Quick and easy is exactly what I want," I assured her. "We're dealing with Hazel Marie, which means we'll be lucky if she even *thinks* of mayonnaise until Mr. Pickens wants a sandwich."

"Okay, then," LuAnne said, opening a recipe book that was full of handwritten or typed recipes. "What I'm going to do is give her some that start with something ready-made. You know, like box cakes, but box cakes that have extra added ingredients that make them special. But tell her that she shouldn't use these when she's entertaining. People will talk about her if she does. She should borrow Lillian or wait till James is well to have a party or a luncheon. People will understand when they hear what happened to him. In the meantime, though, these I'm going to give you will help her put something on the table for her family. She won't have time to do any entertaining anytime soon, anyway. Here," she said, holding out her recipe book, "copy this one down."

LuAnne's No-Cook Barbecue Sauce

Mix together the following ingredients thoroughly:

½ cup catsup
½ cup water
1 tablespoon vinegar (LuAnne uses apple cider vinegar)
½ tablespoon salt
½ tablespoon paprika
¼ teaspoon black pepper
¼ teaspoon chili powder

Preheat the oven to 350°F.

Salt and pepper 4 medium-thick pork chops (you can also use chicken or ribs) and place them in a foil-lined pan or ovenproof dish. Arrange a slice of onion on top of each chop, then pour barbecue sauce over all.

Cover with foil and bake until the meat is done—about 1 to 2 hours, depending on the thickness of the chops.

Remove the foil about 10 minutes before taking the pan from the oven.

Serves 4.

(Not all barbecue has to be done outside on a grill, Hazel Marie. It's safer to put it in the oven and be done with it.)

~

"Now, Julia," LuAnne said, taking the book from me as I finished copying. "Here's another easy one that she can put in the oven and let cook for hours. She can do it early in the afternoon and forget about it until suppertime."

"That's the kind she needs. Let me see it."

"I'll tell you what. Put me down for two days. I'll do the pork chops Monday and this roast the next time. I have a manicure appointment on Tuesday, so let's say Wednesday, if it's not already taken."

"It just happens to be free. I'll put you down right now." And I did, noting that I now had meals for the Pickens family for three days.

LuAnne's Easy Pot Roast

2- to 3-pound roast (eye round works well)

Preheat the oven to 350°F. Put the meat in a Dutch oven and mix together the following:

One 10¾-ounce can cream of mushroom soup
½ soup can of water
½ envelope of Lipton's dried onion soup
(you can also add 1 chopped onion, 1 chopped garlic clove, and 1 bay leaf, if desired)
Dash of Kitchen Bouquet for color

Pour the mixture over the roast, then cover and cook in the oven for 2½ hours or so. Remove the bay leaf, if you're using one, before serving. There will be no need to thicken the gravy—serve it over rice, noodles, or mashed potatoes. The roast will be tender and tasty, and if there's any left over, it will make excellent sandwiches with lettuce and tomatoes. Or you may chop the leftover roast and add it to the leftover gravy to make a hash. Serve it over toasted English muffins.

Serves 6 to 8.

A variation: Instead of a roast, use ground-beef patties. Brown the patties quickly on both sides, then lower the heat to simmer. Mix together the mushroom soup, water, and dried onion soup, and pour over the patties. Cover and let simmer until the patties are cooked through.

(I'm not sure how easy this is, Hazel Marie, so watch her carefully and take notes when she fixes it.)

"Look, Julia," LuAnne said, holding out another recipe. "Hazel Marie has to have this one. No one would believe she hadn't slaved all day over it and it's just as easy as can be. I tell you what—on my first day I'll show her how to make barbecued pork chops and this cake. All she'll need to make on her own will be baked potatoes and a salad."

"Maybe we ought to stick to just a main dish," I said. "I'm not sure she's ready to do two things at once."

"Oh, no, she can do this. It's simple, I promise."

LuAnne's Apricot Delight Cake

1 box Duncan Hines yellow cake mix
4 eggs, beaten
¾ cup Wesson oil
¾ cup apricot nectar (found on the canned-juice shelves)
3 teaspoons lemon flavoring
8-ounce can crushed pineapple (juice and all)

Preheat the oven to 350°F. Mix together all the ingredients and pour into a greased and floured tube pan. Bake for 50 to 60 minutes.

Serves 10 to 12.

Glaze:

2 cups confectioner's sugar
Juice of 2 lemons

Mix together and pour over the cake (when done) while it's still in the pan.
Save some for the top of the cake after taking it out of the pan.

Serves 8 to 10.

(LuAnne says she doesn't serve this cake to company, but I know she does because she served it when the book club met at her house last May. It really is good.)

Chapter 7

By the time LuAnne had left, I was feeling quite pleased with myself. With two cooks and three days lined up, my plan was working. And with LuAnne talking it up on the telephone—which I was sure she was doing at that very moment—I fully expected to have a number of volunteers to fill the rest of the weeks of James's recovery period.

Pushing through the swinging door into the kitchen, I said, "Well, Lillian, that's another one. LuAnne was not only willing, she was so eager that she signed up for two days." I laughed. "My only problem may be slowing her down. I think she would've signed up for even more."

"You got another problem you not even thought of. When you gonna tell Miss Hazel Marie 'bout all them people comin' to her house an' messin' 'round in her kitchen?"

"Oh," I said, stopping abruptly. "I guess I better mention it, hadn't I? Though I can't imagine she won't be thrilled." I walked to the sink and washed my hands. "Anyway, why don't you go on home, Lillian? You worked late last night, and since it's just me I can dip up my own supper. Lloyd's not here, is he? He's at his mother's?"

"Yes'm, he stuck his head in while Miz Conover here an' say he eatin' over there an' stayin' the night to he'p with James."

Murmuring under my breath, I said, "I hope to goodness this doesn't go on too long."

Lillian heard me, as she usually did. "We might have to take a broom to him, he get so used to havin' people waitin' on him."

"I have to keep reminding myself that he really is hurt. It's just that I worry so about Sam and Hazel Marie." I finished drying my hands, then started helping my plate. "You go on, Lillian—I'll clear up here. And first thing tomorrow, I'm going over to tell Hazel Marie that I've signed her up for some cooking lessons."

Lillian got her coat and pocketbook from the pantry and started for the door. Looking back, she said, "You might better put it to her a little diff'rent than that." Taking another step, she stopped again. "An' I forget to tell you, but while you at Miz Allen's house, that man call Miss Hazel Marie again, wantin' to know where she at."

I looked up in surprise. "I hope you didn't tell him. No telling who he is."

"No'm. I jus' say she not here, like the first time, an' he hang up."

"Well," I said, taking a serving spoon from a drawer, "he certainly is persistent. Some people don't know when to quit, do they?"

Lillian opened the back door, then hesitated. "You think I oughta call an' tell her somebody lookin' for her?"

"Goodness, no—she has her hands full without adding a phone solicitor. It couldn't have been important or he'd have left his name and number. You go on home and get some rest. We'll tell her tomorrow."

The next morning, after both Lloyd and Sam had had breakfast—cooked by Lillian at our house since neither was a fan of cold cereal—and Lloyd had left for school while Sam headed upstairs to bed, I rang the doorbell at Hazel Marie's.

Lord, it sounded like bedlam inside. Both little girls were crying—actually, one was screaming—James was clanging his bell, and the telephone was ringing. Hazel Marie came to the door with a harried look on her face. She was still in her robe, her hair uncombed and flat on one side.

"Oh, Miss Julia," she moaned. I thought she was going to cry, but I couldn't determine whether it was because she was relieved to see me or because I was just another demand on her time.

"I'm here to help, Hazel Marie. What can I do?"

"Oh, if you would, please see what James wants. Let the phone go I don't have time to talk to anybody. The babies need changing and I have to get them down for a nap. They've been up since four-thirty." She pushed the hair out of her face, looking distractedly around as if she didn't know what to do first. "And of course J.D. is gone."

"All right," I said. "Go see about the babies, then get yourself dressed. Take your time. I'll handle James."

She gave me a grateful smile, then rushed to pick up the babies. Struggling with one in each arm, she climbed the stairs while I marveled at her strength. Together they must've weighed about as much as she did.

"James," I said as I walked into the room where he lay sprawled out in bed, the covers rumpled and strewn around, "put that bell down. When you need something, ring it once and once only. If somebody doesn't come immediately, it's because they're doing something else."

His eyes got big and his mouth hung open as he saw me—not the one he'd expected at all. I took the bell and put it out of his reach.

"Now, what do you need?" I stood by the bed, my arms crossed, waiting for him to speak.

"Well, ah, I guess I need this tray moved." He pointed with his left hand to the breakfast tray on a table beside his bed. "An' maybe a little bit of toast an' some more coffee. I drink lots of coffee in the mornin'. It gets me goin'."

I looked over the bowl of Cheerios, pitcher of milk, and coffee cup. "You've hardly eaten anything. What's the matter with this cereal?"

"I'm used to havin' me a big hot breakfast. Like grits an' things. That ole cold cereal don't set so good."

"I'm sorry to tell you, James, but you'll have to get used to it. You know Hazel Marie doesn't have time to cook a big breakfast. It's all she can do to manage those two babies. You should be thankful for what you get. I doubt she's had a bite of anything herself." I moved the tray and the table out of the way. "Now, I want you out of that bed. The sheets need changing and you need to be up."

"Oh, no, Miss Julia. I can't do that. I can't put no weight on my ankle, an' it hurt too much to move my arm. I better stay in bed some more."

"Staying in bed isn't good for you. You'll get a clot in your leg, and then where would you be? Now, swing your feet off that bed and sit there on the side while I move this chair." With a lot of pushing and shoving, I moved a large upholstered chair from the corner of the room to the bedside.

"Now, stand up, James. Hold on to me and balance on your good foot. That's the way." I held on to his arm while he moaned, but he did what I told him to do. "Lean on me and take one hop to the chair. Now swivel around and sit down."

He did it, but you would've thought I was putting him through torture. James was not a silent sufferer by any stretch of the imagination.

I stripped the bed, then went to the linen closet for fresh sheets. When I had the bed remade, he turned his face up to me with a mournful look. "Can I get back in now?"

"No, you can't. I'll bring an ottoman so you can elevate your foot. Then I'll make you some toast and more hot coffee. I think you'll find it easier to eat sitting up than lying in bed."

By the time I had his foot situated, my back was letting me know that I'd done enough lifting and pushing and rearranging. I brought James a plate of buttered toast and a large mug of hot coffee, putting it near to hand and telling him to leave his dishes on the table beside him when he finished.

"I'm going to clean up the kitchen, but I'll be back in a little while. I can figure out how long it'll take you to eat, so you don't need to be ringing that bell when you're through."

"Can't reach it nohow," he muttered pitifully.

"We're not going to forget you, James. Don't worry about that. It's just that there's a time and a place for everything, and sometimes we have to get in line and take our turn."

By the time I had the kitchen cleaned and a few toys picked up, Hazel Marie came downstairs, dressed—if you can call it that—in a pink loose-fitting running suit that had nothing but comfort to recommend it. She had brushed her hair and put it in a ponytail, but her face was only partially made up. In spite of having been so lavish with the use of cosmetics before the babies came, Hazel Marie had obviously begun to slack off. Why, there was even an inch of dark roots showing in her part, indicating that visits to Velma had not been high on her priority list.

I peered closer. No eye shadow, either! Things were going downhill fast, which was just one more thing to worry about.

"Well, they're down," she said, blowing out her breath. "Whew, with J.D. gone, it's awful around here with everybody wanting something at the same time. Thank you for coming, Miss Julia—I was about to lose my mind."

"I'm happy to do it. Sit down now, and I'll pour you a cup of coffee. Have you had anything to eat?"

"I'm not hungry," she said, as she sat at the kitchen table. I put two slices of bread in the toaster for her. Then she sat up abruptly. "How's James? He's awfully quiet. I'd better see about him."

"Stay right where you are. He's fine. He's sitting in a chair. I changed his sheets—the whole room was getting a little rank. I'll look in on him in a little while, but I need to talk to you for a minute."

So I did, telling her my plan, although, as I'd told Lillian, presentation is everything. I put it to her not as a way to teach her to cook, but as a way to have meals on her table—along with the recipes that would allow her to replicate the dishes whenever she wanted.

Hazel Marie put her arms on the table and her head down on them, crying. My heart almost seized up at the thought that I'd hurt her feelings. "We don't have to do this, Hazel Marie. Not at all. If you don't like the idea, they can just bring a dish like they'd do anyway."

"Oh, no," she said, sitting up, with her hands covering her face. "I think it's wonderful. It's just . . . I can't believe anybody would do that for me."

"Everybody's eager to do it. Well, the ones I've talked to are, but I'm sure everybody else will be, too. They love you, Hazel Marie, and this is one way they can show it. And everybody knows how interested you are in cooking, so it'll be a real pleasure for them to demonstrate their special recipes."

She wiped away the tears and smiled. I patted her hand and said, "It'd be nice if we could find somebody who's responsible to watch the babies while you're cooking. Mildred and I can do it this Saturday, but be thinking of someone we can get. Now," I went on, "let's you and me go get James and take him into your family room. We'll get him comfortable in the recliner and turn on the television for him. That'll cut down on the bell ringing for a while."

About halfway down the hall, with Hazel Marie on one side of James and me on the other with his arms across our shoulders— I got the one with the cast which was about to drive me to the floor—and him moaning with each hop, I began to think that moving him had not been one of my better ideas.

I steadied myself with a hand against the wall while he rested on one foot like a stork. Maybe a flamingo, one of those thin-legged birds. "Come on, James, take little hops. We're almost there."

"But ev'ry hop jolts me bad," he said, leaning crookedly because I was taller than Hazel Marie. "I may have to go back to bed."

Hazel Marie looked up at him. "It's closer to go on than to go back, James. Just a little farther."

We finally got him to the recliner where he sank down with a deep sigh. Grateful to be free of the burden, we showed him how to manipulate the chair to a comfortable position, with his feet elevated.

"Now you're all set," I said as I turned on the television.

" 'Cept for the remote," he said, reaching out for it.

I gave it to him, then followed Hazel Marie out of the room, conveniently forgetting that the bell was still in the bedroom.

"Go sit down, Hazel Marie," I told her. "Catch your breath for a while. I'll go up and make the beds and straighten a little."

She protested, but I remained firm because she was about wiped out. Going quietly from room to room upstairs so as not to wake the babies, I gave everything a lick and a promise to do better next time.

When I got back downstairs, all was quiet except for a game show on television. I walked in to see about James, asking if he needed anything.

"I'm feelin' like it 'bout time for lunch," he said, barely taking his eyes off the set. Then his head jerked around. "You smell something burnin'?"

"Oh, Lord!" I said, whirling out of the room. "She's in the kitchen."

And sure enough, smoke was drifting out of the kitchen as I ran through the dining room. The smoke alarm began shrieking loud enough to wake the dead and both babies upstairs. Hazel Marie had the back door open while she flailed away with a broom, batting the alarm to make it stop.

"What happened?" I asked as soon as she knocked the alarm off the wall and quiet descended—except for the wailing from the cribs upstairs. "Where's the fire?"

She leaned against the wall and pointed to the sink, where a skillet still hissed as water ran over it. "I was fixing James a grilled cheese sandwich, and the pan just started smoking. I guess it got too hot."

I guess it did, I thought, looking at the shriveled, blackened, water-soaked sandwich in the skillet. "No harm done, Hazel Marie. You go on and see to the babies. I'll fix lunch."

After Hazel Marie's attempt, I felt quite competent making two nicely grilled cheese sandwiches, one for her and one for James. Putting one sandwich, along with a glass of milk, on a tray, I took them in to James.

His mouth turned down at the sight of the milk. "A Co-Cola'd go a whole lot better with that," he said.

"You need the calcium," I said, mainly because I hadn't been able to find any soft drinks. "Good for the bones, you know."

❦

Later, as I dragged myself tiredly into the kitchen at home, I said, "Lillian, I am going to find some help for Hazel Marie if it's the last thing I do." And the way I felt after that strenuous morning, it could very well be the last thing I did.

Chapter 8

Before she could respond, I headed for the telephone on the counter by the refrigerator. "I hate doing this," I said, knowing full well that a ringing telephone was the last thing Hazel Marie needed. "But I forgot to tell her something."

"Tell her 'bout that man callin' her, if that what you forget."

I nodded, listening as the phone rang so long that I was about to hang up and run back over there. When Hazel Marie finally answered, she sounded beside herself, in spite of the fact that I'd spent most of the day helping her.

"Hazel Marie, honey, I'm sorry to interrupt whatever you're doing, but . . ."

"Oh, Miss Julia," she sobbed, "I almost killed him!"

"*Who?*"

"James! He has to go to the bathroom and I tried to help him get up, but he lost his balance and fell back in the chair and I fell on top of him. I don't know what to do and he has to go real bad."

"Okay, listen. Here's what you do: Put the phone down and run to the pantry. Find a fruit jar or some other large watertight container with a lid and take it to him. Pour something out if you have to. Take it to him right now, then come back to the phone. I'll wait."

She gasped at the simplicity of it, flung down the phone, and left. I waited, hearing her footsteps as she ran through the house and hearing also the mumble of their voices as she and James spoke.

"Miss Julia?" she panted as she picked up the phone. "I'm back.

I don't know why I didn't think of that, except he probably wouldn't have used it if I had. But when I told him it was your idea, all he said was, 'I sure hope you close that door.' " She took a deep breath, pulling herself together. "I guess I'll have to go empty it."

"No, that's why I'm calling. I wanted to tell you not to try to move him by yourself. Sam will be over there in a little while and he'll empty it and get him back to bed. I'm sorry, Hazel Marie—I should've thought to tell you before I left."

"That's all right. I'm just, well, I'm not thinking too good myself. Everybody needs something at the same time. I'll be so glad when J.D. gets home."

You and me, I thought but didn't say. "Well, here's something else I keep forgetting to tell you. Lillian says that some man has called you a couple of times, but he doesn't give his name or say what he wants. He just hangs up when she says you aren't here."

"Wonder who it could be?"

"Probably a salesman or somebody wanting a donation. I just thought you should know."

"Well, don't tell him anything," she said with asperity. "I don't need anybody else wanting something from me." Then she giggled. "I might throw that milk carton I got out of the trash at whoever wants another thing. And I mean when James gets through with it, too."

"Lord, Lillian," I said, after hanging up the phone. "To think that just a couple of days ago, I was feeling that all was right with the world. Everybody was happy and settled and getting on with life and . . ." I stopped, put my hand to my mouth and reconsidered. "Well, I guess I wasn't thinking of those poor souls who've had tornadoes, wildfires, hurricanes, floods, wars, lost jobs, and foreclosures. And fairly soon, there'll be snow and sleet and power outages and who knows what else. When you think of all that, it doesn't look as if anything, anywhere, is going right. It's just chaos everywhere you look."

"Yes'm, but that's livin', Miss Julia. Ever'body have to get they enjoys where they can, when they can. Besides, James'll get well, Mr. Pickens'll be back home, an' the babies'll grow up. Nothin' last forever. Least, when you think of all them other things, I hope they don't."

"That's one way to look at it, I guess. Everything—good or bad—will pass sooner or later." I stopped and studied the matter for a minute. "Somehow or another—I don't know why—that doesn't seem very comforting."

"But the Reverend Abernathy say it do. He tell us we live in a transitory world, then he tell us what that mean. It mean something that don't last long, an' we got to take a overview. Which mean lookin' over what happen here an' countin' on what happen hereafter."

"Lillian, that is the most comforting thing you could've said. The reverend is absolutely right, and when things start going wrong we need to be reminded of it. At least *I* do." I sat down at the table and rested my head on my hand. "I declare, I wish Pastor Ledbetter would take some lessons from him. It's our annual pledge time— the Every Member Canvass—and all we hear is how we should be tithing and giving over and above. Then next Sunday one of the elders will tell us how badly we need a youth director, and the Sunday after that a deacon will tell us that the church furnace is acting up. I think I might start going to your church."

"You jus' come on anytime," Lillian said with a little smile. "We be glad to have you. But you might get a little of the same kind of preachin' now an' then, 'cause the Reverend Abernathy say the Lord don't pay no 'lectric bills."

"That's true," I said as we laughed together. "Well, I guess I'd better get up from here and try to line up a few more cooks for Hazel Marie. Sam will be up in a little while, and I expect James will be glad to see him. He's been sitting in that chair all day."

"I 'spect he been sleepin' in it, too. He can nod off jus' settin' in a straight chair, so you don't need to feel sorry for him. I jus' hope this the last night Mr. Sam have to spend over there."

Saying, "I do, too," on my way out, I headed for the new library, where my folder and calendar were, thinking as I went about who I should call next.

Etta Mae, I decided, because her work hours were somewhat erratic and I wanted her to have a choice of days before they filled up—if they filled up. I was somewhat skeptical of her cooking skills, knowing that she patronized McDonald's an inordinate number of times each week, but I couldn't leave her recipes out of Hazel Marie's book. The two women had known each other too long and I myself owed Etta Mae the courtesy of being included and much more than that, if the truth be told. So, figuring that she was home by this time, I dialed the phone in her single-wide at the Hillandale trailer park.

"Etta Mae?" I said when she answered. "This is Julia Murdoch. I have a favor to ask of you."

"Uh, Miss Julia, I really don't think I can go back to West Virginia anytime soon."

"West Virginia? I'm not going to West Virginia or anywhere else, for that matter. No, I'm calling about something else." And I went on to explain what I was doing and what I hoped she could do to help me.

"Recipes? Oh, sure, I can do that," Etta Mae said in a considerably lightened tone of voice. "And I'd love to get in the kitchen with Hazel Marie—that'd be fun. Let me think a minute. I don't do a whole lot of cooking, but my granny taught me how to fix a few things."

"What's a good day for you?" I asked, my calendar at the ready. "Mildred Allen and Ida Lee are going over tomorrow, and LuAnne Conover has Monday and Wednesday. She wants to do two days, but I doubt anybody else will."

"Oh, I can do next Friday, a week from today. I have it off because I'm working that weekend. Would that do?"

"It'll do perfectly," I said, putting her name on the calendar. "Now, Etta Mae, we need a main dish, although you can submit a couple of others if you want to. But the main dish has to be something simple, something you can show her how to make. And remember it's Hazel Marie we're dealing with."

"Okay," Etta Mae said. "I've got the perfect thing right here in my recipe book. One of the shut-ins I look after gave it to me, and I've been meaning to try it. Looks like it can be put together early in the day, then it just simmers for a while. I'll read it off to you."

Etta Mae's Chicken Cacciatore

Flour, salt, and pepper 4 chicken breast halves (with or without bone, as preferred)

Heat 1½ tablespoons of butter and 2½ tablespoons of olive oil in a Dutch oven. Sauté 1 clove of minced garlic, 1 large chopped onion, and 1 large chopped bell pepper.

Add and saute the prepared chicken breasts until the chicken is golden brown.

Then add the following:

2 cups canned tomatoes with juice
1 tablespoon tomato paste
2 tablespoons parsley
1 large pinch each of thyme and oregano (dried is okay)
Salt and pepper to taste
1 cup dry red wine (Burgundy or claret)

Cover and simmer gently for at least 1 hour—longer is fine. Then add 2 cups of sliced mushrooms (preferably fresh, but drained if not) and cook 30 minutes more. Serve over rice.

Serves 4.

(Hazel Marie, even if this comes out right when Etta Mae makes it, if I were you I'd wait for Lillian to look it over before attempting it yourself.)

"That sounds delicious, Etta Mae," I said, more than a little surprised because I'd thought her recipe would be for Hamburger Helper or sloppy joes or some other such throw-together dish. I halfway wished it had been, instead of an untried one. "Now, if you'll make out a grocery list of all the ingredients and drop it off here, we'll have everything at Hazel Marie's ready to go next Friday. But be prepared, because you'll have to show her how to sauté."

"That's no problem," Etta Mae said, laughing. "I've been frying stuff my whole life."

"There's one other thing," I said, thinking that I should put the word out wherever I could, and went on to explain what had happened to James which resulted in Hazel Marie's dire need of help. "So, if you know anybody who could help with him or with the babies or just come in to fix breakfast and lunch, I'll, well, I'll dance at your wedding."

"Shoo," she said, laughing, "that won't be anytime soon. I've been down that road too many times already." Then, turning serious, she went on, "I wish I could come over and help, Miss Julia, but my boss is threatening mayhem if any of us even look like we want time off. But let me think about it. I know a lot of people out in the county, so I might can come up with somebody."

"Lillian," I said, as I pushed through the swinging door into the kitchen, "you won't believe this, but Etta Mae Wiggins gave me what looks like an interesting recipe—except she's never made it, so who knows? Look at this and see if we should try it first."

As I handed her the recipe I'd copied down, the telephone rang and I turned away to answer it.

"Miss Julia?"

"Hazel Marie?" I could barely make out her voice, it sounded so subdued and strained. "What's the matter? What's wrong?"

"Uh, well," she said, half murmuring, "I guess I have to cancel our cooking date tomorrow. I'm real sorry, but it's not a good time for Mildred and Ida Lee to come over."

"Why, what in the world, Hazel Marie? Everything's all set and ingredients have been bought. It's really too late to cancel. We can work around James and the babies, so what's brought this on?"

"Well, uh, you know how somebody's been calling me?"

"Yes . . . ?"

"And you know we've been wanting somebody to help with James?"

"Yes, and . . . ?"

"Well, I guess we might have somebody."

"Who?" I asked, gripping the phone, disturbed at the way she sounded. "It'd be wonderful to have help, but who is it?"

"I don't know how he found out where I live, but he just called. And he's on his way over because he has nowhere else to go. He said he's in a bad way and needs help from his family, and I'm all the family he has."

"*Who,* Hazel Marie? Who're you talking about?"

"My uncle. You remember . . . ?"

"*Brother Vern?* Brother Vernon Puckett? Don't tell me he's back in town."

I had to sit down, so done in by the thought of that money-grubbing, itinerant street preacher back in our lives again—and back just when Hazel Marie didn't need another soul to look after. She already had three needy people—three and a half, if you counted when Mr. Pickens was home, which you might as well—clamoring for her attention. The Lord knew she didn't need another one.

Chapter 9

After hanging up, I sprang from the chair and hurried out of the room. "I've got to get Sam up. Lillian," I called over my shoulder, "don't go anywhere. I'll tell you about it in a minute. Lord, we're in for it now."

Hurrying up the stairs to our bedroom, where Sam was sleeping after being up most of the night with James, I hated the thought of waking him early. But, hesitating only a second before putting my hand on his shoulder, I whispered, "Sam? Can you wake up?"

He turned, looked at me through half-closed, bleary eyes, and said, "Hey, honey. Time to get up?"

"Not quite," I said, sitting on the side of the bed and taking his hand. "But I need you to, anyway. Hazel Marie just called, and that good-for-nothing uncle of hers is back, wanting—no, *expecting*—her to take him in. We need to do something."

Sam sat up, his eyes clearing at the news. "Brother Vern? He wants to move in?"

"That's what it sounds like. Oh, Sam, she sounded like a beaten child, and I just can't stand for her to be under his thumb again—you know how he is. We've got to get rid of him."

"Wait. Wait, Julia. I do know how he is, and he doesn't stay anywhere for long. He may just want to drop by to see her. Maybe hit her up for a little money, then he'll be gone again."

"I don't think so this time," I said, feeling weepy with dismay. "He told her he was in a bad way—so who knows? He may be sick because he said he needed his family at this time. And, as you know, she's the only family he has."

"Hmm," Sam said, "probably the only family who'll give him the time of day. But, look, sweetheart, it's not going to be a problem. Pickens will be back tomorrow and he'll handle Brother Vern. Besides, we can put him to work helping with James." Sam smiled and kissed my hand. "That ought to cut down on how long he stays."

"I wouldn't count on it. If he's sick, he won't be any help—he'll need help himself." I stood up and began pacing by the side of the bed. "I tell you, Sam, Hazel Marie isn't the strongest person in the world and this might be the final straw. I mean, she's barely gotten over the birth of twins, and along with acquiring a home of her own with a full-time husband in it, well, it's a lot to adjust to."

Sam laughed and reached for my hand as I made another turn. "Oh, I think the way Pickens has to travel, he's more of a part-time husband."

"Even worse. He's in and out, and half the time she doesn't know where he is, and now that uncle of hers means to camp on her doorstep. And we haven't even mentioned James laid up in bed, clanging that bell and wanting to go to the bathroom. I tell you, Sam, I don't know how much more she can take. She's already letting herself go, what with dark roots and no eye shadow."

"Well, that's certainly a bad sign," Sam said, grinning, as he threw back the covers and got out of bed. "I'll go on over and see what Puckett's intentions are. But, remember, Pickens will have something to say about what goes on in that house. I don't think he'll take kindly to having another burden put on his wife."

"You're right—I know you're right. I'm worrying for nothing." I sat down in the warm place that Sam had just left. "You think we should call him and let him know what'll be waiting for him?"

"No," Sam said, looking back at me from the bathroom door. "He'll be back tomorrow, and for all we know, Brother Vern will be gone by then. I think we ought to assume this is just a brief visit and it may well be. Once he hears those two babies crying and James moaning and Lloyd running in and out, and Mildred and Ida Lee and you banging around in the kitchen, he may head for the hills before lunchtime."

"And that's another thing," I said. "I talked Hazel Marie out of canceling our cooking session, but I don't know how Mildred will take Vernon Puckett. She's not accustomed to, well, his kind of personality. He'll take one look at all the diamonds she wears and think he's hit the jackpot."

"I wouldn't worry about that," Sam said, turning on the shower. Raising his voice over the roar of the water, he called, "I expect Mildred can look after herself."

Mildred's ability to look after herself was a given as far as I was concerned. If Brother Vern came on too strong, she could and would take him down not one, but several notches, if she took a mind to. No, my real concern was for Hazel Marie. It was the shame and embarrassment that she would suffer if her uncle began to poor-mouth, wheedle, and flat-out beg Mildred for support of whatever ragtag ministry he was currently engaged in.

Just as I finished telling Lillian the new problem we were about to face, the telephone rang.

I snatched it up, wondering what the news would be this time. "Yes?"

"Hey, Miss Julia, it's me, Etta Mae. I just thought of something else to make for Hazel Marie. My granny would be tickled to death to have her recipe for Ritz cracker pie in your cookbook."

Ritz cracker pie? I'd never heard of such a thing, but not wanting to offend Etta Mae or her granny, I said, "Well, I don't know, Etta Mae. Your chicken dish might be all she can handle."

"Oh, that's all right. I can whip it up in a minute and all she has to do is watch. Listen to this."

She read it off to me, then said, "See? Real easy and real good. My granny's been fixing it for years."

Etta Mae's Granny's Ritz Cracker Pie

20 Ritz crackers, crumbled coarsely
1 scant cup sugar
¾ cup pecan pieces
3 egg whites

Preheat the oven to 350°F. Mix the crackers with ½ cup of the sugar and add the pecans. In a separate bowl, beat the egg whites with the rest of the sugar, then fold the cracker mixture into the beaten whites. Pour it all into a greased 8-inch pie plate and bake for 20 minutes. Serve with whipped cream.

Serves 6.

(Hazel Marie, if anybody asks, you can tell them what's in this. Otherwise, I'd keep quiet.)

"Yes, it does sound easy," I agreed, but for the life of me I couldn't imagine what a sweet Ritz cracker would taste like. "So if you want to make it, I'll get the ingredients. But, Etta Mae, let me ask you something while I have you. Did you ever know Hazel Marie's uncle Vernon Puckett?"

"Oh, brother, did I ever. Why?"

"Well, he's now shown up at Hazel Marie's, saying he wants to be with his family in his time of need."

"When has he ever *not* had a time of need?" Etta Mae demanded. "I hope Hazel Marie runs him off, and if she won't, I bet J.D. will. He's nothing but a leech, Miss Julia. He's been trying to get me in a river for years."

"What! Get you in a *river?*"

"For full immersion in running water, which he says is the only kind that takes. And I've already been baptized about three times. I'm not going to do it anymore."

"Well," I said, somewhat taken aback because I'd always thought that once baptized, always baptized. "I don't blame you. Stay out of rivers, Etta Mae—no telling what's in them. Of course, we Presbyterians don't believe in full-body dunking. We just sprinkle a little water on the head, which doesn't soak you through and through, but it sure does mess up your hair. Anyway, I'm hoping Brother Vern is there just for a short visit and that he'll be gone before your cooking day."

"Me, too. But, listen, Miss Julia, there's another reason I called. I may have somebody to help Hazel Marie. She's real good with babies—loves them to death—and, if they don't mind plain country cooking, she's a whiz in the kitchen."

Brother Vern flew out of my head. "Wonderful, Etta Mae. That is wonderful news. Who is it? Do I know her?"

"I think you've met her. It's my granny. She says she's going crazy out in the country by herself. She's been doing for other people all her life, and now with the family all gone, she needs something to do. Idle hands are the devil's workshop, she keeps telling me, and if I don't find her something, she's going to apply at Wal-Mart for the Christmas season. I don't want her working there, but she says her Social Security has stopped stretching and she needs the work."

A vague image of the skinny, fast-talking, gray-haired woman leaning on Hazel Marie reared up in my mind, and I really didn't know what to say. So I temporized. "Well, Etta Mae, I know Hazel Marie would love to have her around, but it might be too hard on your granny. I mean, it'll be a lot of work, what with the babies, James, and maybe Brother Vern, too. I'm not sure she'd be able to handle it."

"Oh, you wouldn't believe the amount of work that woman can put out. She'd love it and it would set my mind at ease, knowing that nobody's going to grab her in the Wal-Mart parking lot. I'll call Hazel Marie right now and tell her that her worries are over."

We hung up as I hung over the counter in dismay, realizing that Granny Wiggins would do nothing but add to Hazel Marie's workload.

Chapter 10

After telling Lillian what Etta Mae had just told me, I sank down in a chair and wondered what in the world to do.

"Mrs. Wiggins won't be a bit of help, Lillian. She's older than the hills and about the size of Lloyd. She can't possibly get James in and out of bed by herself. Oh, she can take trays in to him, but whether she can cook or not, I don't know. And the babies! One of them would drag her down to the floor, to say nothing of trying to manage two. It's just not going to work."

"I think you worryin' 'fore you have to," Lillian said as she came over to set the table. " 'Sides, if she that bad, why didn't you tell Miss Etta Mae she won't do?"

"Because I didn't want to hurt her feelings, that's why. So now her feelings are really going to be hurt when we try her grandmother out, then have to let her go. Oh," I sighed, "it's all a big mess. I've a good mind to move Hazel Marie, the babies, and Mr. Pickens back over here and leave her house to all the sick and ailing and elderly."

"Huh, where you gonna put 'em? You forgettin' that that big bedroom you used to have downstairs be a liberry now?"

"I guess that won't work, will it?" Then I straightened up with determination and said, "Well, if it comes down to it, I'll just buy them another house."

"Miss Julia," Lillian said, frowning at me, "you goin' off about half cockeyed now. What good's that gonna do? Miss Hazel Marie, she feel like she got to take care of James an' her uncle, an' I guess Miss Etta Mae's granny, too, if it come to it, so she won't move out an' leave 'em all by theyselves. You got to come up with something else."

"I know it," I said, sagging back again. "I'm just talking to hear myself talk."

Sam called after Lillian and I had eaten supper and Lillian had left for home. He was at Hazel Marie's, spending another night—the last one, I hoped—looking after James.

"Julia?" he said, speaking softly. "I just have a minute to talk, but wanted you to know that you were right. Hazel Marie's uncle says he's been diagnosed with the high blood, which I guess means high blood pressure, and the doctor's told him he has to get a lot of rest and stay on his diet or he'll have a stroke. So it looks like he's here for the long haul, or at least till Pickens gets home."

Well, that just took the cake. Hazel Marie might as well open a rest home and welcome all comers. The idea of that man just showing up, expecting Hazel Marie to nurse and care for him after all he'd put her through. It beat all I'd ever heard, and I told Sam so.

"You remember, don't you, Sam," I said, "how he treated her and how she showed up at my door, black and blue, and how he's tried everything under the sun to get his hands on Lloyd's inheritance? It wouldn't surprise me a bit if he's as healthy as a horse. I'd demand to see a doctor's report, if it were me, and I expect Mr. Pickens will. What's he doing now?"

"Resting. Hazel Marie had to put him in Lloyd's room—the only empty one left. So Lloyd will be with you tonight, and—this should make you feel better—he'll be with us full time for as long as Brother Vern is here."

"Well, of course I'm glad we'll have Lloyd, but that's his room and he may not appreciate being evicted. Why didn't she put him in James's apartment?"

Sam chuckled under his breath. "James got downright feisty at that idea. Didn't like it a bit, and I don't blame him. That's his home. But I tell you, Julia, I thought they were going to have a knock-down, drag-out fight—James and Brother Vern didn't take to each other at all. James said if anybody was going to live in his house, it would be him and he'd just lie up there by himself and starve to death."

"Oh, my," I groaned. "Well, I hope you get some sleep tonight. I'll be over around nine to meet Mildred and Ida Lee, but I expect the last thing on Hazel Marie's mind now is learning to cook."

❧

I didn't know what to expect when I rang the bell at Hazel Marie's house the next morning, but I thought—wrongly, as it turned out—that I was prepared for the worst. Sam had called earlier and told me that he was staying over to be a short-order cook for what he called all the boarders, while Hazel Marie saw to the babies and Lloyd took breakfast orders from James and Brother Vern.

And now, as I stood waiting to be admitted, sniffing at the sight in the driveway of what had to be Brother Vern's old, listing-to-one-side Cadillac—burnt orange and white, looking like a reject from a Florida used-car lot—my bright idea of how to put food on Hazel Marie's table seemed an unworkable trifle. But I'd set it in motion, so there was nothing to do but see it through. At least for this day, which if it turned into a holy mess, I'd cancel the other cooks and shelve my cookbook plans.

Sam opened the door for me, smiled grimly, and said, "Welcome to the madhouse, sweetheart."

I hugged him, having sorely missed him the last few nights. "Go home, Sam, and get in bed. I expect you've been up all night, haven't you?"

"Just off and on. James is doing better physically, but he's all torn up about Vernon Puckett coming in and taking everybody's attention."

"Is Brother Vern really sick?" I whispered as we stood in the front hall, with household sounds reverberating from up and down the stairs.

"Yeah, I guess he is," Sam said, sighing. "Apparently, he does have hypertension. He told us about his dizzy spells—where he had them, how long they lasted—all in great detail, and how the doctor told him he's a stroke waiting to happen. He's on some kind of expensive medication—well, he's supposed to be, but he says he can't afford to have the prescription filled. That was for Hazel Marie's benefit, of course, and she immediately gave him some money, which so far remains in his pocket."

"Which is probably where it'll stay," I said, "waiting for more. But, Sam, does he look sick? Is he on bed rest? How much help— besides financial—does he need?"

"Well, I tell you, Julia, he looks fine to me. His face is a little flushed, but that's pretty much his natural coloring, if I remember correctly. And he's taking seriously what the doctor said about resting—he even suggested moving James upstairs and letting him have the downstairs bedroom with its own bath, so he wouldn't have to climb the stairs. I put my foot down on that, because I saw how quickly he can move when it's time to eat."

About that time, Lloyd came out of James's bedroom, saw us in the hall, and walked over just as one of the babies screamed upstairs. "Mornin', Miss Julia," he said, putting his hands over his ears. "Kinda hectic around here, isn't it?"

I put my arm around his shoulders. "I expect you wish it was a school day, don't you? But we're going to need you when Miss Mildred and Ida Lee get here."

"There they are now," he said, pointing out the door as Mildred's sleek Lincoln Town Car pulled in behind that Popsicle-colored Cadillac in the driveway.

"Oh, my," I said, watching as Ida Lee began unloading bags of groceries from the car. "Where's Brother Vern? Is the kitchen clean?"

"Kitchen's all cleaned up," Sam said, "and Brother Vern's still in bed."

Lloyd said, "I had to take his breakfast to him, 'cause he didn't feel like getting up. Mr. Sam made his famous pancakes and

Brother Vern fussed at me 'cause they got cold on my way up. Even though I hurried."

Sam went out to help unload Mildred's car, and I turned to Lloyd. "His fussing at you is going to stop. He'll probably do it only when nobody else is around, so you tell me if he says anything to you again."

"Well, I don't mind," the boy said. "Sick people get kinda cranky anyway."

"You're very understanding, Lloyd, but I've yet to be convinced that he's really sick. Oh," I said, plastering a smile on my face and turning as Mildred got to the door, a sack in her hand. "Good morning, Mildred. Are you ready to start cooking up a storm?"

"I sure am," Mildred said, plainly in an expectant mood. "Look, I brought in the mushrooms. And good morning to you, Lloyd."

Sam and Ida Lee followed her in, their arms full of grocery sacks, pots, and various utensils. Greetings flowed around us as I relieved Ida Lee of a Dutch oven and a chef's knife, while Lloyd caught an overloaded sack from Sam. Leading them all to the kitchen, side-stepping a stroller on my way, I chattered away, telling them about Hazel Marie's uncle, who'd made a surprise visit.

"But he won't bother us," I said, "and we won't bother him. We're going to have a wonderful time. Lloyd, if you will, run up and tell your mother everybody's here and we're ready to start."

Ida Lee arranged things on the kitchen counter, while Mildred settled herself at the table in the corner of the kitchen, and I began pouring coffee. "Now, Mildred," I said, in an attempt to prepare her, "Hazel Marie's uncle is a case unto himself, I'm sorry to say. If he comes in, you'll just have to overlook him. But he's not feeling well, so you may not get to meet him. Hazel Marie, though, may be a little jumpy and not have her mind too much on cooking—they've never really gotten along."

"Oh, don't worry about me," Mildred said, reaching for the sugar bowl as the array of diamonds on her fingers sparkled in the light. It wasn't that she wore so many rings as it was so many carats in a few. "My family's full of that kind. He won't bother me at all."

Hazel Marie walked in then, looking somewhat distracted and ragged in an old navy running suit that she'd about worn out during her pregnancy and that I now wished she had. She greeted Mildred and Ida Lee, then told us that the babies were down for a nap that she hoped would be a long one. She accepted the coffee cup I handed her and visibly made an effort to face what I feared was a now-unwanted cooking lesson.

"You're all so nice to do this for me," Hazel Marie said, putting on the social smile that she'd learned from me. "I can't wait to get started."

"Well," I said, pulling out a chair, "rest a minute before you start. Has James had his breakfast?"

"Yes, ma'am," she said, "before anybody else. I think he got worried about his bills or something. He sent Lloyd out to check his mailbox real early, which," she went on with a wry smile, "was another thing I forgot to do. Anyway, the two of them have been huddled in there, going over his mail. I think Lloyd's doing the writing for him. I'm not sure the poor thing can even sign his name."

About that time, Lloyd stuck his head in and announced, "As soon as I finish helping James, I'm going to run to the post office for him. If anybody needs me for anything, I'll be at Miss Julia's house working on my computer after that. There're some things I have to look up."

Hazel Marie jumped up and kissed him. "You're real sweet to help James out. My goodness," she said, noticing the stack of envelopes in Lloyd's hand, "he has a lot of correspondence." As Lloyd left, she turned back to us. "Let's get started, Ida Lee, and you better keep me busy. The babies are teething and I didn't get much sleep. I might keel over any minute."

"We'll get our beef stroganoff on in just a few minutes," Ida Lee said. "Why don't you sit down and watch."

"No, I want to do something. But you have to tell me what to do. And, I guess," Hazel Marie said with a laugh, "tell me how to do it."

"All right," Ida Lee said, opening a package of meat. "First, we're going to put our recipe right here so we can follow it and not miss anything. Then we'll cut this sirloin into cubes, about an inch or so in size. Here's a cutting board and a knife. You can start, but be sure to trim off all the fat."

That lasted a minute or so, as Hazel Marie carefully—too carefully—sawed away at the meat. Then Ida Lee took the knife, saying, "You're doing good, but why don't you put the Dutch oven on the stove and put a couple of tablespoons of butter in it. Then you can slice the onions. I'll finish this."

I sat down by Mildred to watch the show, then almost said something to correct what Hazel Marie was doing. Ida Lee beat me to it.

Softly and patiently, Ida Lee said, "It works better if you peel the onions first."

"Oh," Hazel Marie said, "okay."

Before long, they had the meat cubes sizzling in the melted butter, and Ida Lee said, "I'm adding a split garlic clove—see how I smash it to get the peel off? And now, a bay leaf. Watch the meat, and turn it so that it browns on all sides." Soon Ida Lee had Hazel Marie watching and stirring while the meat browned. Ida Lee was watching, too.

"That's good," Ida Lee said. "Now we're ready for the other ingredients. Let's add a teaspoon of salt—that's right, just throw it in. Then a teaspoon of paprika and one and a half cups of water and stir it around a little. Now put the lid on and lower the heat so it will just simmer."

As Hazel Marie slowly and deliberately followed her instructions, Ida Lee remained patient and good-humored.

As Hazel Marie lowered the heat and looked to Ida Lee to be sure she'd done it right, Ida Lee gave her a big smile. "Perfect! The first step is done. You can rest now, because it has to simmer about an hour."

"That's all there is to it?" Hazel Marie noticeably brightened. "Why, I think I could do it by myself now."

"Well, we aren't through," Ida Lee said, "but the rest is just as easy."

Mildred and I had not done any entertaining—no *Have you heard* or *Let me tell you*—as earlier promised, both of us being transfixed by Hazel Marie's ineptness with a knife and by fear of what she might cut. Hazel Marie joined us at the table, her eyes bright from having successfully completed the first step, as she urged Ida Lee to join us.

"I'll just put up what we're through with and clean the counter," Ida Lee said, then looked around as a loud voice called from the front hall.

"Hazel Marie! Where are you, girl?"

I knew immediately who was yelling his head off and turned toward the dining room as Brother Vern approached. Stopping at the door, he looked straight across at Ida Lee in her gray uniform. "Well, now, young lady, I sure hope you know how to cook better'n whoever fixed breakfast," he said, grinning as if he'd paid her a compliment. "Thank the Lord Hazel Marie's hired herself a real cook. What's for dinner? I could eat a horse if you fixed it right."

That was what I call starting off on the wrong foot—the one he always started with and the one he pretty much stayed on.

Chapter 11

There he stood in the doorway, his head swiveling to survey the kitchen and those of us in it, his mouth dropping open at the sight of us staring right back at him. I hardly recognized him—gone was the shoe-black hair, replaced by a frowzy gray mop, while an extra twenty or so pounds had been added to a none-too-slender frame to begin with.

Realizing that four women were gazing at his rumpled pajamas that had seen too many mornings and an unbelted robe that needed to be closed—as did the slightly open fly of his pajamas—he yelped and snatched the robe around himself. Hazel Marie sat frozen stiff in her chair as I jumped up and Mildred leaned over to get a better look.

I grasped his arm and turned him away. "Julia Murdoch, Mr. Puckett," I said, walking him back through the dining room. "You remember me, don't you? Why don't you run upstairs and get dressed—it's eleven o'clock in the morning. Nobody comes to the table in their nightclothes, do they? In fact, you have just enough time to get dressed and go have your prescription filled. Why don't you do that while we get lunch ready?"

I chattered on, talking over him when he tried to speak, and all the while leading him to the foot of the stairs. "Now, Mr. Puckett," I said sternly, "you are a guest in this house so it behooves you to act accordingly. Hazel Marie has her own life to lead, which is what she's doing this morning. You can't expect everybody to change their plans because you've chosen to show up out of the blue. And," I went on, "a word to the wise: Mr. Pickens will be here before long, and I'll advise you to conduct yourself in a respectful way while you're in his home. Otherwise, I doubt you'll be receiving an overly warm welcome."

"Oh, my Lord," he said, his face flushed with embarrassment, "I didn't know we had company. I didn't mean to barge in like that."

"I know you didn't, so it's all right for now. But go on up and get dressed for the day. If you don't want to go to the drugstore, you can entertain yourself with the morning paper for a while. We'll let you know when lunch is ready." In other words, but more nicely put: Stay out of the way and leave Hazel Marie alone.

As he turned and started up the stairs, pulling himself along on the banisters, I said, "And don't wake the babies."

I started back to the kitchen until stopped by a whispered voice calling my name. I went to the door of the bedroom and looked in at James, who was propped up in bed with a pair of earbuds hanging around his neck. As he shifted his position, I heard the rustle and crackle of paper hidden under the sheets. I smiled to myself, thinking that Brother Vern would have trouble finding something to read.

"How are you, James?" I asked, surprised that he wasn't in the den watching television. "You need something?"

"No'm. Lloyd, he let me play his iTunes, so I'm all right. But that ole preacher man, he 'bout to drive me crazy. I was real glad to hear you jackin' him up, 'cause he need it. I can't even watch my shows 'thout him comin' in an' tellin' me I'm wallerin' in hell watchin' them things. He jus' makin' me feel so low-down I don't know what to do."

"I'm sorry about that, James, but you know he's Hazel Marie's uncle so there's not much we can do for now. But," I said, with a smile and a glance toward the front door, "Mr. Pickens will be coming in anytime, and I expect we'll see some changes made fairly quickly."

I hurried back to the kitchen, concerned about Hazel Marie,

who'd been so clearly mortified by the sight of so much of her uncle.

"Hazel Marie," I said, ignoring the strained silence and acting as if business were going on as usual, "has Lloyd already left? I thought he was with James, but he's not."

"Oh," she said, giving me a grateful look, "he was going to the post office, remember? Then to your house to work on his computer. Homework, I guess." She glanced at Mildred and smiled in a self-deprecatory way. "He's already so far beyond me that I don't even understand the assignment, much less be able to help him."

"Oh, tell me about it," Mildred said airily. "I recall when Tonya was in school—of course that was when she was Tony. I told him then that if he didn't get it in school, don't expect to get it at home. But I'll tell you this: I think the teachers assign too much homework, don't you? Children need time to be children is what I think."

"I think so, too," I said quickly, falling in with the change of subject from that which was on all our minds. "Did you see in the paper about that couple who's complaining to the school board because their child didn't get in the school they wanted? Now they're petitioning the board to rearrange all the school districts in the county."

"I did see that," Mildred said. "The whole thing is just ridiculous. Why should every child in the county be uprooted because of one child? Or rather, one child's parents, when the solution is for them to move into the district they want. I've never understood people who think their wants come before everybody else's."

I nodded and started to agree, but Ida Lee said in her mild way, as she lifted the lid of the Dutch oven, "Miss Hazel Marie, I think we can finish this recipe now."

Hazel Marie hopped up, eager to have something to occupy her mind other than the sudden and shameful appearance of her uncle.

"Now the first thing you do," Ida Lee said softly, "is look over your recipe again and be sure you know what comes next. Let's measure out one-third cup of tomato juice and pour it in this small bowl. Then take your measuring spoons and add two and a half tablespoons of flour. Smooth the top of the spoon with your finger so you have the exact amount. That's right—now stir it together."

While Hazel Marie stirred, Ida Lee went to the refrigerator and took out a large container of sour cream. "Now we'll add two cups of sour cream. Just spoon it out, then stir it in."

Hazel Marie looked at the sour cream container. "Don't we have to measure it?"

"No, because, see? This is a pint container and two cups equal one pint."

"Oh, my," Hazel Marie said, "I didn't know you had to know arithmetic. No wonder I keep messing up."

"You're going to be fine," Ida Lee assured her. "And the more you do it, the more you'll know without having to look anything up. I expect every cookbook you have has an equivalency list. Just use that until you know some of the basics.

"Now," Ida Lee went on, "let's add a teaspoon of Worcestershire sauce and mix it all together. Ordinarily at this point, we would stir this mixture into your cooked meat, add the mushrooms, heat it all up, and serve it right away. But since it's not dinnertime, we're going to stop and put the sour cream mixture and the Dutch oven with the cooked meat in the refrigerator. But about thirty minutes before you plan to serve it, take them out and put the Dutch oven on the stove over low heat and let it warm up. Then stir in the sour cream mixture and add your mushrooms. Let it all heat up, but don't let it boil. And meanwhile, have your wide egg noodles ready—just follow the directions on the package—and serve the stroganoff over them."

"Will you write all that down?" Hazel Marie asked. "I mean, in detail, so I won't forget anything." A wail came from upstairs and Hazel Marie lost interest in beef stroganoff. "Oh, they're awake." And off she took.

"Julia," Mildred said, "we could watch the babies if Hazel Marie wants to keep on cooking."

"That's nice of you, Mildred," I said, "but it looks as if the lesson is over, so our timing seems to be right. You are through, aren't you, Ida Lee?"

"Well, Mrs. Allen wanted us to make a biscuit tortoni for dessert, but I can do that while Mrs. Pickens watches." She smiled as she began to gather the ingredients she'd need on the counter. "Actually, we should've made that first because it has to freeze. But I wanted to make sure her main dish was done."

In a few minutes, Hazel Marie came back to the kitchen, lugging those two fat babies, one in each arm. She moved two high chairs from a corner with her foot and strapped a baby into each one. "Here we are," she said, smiling at her little girls. "Who's ready for some green peas?"

"Ugh," Mildred said, shuddering at the baby food jars that Hazel Marie took from the pantry. "I would offer to feed them, Hazel Marie, but I don't think I can."

Hazel Marie laughed as she tied a bib around each little neck. "It does look awful, but they love it. Ida Lee, I guess my lesson had better be over. These two will be up for several hours now, but I do thank you so much. It's such a relief to know that supper is ready. Well, I mean I know I have to heat it up and then it'll be ready. But I thank you so much—I would've never known how to do it without you."

Ida Lee smiled and began crushing macaroons for the biscuit tortoni. "I'll go ahead and fix the dessert since we have everything here. One little tip, though: When you plan a frozen dessert you can make it the night before and be done with it. And later this afternoon, you might want to make a tossed salad, but that won't take long. I have everything you'll need in the refrigerator."

"That's wonderful," Hazel Marie said as she spooned baby food into eager mouths, adeptly angling the spoon away from grasping hands. "J.D. is going to be so surprised. I can't wait to serve it all."

Then she stopped with spoon in midair. "Oh!" she said. "I've got to fix some lunch, too, don't I? James and Uncle Vern are probably starving. Here, little girls, hurry and eat up."

"You know," I said, noticing that Hazel Marie was losing the joy of cooking at the thought of having to do more of it, "that's the problem with cooking. It never ends. By the time you clean up from one meal, it's time to start the next one."

"That is the truth," Mildred said, sighing, as if she had that problem every day of her life. "A woman's work is never done, is it?"

I started laughing—I couldn't help it. "Mildred, here you and I are moaning about all the work that feeding a family entails, and we rarely put a foot in the kitchen. Ida Lee, you must think we're crazy."

Ida Lee smiled almost to herself and shook her head. "No, ma'am. I know what you mean. But, Mrs. Pickens, I can put some lunch together if you'd like. What were you going to serve?"

"Oh, no, Ida Lee. I appreciate it, but I'm getting real good with grilled cheese sandwiches. I'll do them as soon as I finish here."

"All right," Ida Lee said, raising her voice as she began to whip the cream for the tortoni. "But I'll put the sandwiches together for you, and all you'll have to do is grill them."

"I'll do that," I said, getting up from the table. "Mildred, would you and Ida Lee like to stay for lunch?"

"Thank you, but no," Mildred said, shielding her eyes from the feeding frenzy of the babies. "As soon as Ida Lee finishes, we'd better run on."

By the time the babies began refusing another spoonful and Hazel Marie started washing strained beef and pureed peas off their faces, necks, and hands, Ida Lee was sliding a loaf pan of biscuit tortoni into the freezer.

"Hazel Marie," I said as I laid out bread slices and opened the mayonnaise jar, "I hope James and your uncle really like grilled cheese sandwiches. You have enough cheese here to feed an army."

"I think James is getting kinda tired of them," she said, lifting the babies out of the high chairs. Pushing the chairs back out of the way, she pulled out two little jumper chairs and plopped a baby in each one. "I don't know about Uncle Vern. He hasn't been here long enough. But cheese will keep a long time while sandwich meat won't. At least," she said, smiling, "I've learned that much."

Ida Lee glanced at my sandwich layout. "You might put a slice of tomato on each one," she said to me. "That grills up nicely, and will make a change from plain grilled cheese."

So I did, while Ida Lee cleaned off the counter and put mixing bowls in the dishwasher. "Ida Lee," I said, noticing that Mildred and Hazel Marie were cooing over the babies and paying no attention to us, "I can't tell you how much I appreciate what you've done this morning. You're an excellent teacher, and even I might learn how to do it with your instructions. Not that I want to, but I mean you were so patient and encouraging with Hazel Marie that she's beginning to feel quite competent."

"I was glad to do it," Ida Lee said, smiling.

After seeing Mildred and Ida Lee off, effusively thanking them both, I returned to the kitchen, where Hazel Marie was heating a skillet for the sandwiches. By this time, she was looking fresh and pretty, flushed with the morning's success—excepting her uncle's untimely appearance—and I was justifiably pleased that it had all been of my doing. What a wonderful idea a recipe book and cooking lessons had been!

Needing to get home, I served two sandwiches to James, who was still in bed, and helped Hazel Marie prepare a plate of sandwiches for the kitchen table, then I made my exit, leaving Brother Vern to her.

I had no desire to see any more of him than I already had, much less have lunch with him. I did, however, hate to miss seeing Mr. Pickens's reaction when he got home and found another ailing guest there.

Chapter 12

❧

I sat at my own kitchen table and looked over the plate of tuna fish salad and cantaloupe slices that Lillian had set before me. "Thank goodness it's not grilled cheese," I said.

"I jus' fixed one for Lloyd," Lillian said, her eyebrows raised. "An' almost made one for you, too. I thought you liked grilled cheese."

"Oh, I do, but I've had enough of them lately." Then I went on and told her about the morning's cooking lesson, including the sudden appearance in the kitchen of a barely covered Brother Vern. "I thought Mildred's eyes were going to pop out of her head."

"Oh, poor Miss Hazel Marie," Lillian said, shaking her head. "I 'spect she shamed to death with Miss Mildred Allen and Ida Lee there."

"She was," I said, "but Mildred and Ida Lee have such good manners that they carried it off without turning a hair. They didn't make one comment or ask any questions—just acted as if nothing untoward had happened. I really admire that ability and always try to emulate it."

Lillian grunted in response.

"Do you remember that woman?" I went on. "I can't recall who she was, but I told you about her. Anyway, the one who served soup at her first dinner party after she married and her new husband slurped it? She didn't correct him or mention it any way. She just never served soup again when they had guests. That's what I call marital diplomacy. And what about the woman whose guest was so embarrassed because one of those little cherry to-matoes squirted across the table when she tried to spear it? In just a few minutes the hostess did the same thing on purpose. But as tactful as those women were, I expect even they would've been discomposed if they'd had somebody like Brother Vern on their hands."

"Uh-huh," Lillian said. "You better quit talkin' an' eat something."

So I did, thinking over what I could do that afternoon with Sam still sleeping and Lloyd still busy with his homework.

Emma Sue, I thought. After one successful cooking lesson, it was time to fill in my calendar with more cooks. I say *successful,* but of course the proof of the pudding would be how well Hazel Marie completed the recipe and got her first attempt on the table.

But I put those thoughts aside and called Emma Sue to be sure she was home. I almost had to make an appointment to see our pastor's wife, she was always so busy with first one thing, then another. If it wasn't a meeting at the church, it was visiting the sick and shut-ins, or preparing a dish to take to a new member, or collecting clothes for a missionary, or soliciting donations for some worthy cause. She did good works from sunup to sundown, never stopping until a migraine put her in bed for two or three days.

Because of Emma Sue's proclivities, I was always leery around her for fear she'd give me something to do. That's the problem with these active do-gooders: They try to rope everybody else into their enthusiasms. Whenever I know I'm going to see her, I make a mental list of all I have to do so I have a ready excuse not to take on anything else.

When we were settled at Emma Sue's table—cups of hot spiced tea before us—and I'd told her about the cookbook I was putting together for Hazel Marie, a look of profound gratitude swept over her face. Emma Sue was essentially a needy person, who, I'm sorry to say, rarely got the credit or acclaim that she both craved and deserved.

"That is so thoughtful of you, Julia," she said. "And to think you want *my* recipes."

"Well, not all of them. Just a few favorites to remind Hazel Marie of you and only those you think she can manage to fix. I know you have some excellent main dish recipes that wouldn't be too involved for her. Remember that she is nowhere near your level of expertise."

As Emma Sue glowed under my complimentary words, I mentally asked for forgiveness because, in reality, she was a terrible cook. A willing, eager, and generous one, but terrible even so. The few times a year she had a luncheon or, even rarer, a dinner party, I snacked before leaving my house because I knew half of what she served would be inedible—undercooked, overcooked, or a concoction of flavors no other cook would ever put together.

I learned the reason for that one time when I offered to help her in the kitchen: She substitutes. I watched as she looked through her spice shelf for paprika to sprinkle over a plate of deviled eggs.

"Oh, well," she said, grabbing a jar, "I guess I'm out. But all I want is a little color, so this'll do." And she covered those eggs with enough cayenne pepper to burn a hole in the roof of your mouth.

And she once told me of the time, not long after she and the pastor were married, when they were in their first pastorate. They were serving a small, rural church of some sixty or so members, barely half of whom attended services on a regular basis, so naturally, she said, she and the pastor were eager to receive a call to a larger congregation. Every stranger who appeared for Sunday worship put them in a state of high anticipation because he could have been a member of a pastor-seeking committee checking out the pastor's expository style and delivery before issuing a call.

On a certain Sunday, she told me, when the ladies of the church had prepared a covered-dish luncheon, a nattily dressed stranger had appeared and, being warmly greeted, had stayed for lunch. Emma Sue had prepared a chocolate pound cake as her contribution to the luncheon, but unhappily found as she'd mixed it early that morning that she was out of vanilla extract. It was too early for a grocery store to be open, which wouldn't have helped her anyway since the pastor frowned on unnecessary purchases on the Lord's Day. So Emma Sue had substituted lemon flavoring in the chocolate cake.

Knowing what she'd done, the pastor tried everything he could think of to steer the stranger away from Emma Sue's cake, but the man was having none of it. He took a large slice, ate it with relish, then declared it was the best cake he'd ever tasted.

Emma Sue still credited her cooking skills with setting the pastor on his rise up the ladder of ministerial success.

"Stop writing a minute, Julia," Emma Sue said after she'd recommended a particular recipe from the cookbooks she'd spread out on the table. I'd been concentrating on copying a few of them into my notebook and had not noticed how quiet she'd become.

Putting down my pen, I glanced up at her, noting the look of stress on her face. "What is it, Emma Sue?"

"Well, I know you're not a Bible scholar, but you do have some common sense and I'd like to have your opinion about something."

Have I mentioned that Emma Sue could be blunt to the point of giving offense? I've never forgotten the time she ran up to a woman she barely knew one Sunday after the services and asked her forgiveness. "For what?" the woman had asked.

"For thinking so badly of you because of all the eye makeup you wear," Emma Sue had answered. "I'm terribly sorry and I hope you'll forgive me." She was perfectly sincere about it, even though the woman had been completely unaware of Emma Sue's disapproval of eyeliner.

I leaned back with a sigh. "I'll try, Emma Sue. What is it?"

"It's about Mary and Martha. I just can't figure it out."

"I don't think I know them."

"Yes, you do. The two sisters, you know, from the Book of Luke, where it tells about Jesus coming to visit and Martha doing what any hostess would do. She stayed in the kitchen, cooking and preparing a fine meal for all the guests, then was left to clean up by herself. And all the time she was working her fingers to the bone, her sister was sitting at the Lord's feet, listening to Him talk without lifting a finger to help. And when Martha complained about it, the Lord rebuked her and said that Mary had chosen the better part. And I know I shouldn't question it, but it just seems to me that *somebody* had to feed those people."

I sighed because Emma Sue couldn't get those two sisters off her mind, and I'd heard this story from her before. "Well, as you say, Emma Sue, I'm no Bible scholar, but maybe we're not supposed to take it literally. Maybe it's figurative or something."

"Oh, I know that," Emma Sue said. "It teaches us to put spiritual matters first and not fill our days with mundane busy work like Martha, who was cumbered with much serving. While at the same time her sister was sitting around doing nothing, yet it says that was the good part. Now it seems to me to be saying that both of them should've just let everybody—and I'm talking about *guests* in their home—go hungry.

"Oh, Julia," she went on, as the tears I'd been expecting filled her eyes, "I try so hard to choose the better part, but I'm forever in the kitchen, and if I never had to put a foot in it again I'd be happy. But Larry expects three meals a day, every day except for when Rotary meets. And I thought when our boys were grown and gone, we might just occasionally eat out somewhere." She snatched a napkin from the holder in the middle of the table, knocking over a salt shaker, and pressed the napkin to her overflowing eyes. "I get so tired, and I'm just so . . . so *cumbered*."

"There, there," I said for lack of anything else to say, as I put a comforting hand on hers. "I understand, Emma Sue. People load you down with work because you're so willing and eager to help. But sometimes you have to put your foot down and say, 'No.' You can't do everything, you know. And as far as the pastor's concerned, he's like any other man. If he comes home and dinner's on the table, he'll eat it and not give it another thought. But what if he came home and dinner was not on the table and not even started? What if you simply announced that the two of you were going out to eat?"

"Oh, Julia, I couldn't do that. He *expects* dinner on the table. And if it wasn't, all he'd do is look disappointed in me and go fix a peanut butter sandwich."

"Then let him while you go out."

"By *myself*?"

"Why not? Sometimes you have to show a husband that you mean business." Of course, all the while I was telling her what to do, I was recalling the long, dry marriage to my first husband and realizing that there was a lot of Wesley Lloyd Springer in Pastor Larry Ledbetter. Both had unshakable ideas of what a woman's job was and where her place was, as well. I would've never dared to contradict Wesley Lloyd or failed to have his dinner, via Lillian, on the table when he walked in at 5:45 every evening except Thursdays, when, unbeknownst to me, he was visiting his paramour while I thought he was doing bank business.

But those days were gone forever for me, now that I had Sam, who was the most thoughtful of men, except when he took off fishing or world traveling for days at a time.

So, having been through a similar marriage as Emma Sue was currently in without being able to make any changes, I was a poor one to be giving advice. Gradually, Emma Sue's tears dried up and, as she wiped her face, she said, "I'll be all right, Julia. I just get down sometimes, but whatever cross I'm given to bear, I know the Lord will help me carry it."

I didn't know what to say to that. All I could think of was what a crying shame it was for a wife to think of her husband as the cross she'd been given to bear. Of course, Wesley Lloyd had been mine to bear until a sudden heart attack in his new Buick Park Avenue lifted it from me.

Emma Sue blew her nose, then, as she lifted her head, a troubled frown appeared on her forehead. "Wonder what she served," she said.

Still thinking of bearing crosses, I was confused. "Who?"

"Martha, of course," Emma Sue said. "Imagine a dozen or so people dropping in for lunch. What in the world would she feed them?"

"I don't know, Emma Sue, but lamb would be my guess. Or a fatted calf. Maybe in a stew so she could extend it with other things."

"Well, I guess she'd have to, especially after her brother was raised from the dead. Do you realize he hadn't eaten in four whole *days*!"

❧

It took a while but I was finally able to distract Emma Sue by praising the tuna casserole topped with crumbled potato chips that she'd taken to the last covered-dish supper. Then I was able to turn her attention to my mission by asking for the recipe for her famous dump cake that she dumped on anybody who was ill, pregnant, or celebrating some event.

Emma Sue's Famous Dump Cake

21-ounce can cherry pie filling
2 cups yellow (or white) cake mix (about half a box)
1 stick margarine, cut into small pieces
1 cup chopped pecans

Preheat the oven to 350°F. Butter an 8 × 8-inch square baking dish. Dump the cherry pie filling into the dish. On top of the pie filling, sprinkle (don't stir) the cake mix. Scatter the margarine over the mix. Then sprinkle the pecans over the top. Bake for 35 to 45 minutes until the top is brown. Serve with ice cream.

VARIATIONS: Use apple, blueberry, peach, strawberry, or pineapple pie filling instead of cherry pie filling. You also may sprinkle shredded coconut over the top along with the pecans.

Serves 4 to 6.

(This recipe is justly famous, Hazel Marie, and you know why–it's Emma Sue's signature dish for any occasion. She's brought it to us often enough.)

⌒〜᥈

"Hazel Marie will be thrilled to have this recipe, Emma Sue," I said. "And I know her family will enjoy it." I didn't mention that Hazel Marie herself didn't like dump cake.

"Well," Emma Sue said, wiping the last of her tears away, "tell her she should use a square tinfoil pan if she's taking it to somebody. That way she won't have to worry about getting her Pyrex back. I figured that out after I realized I was spending a fortune on Pyrex dishes. Nobody ever returns them."

"I'll be sure to do that. But now I need a main dish recipe and, remember, it should be one that you won't mind showing her how to make. And, by the way, what day would be good for you? Next week is all taken care of."

We studied the calendar and she chose Tuesday of the following week. "I can do it then," Emma Sue said. "I have a ten o'clock meeting that will run through lunch. I could go by Hazel Marie's about one, before the Christmas pageant committee meets. We'll have time to throw it together in between."

"Well, Emma Sue, I don't know about throwing something together. Hazel Marie needs *details*."

"Oh, she won't have any trouble with this," Emma Sue said. "Really, throwing together is all you do. Here—read it and see."

Emma Sue's Good Beef Stew

3 pounds lean stew meat, trimmed and cubed

Preheat the oven to 300°F. Put the meat in a large Dutch oven, then drain each of the following (saving juices) and add to the meat:

16-ounce can English peas
16-ounce can sliced carrots
16-ounce jar small onions
16-ounce can green beans

Then add:

16-ounce can whole tomatoes (plus juice)
10¾-ounce can beef consommé, undiluted
½ cup dried bread crumbs
½ cup dry red wine
⅓ cup flour
1 tablespoon brown sugar
2 tablespoons Worcestershire sauce
2 teaspoons salt
¼ teaspoon black pepper
1 bay leaf
1–2 teaspoons Kitchen Bouquet, for color

Mix well, cover, and put in the oven for 2 to 3 hours, stirring occasionally and adding small amounts of drained juices if needed. Remove the bay leaf. Serve over wide egg noodles.

Serves 8.

(This recipe looks as if it will feed a crowd once or your family for two or three days.)

"Now, Julia," Emma Sue said, "I know it calls for wine, but don't let that upset you. I use cooking wine, which is nonalcoholic and perfectly fine for a Christian cook."

If I stayed around Emma Sue for any length of time, she could send me around the bend. I looked her straight in the eye. "I'm not upset because I didn't even notice. Besides, I doubt that a half a cup of wine that will cook down anyway would corrupt any cook—Christian or not."

"Oh, Julia," she said as tears sprang up in her eyes.

I had to quickly reverse myself, apologize, and thank her again and again. Then I got myself out of there before I said something worse.

Chapter 13

When I got home, I expected to find Sam up early because he'd be spending the night in his own bed instead of staying with James. With Mr. Pickens back home, we would be reverting to our normal sleeping arrangements, and that thought was putting a spring in my step. Our bed had been awfully lonesome the last few nights.

As I passed through the kitchen on my way to him, Lillian stopped me with an announcement. "Lloyd, he say to tell you he gonna eat at his mama's an' spend the night, too."

I turned to her. "Where's he going to sleep? Every bed in the house is taken."

"He say the couch'll do him, an' Mr. Sam, he say he already take a million naps on it so Lloyd won't have no trouble gettin' a good night's sleep." Lillian washed her hands at the sink as I started toward the living room. "Oh, an' Lloyd say his mama's cookin' smell real good, so he stayin' to try it."

"Well, good. Let's hope she gets it on the table the way it's supposed to be. Did Mr. Pickens get home?"

"Yes'm—that's another reason Lloyd stayin'."

I smiled at that, my heart melting at the thought of how good a father Mr. Pickens was proving to be. Hazel Marie could've done a lot worse than to choose him. In fact, in the past she *had* done a lot worse.

"Go on home, Lillian," I said. "Sam and I can put something together for dinner, or . . ." I stopped, recalling my conversation with Emma Sue. "Or we'll go out for a change."

Sam and I had a lovely evening in the clubhouse dining room, our catching-up conversation interrupted now and then to greet people we didn't often see. Sam and I had each been members of the country club before we married, although neither of us played golf or tennis or, for that matter, lolled around in bathing suits at the swimming pool. Wesley Lloyd Springer, my unmissed first husband, used our membership to entertain bank customers and to make sure he was seen among the movers and shakers of the community. In his business, he'd said, it was essential that he appear socially involved, although I had been cautioned against using the membership too often.

Sam said he had joined so that he could play bingo every Tuesday night, which made me laugh at the thought of him hunched over trying to fill his card while all the widow ladies hovered around. The last thing Sam Murdoch would be interested in was bingo, much less a swarm of hovering widow ladies.

While we ate I told him all about Brother Vern's embarrassing appearance, as well as about Hazel Marie's cooking lesson, reiterating my admiration for Ida Lee. And he told me of his nights alone with James and, taking my hand across the table, how he was looking forward to being in his own bed. My face glowing, I glanced around to see if anyone had heard him.

"James should be able to manage the stairs to his place in a day or so," he went on, sliding his hand back as an unobtrusive waiter offered coffee. "That ankle is still swollen but not as badly as it was, and I think there's an old walking stick stuck back in a closet somewhere over there. I'll look for it tomorrow and let him try walking around a bit."

"Just don't let him fall and break something else. But I'll tell you this, Sam—James will be more than ready to be back in his own apartment. He's still not getting along too well with Brother Vern."

"Well, who does?" Sam laughed. Then turning serious, he

said, "But when James is able to go back, you know what that'll do, don't you? It'll free up a nice private room and bath downstairs for Brother Vern, and he may settle in for a long stay."

"Oh," I said, rolling my eyes, "I'm hoping Mr. Pickens will nip that idea in the bud. But you know how easily swayed Hazel Marie is—Vernon Puckett will play on her compassion, make her feel sorry for him, and she won't be able to turn him out. She may end up having to choose between her uncle and her husband." I leaned forward and lowered my voice. "I tell you, Sam, it's a recipe for trouble any way you look at it. We may have to resort to making things so uncomfortable for Brother Vern that he'll *want* to leave."

Sam laughed and shook his head. He put his napkin beside his plate, raised his eyebrows to be sure I was ready, and stood. As he moved my chair, he said, "I expect they can handle the situation. We can sit this one out."

Well, we'll see, I thought as we walked toward the lobby.

⟐

None of the Pickens family was in church the next morning, not even Lloyd, and I missed having him beside me. I occupied myself during the service—except when interrupted by having to stand and mouth a hymn—by imagining the turmoil in that household with James and two babies needing immediate attention and Mr. Pickens and Lloyd trying to cook breakfast and Brother Vern either listening to a Sunday sermon on the radio or trying to preach one himself to anybody who'd listen. With that picture running in the background of my mind, I realized that Pastor Ledbetter was preaching a fairly satisfactory sermon himself for a change. For weeks we had been subjected to hearing all the details of the tour to the Holy Land that a church group had taken back in the summer. I was tired of hearing about it, and so was Sam, since he'd experienced the tour firsthand. It was almost a relief to hear a biblical expository sermon, even though his subject concerned the need to dig down deep to keep the church solvent, which, according to him, was merely our reasonable sacrifice.

⟨~❧⟩

Just as we'd settled ourselves in the new library with the Sunday papers, anticipating a leisurely afternoon, the phone rang for Sam.

After hanging up, he turned to me. "Pickens found that old walking cane and wants to see if James can get around with it. Old man Puckett says he's too weak to help, so Pickens wants me to come over. Want to go?"

"Yes, I'll go with you, although to tell the truth, I may be better off not knowing what's going on over there. I must say, though, that out of sight, out of mind is not working real well."

We walked the four blocks, even though I regretted every step. October was beginning to show its colors in more ways than one, and we were thoroughly chilled by the time we got there. Mr. Pickens answered our knock, greeting us with a tight look on his face.

"Come in," he said, shaking Sam's hand. "Glad to see you," And to me, "Hazel Marie's in the kitchen making coffee." Which I took to mean she probably needed help.

I walked back through the hall, glancing into the living room as I passed. Brother Vern was stretched out in Mr. Pickens's favorite chair, his feet crossed on an ottoman, while Lloyd, who waved at me, was on the floor with the babies. They were rolling around on a quilt with all kinds of rattles and spinning toys spread around them.

"Hazel Marie?" I said as I entered the kitchen. "Can I help?"

"Oh, Miss Julia," she said, relief in her voice as if I were a lifeboat in a storm. "I'm so glad to see you, but I don't think anybody can help. Things're going from bad to worse. Uncle Vern expects so much from all of us, and J.D. is holding his temper but it's an awful strain on him, and the babies aren't sleeping because they're teething, and James and Uncle Vern are at each other's throats. I don't know how we're going to get through it all."

"Well, first things first," I said, guiding her to a chair at the kitchen table. "Do you have the coffee on?"

She nodded and I sat down beside her. "How did your dinner go last night?"

Her face immediately brightened. "Oh, you wouldn't believe how good it was! It all came out just like Ida Lee said it would, except the noodles got all mushed together. I think I cooked them too long, but they tasted all right. I'm going to send Ida Lee some flowers in the morning. J.D. was amazed—he loved it. All the men had two helpings and Uncle Vern would've had three if there'd been enough. Even James said he had to hurry and get well or he'd lose his job in the kitchen." Then she sighed. "I just hope I can do as well the next time."

"You will, but see, that was one thing that went fine, so don't let yourself get down. If Sam and your husband can get James walking on his own, why then everything will start looking up."

"I don't know, Miss Julia." She sighed again and began twisting a napkin around and around. "Uncle Vern keeps at me to move James out. He'll ask whether James has any family we could send him to, or he'll say that James is taking advantage of me and he's really not that bad off. He told me this morning that he has a few things in storage—some books and copies of his sermons that he needs to get out. He drove over this morning to check on them and came back hinting that the room where James is would be perfect for him."

"Why, that sounds like he intends to move in for the duration."

She nodded. "He does, but for the duration of what, I don't know."

"Well, I'll tell you for what. For as long as your husband will put up with him. You have to let Mr. Pickens handle him, Hazel Marie. With your sweet nature, Brother Vern will run all over you. You must just stay out of it so that when Mr. Pickens has had enough, you don't start feeling sorry for your uncle. Your responsibility lies with your husband and children. They should be first and foremost, regardless of what Brother Vern wants."

"I know," she agreed, wiping her eyes. "But I do feel sorry for him." She sniffed. "Occasionally, I mean. Not all the time."

Chapter 14

I carried a tray laden with cups, saucers, and the coffeepot to the living room, making a wide detour around the edge of the room to avoid stepping over or on a baby. Setting it on the coffee table, I directed a hard look at Brother Vern, who had not moved a muscle to offer any help. He just lolled in that easy chair and watched, a pair of bedroom scuffs dangling from his sockless feet.

Hazel Marie followed me with a plate of cookies—Pepperidge Farm Milanos. She poured coffee for Brother Vern and took the cup to him. Instead of taking it from her, he pointed to the table beside him and she set it down.

"I take two sugars and a dab of cream," he said.

And I guess you want it stirred, too, I thought, which Hazel Marie ended up doing. My mouth tightened into a thin line as she waited on him.

My attention was taken by a commotion in the hall and I walked out to watch the rehabilitation therapy of James. Mr. Pickens was on one side and Sam on the other, with James teetering on one foot between them, holding onto a wobbling cane with his left hand. The cast on his right hand had been rigged up into a sling and was of no use to him. His left hand wasn't much better, nor was the still-bound left ankle, which he barely let touch the floor.

"It don't feel right," James said, a look of stress on his face. "I never been much of a left-handed man. I do ever'thing right-handed, an' I don't think this ole walkin' stick gonna hol' me up."

"We're right here, James," Sam said. "We'll catch you if you start to fall."

Mr. Pickens said, "Just think how much better you'll feel if you can get around on your own. Besides, the Panthers are playing today. You want to watch the game, don't you?"

"Le's keep on, then," James said, as he set his sights on the family room where the television set was.

I shook my head and turned back in to the living room. It was going to be a while before James would be able to trust his own two feet. When Sam and Mr. Pickens got James settled in front of the television set, they came back into the living room. Hazel Marie handed out coffee cups and offered around the plate of cookies, from which Brother Vern took two more.

"I got the high blood and the high sugar," he announced, "but these're too little to do much damage."

My eyes rolled just a tiny bit, but I didn't say anything. Hazel Marie sidled up to me and whispered, "I'm so glad you and Mr. Sam came over. I hope you can stay all afternoon. It gets kinda tense when J.D. has to talk to Uncle Vern by himself."

So we continued our Sunday afternoon visitation, chatting comfortably while Lloyd played on the floor with his sisters. They seemed to love him, pulling themselves along to climb up on him, laughing and gurgling, reaching for his glasses, and examining his hair.

Mr. Pickens sat and watched, his face a picture of contentment. I couldn't help but wonder if he was ever jolted by the way his life had changed. When we first met him, he was an unsettled man, bouncing from one woman to another, stopping now and then to marry a few, then pulling free and taking off again. Of course, Hazel Marie had caught his eye as soon as he saw her picture, and when he saw her in the flesh, well, I thought his bouncing days were over. It hadn't been that simple, though, because they'd had their ups and downs and, I'll tell you the truth, I had begun to think that she would be better off without him.

Then the babies came, or rather, they made known their imminent arrival, and Mr. Pickens decided it was high time to settle down for good.

I just hoped it would last.

Sam and Mr. Pickens began discussing the repair of the roof, necessitated by a fallen tree back in the summer, while Hazel Marie took coffee and cookies to James in the room across the hall.

Brother Vern, who was finding it hard to stay awake, suddenly roused himself. "Hazel Marie, I need some more coffee over here."

She quickly veered over to him and refilled his cup.

"That'll do," he said. "Now, folks, settin' around visitin' is all well and good, but it being a Sunday, I think a Bible lesson might suit better. Lloyd, run up and fetch my Bible."

Lloyd sat up, holding a baby and sending a questioning glance toward his mother, then toward Mr. Pickens.

I smiled and intervened. "We looked for you in church this morning, Mr. Puckett, which was when we had our Bible lesson. But I guess you decided to sleep in. Lloyd," I went on, "hand Julie to me, then you come sit beside me with Lily Mae."

He quickly complied, laughing as he said, "I'm not sure which is which. Mama needs to put different colors on them so I can tell them apart."

Brother Vern didn't pursue his Bible lesson suggestion, watching as we played with the babies. But he wasn't through by a long shot.

Mr. Pickens seemed to be keeping a watchful eye on him, but staying silent even when Hazel Marie was given orders. From the look on Mr. Pickens's face, though, he was keeping a mental list of demerits against Brother Vern, and I wondered when he would reach the end of his tether. The problem, as I saw it, was whether he'd send Brother Vern packing or start packing himself. Mr. Pickens had never been much of a family man to begin with.

But he was making an effort to keep the peace—something he rarely bothered to do. Watching Lloyd and me with the babies, he said, "I think those little girls take after you, Miss Julia. They both have minds of their own."

We laughed, but it pleased me to think that I might have some influence on their little lives, even though they weren't a lick of kin to me.

Then Brother Vern, not knowing when to leave well enough alone, decided to make another pronouncement. "They're fine-lookin' babies, all right, but it's too bad one of 'em couldn't of been a boy. Every man wants a son."

Lloyd stopped bouncing Lily Mae on his lap and Hazel Marie's eyes suddenly filled. I gaped at Brother Vern, astounded at what had come out of his mouth. Here he was, making a critical statement like that when, as far as I knew, he'd never had a child, regardless of gender, of his own.

Mr. Pickens aimed a hard look at him and held it there. His face tightened as he strained to hold his tongue. "Why," he asked—and it wasn't a rhetorical question—"would I want a son when I already have one?"

He aimed a tight smile at Lloyd, as I felt the boy relax beside me.

"Well," Brother Vern said with an ingratiating grin, "you know."

"No, I don't," Mr. Pickens said, his voice hardening as those black eyes swiveled toward Brother Vern again. "In fact, it's a good thing we didn't have a boy. He'd never be able to measure up to the one we have."

Lloyd's face was glowing by this time, a little red, too, as Mr. Pickens praised him.

Hazel Marie jumped up. "More coffee? I can put some more on if anyone wants it."

Sam said, "No, don't do that, Hazel Marie. We've got to go and let you folks have supper. Unless," he paused for effect, "you want to sample my world-famous pancakes. Why don't I cook up a batch for us all?"

"Yeah, let's do that," Lloyd said, putting the baby on the floor, where she started crawling toward her daddy. "I'll help you, Mr. Sam."

"Pancakes is not on my diet," Brother Vern announced, as I wondered if half a dozen cookies were. "All that syrup'll send my sugar sky-high."

I stood up to help in the kitchen. "That's all right, Mr. Puckett. We'll fix you a salad. Hazel Marie, let's set the table."

I declare, it's too bad when a good idea—even one from Sam—turns out to be not so good. Which is what happened to that one. First of all, Hazel Marie was out of eggs, so Mr. Pickens had to go to the store, taking a list of a few other things she was out of—bacon, syrup, milk, and pancake mix. While we waited for him to return, the babies got fussy, so they had to be fed, their two high chairs taking up half the kitchen. Then James got restless, so as soon as Mr. Pickens returned, he and Sam helped him to the kitchen table, where he proceeded to critique Sam as he made pancakes.

And Hazel Marie didn't have a griddle, so Sam used two frying pans, neither of which worked too well, not having been properly cured. As it always turns out with pancakes, we had to eat in shifts, James being served first, then Lloyd and Mr. Pickens. When Hazel Marie finished with the babies, Sam handed her a plate, then one to me. He ate last, after making another batch for all the second helpings.

I took a salad into the living room to Brother Vern, who still had not bestirred himself, not even to get to the table. He didn't like the looks of the salad, telling me he was accustomed to a big supper and he didn't know if a bowl of greens would last him through the night.

"I'll bring you a glass of milk," I said. "That should hold you."

When we'd all eaten, Hazel Marie and I were left to rinse the sticky plates and load the dishwasher. I was glad to have her alone for a few minutes.

"Hazel Marie, have you heard from Etta Mae?"

"She called this morning and told me about her granny. She's coming in the morning just to try it out. Did Etta Mae talk to you?"

"Yes, and I don't know what I think about it. I tried to hint around that her granny might be a little old to take on two babies, but she insisted that wouldn't be a problem. But, Hazel Marie, if you aren't comfortable with it, just have Mr. Pickens tell her it's not working out."

"Well," Hazel Marie said, stopping with a plate in her hands as she thought about it, "I might as well talk to her, kinda feel her out to see how she'd do, but you know how I am about babysitters."

"I know, but as you interview her, you should get a feeling for how she'd work out. And, remember, you don't have to hire her."

"I wouldn't want to hurt Etta Mae's feelings, and it wouldn't be like I'd be leaving them with her—I mean, I'll be right here in the house—so maybe her granny could entertain them while I cook. LuAnne is coming tomorrow, isn't she?"

"Oh, she'll be here, all right. She's looking forward to it."

"And you, too?"

"Yes, if you want me. And, while you're mixing and stirring, I'll keep an eye on Granny and see how she does with the babies."

Hazel Marie smiled. "I was hoping you'd say that."

Chapter 15

Lloyd came home with us that evening because, as he said, our house was four blocks closer to school—four blocks he wouldn't have to walk. And, of course, Brother Vern was still ensconced in Lloyd's room at his mother's house—another reason to spend the night with us.

I had a fitful night—whether because I had too much on my mind or too many of Sam's pancakes in my stomach, I couldn't tell. Whichever it was, I was anxious the next morning to get to Hazel Marie's, arriving about nine o'clock to a house in turmoil. Nothing unusual was going on, just the normal run-of-the-mill activities of too many people wanting too many things at the same time. Hazel Marie was upstairs dressing the babies, James was still in bed but wanting help to get up, Mr. Pickens was putting breakfast dishes in the dishwasher, a tight look on his face, and Brother Vern, still in his robe—but belted this time—was watching a televangelist on the television set.

I decided that the better part of valor was to stay clear of the kitchen while Mr. Pickens was there and, after speaking to him—and getting a short reply—quickly left him to it. He was in no mood for friendly banter, so I went on into the family room to see what Brother Vern was up to.

"Good morning, Mr. Puckett," I said decisively. "We're having company this morning, so perhaps you should get dressed."

He looked over his shoulder at me. "Again?"

"Yes. Two ladies, perhaps three, will be here any minute.

Anyway, I thought you disapproved of watching television, so I'm surprised to see you doing it."

"It depends on what's on. Now this preacher here," he said, pointing to the screen, where a young man with a mustache on his face and a Bible flopping over his hand was holding forth, "he's got a fairly good presentation. Watch him—see how he walks back and forth? That keeps the congregation's attention so nobody goes to sleep on him. And see how he whirls around when he gets to the meat of his message? That's pretty good pulpiteering."

"Well, I declare. I didn't know there was so much to it."

"Oh, there's lots to learn, an' I've taught a many of 'em. I could give this one some pointers he don't know, too."

"I expect you could," I said offhandedly. I wasn't interested in the finer points of preaching on television. Or preaching anywhere, for that matter. "But you do need to turn it off and get some clothes on."

About that time, both babies started crying their lungs out. Although the wails were loud enough to reverberate from upstairs, I was already familiar enough with the sound to know that they were not hurt, just unhappy about being washed and dressed.

Brother Vern, however, frowned and pinched up his mouth. Turning off the television, which had been about drowned out, he said, "Hazel Marie needs to git them young'uns under control. Spare the rod and spoil the child, I always say."

"*Mr. Puckett!*" I said, shocked. "Those babies aren't even a year old. If anybody picks up a rod around here, it'll be taken to an adult, not an infant."

"Well, I'm just sayin'."

"I hear what you're saying, but their daddy better not." And I turned around and walked out, fuming. Why is it that people who've never raised a child can tell you how it should be done? You'd never catch me being so presumptuous.

Just as I crossed the hall, LuAnne, loaded down with bags of groceries, rang the doorbell. I let her in and relieved her of half the burden. We headed for the kitchen, LuAnne talking a mile a minute, excited about giving a cooking lesson.

Mr. Pickens was quick to abandon the kitchen to us as he headed upstairs to say good-bye to his wife and children. While we were unpacking grocery sacks, I heard him leave for his office, most likely relieved to be doing so. I glanced out the window and saw him walk purposefully toward his sleek black sports car, slipping on his dark aviator glasses against the glare as he went. And probably also to keep his gaze from burning up whatever it landed on. I shuddered and determined to stay out of his way.

While LuAnne and I sat at the table to await Hazel Marie, I leaned over and whispered, "I thought I'd never see the day when Mr. J. D. Pickens, PI, would be washing dishes."

"I expect," LuAnne whispered back, "he didn't, either."

Hazel Marie walked in, pushing her hair off her face and looking as if she'd been up half the night. "Well, they're down, but I don't know for how long. Morning, LuAnne, how are you? I'm really looking forward to this and I thank you so much for doing it."

LuAnne jumped up and began bustling around, opening the packages of pork chops, arranging ingredients, and making a great show in general of preparing to prepare a meal.

"Now, Hazel Marie," she said, "you just watch what I do. It's so easy, you'll be amazed. First I'm going to put the chops in this Pyrex dish and put a slice of onion on each chop. If you slice the onion under running water, it won't make you cry. Some people hold a match in their mouth, but that doesn't work for me. Now I'll mix the barbecue sauce. See how I do it? Then you pour the sauce over the chops, onion, and all—like this—then you cover the dish with tinfoil. Tear me off a piece of tinfoil, will you?"

And that was the extent of Hazel Marie's contribution—tearing off a length of tinfoil and handing it to her. Thinking back to Ida Lee's hands-on teaching method, I wondered how much Hazel Marie had learned by being a mere observer.

"Now," LuAnne said, "let's put this in the refrigerator. What time do you eat supper? About six? Okay, take it out about four o'clock and put it in a 350-degree oven. Oh, you better take it out earlier than that—let it come to room temperature before putting it in a hot oven."

"Why?" Hazel Marie asked.

"Because the glass dish might break, that's why." Hardly stopping to explain reactions to sudden temperature changes, LuAnne went right on. "You can put your potatoes in to bake at the same time, get your salad made, and you'll be through. Now let's do your cake. You'll love this, Hazel Marie. Watch me while I put everything in one bowl and mix it together. Well, everything but the glaze. That goes on when the cake is done."

I sat at the table watching as LuAnne combined the ingredients for the cake. Hazel Marie leaned against the counter watching along with me. LuAnne didn't let her crack an egg even.

When LuAnne put the tube pan filled with cake batter into the oven, she washed her hands and said, "Whew, what a morning. I'm about tired. How about you, Hazel Marie?"

"I could sit for a while," Hazel Marie said, as I remembered that she'd been up half the night, and leaning over a counter with nothing to do hadn't been very restful. "I'll pour us some coffee."

I'd hardly had two sips of mine when the doorbell rang. Hazel Marie jumped up and hurried out, wondering who could be wanting something now.

While she was gone, LuAnne whispered to me, "Where's her uncle? I heard how he goes around half naked and I wanted to see him."

"Did Mildred tell you that?" I demanded. "I'm surprised she'd repeat such a thing. Mr. Puckett didn't know we had company. He's not well, you know, and has to spend a lot of time in bed. He was terribly embarrassed, so I expect you're out of luck."

"Too bad." LuAnne giggled.

I let it go, because if I made one critical comment about Hazel Marie's uncle, it would be spread all over town by lunchtime and it was nearly twelve already.

We looked up as a scurry of footsteps approached. Hazel Marie said, "Look who's here," and in walked Granny Wiggins, her bright eyes darting around as she smiled broadly.

She was no bigger than a minute, but there was something about her that made you think she was in constant motion. Her wrinkled face was animated and her dark eyes were alive with interest in the surroundings. She was wearing a cotton housedress and a heavy cardigan, her skinny, stockinged legs ending in huge white tennis shoes, reminding me of a big-footed bird. A bun sat on the back of her neck, her hair pulled back on her head so tightly that it was as good as a facelift. Her knuckled hands were red and rough, a testament to the years of hard work behind her.

Hazel Marie introduced us and offered coffee, which Granny Wiggins eagerly accepted. "I like my coffee," she said, perching on the edge of a chair as she generously sugared it. "It's a pure pleasure to meet you ladies. 'Course I know all about you, Miz Murdoch. My Etta Mae just thinks the world of you, so any friend of hers—and so forth."

Before I could answer, she turned those bright black eyes on LuAnne. "But I never heard of you, which don't mean nothing 'cause I don't get around like I used to. You a Baptist?"

"Uh, no," LuAnne said, taken aback by the sudden change of subject. "I go to First Presbyterian."

"Well, I guess that's all right," Granny said. "The older I get, the more I think there's hardly a lick of difference between 'em, just so you go somewhere. 'Course my preacher wouldn't agree with me, and I doubt yours would, either. They all want you and your pocket purse comin' in their doors. Well," she went on, draining her cup, "this is nice and all, settin' here talkin' and visitin', but I come to work and there's one thing I want to know. Where's them young'uns at?"

Chapter 16

⁊✍

"Oh, they're sleeping," Hazel Marie said. "They still take a morning nap, but they'll be up soon."

"Well," Granny Wiggins said, hopping up from the table and going to the sink where mixing bowls and spoons were haphazardly stacked. "I didn't come to be comp'ny, so I'll clean up this mess. You let dirty dishes set around long enough, you'll be scrubbin' on 'em all day."

I refrained from glancing at LuAnne, who had been the one to leave the sink full and the counters unwashed. "My goodness, look at the time," LuAnne said, standing, "I better be on my way. Leonard will be wanting his lunch. Hazel Marie, that cake should be done in about thirty more minutes. You can test it first, and if it's done, pour about half the glaze over it while it's still in the pan. Let it cool a few minutes before turning it out, then drizzle the rest of the glaze over the top."

Hazel Marie got a blank look on her face, but followed LuAnne to the front door, thanking her for the lesson.

When she came back, she said, "Wonder how you test a cake?"

"I don't know," I said, a little put out that LuAnne had given such meager instructions. It's the basics that a noncook needs to know—like, when she's told to boil water, she also needs to be told how much, how long, in what, and what to do with it when it's boiled. "Let's call Lillian and ask her."

Granny wrung out a sponge and started scrubbing the countertop. "You wanta test a cake, take out a broom straw an' poke it in. If it comes out with batter on it, it ain't done."

Hazel Marie said, "A broom straw? From a broom?"

"Oh, I know," I said. "Lillian uses a toothpick. I've seen her do it. If you have some toothpicks, Hazel Marie, use that instead. Although," I went on diplomatically, "a straw from the top of a broom might do as well."

Which was exactly what Granny Wiggins used, there not being a toothpick in the house. She showed Hazel Marie how to do it, declared the cake done, took it out of the oven, watched as Hazel Marie poured the glaze over it, then ran a knife around the edge of the tube pan and turned out the cake. It looked and smelled wonderful.

While Hazel Marie and I were admiring the cake, Granny Wiggins whirled around. "Where's your vacuum? Might as well get the front rooms done while I can."

"In the hall closet," Hazel Marie answered. "But I try to keep things quiet while the babies are napping."

"Oh, honey, you don't want to do that," Granny said. "Get 'em used to household noises early on an' they'll sleep through anything." And before Hazel Marie could suggest otherwise, off Granny took to find the vacuum cleaner, assuming, I supposed, that she'd been hired.

So much for Hazel Marie's interviewing skills.

Brother Vern showed up in the kitchen looking put out, but at least he was dressed for the day. "Hazel Marie, who's that bossy ole woman in there running the vacuum? She told me to get up and get out so she could move the recliner. And," he said, as if Granny had exhibited the height of arrogance, "she barged in right in the middle of a rerun of the Gaither show."

"Well," Hazel Marie said, stymied by having to referee another clash of egos, "she won't be long. Maybe the Gaither show will still be on."

Brother Vern didn't like that one bit. "I never seen a house run so slipshod, Hazel Marie. If it's not one thing, it's two more. What with James layin' in there wantin' to be waited on hand and foot and comp'ny comin' in and out all day long, and you droppin' everything to take care of caterwaulin' babies, there's no peace anywhere. You got to take hold an' get things on a even keel. I need my peace an' quiet—the doctor said so. And ever time I turn around, somebody's interruptin' an' disruptin' whatever I'm doing."

Under her uncle's barrage of criticism, Hazel Marie looked ready to cry. But I didn't. I looked—and *was*—ready to lay him low.

Just as I opened my mouth to tell him off, we heard James and Granny Wiggins going at each other.

By the time I reached the back bedroom, James, looking somewhat distressed, was sitting in a chair, watching as Granny stripped his bed.

"Why, James," I said, "did you manage to get up by yourself? Your ankle must be a whole lot better."

"No'm," he said, shaking his head as if to clear it. "That lady, she got me up 'fore I knowed I was up."

Before I could express amazement at such a feat, Granny Wiggins snapped a sheet over the bed and said, "They's nothin' to it. I got no use for layin' up in bed all day long when you can be up and doin'. I'm gonna get him to the TV an' keep that preacher man off his back for a change."

I'd never seen such a grateful look as the one that James gave Granny Wiggins then. I helped her walk James to the family room, marveling as we went at how well James managed under her encouragement and with the walking stick.

Following Granny back to the kitchen—it was all I could do to keep up with her—I heard her ask Hazel Marie, "Who is that feller in yonder?"

"That's James," Hazel Marie said. "He works for us, but he had a bad fall and is out of commission for a while."

"Well, I can't do much for broke bones," Granny said, "but if you got a footbath I can cure that sprained ankle. Or a deep pan'll do. All he has to do is soak that foot in hot Epsom-salts water and it'll be fit to walk on before you know it."

"I don't know what a footbath is," Hazel Marie said, "so I guess I don't have one."

"That's all right. I'll bring whatever I can find and some Epsom salts tomorrow. We'll have him right as rain in no time." Granny stopped, cocked her head, and said, "Them babies is awake."

And off she took, Hazel Marie, calling, "Wait, wait!" right behind her.

I stayed where I was, figuring that I was better off staying out of the struggle between them over baby care. I wasn't that good at it anyway.

While they were upstairs, Brother Vern stuck his head in the door and said, "I've got to go out for a while if anybody needs me. If I find a parking place on Main Street, I might take a walk. Doctor's orders, you know."

"Good idea," I said, hoping he'd take a long one. "I'll let Hazel Marie know."

As he went out the front door, Hazel Marie and Granny came back, each with a fussy baby in arm.

"Now, Miz Pickens," Granny said as she sat at the table, holding one of the twins, "you jus' give me what you want this young'un to eat and I'll feed it right here."

"Well," Hazel Marie said, looking slightly bulldozed, "I usually put them in the high chairs and feed them there."

"That's what you have to do when there's two of them and one of you, but since there's two of us, it's better to hold 'em in your lap. That way, they get the lovin' along with the feedin'."

So that's what they did, but I declare, it looked as if only half the strained food got in the babies' mouths. The rest was spread all over the front of the feeders. The babies did not eat well, both fussing and waving their arms and carrying on. I would've thought that the baby who Granny held was unhappy about being in a strange lap, but the other one was just as bad and maybe worse.

"They're teething," Hazel Marie said, "so they don't feel good."

"What they need," Granny said, "is a sugar tit. Get me two little squares of clean cloth, some sugar, and a little bourbon, and I'll fix 'em up."

"Bourbon!" Hazel Marie was shocked. So was I.

"It won't be enough to hurt a fly, just enough to give 'em some relief. And if you're worried about the sugar, you can just take a little bourbon on your finger and run it over and 'round their gums. That'll do just as well."

"Well, I'm sorry," Hazel Marie said with more spirit than she usually displayed, "but we don't have any bourbon. And even if we did, I wouldn't give it to my babies."

"Oh, that's all right," Granny said, not at all cowed by the rejection of her prescription. "Who knows? That little bit of spirits could start 'em off on the road to destruction. Or so the preachers say. I 'spect you can find something at the drugstore that'll do as well or better. A teething ring wouldn't hurt, either. Well," she said, taking her baby to the sink to repair some of the damage, "I think this one's through. Why don't I take 'em both into one of them livin' rooms you got in yonder and play with 'em for a while? That way, you can visit with Miz Murdoch."

Hazel Marie got Granny and the babies situated on the floor of the main living room, then arranged her chair in the kitchen so she could watch them.

"Oh, me," she said tiredly, "I don't know if this is going to work or not. What do you think, Miss Julia?"

"I think she's good-hearted and capable, but I doubt she can keep up this level of activity. She's cleaned the kitchen, vacuumed the entire downstairs, changed James's bed and got him up, fed one of the babies, and she's still going strong. But you'll have to be firm with her, Hazel Marie, because she does seem a little headstrong."

"She sure does." Hazel Marie leaned back to look across the dining room table so she could see what was going on in the room beyond. We could hear the babies laughing and cooing at whatever Granny was saying to them. "I'm not sure she'll be much help if I have to watch her every minute. I mean, what if she hadn't mentioned bourbon, just went ahead and gave it to them? Of course, she couldn't have because we don't have any, but what else could she come up with that I might not know about?"

"I think," I said, attempting to put her mind at ease, "you should keep a close eye on her for the first few days and see how she does. You noticed, didn't you, how quickly she backed down when you said no to the bourbon? That says a lot about her right there. And remember this. She's not going to do anything that you won't know about. She talks too much for that."

"I hope you're right." Hazel Marie sighed deeply, glanced again at her babies, then said, "I'll talk to J.D. tonight and see what he thinks."

"Now *there's* the answer to your worries," I said. "You have to have Granny here when he's home. See how they get along, and let her realize that he's watching everything she does. Hazel Marie," I went on as I put my hand on her arm, "I am convinced that the presence of a strong father keeps children safer than anything else you could name. Nobody's going to be careless with those babies once they've met Mr. Pickens."

She smiled as a dreamy look spread over her face. "He's so good, isn't he?"

Chapter 17

Well, I wouldn't go quite that far in assessing Mr. Pickens's virtues, but I took myself home more determined than ever to do what I could to settle that household down. It might mean putting a bed in my own living room for James and shaking Brother Vern until his teeth rattled, but something had to be done.

Just as I pulled the car into our driveway it occurred to me that I might have more to worry about than either James or Brother Vern. Now, everybody knows that it's not my custom to meddle in other people's business, but I was unnerved as I realized just how unaware Hazel Marie seemed to be of her husband's discomfort.

I sat there for a few minutes thinking over the day—something in the back of my mind was bothering me. Well, a lot of things had been bothering me throughout the day—LuAnne's carelessly given cooking lesson, the fussy, unhappy babies, Brother Vern's castigation of Hazel Marie, James's drawn-out recovery, not to mention Granny Wiggins's medical advice of Epsom salts and bourbon. But there was something else.

As I went back over the events of the day that might have created the underlying fretful feeling I was having, I suddenly leaned my head against the steering wheel in despair. Mr. Pickens's tight-lipped silence, his curt response to my greeting, his early departure from home that morning, his active dislike of Brother Vern, and my sure knowledge of his habit of picking up and moving on—all of this flashed through my mind. What in the world would he do when he learned that that little dust devil Granny

Wiggins had been added to the mix? I recalled wondering the day before how Mr. Pickens was adjusting to a settled married life, and here I was wondering how long he would tolerate such an *un*settled married life as he now had. I happened to know that men like pleasant and comfortable routines in their homes. They want to come home to order, especially if their working hours are hectic and disorderly, as Mr. Pickens's assuredly were.

Maybe, I thought as I raised my head and gazed unseeingly out the windshield, this was not the time to worry about Hazel Marie's ability to put meals on the table. Maybe I ought to discard my idea of providing recipe books and cooking lessons, which only added to the tumult, the number of people underfoot, and the general discord of the household.

Maybe, instead of concerning myself with improving Hazel Marie's cooking skills, I ought to turn my attention to improving Mr. Pickens's surroundings so he'd stay happy and in place.

I nearly jumped out of my skin when there was a sharp rap on the car window. I turned with a gasp, and the face looking back at me startled me even more.

"Thurlow!" I said, opening the car door. "What do you mean sneaking up on people and scaring them half to death?"

He stepped back as I got out of the car. "Well, what're you doing sitting out here in the car? Murdoch run you out of the house?"

"Oh, for goodness sakes, no, he did not run me out of the house. I was just . . . It's none of your business what I was doing." I closed the car door and tried the best I could to compose myself. Feeling a nudge against my knee, I glanced down and saw Ronnie, Thurlow's huge spotted Great Dane, looking expectantly, I assumed, for a handout. "Anyway," I went on, heading for the front door, "since you're here, it's too chilly to stay outside. But you might as well tell me now: Is this a social visit or have you come to complain about something?"

"I've come to complain, which I have every right to do," Thurlow said, lifting his head in that arrogant way of his as he followed me to the door. Ronnie walked right beside him, as if he'd been issued an invitation as well. His tail, wagging fiercely, flapped against the door frame.

Thurlow himself was in his usual getup—baggy trousers, plaid shirt half in and half out, work boots, and a greasy-looking canvas coat. I had heard several reports that Helen Stroud had taken him in hand, cleaned him up, and demanded he buy new and decent clothes. She'd even gotten him to church, but I didn't know how long that had lasted. Everyone kept expecting news of a wedding, even though the two of them were so ill suited that few of us could fathom such an outcome.

"Well, come on in and let's hear it." I held the door open, hoping to get it closed before Ronnie romped in. I didn't make it, for he barreled his way into my house as if he owned it and sprawled out on the Oriental in my living room.

Now, if you should think that I was being less than welcoming, you'd be correct. And if you're inclined to think that Thurlow was to be pitied, dressed as he was like a Main Street bum, I assure you that he could buy and sell more than half the residents of Abbotsville. In addition, Thurlow was no gentleman, and he had a way of getting under my skin like no other. He didn't care what he said or how he said it, belittling women in general and, seemingly, me in particular. I always tried to avoid him, but here he was with another grievance, which would be merely one more out of many.

After he was seated on my Duncan Phyfe sofa and I in a Victorian chair across the room from him, he proceeded to tell me the purpose of his visit.

"Well, Madam Murdoch," he began, "I hear you're preparing a cookbook and I've been waiting for you to ask for my recipes. So far, you haven't, and I want to know why not."

"Why, Thurlow," I said, taken aback at his demand, "I didn't know you wanted to be included. In fact, I didn't know you cooked."

"How do you think me and Ronnie eat? Of course I cook,

though probably not the fancy dishes you require. But that don't mean I want to be left out when you're running all over town getting recipes from every Tom, Dick, and Harry you can find."

"I hardly think . . ."

"Yeah, and half the women you're getting recipes from don't even know how to boil water. They all have cooks to do it for them."

"Maybe so, but . . ."

"No maybe about it. I keep up with what's going on, don't think I don't, and you ought not to leave me out just because I don't waste my money on kitchen help."

"Oh, I'd never think you wasted money on anything," I assured him, for he certainly didn't. In fact, a lot of us wished that he would. "But I didn't intend to offend you by not asking for yours. I merely thought you wouldn't be interested."

"Let me decide when I'm interested and when I'm not. Now, I know you're trying to help that woman you took in when nobody else would. Not everybody would welcome a husband's discards like you did, even if he was dead, and you may not think it, but I always admired you for that."

"Well, ah, thank you," I murmured and added, "I guess," under my breath. But I was on guard, because I didn't want Thurlow to go off any more than he already had about Hazel Marie's less than appropriate relationship with Wesley Lloyd Springer. That was in the past, and I powerfully resented the subject being brought forth again by anybody.

"Yeah," he said, unable to leave well enough alone, "everybody still wonders how you and that woman can get along like you do. Considering everything."

"My *friend,* Hazel Marie," I said as firmly as I could, "is a properly married woman with a decent, hardworking husband and small children. Anything I do to help her is my business and not open to discussion or criticism."

"Oh," Thurlow said with a wave of his hand, "don't get your back up. You're too sensitive on the subject. All I want to do is give you one of my recipes, and that woman can use it or not—it don't matter to me."

"For the last time, Thurlow, she is not *that woman*. Her name is Hazel Marie Puckett Pickens or, better still, Mrs. J. D. Pickens, and you'd better not let her husband hear you run her down. He is not a man to take something like that lightly."

"Well, I guess I ought to be quaking in my boots, but I don't quake so easy. Now, do you want my recipe or not?" He pulled out a folded sheet of paper from his back pocket and leaned over to give it to me.

I had no conception of what his recipe would be. For all I knew anything made from it would be inedible. I thanked him, determining at the same time that before recommending it to Hazel Marie, I'd have Lillian look it over, if she could read the handwritten scribbles.

"Now, that one," Thurlow said, all business now, "is for home-made soup, and I got plenty more if you need 'em. But I call this one Throw-Everything-In Soup—whatever you got can go in it. It'll make enough for two family meals at least. Three or four for me. I make it on a Sunday afternoon and have almost a week's worth of suppers from then on, if I don't give too much to Ronnie. He likes it, too. And the next one . . ." He stopped and looked at Ronnie, whose stomach growled with an imminent threat. "Ronnie!" Thurlow yelled as he sprang off the sofa. "Get up from there and get outside!"

Ronnie hopped to his feet, then spraddled out his front legs with his head bent between them. He started coughing deep in his throat.

"My word," I yelped, springing up, too. "What's he doing?"

"He's throwin' up, that's what. Get out here, Ronnie." Thurlow had the front door open, but Ronnie was in the throes of power-ful stomach spasms and couldn't move. Thurlow ran back to him, lifted him with a mighty effort, and dragged him out on the porch, where Ronnie emptied his stomach all over my front steps.

"Well," Thurlow said, surveying the scene, "at least he got outside. But don't worry about him. He does this off and on whenever he eats something he shouldn't. He's all right now. Just take a hose to this, Madam Murdoch, and nobody'll know the difference. Tell that woman I hope she enjoys the soup."

I stood there, outraged at being left with Ronnie's mess, as the two of them walked away, unconcerned and unapologetic.

"Well, I never," I said, but of course I was speaking to myself and went right on doing it, employing some choice epithets for sick dogs and their owners.

But what was I to do with Thurlow's recipe? If Hazel Marie tried it, would everybody in the house come down with Ronnie's ailment? That's all Mr. Pickens would need to make him look for greener fields. Of course I could conveniently overlook Thurlow's recipe, but he'd be sure to know it wasn't in the book. I'd never hear the end of his complaining. But if Ronnie's stomach upset was the result of Thurlow's cooking—and what else could it have been?—I needed to make sure the Pickens family never suffered a similar affliction. A caution, a warning of some kind, would have to be included with anything that had Thurlow's name attached.

Thurlow's Throw-Everything-In Soup

(Just as he gave it to me)

Take a large pot and put in a pound or more of good stew meat, cut in chunks and trimmed of fat if you're a picky eater. Cover with water, add a large onion, quartered, and simmer until the meat is no longer pink. Skim off any scum. Add 1 or 2 large cans of tomatoes. Drain a small can each of green beans, lima beans, and corn niblets, saving the juice (except from the green beans—it's awful) and add the vegetables to the pot. Add a bay leaf if you have it, and salt and pepper to taste. Cover and let simmer all morning or afternoon.

About an hour before eating, add 1-inch chunks of 2 potatoes and 2 or 3 sliced carrots. Cover and continue simmering until the potatoes are done.

At this point, taste again. You may need to add more salt and a small can of tomato sauce to make it richer. If your tomatoes taste too acidic, as they can at certain times of the year, add 1 teaspoon of sugar, stir, and taste. Keep adding sugar, a little at a time, until it tastes right. Throw out the saved juice. You don't need it. Remove the bay leaf before serving.

You can add anything else you want to this soup: shredded cabbage, celery, English peas, and so on. You'll need cornbread to go with it.

It'll feed Ronnie and me for three or four days, so do the math.

(For heaven's sake, Hazel Marie, talk to me before you try this. You won't believe what Ronnie did.)

Chapter 18

⁓

Rubbing my hands, which were half frozen from handling the hose I'd used to clean the steps, I went into our lovely new library and sank into a leather chair. Resolutely putting any decision about Thurlow's recipe on the back burner and giving thanks that he apparently hadn't known about the lessons, I turned my mind to dealing with Hazel Marie's frenetic household. My first impulse was to go upstairs and discuss the problem with Sam. Or, even easier, go to the kitchen and ask Lillian's advice.

But I couldn't move—the whole state of affairs was weighing too heavily on me. Taking one problem at a time, I knew that the only thing under my immediate control was the recipe book and the hands-on cooks. I could table the book and cancel the cooks, which would immediately cut down on the number of people tromping in and out of the Pickens house. And also, I realized, make Granny Wiggins redundant. Hazel Marie would no longer need someone to watch the babies if she didn't have to be in the kitchen.

But of course she *did* have to be in the kitchen—or *somebody* had to be—which brought up the problem I'd started with: feeding that crowd for as long as James was laid up. And I knew that two or three outstanding meals a week prepared by his wife could go a long way toward keeping Mr. Pickens content. Men do like to come home to a table laden with good food.

Be that as it may, though, good food and plenty of it wouldn't be enough to balance out the discord in the rest of the house. And that brought me to a decision: The last one in should be the first one out, and that was Brother Vernon Puckett. I didn't count Granny Wiggins because she was on a trial basis and didn't live there anyway.

The ring of the telephone startled me and I hurried to the mahogany desk to answer it.

"Julia?" Mildred Allen asked as if she wasn't sure who had answered.

"Why, hello, Mildred. I hope Hazel Marie told you how much everybody enjoyed your recipe. I know that Mr. Pickens just beams every time he thinks of it." Actually, I didn't know any such thing, but it never hurts to be complimentary whenever you can.

"Oh, she told me, and I'm so glad. Ida Lee and I talked about how much we enjoyed the morning, so if you need another lesson just let us know. But, Julia, I want to ask you about something else. Just what kind of preacher is Hazel Marie's uncle?"

That stopped me for a minute. "Well, uh, why?"

"He called on me a little while ago and I must say he was most pleasant company. I'd never had the opportunity to actually talk with him, but I found him very courteous and attentive, and I'm intrigued by the new ministry he's planning. So I wonder if you could tell me a little about his background."

"I would if I could, Mildred. But the fact of the matter is, I don't know that much about him. All I know is that he and Hazel Marie have had a testy relationship over the years I've known her, but if you're asking about his educational background, I'm not sure he has any."

"Oh, really? Well, he seemed quite earnest and sincere. I'd go so far as to say *burdened,* and it doesn't take an academic degree to move a tender heart the way his has been moved for the down-trodden among us."

"I daresay," I murmured, wondering what Brother Vern was up to now, although it was plain to me that Mildred's diamonds had whetted his interest.

"Anyway," Mildred went on, "he has a special ministry in mind that would benefit the community, but he needs start-up money. I told him I would consider sponsoring him."

"Mildred," I said, immediately on my guard, "you've put me in a difficult position. I want to be honest with you, but I also don't want to run Hazel Marie's uncle down. He's not well, you know, and for all I know he may have had an awakening that's put him on a different track." I paused, wondering how much to say, then decided that I couldn't hold back. "And of course I don't want to be unkind, so I'll put it this way: From the experiences I've had with Vernon Puckett, I wouldn't trust him as far as I could throw him."

Mildred laughed. "Oh, Julia, you don't mean that. He is so concerned about Hazel Marie, and he's determined not to be a financial burden on her. And he did tell me about his physical condition, which truly hampers him as far as an active ministry is concerned. But he's anxious to pull his own weight and become self-sufficient again. And perhaps contribute to household expenses." She paused as I had, then, as if deciding to say what was on her mind, she lowered her voice and said, "I didn't know that the Pickenses were under a financial strain."

"*What!* Did he tell you that?"

"Well, no. But he implied that they were having a hard time making ends meet."

"The only hard time they're having is putting up with him." I was so furious I could hardly speak. "Mildred, don't be taken in. I assure you that the Pickens family is well taken care of." But at that point, I had to recalculate. I knew that Mr. Pickens had been reluctant to marry money—I'm speaking of Lloyd's money, his inheritance from his father, Wesley Lloyd Springer. Which, of course, benefited Hazel Marie as well. I'd assumed they'd come to terms with that, but if they hadn't, and Mr. Pickens was just bullheaded enough to demand that they live on his income, they might very well be under a financial strain. But I wasn't about to discuss that with Mildred, and it infuriated me to learn that Brother Vern had brought it to her attention.

And, if it were true, how did Brother Vern know when I didn't?

⌒〜⌒

After ending the phone call, I tapped softly on the door of the old sunroom upstairs, newly turned into Sam's office. I rarely disturbed him when he was working on that monumental legal history of Abbot County, which he might never finish, seeing that lawyers and judges kept getting into debt, tax arrears, and general all-around hot water, but this was one of those rare times. "Sam? It's me."

"Come in, sweetheart," he said, opening the door. "I'm glad to see you."

"I don't want to interrupt you, but . . ."

"You can interrupt me anytime you want. Here, sit down—I'm more than ready for a break. What's on your mind?"

I took a seat in a chair beside his cluttered desk, as he got comfortable in the creaky old chair behind it.

"It's Hazel Marie and Mr. Pickens," I said in a rush. "Plus two babies, Brother Vern, James, Granny Wiggins, and now Mildred Allen. Add on Hazel Marie's inability to cook decent meals day in and day out, and James's inability to do for himself, and Brother Vern's inability to keep his mouth shut. That's what's on my mind."

"Whoa, whoa now," Sam said, holding his hand up and looking at me over his glasses. "Back up and tell me slow."

So I did, ending up by saying, "And now Brother Vern has gone poor-mouthing to Mildred, telling her that they're under a financial strain and he wants to start some kind of new ministry to help out. Have you ever heard of such a thing? I hope you haven't, because it's not true, is it? I mean, they have plenty to live on, don't they?" If anybody knew the true financial situation of the Pickens family, it would be Sam, who, along with Binkie Enloe Bates, was entrusted with the care of Lloyd's inheritance.

By the time I'd finished, Sam was frowning. He took off his reading glasses and rubbed his eyes. "I can assure you that they have plenty to live on. Hazel Marie gets a sizable check every quarter, just as you do. But what she does with it is another matter. She may spend it all on Lloyd, which is what it's for primarily, or she may be saving it for him—it's really up to her until he reaches maturity. But you know all that," he said, absently moving some papers on his desk.

"Well, I think you should talk to Mr. Pickens and find out what's going on. They're certainly having unexpected expenses with so many in the house, and he needs to use whatever's available." I leaned forward. "Talk to him, Sam. I can't bear to think of them having money problems when there's no need for it."

"No, honey," Sam said, shaking his head, "it's not my place to talk to Pickens about his financial affairs. And Binkie would be the one to talk to Hazel Marie. She can reassure her as to how the funds are to be used." Sam pursed his mouth, tapped a pencil, then looked straight at me. "You do realize, though, that if Hazel Marie is putting it aside for Lloyd because Pickens won't use it, Brother Vern will consider it ready-made to tap into. If he knows about it, that is."

"Oh, Sam, she can't give it to him, can she?" That possibility shot through me like a red-hot poker.

"No, no, she won't do that. *Can't* do that without running the risk of losing Lloyd. The court keeps a careful eye on how his money is used while he's underage. No, what I'm talking about is the stress and strain of having to turn her uncle down if he should learn that that money—which she has access to—is just sitting there."

"Oh, my goodness, yes," I said, clearly seeing what Hazel Marie would be in for. "He'd be after her constantly and she's just gullible enough to *want* to give it to him, but honest enough not to. She'd be whipsawed to within an inch of her life." Then I saw the solution. "There's only one thing to do, and that's to encourage Mildred to sponsor his new ministry—whatever it is. She has more than enough to afford to lose some and, knowing her, she'll keep him on a short leash anyway."

"You really want to put your friend in a position to be taken for a ride?"

"I've already warned her in no uncertain terms. She knows what I think of him, so my conscience is clear. Now," I said, rising to take my leave, "I need to find out just what he has in mind for this new ministry and how he expects to make money from it. Whoever heard of an honest ministry making money anyway? And if it involves Hazel Marie in any way, shape, or form, like having Bible studies at her house or anything of the like, we'll have to put a stop to it."

❧

"Mildred?" I said when she answered the phone. "It's Julia again, and I'm wondering if Mr. Puckett told you what kind of ministry he's thinking of starting."

"Why, Julia, I didn't think you were interested. What's changed your mind?"

"Nothing's changed my mind and I'm not interested, except insofar as it affects Hazel Marie and her family. That's why I'm asking. Mildred, she can't possibly take on another chore, task, or burden, so if he has in mind anything that adds to her load, I'm going to be most upset."

Mildred laughed. "Well, you don't have to be upset, because Mr. Puckett's idea is to rent a place somewhere on the other side of Main Street, maybe near the bus station, to catch, as he says, the wayfarers. He wants a place with a small office he can use to place orders, keep records, and oversee what goes on, all of which will keep him out of the house during the day. Of course he'll have to hire a few people, although he intends to rely primarily on volunteers for most of the work. He's not physically able to do any of the actual work himself, you know. He'll only supervise."

"I see," I murmured, picturing Brother Vern enthroned as the ministry executive sitting behind a desk, answering the phone and giving orders. "But I still don't know the kind of ministry he's planning."

Mildred laughed again, enjoying this entirely too much. "Well, you should know," she said. "He got the idea from you."

"*Me?* That's impossible. The only time I've spoken to him was to tell him to put some clothes on."

"Then he must've heard it secondhand, because he told me that when he saw Hazel Marie learning to cook, he knew what the Lord wanted him to do. He's going to open a soup kitchen, Julia, which you have to admit is really needed. And you may not know this, but I've been feeling a call to finance some charitable organization. I've been awfully lax here lately, and Mr. Puckett's desire to feed the hungry, both physically and spiritually, sounds like just the thing for me to do."

I closed my eyes, swaying at the thought of a soup kitchen run by Brother Vern and financed by Mildred Allen. All they needed to do was to rope in Thurlow Jones and use his recipe for Throw-Everything-In Soup.

Chapter 19

"Well, Mildred," I finally managed to say, "I hope it works out, not only for Hazel Marie's sake but for yours. But how in the world does he expect to make a soup kitchen into a paying proposition? It sounds like a money pit to me."

"Oh, he's thought it through. Besides, he's had experience with similar projects and knows just what to do. All he needs is the capital to keep it going for about a year, then he has every expectation that either the city or the county will take it over. And he'll be applying for a government grant, too. When he gets that, the place will practically run itself."

I just closed my eyes, wondering how I could've ever thought that Mildred Allen had her head on straight. This was going to turn into another bright idea foisted onto Abbot County taxpayers.

I had one last piece of advice for Mildred, then I was going to leave it alone. "Just be sure that you watch him like a hawk, and don't be surprised if he has trouble getting volunteers and you have trouble getting donors."

"Well, I was going to ask you . . ."

"Don't," I said before she could finish. "My donations for the year are already pledged." Then, biting my lip, I reconsidered. If a soup kitchen would keep Brother Vern occupied and out of Hazel Marie's hair, then perhaps I should help it along a little. "However, when the ministry's up and running, I might be able to make a contribution. I want to see how it goes first."

"Good," Mildred said, sounding pleased with herself. "I'll hold you to that."

"It'll depend on one condition," I said, thinking fast. "He has to rent a place with room for him to move into. And that's something you should require, too, Mildred. He needs to be on the premises at all times, not free to run hither and yon to keep bothering Hazel Marie. I want him out of that house."

I knew it would take time for Brother Vern to implement his plan, which meant that we'd have to keep putting up with him for a while. Yet the prospect of his soon being out of the house was like a light at the end of a tunnel for me. And I was sure it would be for Hazel Marie as well, although she'd be unlikely to admit it.

❧

With a load of worry about to be lifted, I sighed and moved on to more recipes and lesson schedules. Reminding myself that anything worth doing is worth doing well, I put on a coat, took up the folder with my calendar, and told Lillian I'd be back soon.

"It gettin' close to suppertime," she said. "When you be back?"

"I won't be long. I have to go to Binkie's now or I'll never catch her. She doesn't get home till suppertime."

Driving to the townhouse where Binkie and Deputy—now Sergeant—Coleman Bates lived, I wondered what kind of recipes Binkie would offer. She'd been married some few years by now, but her active law practice had prevented her from developing many culinary skills. And not just culinary ones, but the whole gamut of domestic skills as well. I figured that Binkie's offering wouldn't be much beyond *Remove wrapping and place in microwave.* But I wanted at least one recipe from her and Coleman and, if it was simple enough for Binkie to prepare, I knew Hazel Marie would have no problem with it.

Binkie was so busy, what with her law practice and all, that I always hesitated to take up any of her time when she was home. The baby, little Gracie, had begun to walk now or, rather, toddle around, and it worried me to death that her parents were so busy.

I just have to say it: I wished Binkie would stay home and raise that child herself. On the other hand, if she did, I'd have to find another lawyer to look after my interests, and Lloyd's, too, so I couldn't wish it too hard. And, of course, Binkie had excellent help in Mrs. Collins, who not only took care of Gracie, but also prepared dinner for Binkie and Coleman several evenings a week. And I must say that those two were hands-on parents when they were home. The weekends were totally devoted to Gracie, and usually were filled with one activity or another for the three of them. They were forever hiking the mountain trails, camping out, or taking trips to that big aquarium in Atlanta or to the science museum in Charlotte, where Gracie could touch some static-electricity thing that made her hair stand on end.

Anyway, when I arrived at Binkie's townhouse and told her what I was doing and what I wanted from her, she threw back her head and laughed.

"Oh, Miss Julia, you know I'm not a cook. Coleman and Gracie would starve if it was left to me. You better ask somebody else."

"No, Binkie," I said. "The beauty of this book will be having recipes from people Hazel Marie knows. Even if she never uses a one, it'll be something she'll treasure and enjoy just reading. Now, if it's at all possible, I'd love for you to find time to make your favorite main dish recipe in Hazel Marie's kitchen so she can learn how to do it."

Binkie looked at me in wonder as she tried not to laugh in my face. "Miss Julia, Coleman would love for me to find time to make something in *our* kitchen."

Although I longed to fill another square on my calendar, I quickly backed down. "Oh, I understand. I know how busy you are. Let's not worry about that, but I'd really like at least one main dish recipe from you to go in the book."

"Well, okay, since you're letting me off the hook. My mom is forever sending me recipes and, knowing her, they're her way of hinting that I should be more domestic. But I only have to please Coleman and, believe me, I keep him happy." And she laughed again. "But I warn you. The only meals I ever cook are the quick and simple kind. There're too many fun things to do than stay in a kitchen all day."

"Quick and simple will be perfect for Hazel Marie. She doesn't mind staying in the kitchen all day, but I want her to have something to show for it when she does."

"Okay, then," Binkie said, getting up from the floor, where she'd been playing with the baby while we talked. "Mom sent me one that I've made a few times. It's so easy even I couldn't mess it up. Coleman really likes it, too."

She went into the kitchen and came back with several laminated sheets of paper. "My mother!" she said. "She's so particular about everything. No wonder I drive her crazy with the way I keep house. All I can say is 'Thank goodness for Mrs. Collins.' But look these over, Miss Julia, and see what you think." She handed a sheet to me, saying, "Here's the one I was thinking of. It's for corn chowder and it's great on a cold evening."

Looking it over, I said, "Hazel Marie can probably manage this. In fact, it looks so good I'm going to give a copy to Lillian."

"And here's an easy one for spaghetti—the only thing I cooked in law school." Binkie smiled, recalling her school days as she looked it over. "That, and grilled cheese sandwiches. We grilled those with a hot iron." She laughed as she handed me a handwritten, food-spattered page torn from a yellow legal pad.

"My goodness, Binkie, there's hardly a measured amount on here. How do you know how much of anything to put in?"

"I don't," Binkie said, blithely admitting her haphazard cooking method. "But that's the beauty part. How it turns out is always a surprise. But, look, here's a list of take-out restaurants. To be on the safe side, you ought to include that, too."

"I don't think so, but what about a dessert? You have anything easy, something she can't mess up? I want her to have some successes, so she won't get discouraged."

"Well, here's one for peach cobbler that Mom used to make in the summer, when peaches are fresh. I've made it, too, a couple of times and it's worked for me."

"Good. I'll take it. What else do you have?"

"That's about it," Binkie said. "I mean, I have lots of recipes, but not many I've actually tried. Tell you what, though: Coleman'll be home in a few minutes, and he has a special recipe that's outstanding."

"Coleman cooks?"

I knew that Coleman did more with and for the baby than your average father, but I had no idea that he was handy in the kitchen as well.

Binkie laughed. "Coleman grills," she said. "So maybe his would be more for J.D. Let's hope *he* knows how to cook."

"Well," I said, "if Hazel Marie's skills don't soon improve, I expect Mr. Pickens will either learn or go hungry."

"I just thought of something that's really easy," Binkie said, brushing back her hair. "No cooking involved, so either one of them can do it. You take a flat serving dish, like a platter, and spread out one large can of refried beans. Just smooth them out with a spoon to the edges of the dish. On top of that, spread a can of guacamole dip, then do the same with a large carton of sour cream. Then you sprinkle a layer of grated cheddar cheese on top and end with sliced black olives. You can serve it with any kind of corn chips you like."

After furiously jotting down the ingredients as she listed them, I then looked over my notes. "And you don't cook any of this?"

"Nope. Right out of the cans and onto the plate—the kind of recipe I like."

"And what do you call it?"

"Beats me. Taco dip, maybe. Or, I know—call it Binkie's Special Dip."

"Well, it does sound tasty," I said, somewhat skeptically. "But it hardly qualifies as a whole meal."

"No, it's an appetizer, but Coleman could make a meal of it," Binkie said, laughing, "and occasionally, J.D. might be happy to get it, especially if he has a couple of bottles of beer on hand."

"I hardly think . . ."

"Oh, Miss Julia, I'm just teasing you."

Binkie's Law School Spaghetti

Brown 1 pound of ground chuck with about ½ a medium onion, chopped. Season with salt, pepper, and garlic powder. Cook and stir until the onion is soft and the beef is no longer pink.

Add:

6-ounce can tomato paste
6 ounces water
15-ounce can tomato sauce
2 large or 3 medium bay leaves
Sprinkle of oregano (more or less)
Sprinkle of chili powder (more or less)
Sprinkle of paprika (more or less)
Salt and pepper, to taste

Simmer, stirring occasionally, for about 1 hour or until you're ready to eat. Remove the bay leaves before serving. Serve over angel hair spaghetti.

Serves 6.

(Hazel Marie, don't be afraid to try this. If Binkie can make it, so can you.)

Binkie's Mother's Corn Chowder

Fry 4 or 5 slices of bacon in a medium saucepan. When crisp, remove the bacon and add a small onion, diced, to the bacon grease.

Turn the heat to low (very low) and put one 20-ounce log of frozen creamed corn, yellow or white, in the saucepan (Hazel Marie, remove the wrapping first), turning the log occasionally until the corn is thawed. Stir well.

Add 2 cups of milk and salt and pepper to taste, and heat but don't boil. Ladle into bowls, crumble the bacon on top, and serve with cornbread.

Makes 2 servings.

(Binkie said that this is a good winter recipe when fresh corn is hard to find.)

Binkie's Fresh Peach Cobbler

Preheat the oven to 350°F. Stir together 2 cups of fresh peaches (peeled and sliced) and ¾ cup of sugar and let sit to form juice while the batter is prepared.

Batter

Melt ¾ stick of butter in a Pyrex pan. (Microwave it, Hazel Marie. Never put a Pyrex bowl on a hot stove eye.)

Blend together the following and pour over the melted butter:

¾ cup sugar
¾ cup plain flour
2 teaspoons baking powder
¾ cup milk

Add the peaches and juice to the batter *without stirring* and bake for 30 minutes or until the top is brown.

Serve warm with vanilla ice cream.

Serves 6.

(This sounds very much like the one that Lillian makes, so check with her if you have trouble.)

Chapter 20

Just about the time I finished copying Binkie's recipes, Coleman came in, looking handsome in his dark blue uniform, but creaking and squeaking from all the paraphernalia strapped around his waist. Squealing with delight, Gracie ran to him as soon as he came through the door. He picked her up, then threw her in the air, making me gasp in fear.

"Guess what, Coleman," Binkie said, giving him a quick kiss. "Miss Julia wants your recipes for the cookbook she's writing for Hazel Marie."

"Hi, Miss Julia," he said, smiling in welcome. "What's this? You know I'm no cook."

"Yes, you are," Binkie said. "I told her about your shish kebabs, and she thinks J.D.'s going to need it."

"Oh, well, yeah, that is a good recipe," he said, handing Gracie to her mother. "Let me get some of this stuff off and I'll find it for you."

In just a few minutes, Coleman came back to the living room, sans utility belt, handgun, handcuffs, walkie-talkie, and sundry other items, ready to share his recipes.

"Now this one," he said, handing me a splotched and smeared page. "I don't remember where I got it. But it's good, and even better," he went on, cutting his eyes at Binkie, "if the lady of the house fixes the marinade."

Binkie laughed. "I do most of the time, don't I? Thing of it is, Miss Julia, somebody has to make the marinade and cut up the steak the day before the cook plans to do the grilling."

"Yeah," Coleman said. "It's better on the grill, but I've done it under the broiler in the oven. But if you do it inside, you're gonna have smoke—the marinade sizzles and spatters so much. Tell Hazel Marie to be prepared for the smoke alarm to go off."

"Unfortunately, she's used to that. But maybe I shouldn't mention using the oven."

"I don't blame you," he said. "But if you're gonna put my recipes in your book, put this in, too. I don't have it written down, since it's just one extra ingredient for grilling hamburgers."

So I wrote down what he told me, and hoped that, if Mr. Pickens bought a grill, he'd use it himself and keep Hazel Marie far from it.

"Okay," Coleman said, "I'm gonna do something that might not be on the up-and-up—claiming something that's not really mine. But it's Lillian's lemon pie, and my absolute favorite. I keep hoping my wife'll make it for me, but so far, no luck." He gave Binkie a mock glare, and she gave him one right back.

"Well, bless your heart, Coleman," I said. "I'll ask Lillian to make one for you. We don't want you to feel deprived."

"Yeah, poor thing," Binkie said, squeezing his muscular arm. "He looks deprived, doesn't he?"

I declare, those two act like they're newlyweds, which on occasion can be embarrassing to an onlooker. Still, it's most encouraging to see a young couple so in love, despite the fact that they've rearranged a few of the traditional rules and roles.

As I copied Coleman's recipes, a part of my mind was pondering Hazel Marie's situation and wondering if she and Mr. Pickens could benefit from the unusual, but obviously working, example in this household. Probably not, I mentally sighed, for how often do we see ourselves as others see us? Hazel Marie's problems—both present and potential—were plain to me, but clearly not to her.

One thing at a time, I told myself, as I erased a mistake I'd made, and kept on copying.

Coleman's Shish Kebabs

3 pounds lean beef (round, chuck, or sirloin) cut into 1½-inch cubes

Cover the beef cubes with California Marinade (below). Refrigerate 12 to 24 hours (use longer time for lesser cuts of meat to tenderize), turning occasionally.

Fill 6 skewers, alternating the meat cubes with mushroom caps, tomato wedges, and parboiled green-pepper wedges and onions.

Grill over hot coals to the desired doneness of meat, brushing with the marinade occasionally. May also be broiled inside in the oven, but your smoke alarm may go off.

California Marinade

Thoroughly combine 1 cup of salad oil, ¾ cup of soy sauce, ½ cup of lemon juice, ¼ cup *each* of Worcestershire sauce and prepared mustard, 2 tablespoons of salt, 1 tablespoon of coarsely cracked pepper, and 2 cloves of minced garlic.

Serves 6.

(It might be better to let Mr. Pickens cube the meat, Hazel Marie. He's probably had more practice with a knife than you.)

Coleman's Hamburgers on the Grill

¼ pound ground chuck (80% lean to 20% fat) for each patty

Add salt, pepper, garlic powder, and Worcestershire sauce, mixing well. Shape into 4 patties.

Sprinkle each patty liberally with Montreal steak seasoning.

Grill to the desired doneness.

(Be sure to give Mr. Pickens lots of compliments when he grills, Hazel Marie. That way, he'll be eager to do more of it.)

Coleman's Favorite Pie

1 envelope unflavored gelatin
1 cup sugar
½ teaspoon salt
4 eggs, separated
⅓ cup lemon juice
⅔ cup water
1 teaspoon lemon peel grated
1 cup whipping cream whipped
1 baked and cooled 9-inch pastry shell
Mint sprigs for garnish

In a saucepan, thoroughly mix the gelatin, ½ cup of the sugar, and the salt.

In a separate bowl, beat together the egg yolks, lemon juice, and water. Stir into the gelatin mixture. Cook and stir over medium heat just until the mixture comes to a boil. Remove from the heat and stir in the lemon peel. Chill, stirring occasionally until partially set.

Beat the egg whites until soft peaks form, gradually adding the remaining ½ cup of sugar, beating until stiff peaks form. Fold into the cooled gelatin mixture, then fold ½ of the whipped cream into that. Pile into the prepared pastry shell and chill until firm.

Garnish each slice with an additional spoonful of whipped cream and a sprig of fresh mint. This pie slices beautifully and holds its shape—perfect for serving at the table.

Serves 8.

(This recipe is Lillian's Lemon Chiffon Pie, Hazel Marie. Coleman wanted his name on it because he likes it so much.)

Chapter 21

When I returned home, I found Sam, Lloyd, and Lillian waiting dinner for me. Apologizing for being late, I quickly sat at the table and began to recount my visit with Binkie and Coleman, marveling aloud at how Gracie had grown. We were still at the table, catching up with the day's events, when Hazel Marie called.

"I'm so sorry for calling at dinnertime," she said when Lillian called me to the phone, "but I have to ask you something."

"It's all right, Hazel Marie—we've finished. Is anything the matter?"

"I'm not sure, and I hate to ask you because I know you have things to do. But Granny Wiggins just called and said she's coming in the morning to doctor on James's foot. I told her I didn't need her till Wednesday, when LuAnne will be cooking again, but she said treatment couldn't wait and I'd thank her when she had James up and walking. So," Hazel Marie stopped and drew a deep breath with a little rasp in it, "so could you come over, too?"

"Well, of course," I said, mentally rearranging a few minor tasks on my to-do list. "What exactly is she planning to do? Did she say?"

"Just that she's bringing Epsom salts and her big canning pot, so I guess she'll soak James's foot. Unless she's planning to put it up for the winter."

I laughed. Hazel Marie wasn't known for having a sense of humor, but occasionally she'd surprise me—mainly because she never realized when she'd said something funny. "Well," I said, "I'd rather see her do that than *dose* him with it."

"Why? What would it do?"

"Clean out his system like nobody's business, and with the shape he's in, that's the last thing he needs."

"Oh, my," Hazel Marie said, taking me seriously. "You think she'd do that?"

"No, no, she won't." But I wasn't all that sure what Granny would do, so I looked on the bright side. "She'll just let his foot soak in it, I expect. But don't worry, Hazel Marie. I'll be glad to come over and, between the two of us, we'll make sure it all goes on James's foot and not in his mouth. By the way, how did Lu-Anne's dinner go?"

"Everybody loved it," she said. "There was only one problem: I didn't have enough pork chops. Uncle Vern would've had two if I'd had them, but I didn't. Do you think I could double the recipe next time?"

"I'm sure you can. Just fill two Pyrex dishes with pork chops and double the sauce recipe. You can bake them both at the same time."

"Will I need to double the oven temperature?"

Oh, Lord, even I knew better than that. "No, Hazel Marie, don't do that. You'll burn them up. The same temperature will do for both."

"Okay," she said, then after a pause: "Maybe that's why my baked potatoes were little nubs when I took them out."

I just closed my eyes and shook my head. Sometimes it was hard to remember that Hazel Marie had many outstanding qualities that could almost completely cancel out any deficiencies she might also have.

So I was knocking on Hazel Marie's door bright and early Tuesday morning, knowing that country people get up before the sun, and I was fully intent on being there before Granny Wiggins arrived.

Mr. Pickens opened the door, said, "Welcome to the mad-house," shoved his dark aviator glasses on his face, and walked out as I walked in. That didn't bode well for a good start to the day and, from the sounds in the house, nobody else was having a good start, either.

I put my coat and pocketbook on a hall chair and went into the den, where the television was tuned to a quartet blaring forth. Brother Vern, still in his pajamas and that seedy bathrobe, was sitting on a footstool, hunched over, glued to the television screen, an empty cereal bowl and coffee cup on the floor beside him. A sugar bowl, an open cereal box, and a half-empty bottle of milk were there, along with pages from the morning paper scattered across the floor.

Turning his head as he heard me walk in, his face lit up as he said, "You're just in time! Don't you want to cook us up a big pot of grits and some sausage gravy?"

"No," I said as serenely as I could, thinking that Brother Vern could trash a room quicker than anybody I knew. "I don't believe I do. In fact, I'd suggest that if you want grits and sausage gravy, you hightail it to the kitchen and cook it yourself. And fix enough for everybody in the house while you're at it."

At the shocked look on his face, I calmly went on. "It'll be good practice for you, since I hear you'll be cooking great quantities of soup fairly soon. I'm sure Mrs. Allen will appreciate hearing that you're so eager to start your new mission that you're helping out in the kitchen here."

"Well, I . . ." he started, then pulled himself together to instruct me in the finer points of ministerial work. "Now you know, Mrs. Murdoch, that there's a great, wide difference between workin' in a woman's kitchen and feedin' the hungry in a mission dedicated to the needs of the downtrodden."

That just flew all over me. As babies screamed upstairs and James's bell started jangling, I reached over and slapped off the television. Brother Vern cringed as I leaned over him. "It's time you got up from there, taking your dirty dishes with you and getting some clothes on. Then you can get yourself back downstairs and start cleaning up the kitchen. Your mission this morning is going to be dedicated to the needs of this household, or else . . ."

I stopped, wondering what the *or else* could be. "Or else," I went on as I thought of something, "I will tell my very good friend Mrs. Allen that you're not worth spending one cent on. And if you've let that milk spoil, you can go to the store for more. Get a gallon this time."

And I flounced out to stand in the hall to pull myself together. While doing that I heard the clink of dishes as he gathered them up. I smiled to myself and headed for James's room to put a stop to that jangling bell.

It stopped in midjangle as I walked in. James sheepishly placed the bell on the bedside table, then said, "I guess I didn't 'spect you today, Miss Julia. How you doin' this mornin'?"

"Quite well, thank you." I stood by the bed, clasping my hands at my waist, while I surveyed the rumpled sheets, the remains of cold cereal on a tray, and the opened envelopes strewn across the bed. "What do you need, James?"

He turned his head and sighed deeply. "Oh, Miss Julia, I need lotsa things, but don't look like I'm gonna get 'em."

"Name one, and let's see."

"I need to be up from here an' on my own two feet again. It ain't like me to be laid up in bed 'thout even bein' able to help myself. I'm jus' a burden to Miss Hazel Marie an' a millstone 'round Mr. J.D.'s neck. An' I can't do nothin' but lay here an' let 'em do for me like I was one of them babies that's always needin' something, too. I ain't good for nothin', an' that's a fact."

"I wouldn't go that far, James," I said, moved in spite of myself. "I know you're tired of being so limited, but here's some good news. Granny Wiggins will be here soon, and she says she's going to doctor you up."

James pulled the covers up to his chin. "What she gonna do?"

"I'm not entirely sure, but it has something to do with Epsom salts."

"Oh, Lordy, my mama used to dose us with that ev'ry spring that rolled around." James reached toward me with his good arm. "Miss Julia, don't let her give me that stuff. I won't ever make it to the bathroom on this bad foot. I'll have to jus' stay in there all day long an' pro'bly all night, too."

"No, James, she's not going to dose you with it. She's going to soak your foot and ankle in it. I don't think it'll do any harm at all and may do you some good."

"You sure she won't make me take it?"

"That's why I'm here—to be sure it goes on the outside and not in the inside."

"Then," James said with relief, "I'm glad you here. You stick around, Miss Julia, and watch her. That ole woman quick as a snake an' she likely ram it down my throat 'fore I know what happen."

"Then I'd keep a tight rein on . . ." The doorbell rang, stopping me. "That must be her now. Why don't you swing your feet around and sit on the side of the bed. That way, you'll be all ready for soaking."

I hurried to the door and found both Granny Wiggins and Lillian waiting. Granny Wiggins breezed in, carrying a large, deep pan with a brown grocery sack in it. "I hope that feller's ready for some doctorin'. Stay in bed long enough an' a body won't ever get up. That's why you got to be on top of things, get movin' an' nip it in the bud."

Lillian came in behind her, giving me a raised-eyebrow look as she did. "I come to do a load of washin' for Miss Hazel Marie," she said, keeping her eyes on Granny, who was headed down the hall to James's room.

"That's thoughtful of you, Lillian," I said, shutting the door against the cold. "I know she'll appreciate it. But first, let's see what Granny's going to do."

We hurried to James's room and met Granny on her way out. "He needs to be got to the kitchen," she said, almost ramming me with that huge pot that was big enough to hold a half dozen Mason quart jars at one time. "I've tried luggin' this pot full of boiling water before, an' let me tell you, it's heavy. Better to get him to the water than the water to him." And off she took to the kitchen, not wasting a glance on Brother Vern as he scrambled up the stairs.

Lillian and I looked at each other, then at James clutching Sam's robe around him as he sat on the side of the bed. "I guess it's up to us to get him there," I said. And we did, although it wasn't easy because James and I both almost fell when he stabbed my foot with his cane.

We got him settled in a kitchen chair and watched as Granny put her pot on the stove, turned the eye to high, and began filling the pot with water.

"Uh, Miss Granny?" Lillian said as she watched the process. "It might be better to put the pot where you want it on the floor, then use that kettle to pour hot water in it. That way we won't have to lift something so heavy. And so hot."

"Why," Granny said in wonder, "that's a thinkin' woman right there. We'll do it that way an' not run the risk of scaldin' somebody."

James looked up at me, his eyes wide with fear. "She gonna scald me?"

"No, no," I assured him. "She'll temper it with cold water to make it just right." I leaned down to whisper, "Don't worry, James—we're watching her."

Granny did just as Lillian had suggested, then took from her sack a box of Epsom salts. She poured about half the box into the hot water, then stirred it good. "While that's coolin' a little," she said, "let's get that bandage off." Snatching up James's leg, she clasped his foot between her knees. James yelped at the suddenness of it just as Hazel Marie walked in. She took one look at what was going on and collapsed into a chair.

Granny gave her a quick smile and said, "We'll bind him up again when I get through doctorin'. But right now we gonna unbind him just like he was Lazarus."

James looked at me. "Lazarus?"

"It's all right, James," I said, patting his shoulder. "It's just a manner of speaking."

Granny unhooked the metal clasps and, to my dismay, put them on the kitchen table. Then she began unwinding the Ace bandage. "This thing's seen better days," she said, letting the ends fall to the floor.

"Let me have it," Lillian said, reaching for it. "I'll put it in with the washin'."

When James's foot was finally uncovered, we could see that the ankle and top of the foot were still swollen and beginning to turn a dusky yellow.

Hazel Marie leaned over to survey it. Then she said, "My goodness, James, that looks awful." Which wasn't exactly the kind of encouragement he needed.

Granny gave the foot a professional examination, turning it to one side and another, James moaning with each turn. "All right now," she said, "you just put that foot right down in the pot. I got enough water in there to come halfway up your leg."

"It might be too hot," James said, apprehension growing on his face as steam billowed up from the pot.

"No, it's not," Granny said. "I done tested it with my elbow. Stick that foot in there."

James lowered his foot, jerked it out, then lowered it again, testing the water gradually until the foot and ankle were all the way in. "It don't fit," he said.

Lillian, Granny, and I leaned over to look in the pot. Sure enough, the foot was on the bottom, but James's toes were bent up on the side.

"That's the biggest foot I ever seen," Granny declared, "but it won't hurt you to cock them toes up like that for a while. Now don't that hot water feel good?"

James, slightly amazed that he wasn't being scalded, admitted that it did.

"Well, you just set back an' enjoy it," Granny said. "I'll put in some more hot when it starts coolin' down. We want it to stay hot so the salts'll draw out all that poison."

"Poison?" James asked, apprehension flooding his face again.

"The swelling," I quickly interpreted. "Rest easy, James—I think this is going to do you some good."

"You're mighty right," Granny affirmed. "Now, Miss Lillian, let's you an' me go strip this feller's bed an' get that washin' machine a-goin'. Maybe by that time them young'uns'll be up."

Hazel Marie leaned her head on her hand, murmuring, "Oh, I hope not."

Chapter 22

That evening, as I told Sam and Lloyd about the house call that Granny had made, Mr. Pickens phoned, asking for Sam.

"Is everything all right?" I asked as Sam hung up.

"Apparently not," he said wryly. "James and Brother Vern got into it before Pickens got home, and now James insists on moving back to his apartment. Pickens wants help getting him up the stairs."

"I'll help," Lloyd said, hopping up to get his coat.

"How's James going to get up those stairs?" I asked. "He can barely hobble to the bathroom as it is."

"I know," Sam said, shrugging on his coat, "but he's bent on trying it. Maybe Granny's doctoring really has helped."

Deciding to go with them, I wrapped up against the cold and rode with them to the Pickenses' house. When Mr. Pickens let us in, the house was silent—no babies crying, no television preacher ranting, no bell tinkling from James's room. The quiet seemed ominous, as if everything were poised to cut loose at any minute.

"Thanks for coming," Mr. Pickens said. "I don't know what else to do but get him up there. Hazel Marie's putting the babies to bed, but she tried all afternoon to talk him out of it. She's pretty upset about James being out there by himself, but he's determined to go. Says he'll crawl if that's the only way to get there."

We all trooped back to James's room and found him sitting on the side of the bed, Sam's bathrobe and one tennis shoe on, the other shoe sticking out of a full shopping bag on his lap. He was ready to go.

"You sure about this, James?" Sam asked.

"Yessir, I am," James said, his face stretched thin with determination—and, it seemed to me, hurt feelings. "Mr. Sam, you know I'm not one to stay where I'm not wanted, an' I been tol' my welcome already wore out 'round here. Lloyd," he said, holding the bag out to him, "you take care of this for me. It's got all my val'ables." Lloyd nodded and, with a serious look on his face, accepted the bag as if it indeed held valuables. He clasped it close, the papers inside rustling against his chest.

"Look, James," Mr. Pickens said, "Vernon Puckett does not speak for us. You know we want you and we want you right here where we can take care of you. This is your home."

"Nossir." James shook his head. "My home's out the door and up them stairs out yonder. That ole preacher man want me outta here, so I'm gonna go. I like it better up there anyway."

"But," Sam said, "what if you need help once you're out there? Don't you think you'd be better off to stay where you can be looked after?"

"Nossir, I done thought it all out. Y'all jus' help me one time up them stairs, an' I won't be no more trouble. An' Miss Hazel Marie don't have to come look after me—the bathroom is real close up there, an' she don't have to climb no stairs, either. Somebody can just slide trays halfway up an' I'll crawl down an' get 'em. I won't be no trouble. An'," he said, pushing himself off the bed with his left hand and balancing on one foot, the Ace-bandaged one held high, "that ole man can stop pickin' on her an' on me."

There was nothing for it but to help him outside and up the stairs to his apartment over the garage, Sam and Mr. Pickens on either side of him. Lloyd had run ahead and turned up the heat, leaving the shopping bag on James's bed, then he ran back to bring up an armful of pillows.

We got James settled and turned to leave, looking back at him propped up in his own bed, his bag close beside him, the remote on his lap, a glass of water and the phone on a nearby table.

I didn't feel good about leaving him alone, but truthfully I couldn't have lived in the same house with Brother Vern, either. Lloyd had made another trip to the house, bringing back a bag of Doritos, an apple, and two bottles of Sprite.

"It's all I could find, James," he said. "But I'll go to the store for you tomorrow. You might need some snacks."

"I 'preciate it, Lloyd. You a good boy, an' I'm gonna do something real good for you one of these days, see if I don't." He lay back on the pillows and sighed. "An' for Miss Granny, too, 'cause if it wadn't for her I wouldna made it up here. Y'all leave me my walkin' stick real close, an' I'll be all right."

The last thing Mr. Pickens did right before closing the door was to tell James to use the phone if he needed anything. Shaking his head as we started toward the house, Mr. Pickens said, "I don't like this one bit." Then he sighed heavily and went on. "Especially since it probably means we've got Brother Vern for good."

Maybe not, I thought.

On my way to retiring for the night, I tapped on Lloyd's partially open door, then stuck my head in. "Bedtime, honey."

"Yes'm," he said, blinking, as he looked up from his computer. "I'm almost through here."

"Don't stay at it too long. You'll ruin your eyes."

He grinned at me, wished me a good night, and turned to peer again at the computer screen. I went to bed.

After turning over for the upteenth time that night, I slipped out from under the covers and, grabbing a robe against the chill of the house, tiptoed out of the room to go downstairs. Sam moaned as I left, but I knew he'd sleep better without my thrashing around half the night.

I went into our new library and stood close to the fireplace, where the last of the embers still glowed. I didn't turn on a lamp, for the room was lit by a huge harvest moon, seemingly hanging right outside the window. Besides, my thoughts needed the dark, and I welcomed the shadows that flitted across the room, as the wind, which had picked up considerably, whipped through the trees and bushes in the yard.

I went to the side window and looked out, seeing how bright the street and yard were in the moonlight. A Comanche moon, I thought, and shivered, thinking of the pioneers who had dreaded those bright nights when painted bodies slipped across the plain to wreak devastation. Pulling my robe closer, I went back to the fireplace, took a chair, and thought of closer perils.

The recipe book was growing apace by this time, and I should've been elated by its progress. I wasn't. I had lost my enthusiasm for it, and wondered why I didn't just wrap up the whole project and quit. Hazel Marie had too much on her hands to take on anything else, and as far as her learning to cook was concerned, this wasn't the time to teach her. She could just offer grilled cheese sandwiches and cold cereal. Serve that often enough, and James would get well and Brother Vern would leave.

Or Mr. Pickens could bring in take-out food, except he wasn't at home long enough to bring in anything. At any minute he would have to pick up and leave on another case—insurance fraud or whatever. It was the whatever that worried me. . . .

I sat up and looked around—a noise, a sliding shuffle. On the stairs? In the kitchen? Was somebody else up in the middle of the night?

I sat still, waiting to hear it again, then decided it was the wind. But it wasn't. The lock clicked on the kitchen door, then I heard the soft sound of the door being eased closed. I hopped up and ran to the window overlooking the backyard. Just as I got there, a small figure dashed from the corner of the house and ran across the yard toward the gate behind the arbor.

Lloyd! What was he doing sneaking out of the house at midnight? Where was he going? I started to rap on the window, then knew he wouldn't hear it or, if he did, it would scare him to death.

What to do? Go wake Sam? Get dressed and go after him? No, he'd be gone and out of sight before I turned around good.

I ran from the room as a dozen awful possibilities ran through my mind. I'd heard of children slipping out of the house to party somewhere, or to meet and drive around looking for trouble, or to see a girlfriend. But Lloyd didn't have a girlfriend. Did he?

I snatched Sam's raincoat out of the pantry, pulled my bedroom slippers on more tightly, and headed out the door, fast on his heels. Running across the yard, the wind whipping through the huge coat, my robe, and my nightgown and playing havoc with my hair, I had one thing on my mind—where was he going? Oh, and what would he do when he got there?

Pushing through the back gate and getting scratched by branches of a forsythia bush, I popped out onto the sidewalk. Looking both ways, I caught a glimpse of a dark figure rounding the corner a block away. His mother's house, I thought with relief, then thought better of it. If that was his goal, why at this time of night? Would it frighten her if he showed up unexpectedly? Wake up the babies? The whole house? What was so urgent that he would rush through the night to get there?

I hurried after him, staying in the shadows as much as I could, not wanting him to know I was sneaking after him. But I had to see where he was going. For all I knew, he'd veer off to somebody else's house or hop into a car on the street. It wasn't that I didn't trust him—it was that I didn't trust whoever he might be meeting.

It was cold and I wasn't dressed for it, but I was too concerned for Lloyd to give it much thought. The wind would die down, then a gust would almost pin me to the fence around the Baldwins' yard. A stoplight danced in the wind away off down the street, and power lines bounced above my head. The worst of it, though, was when the wind billowed Sam's raincoat out like a sail, then breezed all the way up my nightgown while whipping my hair all over my head and into my face.

As Lloyd drew near his mother's house, I hurriedly closed the distance between us. I wanted to get just near enough to see him safely into the house, then I'd go home. I stopped behind the large oak tree on the edge of the yard, recalling a time when Lloyd and I had done the same thing in the same place some while ago, and peered around to make sure he went inside.

As much as I strained to see into the shadows on the front porch of the dark house, I couldn't make out a thing. In fact, I'd lost sight of Lloyd altogether. Thinking he might have gone to the back door, I edged onto Hazel Marie's yard and slipped beside Mr. Pickens's low-slung sports car. Where did that boy get to?

Maybe he'd cut through the yard and was now high-tailing it to somebody's house two blocks over. I'd never find him if that was the case.

Bent against the wind, I held my coat close, and ran for the back corner of the house. Stooping over to look around the edge, I hoped to see him going in the back door. But I didn't. As the moon slid behind a bank of clouds, the whole world went as black as pitch and, feeling safe in the dark, I gradually stood up. Peering intently all around the backyard, I saw no movement, heard no sound.

Until there was a soft tap-tap-tap against James's door up on the landing of the stairs beside the garage, and there stood Lloyd waiting to get in.

I couldn't make out the door opening, but James's lowered voice wafted across the yard. "Come on in here, boy. I was 'bout to give you up."

Lloyd went in, the door closed, and all was dark again. Then a yellowish light appeared behind the drawn shades on James's windows.

I didn't know whether to stay or to go. What in the world were those two doing? They couldn't be up to any good if Lloyd had to sneak out in the dark of the night to do it. I stood there, about to freeze to death, wondering if I should wake Mr. Pickens. Or just go up there myself, knock on the door, and demand to know what was going on. But would Lloyd ever trust me again if he knew I'd followed him?

The thing to do, I told myself, was to find out what they were doing without letting them know I was doing it. With that in mind, I scurried over to the garage and started climbing the stairs to the apartment, hoping to be able to see inside or at least to hear something.

The stairs weren't all that steep, but the higher I climbed, the more the wind gusted around me. I gave up trying to keep my hair from flying everywhere—it was already sticking straight out from my head—and concentrated on getting it to the landing without making any noise.

When I was two or three steps from the landing, the door swung open and, just as I was rising up out of the shadows on the stairs, Lloyd, backlit by lamplight, started to walk out. He came to an abrupt halt, his mouth falling open in shock. Then he let out a high-pitched scream that filled the night with ripples of terror, scaring me so bad that I fell back against the railing. Behind him, James yelled and tried to come to his aid but tumbled out of bed as Lloyd jumped back inside and slammed the door. Lights came on in the Pickenses' bedroom, then the hall, and I knew Mr. Pickens was going for his shotgun.

I stumbled down the stairs, half running, half sliding, grabbing the handrail to keep from falling, then ran across the yard and out onto the sidewalk. I ran as fast as my bedroom slippers would let me, panting with every breath, as I heard doors slamming and Mr. Pickens yelling, "What's going on out there! James, you all right?"

I didn't stop. I didn't want to explain. Thoroughly ashamed of mistrusting Lloyd, I wanted to be home where I could pretend I'd never been out.

Chapter 23

Hurrying inside my own house, breathing heavily, I sideswiped a kitchen chair, then limped to the pantry to hang up Sam's coat. Brushing my hair back with my hands, I determined that if Velma ever used that new hairspray on me again I'd stop going to her. Nothing is worse than hair that's stiff as a board in a windstorm.

I raced up the stairs, wondering if Lloyd would stay at his mother's or be right behind me to finish the night here. Once in bed, I cowered on my side, frozen half to death but afraid to snuggle up to Sam. One touch of my cold feet and he'd hit the ceiling.

I thought I'd never get to sleep, not only for listening for sounds of Lloyd returning, but also because so many thoughts were running through my head. What were Lloyd and James up to? How would I explain my presence to the boy? How would he feel about being spied on? On and on it went, until I woke with a start and found the bed empty beside me and the clock reading almost nine on Wednesday morning.

Lord help me, I thought as I hopped out of bed. Not only would I have to come up with an explanation for Lloyd, but I was going to be late for LuAnne's second cooking lesson at Hazel Marie's.

I hurriedly dressed, all the while dreading the coming day, and went down to the kitchen.

"Sorry I'm so late, Lillian," I said. "I didn't sleep well, then ended up oversleeping." Looking around and finally coming fully awake, I went on. "Where's Sam? Did Lloyd eat here or at his mother's? I don't need any breakfast, Lillian. I'll get something at Hazel Marie's. I've got to get going. LuAnne's probably already there."

"Jus' slow down," Lillian said. "Miss Hazel Marie called and say you don't need to come. Miz Conover already been there and dropped off her roast ready to go in the oven. Miz Conover say Miss Velma working her in this morning to do her color over 'cause she don't like how it turn out the first time, so she don't have time to give a lesson. An' Mr. Sam, he go eat breakfast with his friends downtown, an' I guess Lloyd, he stay at his mother's last night, so he in school now."

"Oh, yes, I guess he did." That wasn't a good answer because Lillian raised an eyebrow. She knew that I always knew where Lloyd spent the night. "I must've had a worse night than I realized, so I'm just as glad not to have to watch another cooking lesson, which wasn't much of a lesson the way LuAnne did it the first time. But she has some nerve to be so high-handed about the second one.

"Anyway, I hope Sam comes home with all the news in town. That bunch he has breakfast with every week seems to know everything that goes on." Trying to change the subject because I didn't want to discuss the previous night with anyone until I'd explained myself to Lloyd. If I *could* explain myself—I still didn't know how I'd manage that.

And that's the way the morning went, Lillian watching me from under her eyebrows and me pretending I didn't have a care in the world. Until Hazel Marie called.

"The babies are down for a little while," she said, "but I had to tell you what happened last night. We had some excitement!"

"Oh? What happened?"

"Well," she said as if settling in to tell the tale, "somebody screaming woke us up and J.D. was out of bed in a flash. He ran outside and, lo and behold, it was Lloyd, who'd been scared to death by somebody trying to break into James's apartment. Can you believe that!"

"My goodness," I said, sounding properly concerned. "Who was it?" I asked only because it was the normal question to ask, but not wanting an answer.

"Nobody knows! James said he got only one eyeball on it and he thought it was somebody in a Halloween costume, and Lloyd said it looked like a witch to him."

A *witch*! I would've been insulted if I hadn't suddenly realized that I was in the clear. Nobody knew I'd been there! Thank you, Lord.

"Ooh," Hazel Marie said, "I'm still shaking at the thought of somebody sneaking around the house. I mean, I know it's October but it's not Halloween yet. J.D. looked everywhere, but he didn't find anything, but we sure didn't sleep well after that."

"I can imagine," I murmured. "But, Hazel Marie, what was Lloyd doing there? He went to bed here last night."

"That boy," she said with a sigh. "I never know whether to be proud of him or be mad at him. He said he got worried about James being up there by himself and decided to run over to check on him. But in the middle of the night? Anyway, he stayed on over here—I started to call and let you know but he said you were sound asleep. But let me tell you this. After we got James up to his apartment last evening, nothing would do but Uncle Vern had to have the downstairs bedroom. So I had to change the sheets and straighten up in there so he could move in. I didn't have time to clean Lloyd's room after Uncle Vern left it, so Lloyd ended up on the sofa again. I tell you, it's like musical beds around here."

"It certainly sounds it," I agreed, feeling better and better as I realized I would not be called to account. Except, I mused, I wasn't overly convinced of Lloyd's reason for slipping out of the house to make a midnight visit.

❧

In spite of my increasing qualms about continuing with the recipe book and cooking lessons, especially after learning that LuAnne hadn't followed the rules, I found myself in a tight spot early that afternoon. After stewing half the day over how to redeem myself with Lloyd—in case he'd realized sometime during the day exactly who that witch had been—Corinne Neely, a member of the Lila Mae Harden Sunday school class and a renowned busybody, called. She just knew I'd want to know that Miss Mattie Freeman's feelings were hurt because I hadn't asked her to contribute a recipe, especially since I'd gotten recipes from everybody else in town.

I tried to explain to Corinne that I was having second thoughts about the whole project and, besides, I had collected only a few recipes, and they were from nowhere near everybody in town.

"Yes, but," Corinne said, "Miss Mattie's eyes tear up every time she thinks of being left out. I knew you'd want to know."

Well, no, I hadn't wanted to know, but, sighing, I capitulated and agreed to include Miss Mattie. With Thurlow and now Miss Mattie knocking down my door with recipes in hand, I decided that maybe the thing to do would be to continue with the cookbook idea, but leave off the lessons. Besides, who would want either Miss Mattie with her walker or Thurlow with his dog in their kitchen?

So to that end, I decided to call Miss Mattie as if she were next on my list and make no mention of Corinne Neely's meddling. Actually, I always telephoned before calling on Miss Mattie. Of course, it's only a courtesy to phone before visiting anyone, but with Miss Mattie it was a necessity. She took a morning nap and an afternoon nap every day of her life, so if you wanted to see her you had to let her know you were coming by so she'd be up.

Miss Mattie was somewhere in her upper eighties—I don't know how far up, since the precise number of one's years is never a matter for discussion. She was a wide woman—not overweight, just one of those women who'd been born wide and stayed that way. Her legs, slightly bowed, were like toothpicks and she used to spend a lot of time adjusting her stockings, which tended to sag and bunch around her ankles. Now she simply let them sag and bunch.

Miss Mattie's mind was still as clear as a bell most of the time, but her body was giving out on her. She couldn't get around very well, although the walker she used was a great deal of help to her. Not to anyone else, though, because she couldn't see well enough to watch where she put the walker's legs—which, like as not, could be on your foot. And, bless her heart, she had the worst time getting up out of a chair. So whenever she went to a party—she never turned down an invitation—she'd find the most comfortable chair in the house and sit there until it was time to leave. And that was always a sight to see, for she would grasp the arms of the chair and start a rocking motion, back and forth, working up enough momentum to catapult herself out of the chair.

And every Thursday morning that rolled around, Miss Mattie went to Velma's for her ten o'clock hair appointment. Only the direst necessity could prevail on those of us who knew her schedule to also be driving on Thursday mornings. I think I've mentioned that Miss Mattie couldn't see well, but she could drive. Or rather, she did drive, whether she could see or not. Velma's Cut 'n' Curl was only about ten blocks from Miss Mattie's house, with one left turn to be made on the trip. And one stoplight, which Miss Mattie totally ignored because it had been up for only ten years or so and she wasn't used to it. But off she'd take at a quarter to ten, and woe be to anyone between her and the beautician's chair. She could barely see over the steering wheel, so her head was always cocked up, turning neither to the right nor to the left, steering straight for Velma's.

I made it a policy to stay home on Thursday mornings, but one morning I had to be out and, I know you won't believe this, but that new sheriff had assigned a patrol car to the intersection where Miss Mattie consistently tooled through the stoplight—red, yellow, or green, it didn't matter.

At first, I'd thought the police officer was there to give her a ticket, but that wasn't the case at all. He was there, standing in the middle of the intersection, to wave her safely through, regardless of the color of the light.

I decided, then and there, that my vote would always go to that sheriff, who understood and sympathized with the limitations of age.

Chapter 24

Enough reminiscing, I thought, and gathered myself to call Miss Mattie and have it over with. So I did and, after explaining my purpose as if assuming she knew nothing about it, she was pathetically grateful for being included.

"I thought you'd left me out, Julia," she said.

"Why, I've only just started, and I'd never leave you out. You're such a good cook that Hazel Marie would have my hide if I didn't include something from you."

That pleased her, but not enough to change her daily routine. "Well, you've called too late for a visit today," she said, although it was only a little after two. "I'll have to read them to you over the phone. It's about time for my rest, and you know how Dr. Hargrove is about following his orders. Hold on while I get my card file."

Well, Lord, I thought, let's don't let anything interfere with nap time, as I sat tapping my pen, waiting for her to return.

After fumbling and dropping the phone, Miss Mattie finally said, "Here's one you have to have. Are you ready?"

"Ready and waiting. Go ahead."

Miss Mattie's Lemon Dessert

Two 3¼-ounce boxes lemon pudding mix (not instant)
1 large angel food cake (from bakery)
10-ounce package frozen raspberries
½ cup sugar
Whipping cream (or Cool Whip)

Make the pudding according to the directions on the box.

Crumble half of the cake into large chunks and place in a 9 × 11-inch Pyrex dish. Pour half of the pudding over the cake. Add another layer of crumbled cake, and top with the rest of the pudding.

Refrigerate for 2 or 3 hours or overnight.

About an hour before serving, pour the raspberries into a bowl and sprinkle the sugar over them to form juice.

Cut the cake into squares, and top with the sweetened raspberries and a spoonful of whipped cream.

Serves 12.

(This was supposed to be a main dish recipe, Hazel Marie, but you know how Miss Mattie is.)

❦

"That sounds so good," I said, "and easy, too. But, Mattie, I really need a main dish recipe."

"Hold on—I'm getting to that. But here's one she has to have—it's perfect as a Christmas dessert after a large meal."

Miss Mattie's Heavenly Hash

8-ounce can pineapple tidbits
½ pound miniature marshmallows
½ pound pecans, chopped
6-ounce bottle Maraschino cherries (chopped)
1 pint whipping cream

Pour the juice from the pineapple over the marshmallows in a bowl and let stand about 30 minutes. Then add the pineapple tidbits, pecans, and cherries. Mix together. Whip the cream and fold into the fruit mixture. Serve in festive glass bowls or cocktail glasses. Makes a beautiful, light dessert for the holidays.

Serves 12.

(Would you believe that Emma Sue once said that the name of this recipe was sacrilegious? She told Miss Mattie she should call it something like "Yum-Yum Hash" or "Whipped Cream-Cherry-Pecan-Pineapple Goody." I can't help but worry about that woman.)

❧

"All right," I said, "I have it, but I do need a main dish recipe."

"Just wait a minute," Miss Mattie said. "Since we're on Christmas recipes, here's another one she'll love."

Miss Mattie's Hot Spiced Tea

Make tea, using 2 quarts of water, 6 tea bags, and 2 cups of sugar. Allow to steep.

Meanwhile, in a separate saucepan, simmer 4 sticks of cinnamon and 3 tablespoons of whole cloves in 2 quarts of water. This makes the house smell wonderful.

In a very large container, pour 1 can (23 ounces) of unsweetened pineapple juice. Dilute a 6-ounce can *each* of frozen limeade, lemonade, and orange juice, according to the directions, and add to the pineapple juice.

Add the tea, then scoop out the cinnamon sticks and cloves from the spice mixture and add that liquid, too, stirring well.

This recipe makes well over 2 gallons, so you should have smaller containers ready after all the ingredients are mixed. Miss Mattie has used well-washed milk cartons as well as various plastic containers. It will freeze well; just thaw and heat the contents of a container in a saucepan.

(Hazel Marie, there are all kinds of recipes for instant spiced tea—some with little red-hot candies in it—that are easy to make. But I can confirm that this recipe is worth the time and trouble—not that I've ever made it myself.)

"Mattie," I said, trying to uncramp my fingers while wondering if her hearing had gone the way of her eyesight, "that sounds awfully involved. Let's find a simple *main dish* recipe now."

"All right—let me look." I could hear her shuffle through cards, then groan as she bent over to pick up a few that she dropped. "Oh, here's one. Take it down, Julia."

Miss Mattie's Cheese Wafers

2 sticks butter
2 cups all-purpose flour
2 cups Rice Krispies
½ teaspoon salt
Dash red pepper flakes or Tabasco
½ pound sharp cheese, grated

Preheat the oven to 375°F. Mix the ingredients together with your hands, pat out into small wafers, and place them on a cookie sheet. Bake for 12 to 15 minutes. Store in an airtight container.

(You can't have a tea or a coffee without having a tray, preferably silver, of cheese wafers, Hazel Marie.)

By the time I'd written down all of those unasked-for recipes, I was feeling mildly testy. "Mattie, I need at least one main dish recipe. I can't use any more holiday recipes."

"*Well,* Julia, it's almost Christmas, or haven't you noticed? Believe me, Hazel Marie will be thrilled to have them. But," she said, capitulating, "if you insist, try this one. And be sure to put down that's it's an old family recipe and nobody else in town has it. I give it only to special people."

"She'll appreciate that, Mattie," I said and poised my pen.

Miss Mattie's Deviled Crab

Make a white sauce, using:

2 tablespoons butter
3 tablespoons all-purpose flour
1¼ cups milk
1 teaspoon salt

Add to the sauce:

1 pound crabmeat (picked over to remove all shell fragments)
1 teaspoon dry mustard
2 hard-boiled eggs, chopped
1 teaspoon onion juice or grated onion
1 tablespoon Worcestershire sauce
Dash red pepper
Dash paprika

Mix all the ingredients well and put into 6 to 8 individual shells or ramekins. Sprinkle the tops with bread crumbs and dot with butter. Bake in a moderate oven until brown and bubbly, about 20 to 30 minutes.

(Hazel Marie, Lillian says a moderate oven means 350°F. Wonder what Emma Sue thinks about the name of this recipe.)

Frowning at the directions, I recognized the recipe as the same one that Ida Lee had offered. *Old family recipe, my foot,* I thought, but only said, "Oh my, a white sauce? I'm not sure Hazel Marie can manage that."

"Of course she can," Miss Mattie said. "But if she can't, it won't hurt her to learn. And if you're so intent on main dishes, here's another one."

Miss Mattie's Chicken and Rice Casserole

Preheat the oven to 325°F. Salt and pepper 4 to 6 chicken breast halves (no flour) and brown in a skillet with 1 stick of butter or margarine. Remove and place in a casserole.

In the same skillet, sauté 1 small chopped onion, 1 cup of uncooked rice (not minute rice), and 1 clove of minced garlic, until the rice is brown. Spoon this mixture over the chicken breasts.

Then mix together:

10¾-ounce can cream of mushroom soup (undiluted)
2 chicken bouillon cubes, dissolved in 2 cups water

Pour this over the chicken and rice mixture, then add one 4-ounce can of mushrooms, undrained, and cover the dish tightly with foil. Bake for 1½ hours. If the rice hasn't absorbed all the liquid, continue baking for another 15 to 20 minutes.

Serves 4 to 6.

(This looks easy enough, Hazel Marie, but it was like pulling teeth to get it out of her.)

"Is that enough for you?" Miss Mattie said. "I have plenty more, but you'll have to call back. I can't stay on the phone all afternoon."

I quickly thanked her, assured her how appreciative Hazel Marie would be, and got off the phone so she could take her nap. When Miss Mattie's routine is disrupted she can get downright snippy

Chapter 25

I'd barely hung up when I heard a commotion in the kitchen as Lloyd came in from school. I started to sit and wait for him to come to me, then decided it would be better if Lillian heard what had happened. That way I wouldn't have to repeat it to her and take the chance that she'd figure it out from the way I told it. She'd hear all about it sooner or later, anyway.

Sure enough, when I got to the kitchen, Lloyd was hanging on the counter, talking away about his frightening experience of the night before.

"I tell you, Miss Lillian, whatever it was, it scared the daylights outta me!" Lloyd was saying. Then he swung around as I entered and started all over at the beginning.

"Miss Julia, you won't believe what happened at James's last night! He'll tell you. He saw it, too. Just ask him. We both saw it, just rising up out of the dark, right there on the landing! If I'd stepped out one minute earlier, we'd of run into each other right there on the stairs. No telling what would've happened then!"

"Oh, my Jesus!" Lillian said, holding her hand over her heart. "What you reckon it was?"

"Well," Lloyd said with a firm nod of his head, "I think it was a witch. Or maybe a tramp looking for a warm place to sleep. Or maybe somebody who thought Halloween came early this year." He thought for a minute, then went on. "James didn't know what to think at first, but after it was gone, he thought it could've been an escaped convict. He said he even saw some stripes, but I didn't. So now he's gotten leery about staying up there by himself.

Except Uncle Vern has his bed, so he's kinda stuck. I may have to stay with him and sleep on a pallet."

"Let's not make too many plans right now," I said, trying to make light of whatever it was that he'd seen. "It sounds as if you've had enough excitement to last you awhile."

"That's right," Lillian agreed, taking a plate of chocolate chip cookies to the table. "We all need a little snack to settle us down. Miss Julia, you want coffee or hot chocolate?"

"Coffee, but I'll get it." And I did, bringing a cup to the table for her as well as for myself. Lloyd had hot chocolate.

As we settled around the table, I knew it was time to put the question to Lloyd. I dreaded it, because the more we talked about his harrowing experience, the more likely it was that the truth about the witch would dawn on him. Not wanting to rush things, I stirred cream into my coffee, then opened my mouth to ask the question. Lillian beat me to it.

"What I want to know," she said, both arms leaning on the table, "is what was you doin' over at James's at that time of night in the first place?"

"Exactly," I seconded.

"Well," he said, giving careful attention to spooning up a melted marshmallow. "Well, it's like this. I had a hard time getting to sleep last night because of worrying about him. You know, if he needed anything or what if he fell again or, well, if he was warm enough. It was awfully cold last night, you know."

I nodded. I knew.

"Anyway," Lloyd went on, "I decided I better go over there and check on him. So I did, and he was fine, and I didn't stay long, and when I started to leave, that's when we saw it. Whatever or whoever it was. And that's what I was doing over there."

He stopped, as if he'd run down, and Lillian and I just sat there and looked at him.

"Well, you know," Lloyd said, just a tiny bit defensively. "You know how it is when you get something on your mind. You just have to go see about it."

Of course I knew how it was. Hadn't I done the same thing more times than I could recall? But he wasn't giving us a full account, and I knew that, too. For one thing, he hadn't once looked me in the eye, or Lillian, either. In fact, throughout his explanation he'd looked everywhere but at us—a clear sign of something left unsaid. Lloyd was certainly not in the habit of telling stories, but I wasn't convinced that we were getting anywhere near the whole one here.

Lloyd abruptly stood up, took his cup to the sink, and said, "I told James I'd bring him some snacks. And I want to make sure he's all right, so I better run on."

"Jus' wait a minute," Lillian said, rising from the table. "No need for you to go spendin' money at the store. You can take him some snacks from here." She went to the pantry and began filling a sack with crackers, bananas, chocolate chip cookies, hot cocoa mix, and potato chips. "Can you tote a quart of milk, too? I got one not even open yet."

"Yes, ma'am, I can manage." With his arms full, he left to succor James, seemingly his partner in something he was unwilling to reveal.

When the door closed behind him, I wondered whether I should leave well enough alone and change the subject—to something like, for instance, what we were having for supper. I couldn't stand it, though, so I looked at Lillian. "What do you think?"

"I think they saw *somethin'*, but they's no tellin' what."

"I'm not talking about that. I'm talking about the *reason* he was over there. Lillian, something's going on with those two. They're up to something and I want to know what it is."

"They prob'bly thinkin' up ways to get rid of Brother Vern, which if they did, it would be a blessin' for everybody."

"Well, that's the truth, but Mildred is going to back him in setting up a soup kitchen—against my advice, I assure you. But if that goes through, I've urged her to insist that he live there, too. So that'll get him out of the house and give Hazel Marie some breathing room." I took my lip in my teeth, still unable to accept the explanation that Lloyd had given. "No, I think Lloyd and James are up to something else."

"If it was me," Lillian said with a shudder, "I wouldn't be worryin' myself 'bout what they up to. I'd be worryin' more 'bout that *thing* they saw."

"Oh, Lillian," I said as dismissively as I could, "you heard that wind last night. It could've been a shadow or a half-broken branch hanging down. Neither of them got a good look at it, probably because they'd been cooking up something between them, and had their minds on that. I just want to know what it could be."

"Miss Julia, it prob'bly no more than what Lloyd told us. He a good boy an' he worries about James. You don't have to look no further than what he say."

"Well," I said, rising, "maybe you're right. I don't like feeling that he's being less than truthful anyway. I guess all that we can do is wait and see."

Well, not exactly *all* that we could do, but she didn't need to know that. I intended to keep my eyes open and my ears attuned to any more night missions and, if needed, to follow them wherever they led. I say, *witch!*

Feeling edgy enough to jump out of my skin, I couldn't settle down enough to copy the latest recipes into the recipe book. I had made it a practice to use the pages of a legal pad when recipes were first given to me, then to recopy them in a neat hand onto the blank pages of a very nice book, which would eventually go to Hazel Marie. I used a sharp number-two pencil for their final placement, and if you've ever spilled anything liquid on a recipe written in ink, you know why.

But after having to erase several mistakes, I decided to put recipes out of my mind and do something else. But what? I picked up the newspaper, opened it, and tried to read, but worrisome thoughts kept intruding. Would Lloyd eventually realize who had been on James's landing? Should I just go ahead and confess— clear the air, so to speak, to make it easier for him to admit the real reason he had been there?

And what about Mr. Pickens? The sudden thought of him shook me to the core. I stiffened in my chair, thinking about that sharp, professionally trained mind investigating a possible breaking and entering, or looking for an escaped convict or even for a Halloween prankster. If he started digging into it, there was no telling what he'd come up with—the truth, most likely. The more I thought about it, the worse it got. Once he got on the trail, my goose would be cooked. Which was pretty much how it was already, for I knew there was no way he would leave the report of a prowler around his own house alone.

The newspaper shook in my hands as I pictured being grilled by Mr. Pickens. How long would I be able to hold out? Being basically a truthful person, not long. How embarrassing.

I bent my head toward the fold of the newspaper, my face already burning, and came face-to-face with a want ad in bold type:

FOR LEASE:

2000 sq. ft. building on North Main

Minimal kitchen facilities

Sm. partially furnished apt. on 2nd floor

CALL BILL AT 555-8804

Now, that's what I would call good timing or saved by the bell or the Lord looking after me.

I called Bill, whoever he was, to arrange to see and inspect the building. He sounded as delighted to hear from me as I was to have found him, although I tempered my enthusiasm when he quoted the price.

"You'll have to do better than that," I said, and was about to tell him that I represented a nonprofit organization, but, remembering Brother Vern, thought better of it. "Or there's no need for me to see it."

"Oh," Bill said, "we can come to terms—I'm sure of it. Tell you the truth, ma'am, I'm flat tired of that building settin' empty. Vandals and so forth, you know, while property taxes and insurance keep on a-goin'. Tell you what—I'll make you a good price the first year, then we'll talk again after that."

One year was about all Brother Vern was good for, so I asked, "When could I see it?"

"Right now?"

So off I took to meet Bill Whoever at the empty building on North Main, not all that far from the bus station if you didn't mind walking a mile or so. Seeing that ad was as if it had been meant to be, if only the thing had a roof, a furnace, and no rats or termites. Driving along, I was exhilarated at the thought of getting Brother Vern out of Hazel Marie's house and, hopefully at the same time, distracting Mr. Pickens from looking deeper into a possible garage-apartment invasion.

Maybe the building would need painting. Mr. Pickens could paint. He'd certainly be called on to help Brother Vern move and get him settled into his new place. There were all kinds of jobs I could think of that would keep Mr. Pickens too busy to be digging around in a cold case.

Chapter 26

I pulled to the curb in front of 1022 North Main, which was so far north of downtown that it was almost out of town. Anybody coming in on a Greyhound bus would have a fair trek to get a handout, but there looked to be a goodly number of locals standing around that might welcome a bowl or two of soup.

I looked out the car window at the redbrick building, featuring a door to the side and a large display window, displaying nothing now but a thick layer of dust. A wire mesh fence separated it from a warehouse of some kind next door while an unpaved alley ran along the near side. Looking out the rear window, I noticed a used clothing store and, across the street on the far corner, MIGUEL'S TACOS, which must have been serving more than tacos from the number of customers going in and out.

When a short, wiry man in a puffy green parka opened the front door of 1022 North Main, I assumed it was time to inspect the building. He met me as I got out of the car, shook my hand, introduced himself as Bill Somebody, slurring the last name so that I didn't catch it.

"Now, don't pay no attention to the state of things," Bill said as he ushered me into a small foyer with stairs running up the side. "The last folks I had in here was a dance studio, which I could've told 'em they wadn't gonna make it, but they give it a good try. Now," he went on, opening a door into an open space that ran the length of the building, "just look at this nice big room."

I nodded without saying anything, but I could picture it filled with folding tables and chairs with men hunched over bowls and

Brother Vern behind a podium, exhorting them from the Scriptures.

"Now, come on down here," Bill said, walking toward the back and pointing out the bathroom as he went. He stopped in a doorway to a small galley kitchen that needed several packages of Brillo pads. "See here, you got your gas stove and your deep sink for washing up. And you got your back door right there with its own Dipsy Dumpster next to it. This place is just the ticket for what you got in mind."

I didn't recall telling him what I had in mind, but I may have. I took it all in and decided he was right. So far, it was just the ticket. It got even better when he showed me into a small office space, complete with a metal desk and a file cabinet, beside the kitchen. Brother Vern would love it.

"Could we see the apartment now?" I asked.

"Yes, ma'am," he said, motioning me out of the kitchen and back into the foyer to the stairs. "You'll like this, though I 'spect you're not the one gonna be living in it."

"Indeed not," I murmured and followed him up the steep stairs.

There were two rooms, one with a sprung sofa and the other with an iron bedstead, a small kitchen I could barely turn around in, and another bathroom, which could've used some rust remover. Although the main rooms were quite large as far as floor space was concerned, head room was another matter. The apartment had obviously once been an attic, so the only standing room was under the peak of the ceiling.

"See?" Bill said. "It's real nice, clean as can be, except for the dust, which an empty building always gets. But you got your privacy up here, a good lock on the door, and everything you need for easy living. Cable hookup, too."

Again, I made no comment one way or the other, knowing that the more interest I showed, the higher the rent. The car I'd driven up in had put me in the high-rent bracket already.

When we reached the foyer again, Bill couldn't stand it. "Well, whatta you think? I can give you a good price on the lease and the first month is free. You can't get no better'n that."

"Well, Mr., uh, Bill," I said, "I am merely an agent here, searching out rental properties for my principals. I will report back to them, and they'll make the final decision. I'm reasonably sure that one or both of them will be in touch with you soon."

"That being the case," he said, reaching into his shirt pocket, "here's my card. Take two, one for each of 'em. My cell's on there, so they can reach me anytime. But you can look all over town, and you're not gonna do any better than right here."

We haggled just a little over the monthly payments, but I knew the place was ideal for Brother Vern's soup kitchen and only went through the formality of rejecting the first quote he made.

⌒〜⌒

Since I was already on the north side and needing a few cards from the Hallmark shop, I decided to go a little out of the way and stop at what answered for a mall in Abbotsville. Of course it was a mall because it was a large enclosed space with JCPenney anchoring one end and a locally owned department store the other, while smaller shops lined the wide hall, in spite of the fact that about a third of the shops were empty and another third had windows pasted over with close-out-sale signs.

As soon as I walked into the main entrance I was engulfed by the odor of popcorn (not unpleasant) and sizzling hot dogs (not pleasant). That was bad enough but not the worst thing about a mall visit, which I made only when I had to. What you really had to watch out for were the walkers—not the kind that Miss Mattie used but the two-footed kind from the various rest homes and retirement villages nearby. Those exercise-determined souls put on their walking shoes and running suits every day of the week and proceeded to the mall, where they strode around and around the interior, bent on strengthening aging muscles, bones, and joints. You had to watch out for them. They'd come at you in a pack, huffing and blowing, intent on making a certain number of laps before giving out. They wouldn't veer from their appointed rounds, regardless of who was in their way. You had to step lively to avoid them, and if you wanted to enter a shop you had to wait until there was a break in the traffic, then pop between them and hope you'd get through before they ran you down.

I made it in, then out, of the Hallmark shop with a small bag of greeting cards, ranging from those that extended congratulations to those that offered condolences. Be prepared, I always say, for whatever occasion that might arise.

Escaping the walking army unscathed, I went out into the bright, cold air and hurried across the parking lot to my car. I was eager to get home and tell Mildred that her search for a soup kitchen location was over. Huddled in my coat, I looked neither to the right nor the left until I got to my car and, in the process of unlocking it, glanced across the lot. Beyond the lines of parked cars clustered near the mall entrances, a familiar-looking one was parked alone, nosed away from the others under a leafless tree on the far edge of the lot, a cloud of exhaust billowing out behind it.

I stopped and stared, wondering if I could be wrong. But no, there was only one low-slung black car with heavy-duty tires, a long antenna whip, and an Abbotsville High sticker in the back window. And only one such car with Mr. J. D. Pickens behind the wheel, his full head of black hair turned away from me and focused on a blond-headed woman—who most assuredly was not Hazel Marie—seated at his side.

I squinched up my eyes, wanting to be sure of what I was seeing, as my heart began to sink. I knew Mr. Pickens had a notable weakness for blond women, and although I couldn't see her face, this one had hair like Dolly Parton. Whatever other attributes she had like Miss Parton, I couldn't tell.

Standing there about to freeze, I recalled stories I'd heard about the mall parking lot being a meeting place for illicit lovers. Regardless, though, of what was right in front of my eyes, I found it hard to believe that Mr. Pickens would engage in something so public. I got in my car and sat, straining over the roofs of the two rows of parked cars between us to see what they were doing. At one point, Mr. Pickens turned his head away from the woman to look out the front windshield, giving me a clear profile view. Who could mistake those dark aviator glasses? He was firmly nailed, but who was the woman?

I had the urge to drive by and get a better look at her, but quickly discarded that idea for fear that Mr. Pickens would come after me.

So I stayed where I was and waited for whatever was going to happen. But they didn't leave and the woman didn't get out. As far as I could tell, there was no touching going on, but those two sure had something to talk about.

I kept sitting and watching, fearing that Mr. Pickens had reverted to his normal gallivanting ways even with a loving wife and a houseful of children waiting for him. Of course that had never deterred any other man who had cheating on his mind. Take it from me—I know.

I turned on the ignition to start the heater, knowing I couldn't sit there much longer—I was low on gas—and knowing that sooner or later somebody would come along and tap on my window to see if I was all right. People can be so nosy sometimes.

Feeling sick to my stomach, I finally gave up and headed home with a heavy heart.

⟨∾⟩

Trying to get that trysting picture out of my mind, I hurried inside to call Mildred. There was more reason than ever to get Brother Vern out of the Pickens house and put Hazel Marie back on track. I needed to get her to Velma's and have her hair cut, colored, and set. She needed new clothes, maybe some with those low-cut necks that showed more than I ever wanted to see of areas that even television newswomen were inflicting on us. Without even hinting to Hazel Marie about the danger she was in, I would have to make sure that she was a worthy competitor to that big-headed blonde in Mr. Pickens's car.

And as for the twins while all this was being done? Well, Granny Wiggins was going to be put to the baby-care test, which meant that I would have to be on the spot to supervise, else Hazel Marie wouldn't leave the house. And if she refused to let the babies out of her sight, I'd just stow that huge twin stroller in my car and use it to walk those babies up and down the sidewalk in front of Velma's for as long as it took to get Hazel Marie beautified again. Maybe Lillian would help.

With all those plans running through my mind, I got Mildred on the phone, described the building I'd found, and told her the price, expecting her to praise me for doing her job for her.

"Well, Julia, I don't know," she said. "I've been thinking over what you said about Mr. Puckett, and I may have been a bit hasty. There are so many good causes around and it seems as if every one of them wants my support. What do you think? Is this a worthwhile venture for me to sponsor?"

I had a great sinking feeling as Mildred appeared ready to renege on her promise to get Brother Vern out of Hazel Marie's house and put him to ladling soup. "Mildred," I said, feeling my way, knowing that the very wealthy can pinch pennies worse than people with empty pockets. "Mildred," I said again, "I know I wasn't enthusiastic at first, but now that I've realized the good that Brother Vern can do in helping his fellow man—and I assure you, he's devoted himself to good works of some kind or another all his life—I am convinced that you wouldn't go too far wrong in backing a soup kitchen in that area of town. It's really needed, and remember, if it gets off the ground, I'm planning to contribute to it, as well. On second thought, though, I may be able to find a little startup money, too. Oh, and think of this: It's only a one-year lease and the first month is free."

"Really?" she asked, perking up at the thought of getting something for nothing. "In that case, I'll do it. Give me the owner's name and number. I'll call him right now and take it before somebody gets in ahead of me."

I gave her Bill's name and number, as well as a caution.

"Maybe you should talk to Brother Vern before you commit your-self, Mildred. The two of you need to go look at the place and make sure that Brother Vern likes the apartment. And you should make sure that he'll handle everything that'll be needed. I mean, like buying supplies, finding tables and chairs, and hiring some help. You don't want to be over there washing dishes yourself."

She laughed. "Oh, Julia, you're so funny."

I ignored that, because I was being serious. "One last thing, but it's the most important. If Brother Vern doesn't move out of Hazel Marie's house, all bets are off. I won't contribute one cent to his soup kitchen, even if it turns out to be the best one in the state and he gets an award from the governor."

Chapter 27

I arose the following morning, rested and relieved that Mildred would be handling Brother Vern from henceforth. Once she had money invested in him, she would have him dancing to her tune. If he thought I was hard on him, he hadn't seen anything yet.

So that was one down for me, but as I turned to the next problem, I could feel my nerves beginning to strum along whatever paths they traveled—my whole being becoming as tight and edgy as a stretched-out rubber band. *Mr. Pickens and another woman!* And him married barely a year—it beat all I'd ever heard.

I took a deep breath to calm down. Why had I thought that his marriage to Hazel Marie would be any different from the two or three others he'd engaged in? Well, for one reason, he'd chased her for years. She hadn't just dropped in his lap, as I assumed his other wives had. And for another reason, none of his previous marriages had resulted in issue, that is, not just one baby but two. You'd think that would be enough to settle him down, but no. What I'd seen with my own eyes proved that.

Well, I couldn't stand around dawdling all day. I'd just struck off one item on my list by clearing the way to oust Brother Vern from the house. It might take a few days to be completely rid of him, but with all he'd have to do to ready his soup kitchen, his days would surely be full enough to get him out from underfoot.

So the next thing to do would be to make an all-day, full-service, complete do-over appointment with Velma for Hazel Marie. And did she ever need it! Bless her heart, she had let herself go simply from lack of time to do any better. Which was all the more reason for me to step in whether she liked it or not. She'd thank me once it was done.

Even though she didn't know it, there was no time to waste with another woman already in the picture, but when to do it? The next day was Friday, so I knew Velma would be booked solid. Her Thursdays and Fridays were always full with everybody getting ready for the weekend. Of course more than half of her regulars never went anywhere over the weekend, but they wanted to be prepared in case something came up.

And, I suddenly realized, tomorrow was Etta Mae's day to show Hazel Marie how to cook that untried chicken dish of hers. I couldn't very well cancel that, especially since Lillian had already bought all the ingredients and had them waiting in Hazel Marie's kitchen.

And Granny Wiggins would be there, too, which would be fine. I'd take her aside and enlist her help by reassuring Hazel Marie that the babies would be well taken care of when and if I could get her an appointment. And of course I'd be there with her and, to tell the truth, I was more leery of spending several hours in Granny's company than I was about taking care of two infants. Granny tired me out with all that running around and talking and housecleaning and whatever else struck her fancy. But for Hazel Marie's sake, I would weather it.

Tired of just standing there, I sat down to think through what had to be done. My first inclination was to tell Sam what I'd seen in the mall parking lot. My second was to confide in Lillian, maybe even Etta Mae. But no, there would be nothing worse than for Hazel Marie to learn sometime in the future that so many people had known of her husband's lack of fealty while she had been totally in the dark. I knew how that felt and it hadn't been good. While Wesley Lloyd Springer, my unmourned first husband, had been cavorting with his other woman, I had been the town's laughingstock. The humiliation I'd suffered had not been forgotten, although I am pleased to say that eventually I had been able to forgive most of those who had trespassed against me.

But I wouldn't put Hazel Marie in the position of being talked about and laughed at behind her back—because the word would get around. Not that I didn't trust Sam and Lillian and Etta Mae—they would never spread gossip—but just as soon as you tell one person a secret, it will spread like wildfire. I don't know why that is—maybe the walls have ears to hear and mouths to leak—but the only way to keep a secret is to keep it. So I'd keep what I'd seen to myself and work behind the scenes to ensure that Hazel Marie could give that Texas big-haired blonde a run for her money.

I lifted the phone and dialed the number of the Cut 'n' Curl beauty shop. Finally getting Velma on the phone after waiting for her to put someone under a dryer, I explained what I wanted.

"Hazel Marie needs a complete makeover, Velma. She's been so tied down with those babies that she hasn't been able to make or keep her appointments—you should see the roots in her hair. She needs everything—the works—so that she comes out of your shop looking like a million dollars. It's something I want to do for her. When do you have an opening?"

"Not anytime soon, Julia," Velma said, sighing as if she were worn to a frazzle. "I am booked way into next week with perms and colors and so forth. What you want will take several hours, and I can't just cancel these people. Maybe sometime in November? Early November, before everybody's getting ready for Thanksgiving?"

"Oh, no," I said. "She can't wait that long. You can imagine the shape she's in. Hazel Marie hasn't had time to take care of herself. She really needs you."

"I really am sorry," Velma said. "I would love to do her, but we have a new stylist who's very good and she doesn't have a lot of clients yet. Maybe she could do Hazel Marie."

I knew what that meant. A new stylist was someone just out of beauty school, which meant she wouldn't know what she was doing. I would never turn a new stylist loose on Hazel Marie. She needed an old hand, a professional who knew how long to let color set up so that she didn't walk out looking like something from a Hollywood freak show.

"No," I said, "that won't do. I know you're busy, Velma, but if you can't do her, I'll try a salon in Asheville. On second thought, though, it might be better to make a trip of it and take her to Atlanta. You know, to one of those high-fashion beauty salons where she can get the full spa treatment plus everything else."

I knew there was no way in the world that Hazel Marie would leave those babies and go to Atlanta, but Velma didn't.

"Oh, you don't want to do that," Velma said, just as I hoped she would. "Hazel Marie is so sweet, I know we can work something out. Let me look at my book."

I waited as Velma checked her schedule, listening to the noises of the shop in the background.

"I tell you what, Julia," Velma said as she picked up the phone again. "Can she come in Monday?"

"This Monday? I thought you took Mondays off."

"Well, usually I do, but I come in now and then to straighten up and check inventory. Hazel Marie has been a good client and, of course, you are, too, and to tell you the truth, I'm eager to get my hands on her. I love a challenge."

"Velma," I said with heartfelt gratitude, "I will dance at your wedding. Thank you, thank you. I'll have Hazel Marie there at nine o'clock Monday morning."

"Tell her to plan to spend the day. If you want the works, I'm putting her down for a mani, pedi, facial, some waxing and color, trim, and styling. Anything else?"

"Well, if you can manage a massage, you might as well add that, too."

Hanging up the phone, I felt a warm sense of accomplishment wash over me. Two items—getting rid of Brother Vern and getting a last-minute appointment with the busiest hairstylist in town—were checked off my list. Now for the most difficult one of all—getting Hazel Marie to leave the babies and into the Cut 'n' Curl for what I knew would be most of the day.

I hoped Granny Wiggins was up to babysitting that long. Well, actually I hoped *I* was up for it, because neither Hazel Marie nor I would be willing to leave Granny alone with them. You'd think that the two of us could handle two babies, but as I thought about what that would entail—feeding, cleaning, rocking, changing diapers, picking up, and holding—I wasn't sure we could do it all. We were going to need more help.

I got up and walked to the kitchen. Pushing through the swinging door, I said, "Lillian, I have a proposition for you."

Chapter 28

It occurred to me that I was spending more time at Hazel Marie's house than at my own, yet there I was again bright and early on Friday morning. But none too early, for Etta Mae and Granny weren't far behind me—Granny with her arms wrapped around her big canning pot with a little canvas duffel bag stuffed inside and Etta Mae with an eager smile on her face.

"We are ready to do some cooking," Etta Mae said as I led them through to the kitchen. "I can't wait to see how this recipe turns out. You can't go far wrong with chicken, though, can you?"

Well, yes, I could, but I didn't bring that up, just welcomed them and hoped for the best. "Hazel Marie is putting the babies down for their nap," I told them, "but she shouldn't be long. Etta Mae, let's get the ingredients out so everything will be ready."

Granny plopped her little duffel bag on the kitchen table, then headed for the back door with the canning pot. "I'm goin' up to soak that feller's foot again. This'll be the third time and it's really doin' him some good. Just like I knowed it would."

I had to agree, for James could now stand on that hurt foot even though he couldn't yet put enough weight on it to walk on his own.

"Does he have a stove up there, Granny?" Etta Mae asked. "I don't want you carrying a pot full of hot water up those stairs."

"He's got everything I need. Just the cutest little apartment you'd ever want to see. And, Etta Mae, I know better'n to try to tote a heavy load up them stairs, so quit worryin' about me."

"I can't help it," Etta Mae said. "I never know what you'll be doing next." But Granny didn't hear it because she was already out the door.

As Etta Mae began to lay out the ingredients for her recipe on the counter, Brother Vern presented himself in the kitchen. I was taken aback because not only was he fully dressed, he was fairly nicely dressed in a shiny gray suit, a florid tie, and highly polished oxfords. His hair was combed, his face freshly shaved, and a cloud of aromatic aftershave floated around him.

"Good morning, ladies," he said, glancing around the kitchen. "It's a beautiful, though chilly, day the Lord has given us. Where is everybody?"

"Well, we're right here," I said, and in an effort to shame him went on to point out that Mr. Pickens had already left for work. "And Hazel Marie is busy with the babies and James is in his apartment soaking his foot."

"And your dear grandmother?" Brother Vern asked of Etta Mae. "Is she coming today?"

"She's helping James," Etta Mae said somewhat shortly, keeping her eyes on the recipe. I could see how leery she was around Brother Vern. He might try to baptize her again.

"Ah," he said, nodding, "always with the helping hand. The Lord blesses those who help others. Well," he went on as Granny came through the back door, "here she is now. Good morning, sister, how is your patient today?"

"Fit as a fiddle," she announced. "Almost. I'm gonna have him walkin' in a day or two. And I'm glad to see you, Preacher, 'cause I hear you've got problems, too. You just set down over there and let me dose you up. I come prepared to do just that." She unzipped her duffel bag and brought out a glass bottle. "Now this," she said with authority, "you won't find a doctor in the land that'll prescribe it, but it's been used for hundreds of years and it's just what you need to bring that high blood down to normal."

Etta Mae's semi-nursing experience immediately put her on guard. "Wait, Granny. He's on medication from his doctor. You can't be dosing him with just anything. What is that?"

"Well," Brother Vern said as he took a seat at the table, apparently willing to be dosed, "I have to admit that I'm not on medication at the moment. I decided against getting that prescription filled. I'm just gonna put my trust in the Lord. He's still in the curin' business if we just trust Him enough to let Him do it."

My eyes rolled back in my head. I knew why he hadn't had his prescription filled—he'd used the money Hazel Marie had given him for other things.

I started to say something, but Granny gave out a cackle and said, "The Lord helps them that helps themselves, brother. Don't you know that? Besides, this is natural medicine straight from the Lord's hands. And quit worryin', Etta Mae—apple cider vinegar won't hurt a flea. Now, Brother Vern, I'm gonna mix this up and I want you to take it down and do it every mornin' from here on out. An' you'll get added benefits, too, if you happen to be sufferin' from constipation or dandruff."

She measured out a dose of vinegar, dumped it into a glass, then added a spoonful of honey "to cut the taste." She filled the glass with warm water, stirred it briskly, then, handing it to Brother Vern, said, "Down the hatch."

He docilely accepted the glass and drank the concoction, shuddering as he handed the empty glass back to Granny.

"This fine Christian sister," Brother Vern bravely announced, "has started me on the road to good health. And what she's done for Brother James just confirms it. He's about to take up his bed an' walk."

"Well," Granny said with a slight blush as she modestly ducked her head, "I wouldn't go that far, but I have had some success in the healin' business."

Etta Mae, ignoring Brother Vern and Granny, beckoned Hazel Marie to the counter and set her to work chopping bell peppers and onions, while she unwrapped the chicken. Butter and olive oil were sizzling in the Dutch oven on the stove.

"The healin' business is exactly what I want to talk to you

about," Brother Vern said excitedly as he stood up. "I'm about to open up a soup kitchen for all those lost souls out there, and it come to me that what many of 'em need besides a bowl of soup is a healin' ministry. They're sick in soul *and body,* and, sister, you have a gift from God that's badly needed. Would you be interested in joinin' up with me in the Lord's work?"

Etta Mae jerked around and opened her mouth to say something, but Granny was already speaking. "Why, I don't know about that. I never thought plain ole common sense was any kind of gift. Besides, I don't hold no truck with faith healers. So if you got that in mind, you can count me out. Ever' one I seen just wants to get on television an' be a big star ridin' around in a Cadillac."

"Oh, I know what you mean," Brother Vern piously agreed, as if he'd never had similar aspirations. "It's a cryin' shame how they carry on, and I know you don't have a cravin' for the big time. But let me tell you this—I had a sign yesterday that the Lord is behind this one-hunnerd percent. I wasn't even lookin' for a cook yet, but one showed up anyway. She's a big, hefty woman and a little long in the tooth, but she knows her stuff. Been cookin' for crowds for a long time down in Florida, so you wouldn't even have to help her 'less you just wanted to."

"I don't do no cookin' for the unwashed," Granny said, setting him straight. "I run a clean kitchen."

"Oh, I wouldn't ask it of you, but if you'd join up with me, you'd really help my soup kitchen get off the ground. The *Lord's* soup kitchen, I mean."

"I'd have to know more about it," Granny said.

"Granny . . ." Etta Mae said with a note of warning, handing Hazel Marie the large can of tomatoes she'd just opened. "When the chicken is just golden," she told her, "pour this in."

"Absolutely," Brother Vern said eagerly. "I want you to know all about it. We'll set down an' make our plans an' it'll be like nothin' else around here. I'm even thinkin' of havin' a praise band playin' while folks come in and eat. That band and the two of us—one ministerin' to the hungry an' the other to the ailin'—why, we'd be bringin' in the sheaves by the armful. We'd put your gift to work an' there'd be blessin's showerin' down on us."

"Granny . . ." Etta Mae said with a sidewise glance as she demonstrated to Hazel Marie how much a large pinch of oregano probably was.

"Hush, Etta Mae," Granny said without looking at her. "I already got this feller's number, but they's no harm in listenin' to him. And what I'm hearin' still sounds like faith healin' to me, includin' a praise band to get folks ginned up. I'll tell you what's a fact, mister—I don't hold with guitars an' bass fiddles an' washboards playin' toe-tappin' music in a worship service. Toe-tappin' is right next door to dancin' in my book, an' that's something I don't do, even if David did."

"Oh, we won't have no dancin'," Brother Vern assured her. "All you'd be doin' is just what you're doin' for Brother James and me. An' you know, sister, if you don't use a gift like you have, you're likely to lose it."

"Well now, you just listen to me real good, Preacher Puckett. I don't claim no gift. My doctorin' is all natural. Anybody can do it, 'cause I use the old tried-and-true remedies. So, take note right now—there won't be no layin' on of hands from me."

"Oh, I completely agree, sister," Brother Vern assured her. "In fact we can call it the Lord's Soup Bowl and *Medical* Mission. That way there won't be no misunderstandin'. The only time I'll mention faith is in my preachin'."

"'Bout time you mentioned preachin'," Granny said. "You got to bring the Lord in somewhere or they's no use doin' it."

"So you'll join me?" Brother Vern was elated. "I'm on my way to a meetin' with Miz Allen, and I can't wait to tell her. I know she'll be thrilled."

I wasn't so sure about that, but, then, I never knew what would strike Mildred's fancy.

"Granny . . ." Etta Mae warned again, then, turning to Hazel

Marie, handed her a bottle of wine. "Pour in about a cupful. Now, Granny," she went on, "we need to talk about this."

"Don't get in a uproar, Etta Mae," Granny said offhandedly. "I'm not sayin' yea nor nay. I'm just sayin' I'll study on it."

Brother Vern suddenly jerked around and yelled, "*Hazel Marie!*" He startled her so bad that she dropped the wine bottle into the Dutch oven, splashing tomato sauce all over the stove.

"*What? What?*" Hazel Marie cried, then her face crumpled as she looked at the mess she'd made.

Quick as a flash, Etta Mae grabbed a potholder and fished out the bottle, holding it over the Dutch oven so the sauce would drip back into the pot. "It's okay, Hazel Marie," Etta Mae said, rinsing the bottle at the sink. "No harm done."

"But what'd I *do*?" Hazel Marie said. "I mean, before I dropped the bottle."

Brother Vern commenced an interrogation. "What was in that bottle? Was it what I think it was? Don't you know better'n to have that stuff in your house? An' put it before me to *eat*? I swan, Hazel Marie, you act like you don't have a lick of sense. You musta been behind the door when it got passed out."

Hazel Marie turned her back to us, lowered her head, and put her hand over her face. That did it for me. I had taken as much as I intended to take. I rose up from the table and opened my mouth to lay Vernon Puckett low. I was too slow.

Granny took two steps and got right up in his face. "'Take a little wine for thy stomach's sake,' Preacher, First Timothy, chapter five, verse twenty-three, or don't you know your Bible? An' I'll tell you another thing. As long as you're puttin' your feet under Hazel Marie's table, you better lay off her an' be thankful she's givin' you a roof over your head." Then Granny poked her finger at him. "You got some nerve, mister, talkin' to her that way. I don't hold with such rantin' an' ravin' as you been doin' to your own kin, so you can count me out of doin' one blessed thing in your, your . . ." At a loss for the name of his enterprise, Granny flapped her arms. ". . . whatever it is."

Etta Mae said, "You go, Granny." But it was Brother Vern who went. Seeing three pairs of angry eyes glaring at him, he turned on his heel and left the room, beaten but unbowed.

But Hazel Marie was hardly consoled. She wiped her eyes, leaned over to look into the Dutch oven, and whispered, "I guess I ruined it."

"No, you didn't," Etta Mae said, smiling, as she put her arm around Hazel Marie. "In fact, a little extra wine will make it all the richer. J.D.'s going to love it."

Chapter 29

I lingered after Etta Mae and Granny left, waiting for a good time to tell Hazel Marie about her beautification session with Velma on Monday. In the meantime, the babies were up, so she was getting ready to feed them. Granny had wanted to stay and help, but Hazel Marie, still suffering from the shame of her uncle's words, insisted that she had things well in hand. I knew her heart was hurting—anybody's would be after such a public dressing-down—so I busied myself with fixing lunch for her and James.

As I crossed the yard with a tray for James, it crossed my mind that, even more than needing an appointment at a beauty parlor, Hazel Marie needed an appointment with a therapist who could help her develop some backbone. Somehow or another, she had to learn to stand up for herself, but how she was going to learn it, I didn't know.

I did know this, though: The more criticism you take, the more beaten down you get. After a while, you begin to believe you're worthless. I didn't want that to happen to Hazel Marie because her worth to me was far above rubies. From that moment, years before, when she'd walked over to comfort me in my living room, thinking I had lost my mind as I unbuttoned my bodice in public to fish out Wesley Lloyd's last will and testament, my heart had gone out to her. And it had stayed there.

Carefully balancing the tray, I carried it up the stairs, tapped on James's door, then pushed on through. "Lunchtime, James," I said, noting how quickly he threw the covers over the papers on the bed. "It's not much, just a couple of pineapple sandwiches, but supper will make up for it. You wouldn't believe how good it's already smelling."

I chatted with him a few minutes, then, seeing a stack of stamped and addressed envelopes on the table beside the bed, I pointed at them and said, "If you want those mailed, James, I'll be glad to do it."

"Well, uh," he said, his eyes darting around, "Lloyd, he say he'd mail 'em for me. I 'spect I better wait on him."

"That's fine, except it might be tomorrow before he can do it. He has some kind of meeting today after school. Spanish Club or some such, so he'll be late getting home."

James frowned. "I sure hate to wait till tomorrow."

"You don't have to. I can drop them off on my way to the bank this afternoon, if you'd like."

"Well, yessum, I guess I do, then." He didn't sound too sure about entrusting his mail to me, but the need to get them off seemed greater than any doubt of my ability to get them to the post office.

After gathering his breakfast dishes to take to the kitchen, I picked up the stack of envelopes and prepared to leave. "How's that foot coming along, James?"

"It jus' about well," James said, his face coming alive. "That Miss Granny, she sure know her doctorin'. I almost can get to the bathroom without holdin' on to the wall."

"That's good to hear. Now, if you don't need anything else, I'll be going. Hazel Marie needs all the help she can get."

"Yes, ma'am, she cert'ly do."

⚬⚬⚬

When I got back to the house, Hazel Marie was spoon-feeding the high-chaired babies. As I entered the kitchen, she wiped her face with her sleeve. Sliding James's envelopes under my pocketbook so I wouldn't forget them, I pretended I didn't notice.

"Etta Mae left this kitchen spotless, didn't she?" I said. "And what about this rice she left? I didn't know you could boil it in its own bag. What will they think of next?" Just talking to give her time to compose herself. "Listen, Hazel Marie, I have an idea. When you finish there, why don't we put the babies on a quilt in the living room and let me watch them for a while? It is so nice outside—Indian summer, I guess—so it would be a good time for you to take a walk. It would do you good to get out by yourself, breathe the fresh air, and just wander around for a little."

"I ought to go to the grocery store," she murmured. "I could do that if you don't mind staying with them. I wouldn't be long. We could take a walk when I get back."

That didn't sound like much, but it was. It was the first time she'd seemed willing to leave the babies alone with me. And even though I was leery of having total responsibility of two infants, it wasn't at all bad. The babies cooed and played with rattles and watched a mechanical whirling toy, while I sat on the sofa and watched them. The only times I had to intervene was when one rolled on top of the other or when they began to scoot off the quilt. And when I had to rescue Lily Mae, who had crawled to her daddy's chair and pulled herself to her feet, then wailed because she didn't know what to do next.

When Hazel Marie got back from the store, she immediately checked on her little girls. Reassured, I think, that they'd suffered no damage while she'd been gone, she quickly put away the groceries.

As we strapped the babies into the twin stroller for a walk, Hazel Marie said, "Oh, guess who I saw at the store—Lillian. She is so sweet, kept asking how I was doing and if she could help in any way. But, you know"—Hazel Marie stopped—"she looked really worried about something. You know how she's always smiling? Well, she wasn't today. Is anything bothering her?"

"Not to my knowledge," I said, wondering if, with my concern for Hazel Marie, I'd neglected Lillian. "I'll talk to her when I get home. But now, let's get outside and enjoy one of the last pretty days."

Our walk wasn't exactly what I'd had in mind—I'd wanted Hazel Marie to have some time to herself—but she told me that she'd never realized how calming and serene the aisles of a grocery store could be. I'd never considered grocery shopping an enjoyable pastime, but I guess doing it without two babies filling up a cart would be a change.

As we strolled along the sidewalk, I ventured to say, "What do you think about Brother Vern's soup kitchen?"

Hazel Marie shrugged her shoulders. "I've only heard bits and pieces, but it won't happen. Uncle Vern has lots of big ideas, but not much follow-through."

"He may surprise you this time. He has Mildred involved with it, and if one cent has passed from her to him, she'll be after him with a horse whip if he doesn't follow through."

Hazel Marie smiled at the thought. "That would be something to see."

"And I don't know if you know this, but their agreement requires him to be on the premises all the time. There's an apartment above the soup kitchen just waiting for him to move in."

She stopped pushing the stroller and looked at me. "Really?"

"Yes, really. And to make sure he actually moves in, I've told Mildred that I'll help fund the mission only on the condition that he lives there. All we have to do now is get him there."

"That would be wonderful," Hazel Marie murmured almost to herself. Then turning back to me, she tentatively asked, "But what about his blood pressure? What if he's not able live by himself? And do all that work? His doctor said he needs rest and the right food and someone to take care of him. I'd feel terrible if something happened to him. Maybe he ought to stay with us."

"Hazel Marie," I said firmly as we stood in the middle of the sidewalk, "I grant you he's getting a lot of rest in your house because he hasn't turned his hands to anything since he first rang your doorbell. As far as the right food is concerned, he doesn't eat it when it's offered or else he eats too much of it. And all that work? Don't make me laugh. That'll be done by volunteers, while he sits behind a desk. Hazel Marie, you have got to let him try this. He can't live on you forever, which I have a feeling he'd like to do. My advice is not to give him any reason to stay and every reason to move out. And do it as soon as humanly possible."

"It would be nice," she said dreamily, as if picturing what it would be like in a house empty of Brother Vern. "I'll see what J.D. thinks."

"You know what he thinks. Frankly, it'd be better for all concerned if Brother Vern moves out on his own than for Mr. Pickens to throw him out. Which it may come down to if you get wishy-washy about him leaving. And," I went on as we began to stroll again, "speaking of Mr. Pickens, I think the two of you deserve a night out together. Maybe a weekend at the Grove Park Inn."

"Oh, I couldn't do that. Who'd watch the babies?"

"I would. And Sam and Lillian and Lloyd and Latisha."

She smiled. "I might not even worry about them with all of you there. And J.D. has mentioned that he'd like to see a movie or something." Then she frowned. "But I look so awful these days. Seems I never have time to fix myself up. Just look at this hair— the color's gone and it's full of split ends. And I've lost so much weight that nothing fits. He probably wouldn't want to be seen with me."

"Well," I said brightly, "I have just the ticket for that." And went on to tell her that, come Monday, when Velma got through glamorizing her, she would have recaptured every bit of her pre-baby allure.

Chapter 30

"Lillian," I said as soon as I walked into the house, "prepare yourself to babysit on Monday. I've talked Hazel Marie into keeping her appointment with Velma. Now," I went on as I put my pocketbook and James's letters on the table and slid off my coat, "if only she doesn't change her mind. Oh, and by the way, she told me she'd seen you at the grocery store and that you seemed concerned about something. Is anything wrong?"

I make it my business to know what's going on in the lives of the people I care about and to do what I can to help. I don't call that meddling. I call it my Christian duty.

"I don't know if it's anything," Lillian said, turning her back to me as she worked at the kitchen counter, "so I 'spect I get over it sooner or later."

That got my attention. "What? What is it? If something's bothering you, tell me and let's do something about it."

"You know I don't like to talk about folkses' business. It's theirs an' not mine, so I best stay out of it."

I walked over and stood beside her so that she had to look at me. "What is it, Lillian? If it's enough to concern you then it's enough to let me help."

"It's not my place to be carryin' no tales." She carefully dried her hands with a paper towel, taking pains to wipe each finger, and in the process to delay revealing her problem.

"Is it something about Latisha?"

"No'm." She shook her head.

"Sam?"

"No'm."

"Lloyd?"

She shook her head again.

"Well, who?" I asked. "Hazel Marie?"

"You gettin' close, but I can't say no more."

"James? Brother Vern? Who else is there?" Then my eyes widened as I knew as well as I stood there who she meant. "Mr. Pickens," I stated in the firm conviction that I was right.

"Oh, Miss Julia, I don't wanta think what I been thinkin', but I saw him in his car with a black-haired, bushy-headed woman an' they was parked way back under a tree in that Lutheran church parking lot, an' it not even Sunday." I thought Lillian was about to cry.

"They Lord," I moaned and walked over to the table to find a chair. I didn't think my limbs would hold me up another minute. Propping my head on my hand in near despair, I asked, "What were they doing?"

"Jus' talkin', it look like, but I didn't get a chance to see much. I passed the church on my way to the store, so I jus' catch a quick look. But I'd know that car of his anywhere, 'less somebody else drivin' it, which I don't think he let anybody do. I tell you the truth," Lillian went on as she joined me at the table, "I like to run off the road when I seen what I seen."

"It couldn't have been a black-haired man, could it? I mean, lots of men have long, bushy hair."

She shook her head. "I don't think so. They was parked at the back of the lot like they didn't want nobody to see 'em, an' I wouldna seen 'em if I hadn't cut down that back street from the dry cleaner's to get to the grocery store." Lillian rubbed her hand across her mouth. "An' I don't think if it was a man, that it look any better than if it was a woman. Maybe look worse."

"Oh, my word, Lillian, I didn't mean that. I meant that it could've been a client wanting an investigation that was really private."

We sat there for a few minutes saying nothing, as we thought of all the ramifications of what she'd seen. I was feeling sick to my soul at the thought of Mr. Pickens on a cheating spree.

"They was another car parked right next to 'em," Lillian said. "A big ole car like what Brother Vern drive, but black, not orange, like his. Nobody settin' in it that I could see."

"So he didn't just pick her up somewhere. They'd arranged to meet there, which means he's known her for a while." I hung my head, wanting to cry. "No telling for how long, which makes it even worse.

"Lillian," I said, reaching over to put my hand on her arm, "I wasn't going to say anything because I believe in giving people the benefit of the doubt. But I saw him with a woman, too—a big-headed blonde—and they were in the parking lot at the mall just the other day. And I've been heartsick about it ever since. And now, to hear that he's fooling around with another one in another parking lot, I just don't know what to think."

"I guess he like them parkin' lots."

"Sounds like he likes more than that." I tightened my mouth at the thought. "Well, one thing's for sure—we have to get Hazel Marie glamorized without telling her why. Thank goodness she's willing to go to Velma on Monday—and not a moment too soon, either." Pausing to consider the situation, I then said, "I don't understand that man. You'd think he'd be grateful for what he has and not go running after something else. You know what they say, though—a tiger doesn't change his stripes. Or is it a zebra?"

"Well, but Miss Julia," she said plaintively as she ignored my rhetorical question, "look like he be more careful if he foolin' around. I mean, he got a office in Asheville, where nobody 'round here see who come an' go. Why he pickin' parkin' lots to meet up with them women? Anybody could see him. *We* seen him, so he not hidin' anything from anybody."

"Maybe that's the thing. Maybe he wants to get caught. Maybe he wants Hazel Marie to run him off so he won't feel guilty about breaking up the marriage." I put my head on the table in despair.

"No, I can't believe that, but I don't know what else to believe. What should we do, Lillian?"

"They's one thing we ought *not* do, an' that's tell Miss Hazel Marie. An' I know you say you wish somebody tell you when Mr. Springer was cattin' around, but I say we don't know enough to be tellin' anybody anything."

"I'm in total agreement with that," I assured her. "We could've misread what we saw, so the thing to do is keep our eyes open for further mischief on his part. If he keeps on meeting strange women, we might have to have a little talk with him."

"Uh-uh, not me. If it come down to that, somebody else gonna have to do the talkin'."

"We'll worry about it later," I said. "What we have to do now is make sure Hazel Marie doesn't find out. I don't think she could handle anything else, as frail as she is now. But Lillian," I went on as another worrisome thought hit me, "what if Lloyd happens to see him parked way off somewhere with one of those big-haired women? You know how that boy rides his bicycle all over town. He'd know Mr. Pickens's car as soon as he saw it, no matter where it was."

"Oh, Law, that would be bad." Lillian stopped and thought for a minute, then she said, "Why don't you kinda talk 'round Robin Hood's barn an' let Mr. Pickens know he got to be more careful where he park?"

"You mean hint around that his secret's out? I might could do that if I catch him in the right mood. Recently, though, I've only seen him going and coming—and he's usually the one who's going. Which puts a whole new light on what he's been doing."

I suddenly smacked the table with the flat of my hand and came to my feet. "Lillian, I'm not going to put up with whatever he's into. I'm already doing my level best to keep him happy. He wants Brother Vern out? I'm arranging that. He wants James on his feet? Who got Granny Wiggins over there with her Epsom salts? Me, that's who. And who's been directing cooking lessons so Hazel Marie can feed him better than he deserves, and who's talked Velma into working on her day off so Hazel Marie can get beautified? Me, again. And for whose benefit has all that been done? I'll tell you—for Mr. Pickens's benefit, that's who. And does he appreciate it? No, apparently he does not. Now we find out that he's willing to throw away a loving wife, two healthy babies, and a fine house. To say nothing of Lloyd, who worships the ground the man walks on." My mouth was so tight by this time that I could hardly get the words out. "I tell you, I am not going to stand for it."

Lillian didn't seem quite as exercised as I was. She looked up at me and said, "What you thinkin' 'bout doin'?"

I paced to the counter and back. "I'm going to give him a few more days. Just until Velma gets through with Hazel Marie and we get Brother Vern moved out. And if I don't see a marked improvement by then, well, we'll have a come-to-Jesus meeting. So, Lillian, you tell me if you see him anywhere in town with anybody—I don't care what color her hair is, I want to know about it. I'm going to straighten him out if it's the last thing I do."

"It jus' might be," Lillian murmured.

"Might be what?"

"The last thing you do." Lillian rose from the table, sighing as she did. "I don't know, Miss Julia, if you oughta 'front him like that. No tellin' what he do, he think we been spyin' on him."

"But that's the thing! We *haven't* been spying on him. He's doing it right out in the open, in plain sight of everybody. What can he expect but to be seen? And eventually to have somebody report him to Hazel Marie? It would just kill her, Lillian, so if he has his eye on somebody else he can just be man enough to tell her to her face. I am not going to have this whole town talking and whispering behind her back while she thinks everything is just fine."

"Uh-huh," Lillian said as she pulled a skillet out of a cabinet and set it on the stove. "Give it a few more days, that be the best thing. It could be we got it all wrong." She turned to look at me. "I thought you said you had to get to the bank 'fore it close."

"Oh, yes, I do. I'm glad you reminded me. And," I said, reaching for my coat, "I told James I'd mail his letters on my way. I'd better get going."

In my hurry, I snatched up my coat and knocked the pile of letters off the table. "Oh, my," I said as five or six envelopes spread out across the floor. "That's what always happens when you're in a hurry."

I stooped down and gathered up the envelopes, noticing as I did some of the addresses. Still leaning over because it was getting harder every day to straighten up my back, I said, "Lillian, come look at this."

Finally regaining my posture, I put the envelopes on the counter for Lillian to see. "I know it's a federal crime to interfere with the mail, but I think it's okay if we just happen to see the addresses. Have you ever heard of any of these?"

Lillian looked them over carefully, turning some toward her to better read them. "I know about this one: US Wounded Soldiers. I seen it on TV."

"You're thinking of Wounded Warriors, aren't you? That's certainly a legitimate charity. But what about this one? Homeless of America? Or this one: Vet-Meds. Is that medicine for veterans or for veterinarians?" I shuffled through the envelopes again. "They're all going to places like Omaha and Delaware and Newark. He doesn't know anybody that far off."

"What that James writin' to all them folks for?"

"I don't think he's writing to them. See, they're all preprinted and self-addressed envelopes—the kind you get in the mail that makes it easy for you to respond in some way." I glanced over all the envelopes, intrigued now by the addressees. "They all look like charitable organizations of some kind, but I've never heard of any of them. The names are all just a little off. And look at this one." I peered at the address: Lotería Internacional de España.

"Looks like international something-or-other in, I think, Spain. It's going to Madrid, and that's in Spain."

"He don't know nobody in Spain, I can tell you that."

"Well," I said gathering up the envelopes, "I better go and get them in the mail. We can only commend him if he's donating to worthy causes, although some of them, well, maybe all of them, seem a little iffy to me."

Chapter 31

I opened my mouth several times that evening to tell Sam what Lillian and I had seen Mr. Pickens doing, but each time I ended up closing it again. I'll tell you this, though: When I thought of how that unstable man was reverting to his premarital ways, I could hardly hold it in. I wanted to tell Sam so bad I could taste it.

With great effort, though, I held my peace because I knew what Sam's response would be. He'd tell me to stay out of it, that it wasn't our business to interfere and that most likely I was worrying for nothing. And eventually he'd work it around so that I'd feel constrained to promise to leave well enough alone.

I knew I couldn't leave well enough alone because the situation wasn't well enough to be left alone. That left me with the possibility of breaking a promise to Sam, so all I could do was avoid making a promise in the first place. Sooner or later, though, I would tell him because I didn't like keeping anything from him and only did it when it was best for him not to know.

So, because I couldn't just sit there saying nothing, which would be unlike me, I came up with another subject that held far less peril.

"I mailed some letters for James this afternoon," I said, picking up my needlepoint. "I couldn't help but see who they were addressed to and, Sam, they were all to what looked like charities of some kind."

"There're all kinds out there," Sam said placidly as he scanned the newspaper.

"Yes, but I'd never heard of any of the ones he was mailing to.

Some seemed familiar but on a closer look, they weren't quite right." I glanced up at him. "Not that I was being nosy. I just couldn't help but see, and neither could Lillian."

"He's probably sending small donations," Sam said, then smiled. "Which means they'll put him on a list, then sell the list, so he'll get requests for more donations. I expect he'll get tired of it pretty soon."

"Well, I don't know. He's doing an awful lot of mailing. Lloyd went to the post office for him at least twice that I know of and each time he had a stack of envelopes to mail. And you know, Sam, that even legitimate charities don't stop after getting one donation. They'll keep on at you." I let my needlepoint drop to my lap. "Besides, why would he be donating to a charity in Spain?"

That got Sam's attention. He lowered the newspaper and looked at me. "In Spain? You sure it wasn't Nigeria? That's a different kettle of fish. Those international things are scams from the word Go. I'll talk to him this weekend and warn him off. They prey on the elderly, you know."

"He's not that old," I said primly, knowing that James was younger than I was. "But do talk to him. I'd hate for him to be sending his money to unworthy causes." I smiled. "I started to say his *hard-earned* money, but that wouldn't be quite right, would it? Would you like a snack before we go to bed?"

"No," Sam said, a gleam in his eye. "I'd rather just go to bed." So we did.

❧

The following morning—Saturday, it was—I stayed home. No cooking lesson was scheduled so Hazel Marie wasn't expecting me, and I didn't want to go anyway. I assumed Mr. Pickens wouldn't be working, although he often did on weekends. But I didn't want to run the risk of having to be civil to him and not be able to.

Instead, I spent the morning on the telephone, checking in

first with Mildred, who reassured me that the soup kitchen was on track.

"We've rented that place you found, Julia," she said, "and I've been busy phoning around to have the utilities turned on. Oh, I tell you, it's invigorating to have something so worthwhile to occupy my time."

"And Brother Vern?" I asked. "What's he doing to help?"

"He's in charge of renting tables and chairs. He wanted to buy them, but I said renting was cheaper until we see how well things go, at least."

"That's good, Mildred. You need to keep an eye on him." Then, not wanting her to have any more second thoughts, I added, "Well, you'd have to for anybody—you know how easy it is to spend somebody else's money."

"Do I ever. Anyway, he's already hired a cook and two workers, so that's a good start. They're all busy cleaning the place and he says it's beginning to sparkle. Cleanliness is next to godliness, you know."

"Uh, Mildred," I said, trying to tread carefully, "I thought he was going to run it with volunteers."

"Oh, there'll be volunteers, all right. But first he has to have something they can volunteer for. You know, serving soup and so forth. But cleaning is hard work, so he happened to meet these people who needed jobs, so they're on the payroll—at least temporarily. He can't do it all himself—I mean with his health issues—and the sooner it gets done, the sooner he can open the doors."

"When does he plan to move in?"

"Well, that's a problem," Mildred said as my heart sank. "I climbed those stairs, which wasn't easy for me, and looked around. Those rooms really need refurbishing. I can't expect him to live there the way it is, so I've called in Miss Parker—you know, the interior designer you used? She's going to fix up that apartment so that it's fit to live in."

"Mildred . . ." I started to issue another cautionary statement, but she didn't give me a chance.

"I know what you're going to say, Julia, but don't. I know what I'm doing and I've given Miss Parker a very tight budget. She's to make it livable, and that's all. In fact, I told her no special or custom orders. She has to buy everything off the rack, so to speak. And, besides, it's giving me something to do." She sighed. "Isn't it wonderful when you find something that's enjoyable as well as being a help to your fellow man?"

I gave up after that, realizing that the more comfortable Mildred made the apartment for Brother Vern, the more likely he was to move in and stay there.

❧

I sat by the telephone for a few minutes, cogitating on what I should do. I no longer felt the urgency of working on the recipe book and scheduling cooks to teach Hazel Marie. Why knock myself out doing things to benefit such a man as Mr. Pickens, who was proving to be a low-down, tom-catting scoundrel?

I buried my face in my hands, just so torn up over the harsh words that were coming to mind. I *liked* Mr. Pickens. Even when he teased me and occasionally laughed at me, I liked him. And I was eternally grateful for his loving treatment of Lloyd. There were not many men who would so unhesitatingly take under their wing what Lillian would call a yard child.

But *why* was he doing what he was obviously doing? I had never pegged him as a man who was so shallow as to look elsewhere just because his wife was burdened with children and couldn't cook worth a flip and was too busy to have her roots colored.

I sighed, then reached for the telephone. The only thing I knew to do was to continue on with the recipe book. Everyone would know something was wrong if I quit in midstream. There'd be questions if I did, especially from Hazel Marie. I couldn't have that because I would have no answers. So I determined to keep on keeping on, and while I was at it I'd add up all I was doing for Mr. Pickens's sake and, when the time came, I would put it to his account in no uncertain terms. Maybe that way, if he walked out on another wife, as he was wont to do, it wouldn't break my heart.

So I called Helen Stroud. I hadn't seen much of Helen since her husband had been convicted and jailed for fraudulent use of money or some such thing, then was found dead in a toolshed, overcome, apparently, by the sight of his erstwhile wife in the company of Thurlow Jones a sight that would undo the healthiest of men. Helen was still coming to church, although there was a period in which she visited several other churches in an effort to rehabilitate Thurlow—which apparently hadn't worked. But she hadn't come back to the Lila Mae Harding Sunday school class, the class of which she'd been either president or teacher for as long as I'd known her.

I couldn't blame her. Every woman in that class knew everything about everybody and made sure everybody else knew it, too. If I'd been in Helen's reduced circumstances, I'd have stayed away, too. She was working now, I'd heard, at another part-time job—she'd had several. She'd been a receptionist for a while at some nonprofit organization, then for an orthodontist, and after that she'd worked in a dress shop in Asheville. It wasn't that she couldn't keep a job—Helen was the most organized and efficient woman I knew. More likely it was because she was ill suited for a low-level job. And the last one hired was generally the first one fired. The economy, you know.

"Helen?" I said when she answered the phone, then went immediately into my song-and-dance about Hazel Marie's plight and my plan to write a recipe book. When I ended by asking for a main dish recipe that she wouldn't mind demonstrating in Hazel Marie's kitchen, I was shamed by her abject gratitude for being included.

"Anytime, Julia," she said. "I would love to do that and at the same time see those babies and visit with you and Hazel Marie. Just tell me when you want me and I'll be there."

"Well, Hazel Marie has something to do on Monday and Emma Sue will be there Tuesday. Any day after that will be fine."

"Then let's do Wednesday morning. No, wait—I have a dental appointment then. And," she went on, a bit sadly, I thought, "I'm working the rest of the week. I'm sorry, Julia, could I do it maybe the following week?"

"Of course, I'll check with you before then. But I'll go ahead and put your recipe in the book."

"Could I have two?" Her eagerness only shamed me more because I was so aware of what a poor friend I'd been during her self-imposed exile from all the social activities of late.

"I'd love to have two from you, but you'll only have to show her how to do one."

"Oh, good, then I'll give you the recipe for lasagna and for shrimp creole. Unless you already have them."

"No, I don't. Which one will you demonstrate?"

"The shrimp creole. It's easier and doesn't take as long to put together. Will that be all right?"

"It'll be perfect."

Helen Stroud's Lasagna

½ pound ground chuck
¼ cup fine bread crumbs
2 tablespoons milk
1 egg, slightly beaten
2 tablespoons Parmesan cheese
2 tablespoons parsley
½ teaspoon salt
⅛ teaspoon pepper
2 tablespoons butter

Preheat the oven to 350°F. Combine all the ingredients and shape into balls the size of marbles. Heat 2 tablespoons of butter in a large skillet or Dutch oven. Brown the meatballs over moderate heat, stirring and turning occasionally, for 10 to 15 minutes.

Mix together the following and add to the meatballs:

Two 10-ounce cans tomato puree and ½ can water
One 6-ounce can tomato paste

Simmer the meatball sauce for up to 1 hour.

To put together, have the following ready:

½ pound lasagna noodles (cooked according to the directions)
4 ounces mozzarella cheese, sliced
1 cup cream-style cottage cheese
¼ cup Parmesan cheese

Spoon 1 cup of the meatball sauce into the bottom of a 9×11×2-inch baking dish. Cover with a layer of cooked lasagna noodles, then layer half of each of the mozzarella cheese, cottage cheese, and Parmesan cheese. Repeat once, ending with sauce. Bake 20 minutes or so. Let stand for 15 minutes before cutting.

Serves 8.

(LuAnne looked at this recipe, Hazel Marie, and said you could use those no-cook lasagna noodles and save having to wash another pan.)

Helen Stroud's Shrimp Creole

2 tablespoons butter, melted
1 cup chopped onions
1 cup chopped green pepper
½ garlic clove, chopped
1 pint stewed tomatoes
⅛ teaspoon paprika
Salt and pepper, to taste
½ pound shrimp, shelled, deveined, and cooked

In a large skillet, sauté the onions, pepper, and garlic in the butter until tender. Add the tomatoes and seasoning. Boil 5 minutes. Add the shrimp and simmer 10 minutes longer. Serve over rice.

Serves 4.

(Lillian said that you should add a couple of teaspoons of salt and a splash of vinegar to the water you boil the shrimp in–it will cut down the fish smell. Also, boil the water first, then dump in the shrimp. Watch it until it comes back to the boil, then remove it from the heat and cover it for 10 minutes. Drain the shrimp. Instead of doing all this, why don't you just buy precooked shrimp?)

Chapter 32

After bringing the conversation with Helen to a close, I forced myself to continue working on the recipe book—more to have something to displace Mr. Pickens in my mind than anything else—so I reached again for the phone. If anyone could lift my spirits it was the Reverend Poppy Peterson, assistant pastor of the First United Methodist Church of Abbotsville.

To tell the truth, I longed to be able to unburden myself of the troubles created by Mr. Pickens's waywardness, and since I couldn't to Sam, Pastor Poppy was the next best person to hear them. She, I knew, would not extract a promise from me concerning any future action I might feel compelled to take and, as a minister bound by the rule of confidentiality—something that did not constrain most people—she wouldn't tell anybody else.

In the end, though, I decided to keep it to myself. I had Lillian, who already knew as much as I did, to talk to, so there was no reason in the world for me to confide in anybody else. Even if I was dying to tell somebody.

Nonetheless, when Poppy answered the phone in her warm, bubbly voice, I could feel myself waver. "Miss Julia!" she exclaimed, as if she'd been just waiting for me to call. "How good to hear from you. What's going on? How are you?"

I almost capitulated enough to ask for a counseling appointment. Instead, though, I managed to say, "Oh, just so-so, Poppy. You know how it is, trying to keep going and get through the day as well I can."

"Uh-oh, that doesn't sound good. Be careful you don't fall into accidie, which I've just been reading about. But you don't have that problem, I'm sure." She laughed warmly. "You're much too busy and involved in things."

"Well, speaking of being involved, I'd like to involve you in something I'm working on." And I went on to tell her my plan for a recipe book for Hazel Marie. "I'd love to include a main dish recipe from you, Poppy, and if you have time, schedule you for a demonstration of how to prepare it. Could you do that? I'd be ever so grateful."

"Oh, sure. I'd love to. Hold on a minute and let me get my card file." She put down the phone. "Here we go," she said a few moments later "How many chicken recipes do you have?"

"Um, I haven't counted, but there're several. Don't worry, though—everybody likes chicken and if you have something different, I'll take it. Read it out. I can tell if I already have it."

She did and I could. "Oh, goodness, Poppy, that's exactly like Miss Mattie's. In fact, it sounds like something Lillian makes, too, which means it's good. Do you have anything else?"

"Let me see," Poppy said, not at all perturbed. "Here's one I almost gave you to start with. It was given to me by a wonderful cook before I went off to seminary. She said it's the perfect recipe for leftover turkey after the holidays." She giggled. "I like it so much, though, that I buy a turkey breast every now and then just to have leftovers for this."

"Okay, let's do that one, then. I know I don't have any turkey recipes."

"Okay, if you're ready. It's one of my favorite company recipes, and this card tells the tale. I've used it so many times and spilled so much on it, I can barely read it."

Hoping she wouldn't leave anything out, I assured her I was ready to write.

Poppy's Turkey Tetrazzini

¼ pound spaghetti, uncooked
2 cups diced cooked turkey
4-ounce can mushrooms
2 tablespoons butter
10¾-ounce can cream of chicken soup, undiluted
1 cup sour cream
Almonds, chopped
Parmesan cheese

Preheat the oven to 350°F. Cook the spaghetti, drain, and put it in the bottom of an ovenproof bowl. In a large skillet, sauté the turkey and mushrooms in butter, then add the soup, sour cream, and almonds, and stir. Add the Parmesan cheese (as much as you want) and pour the mixture over the spaghetti. Sprinkle more Parmesan over the top. Bake 35 to 45 minutes.

Serves 4.

(Hazel Marie, Poppy says she likes either a congealed or a fruit salad with this, maybe some English peas and yeast rolls, which I wouldn't try to make if I were you. You can get them from the frozen section.)

"That sounds good," I said, "and not too hard for Hazel Marie to practice on. I'm sure I don't have that one. Now, Poppy, what day could you go over and show her how to put it together? Any day next week after Tuesday."

"Let me check my calendar. Wednesday might be best for me, if that'll work for you.

"Oh, wait a minute," Poppy went on. "Look at Miss Mattie's chicken and rice recipe. I bet she didn't give you some variations I've tried with it. What you can do is use *boned* chicken breasts— even chicken cutlets work well. All you do is roll them up, then wrap each piece with an uncooked strip of bacon and use toothpicks to hold it on. Then go ahead and brown the breasts, then follow the recipe. Or instead of bacon, you can wrap the breasts in slices of dried beef—you know, the kind that comes in the little jar."

Writing hurriedly to get down the last-minute options, I said, "Don't think of any other possibilities, Poppy. Hazel Marie won't be able to decide which one to use. I'm about lost myself. Thank goodness I'm not the one who'll be cooking."

She laughed, assured me that Hazel Marie would find her recipe as easy as pie, and, after we'd confirmed Wednesday, we hung up.

Then I rose from the chair, took down the heavy dictionary from the shelf, and looked up *accidie,* effectively proving to myself that I didn't have it.

Looking back, though, I admit that I had to struggle almost that entire weekend to keep from being struck down with a case of it. All I wanted to do was sit and stare off into space. I had no energy for anything, mainly because what I wanted to do, I knew I couldn't do—and that was to kick Brother Vern out, get James back to work, and shake Mr. Pickens until his teeth rattled.

After I had sat around as long as I could stand it that Saturday, I got up and went to the kitchen. "Lillian," I said as soon as I entered, "would you mind fixing a nice little lunch for James? I need to speak with him, and I thought I'd take him lunch. It'll relieve Hazel Marie and give him a change, too. Anything but a grilled cheese sandwich."

Lillian looked at me in surprise. "What you got to talk to James for?"

"All those envelopes he's mailing out every other day. He's opening himself up to being taken advantage of and, for all we know, he's involving Lloyd in it, too. Remember, we still don't know the real reason Lloyd made that midnight visit, in spite of what he told us."

"Uh-huh, I 'bout forget about that. But you think James gonna let you in on any secret they got? Them two's thick as thieves. I wouldn't count on gettin' anything outta James if I was you."

"You're probably right, but I told Sam about those envelopes we saw, and he thinks James may be wasting his money by sending donations to scam organizations. He said he'd talk to James, but what is he doing today? Off interviewing some retired judge he wants to write about, that's what."

"Uh-huh, so you gonna do the talkin'."

"No, I'll just feel him out a little. I'll call Hazel Marie and tell her not to worry about lunch for him. And I don't plan to visit with her. I don't want to even *see* Mr. Pickens—I might slap his face. I'm going straight to James's apartment, then back home."

As she began preparing a to-go lunch for James, I called Hazel Marie, then put on my coat. "Where's Lloyd? He's not over there, is he?"

"No'm, he went with Mr. Sam. He tol' you at breakfast he goin' with him."

"Oh, that's right. He's hoping to get some ideas for a paper he has to write." I sighed as Lillian ladled hot soup into a thermos and wrapped two large chunks of cornbread in foil. "I don't know where my mind is these days."

"James," I said as I poured the soup, thick with vegetables and beef cubes, into a bowl. "You are looking so much better. That ankle or foot or whatever you injured seems about well."

He had come to the door fully dressed, limping a little but without the help of a cane. Even his bed was made. Sitting now at his small table, he watched with a leery look on his face as I set out his lunch.

"Miss Granny 'bout cured my foot," he said, still watching me with a hint of suspicion. "But I can't do no work till I get this cask off my arm."

"I know, but nobody's rushing you. We just want you to get well. You must be tired of sitting around all day, unable to come and go like you want to."

"Yes'm, I do get tired of lookin' at four walls, but I keep myself busy. I got the TV an' Lloyd's iTunes an' I got my forms." I placed the bowl of soup and a plate of cornbread before him. "That sure look good. Miss Lillian, she's a cook an' a half." He looked up in alarm as I took a seat across from him. "You gonna watch me eat?"

"No, I'm going in a minute, but, James, it's those forms I want to talk to you about. Just what kind of forms are they?"

"Well, now, Miss Julia," he said, drawing back because I was poking my nose into his business. I knew it and didn't blame him, but the only way to learn something is to ask. "They jus' something I do for the Lord since I can't get to church."

"For the Lord? My goodness, James, how do you figure that? Your mail is going all over the country, not to your church."

"The Lord do his work everywhere," he said with just a touch of piety, "in all kinda ways."

"Oh, of course," I quickly agreed. "But the reason I ask is that I don't want Lloyd involved in anything unsavory. I know he's helping you, which is why I may appear to be meddling in your business. I hope you understand."

"Lloyd jus' fillin' out my forms like I tell him to 'cause I can't write with this cask on. Then he takin' 'em to the post office for me. An' he write the checks for me, too, but I'm pretty good at signin' 'em with my left hand now, so he don't have to sign 'em for me no more."

I nearly fell out of my chair. "He's been signing *checks* for you? You mean, *forging* your name?"

"No'm, it ain't forgin' when I tell him to an' watch him do it an' put down my X with my left hand. Forgin' is when somebody write your name an' you don't know he doin' it."

"I certainly hope you're right." But I didn't know if he was or not. I could just picture our Lloyd brought up on fraudulent check charges. "But let me be firm about this, James. Don't ask him to do it again."

"No'm, I can jus' about manage on my own now. I been practicin' with my left hand, and besides I don't have to send in all them little donations no more."

"So you *have* been sending donations? I thought so, and, James, I'm worried about that. Don't you know that there are people out there who just look for good-hearted people like you to prey on? Those organizations you're sending money to don't exist—your money is going into the pocket of some crook. From the looks of them, they're all scams, every last one."

"Oh, no, ma'am, they're not. They all have these big drawin's an' raffles, an' that was just for the big prizes. They send you little prizes just for sendin' in your form, which they already sent to you. All you have to do is send your entry form with jus' a little donation, like nine dollars or maybe twenny sometimes. An' then I get back all kinda little prizes, you know jus' for enterin', like little stickers an' bookmarks an' notepads with your name on 'em. But the big thing is, you have a chance to win ten thousand dollars an' sometimes even more than that. An' even if you don't win the big prizes, all them nine-dollar donations go to help hurt soldiers an' poor little dogs an' little sick chil'ren."

I just sat and looked at him, astounded at how he'd been taken in. "Well, let me just say this: If you're intent on gambling, you'd be better off and more likely to win something if you played the lottery. At least it's run by the state, which, I admit, can't always be trusted, but at least the lottery has a semblance of legitimacy."

"Oh, no, ma'am," he said, aghast. "I can't do that. I don't gamble. Gamblin's a sin."

"Why, James, what do you think those drawings and so forth are? You're paying for a chance to win money, which is what a lottery is."

"No, ma'am. No, ma'am," he said, closing his eyes and shaking his head, determined not to be moved. "They not the same. One is donations and the other's gamblin'."

"So how much have you won?"

"Don't make no difference now. I'm already through with them little piddlin' prizes. All them nine-dollar checks I been sending in, they done come back to me lotsa times over—that's what you call caskin' your bread on the water, Miss Julia. So don't you worry 'bout Lloyd—he don't need to do another thing for me. I'm gonna start doin' for him now, 'cause I done hit the jackpot."

"My word," I was moved to say after a little more back and forth, as I tried to point out better places to risk his money, like the state lottery, the stock market, or a savings account. I finally had to concede that I would neither change his mind nor get any more out of him. He closed up tight, wouldn't say another word about what kind of jackpot, where it was coming from, or how he happened to win it.

I went home half frightened and thoroughly discouraged, worrying about what James had gotten himself into. I have never believed that anybody will get something for nothing, but I do believe that if something sounds too good to be true, it generally is. The real question, though, was just how involved Lloyd was in this supposed jackpot that James had supposedly won.

Chapter 33

It weighed on my mind all weekend, which was the main reason—other than Mr. Pickens's perverse behavior—I came so close to falling into accidie. Even Sam noticed how quiet I was, how distracted and glassy-eyed I looked, finally asking if I was coming down with something.

"No, I'm all right. But, Sam . . ." I started, then stopped, unsure of which worry should take precedence. Lloyd, James, and Mr. Pickens were going 'round and 'round in my head—to say nothing of Brother Vern, about whom he'd already heard enough—so if I started talking, I wasn't sure which one would come tumbling out.

"Sam," I said again as he looked at me with some concern, even putting aside his book, "I'm not sure what James is up to, but whatever it is, it looks as if Lloyd is in it, too, even though James says he's through using him." Then I went on to tell him of my conversation with James and how I'd been unable to get any details about the jackpot he'd said he won. "And, Sam, Lloyd has been signing James's checks—forging his name! Can you believe that? In spite of all we've done for that boy, teaching him by word and by example the difference between right and wrong, one little request by James has started him on a life of crime. I can't get over it. If there's been one thing I was sure of, it was that Lloyd had a good head on his shoulders. But this . . . well, now I just don't know."

Sam got up and came over to sit beside me on the sofa. He took my hand and said, "Julia, you are worrying for nothing. I know he's signing checks for James. He's helping him pay his bills, which aren't that many because Pickens pays most of them. But Lloyd asked me about it, and I told him he could sign them if James put his X by his name and Lloyd put his own initials next to that. Then I went to James's bank and told them what was going on and to contact me if they had any problem with it. I thought it would be good training for Lloyd to see where money has to go every month."

"Oh, for goodness sakes, Sam, you let me worry myself sick about this and all the time you were encouraging him? Why didn't you tell me?"

"Well," Sam said, smiling sheepishly, "I thought I had. I apologize, honey, because it was not my intent to keep anything from you. You know I don't do that. I guess it just slipped my mind."

I started to reply sharply, then reconsidered. It was true: Sam didn't keep things to himself. I was the one who did that and, sitting there beside him with my hand in his, was still guilty of doing it.

"Well," I said, somewhat mollified, "well, did you know about all the forms those two having been sending in? With checks signed by Lloyd in each one?"

"No, I didn't know that. But," he went on, frowning now, "let's look on the bright side. The bank may reject them."

"Then how could James have won some big jackpot? From what he told me, he had to contribute something to be eligible to win."

"You may be right. But let me suggest something. Let's let Pickens handle this. James is his employee and Lloyd is his responsibility."

That brought me straight off the sofa. "*His* responsibility! Why, I'm not sure I agree with that. I've always thought of Lloyd as my responsibility." Actually, all I could think of was how in the world Mr. Pickens could accept responsibility for a child at the same time he was planning parking-lot trysts with two different women.

"I know you do, but Pickens is his stepfather and wants to be a real father to him. He's concerned about setting an example and encouraging Lloyd to depend on him. And for them to be a family, it may be best if we don't interfere. This is a situation that calls for a good father-son talk. So let's let him handle it."

The more I thought about it, the more I realized that Mr. Pickens stepping into a fatherly role to Lloyd could add another knot to the tie that binds. In the light of that, though, I couldn't help but wonder why Mr. Pickens seemed to be doing everything he could to cut that selfsame tie.

⊷∾⊶

It was later on the same day, as the house grew dim and quiet with a Sunday-afternoon lonesome feeling, that Lloyd himself came sidling up to my desk. Trying to stay busy while Sam worked in his office, I had been neatly recopying scribbled recipes into Hazel Marie's book.

"Miss Julia?" Lloyd said. "Can I ask you something?"

"Yes, you may." I put down my pencil and smiled at him. "What is it, honey?"

"I'm not sure about this, but I think James's feelings got hurt. He didn't say they were," Lloyd quickly added. "It's just that he said he was feeling kinda low-down."

"Well, we can't have that, can we? Who in the world hurt his feelings? Brother Vern again?"

"No'm. I think it was you."

"Me?" I turned around in my chair to look at him. "How could I have hurt his feelings? Why, I even took lunch to him. Oh," I said, reconsidering, "I expect he didn't appreciate my asking him not to involve you in those scams he's been sending money to. I'm sorry that hurt his feelings and I'll apologize to him, but he should've known better."

"No'm, that wasn't it."

"Well, what else did I do?"

"You didn't ask him for any of his recipes for that book you're fixing for Mama. See," Lloyd went on, "he thought that was why you came over, and when you didn't ask, he thought you forgot about it and would call him when you got home. But you didn't."

"They Lord," I murmured, although I do not approve of taking the Lord's name in vain. In this case, however—and in many others—it was a prayer for help. "It just never occurred to me to ask, and I don't know why it didn't. But of course I will, and right away, too. Do you know what recipes he wants to contribute?"

Lloyd grinned. "He said he didn't know any off the top of his head because he just cooks natural-like. But he figured he could come up with something if somebody happened to ask."

"And that somebody would be me, wouldn't it?" I smiled at him. "I will most certainly rectify my lapse. Thank you for letting me know, Lloyd.

"Now, Lloyd," I went on, figuring it was as good a time as any to do a little probing, "you have certainly been a good friend to James. I've been proud of the way you've looked after him and how you've done whatever you could to make him comfortable. However, I am concerned about all the money he's been sending off as donations, but which are really an effort to win more money. I would like to think that you'd be able to discourage him from giving away what he can't afford. Those things are scams aimed at people who are naïve enough to think everyone is as decent as they are."

"Yes, ma'am, I was a little worried about that at first, too. Especially after I saw his monthly bills. I didn't know how much it takes just to buy a few groceries and pay the phone bill and put gas in his truck. And if J.D. and Mama didn't pay his electric bill and heat bill, he wouldn't have anything left. What's left is what he uses to enter contests, but . . ." Lloyd stopped as if he'd come too close to revealing something he wasn't supposed to reveal. His eyes darted around the room. "But, well, he says he's not going to send in any more forms. He's through with them."

"Yes, he told me the same thing. And the reason, he said, is because he's hit the jackpot. Do you know anything about that?"

"Um, well, no'm, not much." Lloyd looked away from me. "I can't tell, Miss Julia. James made me promise not to because he wants it to be a surprise. And it really will be a surprise. I can hardly believe it myself and I saw the letter—I mean the e-mail."

"I wouldn't expect you to break a promise, so we'll have to wait and see, won't we? I hope he won't be too disappointed to find that it's another scam, as seems highly likely to me."

"He told me you said they were all scams and that he'd be better off playing the lottery." Lloyd grinned. "He was really scandalized about that. Said he couldn't believe a fine Christian lady like you would tell somebody to start gambling."

"Yes, and I asked him what he thought he'd been doing sending in all those forms. But," I said, sighing, "it didn't do any good."

Lloyd soon went to his room to do his homework, leaving me to ponder James's big surprise. Lloyd knew more than he was telling—that was obvious. But having escaped the trap of making promises I didn't want to keep, I was somewhat proud of him for having kept his. That didn't stop me from wanting to find out, however.

As I thought over the conversation with Lloyd, I doodled with my pencil on one of the recipes from Miss Mattie that I'd hurriedly taken down over the phone. LOTTERY, I wrote, then underlined it and circled it over and over. LOTTERY, LOTTERY: *LOTERÍA.*

"My word," I said, sitting straight up in amazement. "I've just translated Spanish."

Chapter 34

So James *was* playing the lottery, in spite of his righteous indignation at the thought of gambling. Of course, with that multitude of entry forms he'd been sending in, he might not have realized he was buying a lottery ticket instead of donating to a cause. Although how he'd known about a cause in Spain to supposedly donate to was beyond me.

Well, it was none of my business now that I'd been reassured that Lloyd was not involved. If James had actually won a jackpot, he'd get his wish to surprise us, because I truly would be. And he would be, too, when the Internal Revenue Service came calling.

I went to bed that night dreading the morning, when Lillian, Granny Wiggins, and I would take charge of Hazel Marie's babies. What if one of them got hurt? Or sick? What if they cried all day? What if I had to go get Hazel Marie and bring her home with her hair still wet and bleaching out under a processing cap? In spite of the worrying, however, I slept well and awoke determined to do what I had to do to save Hazel Marie's marriage. The possibility did occur to me that Velma's ministrations on Hazel Marie might not work—that Mr. Pickens was too far gone for a Clairol 126 application, OPI-polished finger- and toenails, professional makeup, and a little cleavage to reverse his headlong course toward strange women. But, I sighed, we do what we can.

I thought I'd never get Hazel Marie out of the house that Monday morning. I insisted on dropping her at Velma's myself because I didn't want her to have an easy way to get home if she suddenly decided she had to check on her babies. But finally, teary-eyed and looking back at the house, she got in my car.

"I've never been away from them so long," she said as I quickly cranked the car and got us on our way. "It shouldn't take but an hour or so, don't you think?"

I was tempted to say, *Have you looked in the mirror lately?* but I didn't. Instead, I said, "Maybe a little longer, but you have your cell phone. You can check in with us and we can certainly let you know if we need you. Try to enjoy it, Hazel Marie. You'll feel so much better when it's done."

"I guess," she said, forcing a little smile. "I know my hair could use some help." She laughed. "I'll probably go to sleep as soon as I get in the chair."

"I hope you do. Just look at this as a day of rest."

Actually it was one of the longest days of my life. I'd never realized how *tethered* one feels when one has to stay inside at the beck and call of an infant—two infants, in this case. Every time I sat down, one of them needed something else. Lillian was wonderful with them, calling them the best babies in the world.

I wouldn't know, having never had the opportunity to compare. But if they were the best, in spite of the constant wails for diaper changes, spit-up wipings, hand-feeding, bottle holding, and on and on, I'd hate to see the worst.

Of course it wasn't all that bad. There were lots of cooings and smiles and gurgles, and I admit to feeling great swells of tenderness as they went down for their naps. Nothing is sweeter than a sleeping baby.

Granny Wiggins was there, along with Lillian and me. She very quickly saw how uneasy I was with baby care, so as soon as I picked up a fussy one, there she was taking it from me. And talk? That woman could evermore talk.

As soon as the babies went down for their morning nap, I'd

thought the three of us could sit around the table, have some coffee, and engage in conversation as we regathered our strength.

But that woman never stopped talking, not even while she pinned an old towel around the broom and went after the dust on the crown moldings. And when she finished with that, she got down on her hands and knees and cleaned the baseboards, still talking. Lillian kept shaking her head at the torrent of words issuing from Granny's mouth. I concentrated on tuning it out.

Hazel Marie called three times during the morning, once to say that she'd forgo a pedicure so she could come on home.

"Don't you dare," I told her. "You're scheduled for the full treatment and, since you're already there, you might as well get it. Everything is fine here, Hazel Marie, and, believe me, if it wasn't, you would be the first to know. I'd be down there in a flash to get you."

I clicked off the phone and turned to Lillian and Granny, who had been listening. "Good thing I made sure that Velma hid her clothes. Although I expect Hazel Marie wouldn't hesitate to run home in a terry-cloth robe if she thought the babies needed her."

Before they could respond, the phone rang again. It was Sam saying that he was bringing lunch. "And for James, too," he said. "How about Brother Vern? Is he there?"

"No, thank goodness," I said. "He'd already left by the time I got here this morning. And so had Mr. Pickens. So it's just three babysitters. And James and you."

I looked forward to a pleasant lunch of take-out sandwiches, especially with Sam joining us, but it didn't work out that way. About the time he pulled up to the curb and came in carrying several bags, both babies woke up and, from the sound of them, were starving to death. So out came the high chairs and the long baby spoons and the jars of pureed food because their needs came before anything else. Granny fed with one hand and ate her sandwich with the other, while Lillian and I took turns, one feeding and one eating. And of course Hazel Marie called again in the middle of the din, and it was all I could do to assure her that we had things well in hand.

After we had the babies fed, washed, and redressed—we'd forgotten the bibs—we adjourned to the living room. Granny spread out a quilt on the floor and put the babies on it. Then she got down on the floor with them, while I marveled at her agility. Frankly, if I'd gotten down there, I'd have needed a crane to get back up. Well, maybe with Sam's help I could've regained my feet, but I didn't want to risk it.

After Sam left, Lillian said, "Wonder how Miss Hazel Marie gettin' along by now."

I looked at my watch. "It's about time for her to call. Maybe she's having a massage and can't get up right now."

Granny glanced up. "Might be her toenail polish's not dry an' she can't put on her shoes. Reckon you ought to call her and let her know we're all right?"

"I don't think so. She'd probably have a heart attack before I could say more than one word."

I leaned back against the sofa, resting from the hectic morning, eventually assuring myself that it hadn't been as bad as I'd expected. Raising my head, I said, "She should be calling to come home in a little while, but if you ladies aren't entirely given out, what do you think of staying on so she and Mr. Pickens can go out to dinner?"

"Why, that's a dandy idee," Granny said. "She'll be all gussied up and ready to knock that man's socks off. I say let's do it. What about you, Miss Lillian?"

"I was jus' thinkin' the same thing," Lillian said. "I can fix us some supper here an' Mr. Sam can eat with us. An' Lloyd an' Latisha will be home from school an' they can, too. 'Course we'll feed James an' I guess Mr. Brother Vern'll be here. Wonder what she got in her kitchen I can cook."

"Whatever you decide to fix will be fine," I said. "One of us can go to the store and get what you need."

So it was decided and, after calling Sam to tell him we'd all eat at the Pickens house and to bring Lloyd and Latisha over with him, I called Mr. Pickens to let him know he had a dinner date with his wife. Unhappily, though, the call went to voice mail, so I had to leave a message, something I hated doing, as I wanted an enthusiastically affirmative response from him.

"What if he can't go?" Lillian asked, a hint of worry in her eyes. "He might be too busy. Workin', I mean."

"He can just *un*busy himself," I said, although what he might be busy doing worried me, too. Nonetheless, I looked over Lillian's grocery list and prepared to head out to the store.

"I'll take my cell phone," I said as I put on my coat, "so if Hazel Marie calls to say she's ready to come home, call me and I'll pick her up on my way back."

"You want me to tell her she goin' out with Mr. Pickens tonight?"

I thought about that for a minute. "No, maybe not yet. Let's be sure he's not on a case first. Besides, she'll be anxious to see the babies and might say she wants to stay home. I think we ought to make it a fait accompli, don't you?"

"No'm I think we ought to set it all up 'fore she knows what we doin'. That way she can't get out of it."

"I agree," I said and left to do the grocery shopping.

❧

Hurrying along the aisles, as I checked off items on the list, I was anxious to finish before Hazel Marie called. If I kept her waiting any length of time, it wouldn't surprise me if she started walking home.

Just as I got the groceries in the car, Lillian called to say Hazel Marie was ready. Perfect timing, I thought, congratulating myself. Now, to try Mr. Pickens again to put him on notice that he was taking his wife out to dinner.

I sat in the car while making the call, wanting it all confirmed before telling Hazel Marie she'd be going out that evening. But voice mail again. Where was that man? And what was he doing that he couldn't answer his phone?

I turned on the ignition and began to weave through parked cars in the lot to the street. Stopped at the edge of the lot by a line of cars waiting at a red light, I tapped my fingers on the steering wheel, even more anxious now to pick up Hazel Marie.

As I waited to pull out onto the street, my gaze wandered until it suddenly stopped on a certain black low-slung sports car only two cars to my right. Straining to see, I made out two heads in the car—one that I certainly recognized on the driver's side and the other with a bushy head of dark hair just as Lillian had described.

Chapter 35

What was the man doing? Looking for another secluded parking lot? No wonder he was going right past the Winn-Dixie. If he pulled in there, he'd be seen by half the town.

I was finally able to get out into the lane of traffic, and my first impulse was to follow Mr. Pickens. But he was three or four cars ahead, and Hazel Marie was waiting. There was nothing to do but turn off and drive to Velma's. And to pretend that I wasn't outraged over a certain husband's flagrant double life, which, I angrily reminded myself, he was making little or no effort to hide.

Hazel Marie was out the door of Velma's salon before I'd come to a full stop. She hopped into the car, talking and asking questions nonstop.

"How did they do?" she asked. "Did they nap? Have they been fussy?"

"Everything went fine," I said, after giving her a detailed account. "And yes, they napped and they haven't been fussy. Hazel Marie, you look like a picture." And she did. Her face had color and so did her hair. Velma had outdone herself in both venues. Hazel Marie was totally remade, except for that loose running suit she had on, which I hoped she'd replace with a form-fitting dress of some kind.

"I hated being away for so long," Hazel Marie said, almost bouncing on the seat. "But, oh my, it was a wonderful day. I told Velma she should advertise Mother's Day Out. I'd be tempted to sign up every week." She turned to look at me. "You're sure the babies are all right?"

"Absolutely sure," I said, thinking that she should've been asking how Lillian, Granny, and I were. "And, furthermore, Lillian is cooking supper for us all, if you don't mind our staying a little longer. We didn't want you to have to come home and undo Velma's work in one fell swoop."

She laughed. "You're all so good to me."

I pulled into the Pickens driveway and drove on toward the garage, parking beside Granny's rusty old pickup. Hazel Marie had the car door open before I turned off the ignition. "Run on in, Hazel Marie," I said to her back. "I'll bring in the groceries."

She was up the back steps, across the porch, and into the kitchen while I was still climbing out of the car. Just as I punched the key to open the trunk, I heard the low growl of a motor. Turning to look, I saw Mr. Pickens's car turn into the driveway. It rolled to a stop behind my car, the door opened, and Mr. Pickens stepped out, a welcoming smile on his face.

"Hey, Miss Julia," he called as he walked over. "Need some help?"

"More than you know," I said shortly, reaching for a plastic grocery bag. I couldn't look at him, much less greet him with any warmth. I knew what he'd been doing.

"Here," he said, "let me take those."

"Get the other two," I snapped, "if you haven't worn yourself out today."

He looked at me quizzically, then grinned. "I've still got a little life left in me."

"If that's so," I said, glaring into those black eyes of his, "then get in there and tell your wife that you're taking her out to dinner. I don't care how you do it—you can sweet-talk her into it or you can lay down the law, but one way or another, you're taking her out. And, while you're at it, make sure you tell her how nice she looks—she's been in the beauty shop all day and deserves a few compliments." I stopped for breath, then went on. "I've been trying to reach you all afternoon, Mr. Pickens, but obviously you were much too busy to answer your phone. My intent was to tell you that you have plenty of babysitters for tonight and that Hazel Marie needs some time with you. And you with her."

He shrugged his shoulders. "She won't go. I've tried."

"Then try again." I switched the grocery bag to my other hand—cans are heavy. "Those babies will be a year old in a couple of months, and today was the first time Hazel Marie has had to herself. She's been nowhere and done nothing but take care of babies and everybody else. It's high time you paid some attention to what's going on in your own house. But no, you're out shilly-shallying around while your wife works herself to the bone."

"Shilly-shallying?" he said, his eyes beginning to dance as a smile lurked at the corners of his mouth. "I don't believe that's what I've been doing."

I nodded, knowing exactly what he'd been doing, and it was worse than shilly-shallying. I wanted to smack him.

"Whatever," I said, because his backyard was not the place to go into detail about his indecent activities. Besides it was too cold. "But attention must be paid, starting tonight. You should tell Hazel Marie to go upstairs and change clothes, and while she's doing that, you can make reservations. And make them somewhere nice. Now go on in there and do it before her hair gets messed up."

Frowning in spite of the smirk lingering at his mouth, he said, "Miss Julia, have I offended you in some way?"

"Offended *me*? I should say not. I can't imagine that you would ever do anything indecent enough to offend me." I was laying on the sarcasm pretty thick, but every time I looked at him, with that innocent and bewildered look on his face, I wanted to smack him good. "Or have you, and I don't know about it?"

"Well, no, not that I can think of, but you sure seem put out with me."

Looking past him, I saw Sam, Lloyd, and Latisha coming down the sidewalk. I shoved my grocery bag into Mr. Pickens's hand. "Get the rest of them, too," I said and walked off to meet Sam.

Lloyd and Latisha raced across the front yard, waving to me as they leapt up onto the porch and into the house. I met Sam by the front steps, walking directly into his arms.

"Oh, Sam," I said, feeling his arms around me.

"Long day, honey? Babies wear you out?"

I nodded my head against his chest, letting him think what he would. I hadn't yet confided in him about Mr. Pickens's two unknown, but distinctively female, passengers, and here, in the cold, darkening afternoon by Hazel Marie's front porch, was neither the time nor place to do it.

❧

I didn't hear how Mr. Pickens talked her into it, but Hazel Marie came downstairs in a slinky black dress, dark stockings, and shoes with heels so high that she teetered when she walked. She was truly stunning, and I could see her husband's eyes light up at the sight. I hoped that light would stay there, and he'd quit that comparison shopping he seemed to be doing.

As they left for dinner, I felt suffused with satisfaction. From the care that Mr. Pickens took in helping Hazel Marie down the steps and into the car, it was clear that my efforts were paying off. The glow didn't continue, though, for I still had a few more hours of babysitting to get through.

"Mama really looked nice, didn't she?" Lloyd said, watching as his parents left for the evening.

"She look just like a movie star," Latisha said as she sat on the quilt, trying to entertain Lily Mae, who was beginning to signal that it was suppertime. "When I get grown, I'm gonna have me a black dress like that, but I'm not just gonna go get something to eat. That's not gettin' the good outta a nice dress like that. I'm gonna go dancin' in mine." She shook a rattle and made a sinuous move with her shoulders. "All night long, too."

"Law, chile," Lillian said, as she picked up Julie, "it'll be a while 'fore you do any dancin'. Miss Granny, if you'll get that other baby, I think they both need changin'."

Granny had been noticeably quiet since we'd all come in. I

thought the presence of Sam and Mr. Pickens had intimidated her, although she was quick to get Lily Mae and follow Lillian upstairs to the changing table. When they came back down, each with a squirming, unhappy baby, they headed straight for the kitchen and set them up to be fed.

"Let me do that, Mrs. Wiggins," I said, reaching for the baby food jars that Hazel Marie had selected. "You've had a long day and probably want to be home before it gets too dark."

She glanced out the window. "I guess I better, at that. I can't see all that good in the dark. You sure you got enough hands to take care of these babies?"

"With Sam here, and the two children, I think we'll be fine."

"Well," Granny said as she slid into her coat, "Mr. Sam looks like a fine man to have around, but I've yet to see a one that could take over baby tendin'. Seems like the Lord aimed that job for womenfolk."

Before I could respond, the front door opened, then slammed closed hard enough to shake the walls. Both babies jumped and started crying.

"The workingman is home!" Brother Vern announced loudly. "Hope somebody 'round here's got supper on the table."

Chapter 36

⟨～⟩

"He soundin' too happy to suit me," Lillian said, as the baby girls wailed from their high chairs. Lillian motioned to me to start feeding them as she patted hamburger patties into shape. "Wonder what he up to now."

I didn't respond because I was trying to get the lid off a jar of pureed carrots. Just then, Lloyd and Latisha eased quietly into the kitchen, apparently getting out of Brother Vern's line of fire.

"Anything we can help with?" Lloyd asked over the din the babies were making.

"I can feed them babies," Latisha said with an eager look at the jars and long spoons.

"Why don't you two run up to the apartment," I suggested, "and see if James wants to come down for supper? Lloyd, you and Sam can help him on the stairs if he does."

The two children ran out just as Granny Wiggins changed her mind about leaving. "On second thought . . ." she said as Brother Vern loudly greeted Sam in the living room. She shed her coat, slung it over a chair at the table, took the jar of carrots from me, and, with a quick twist of her wrist, had the lid off. "I think I better stick around," she said, "at least till we get these young'uns fed and in the bed. Miz Murdoch, you set down right here an'put something in that littl'un's mouth. I'll tend to this'un."

I did as directed and the noise level immediately went down. "I'm worried about you getting home before dark," I said, carefully aiming a loaded spoon toward an open mouth.

"Oh, don't worry about me. My ole truck been down that road

so many times, it can find its own way home. But Miss Lillian's got all these folks to cook for an' she can't do two things at once. I never yet left anybody in need, an' it sure looks like that's where you are. Just shovel it on in, Miz Murdoch—it don't need no chewin'."

Lloyd and Latisha came rushing back into the kitchen, bringing with them a gust of cold air. "James can't come down," Lloyd said. "He's not feeling good, but I'll take him a tray just in case he can eat something. He's acting pretty sick."

Mopping carrots off Julie's arm, I said, "Ask Sam, if you will, to go check on him. We might need to run to the drugstore before it closes."

It didn't come to that, however, for Sam said that James was able to force himself to eat two hamburgers, a helping of baked beans, and a salad. "But," Sam told me, "he's down in the mouth about something. I tried to find out what was wrong, but all he'd say was that he didn't feel worth shooting. Then hold his head and moan. I'll look in on him tomorrow, be sure he's all right."

Granny faked out a little grasping hand as she fed Lilly Mae. "Well," she said, "I 'bout cured his foot with Epsom salts, but I got my doubts about working on his head."

⁘⁘⁘

I won't give a detailed account of the rest of the evening. Anyone who's had a houseful of children, including infants who needed to be fed, changed, and put to bed, plus someone like James, too wobbly on his feet to come to the table, and a loud, unwanted guest at the table, every one of them hungry for supper, will pretty well know how it went.

By eight-thirty, though, the house was quiet, and Sam and I had a few minutes alone in Hazel Marie's living room. Actually, we'd had more than a few minutes alone in her kitchen washing dishes. After we'd all eaten, I insisted that Lillian go home. Latisha needed to be in bed—both she and Lloyd had school the next day—and Lillian had put in a long, full day. Granny Wiggins left at the same time, with Brother Vern walking her out—an uncommon and surprising courtesy on his part. I could hear her talking until her voice was drowned out by the racket her truck made when she cranked it.

Lloyd went upstairs to his room, which Hazel Marie had restored to its original state after Brother Vern's occupancy. And Brother Vern? Well, he was ensconced in the recliner in the family room—Sam's erstwhile office when he lived in the house—with his eyes glued to the television set.

"It behooves a preacher of the Gospel," he said with a pompous tug of his jacket, "to keep up with the shows they run just like the folks that set in the pews do. That way, a preacher gets to know what kinda vile goings-on is runnin' around spreadin' their influence in their minds. And I tell you, the worst for family watchin' is them housewife shows in all them cities across the country. They're a indication and a *indictment* of which way this nation is headed." And, with that pronouncement, he left Sam and me in the living room while he settled himself in front of the television set to gather sermon material.

"I don't know how Hazel Marie does it day after day," Sam said, leaning his head back on the sofa. "One afternoon of it is enough for me."

I patted his thigh. "It was good of you to walk Julie like you did. She did not want to be put down." I smiled, remembering that baby on Sam's shoulder as he paced up and down the hall, patting her back until she fell asleep.

"It was nice," he said, smothering a yawn, "but thirty minutes of it was long enough." His head came off the sofa at the sound of a growling motor. "I think they're home."

Hazel Marie and Mr. Pickens came through the front door, she with a glow of happiness on her face and he with a self-satisfied smile on his. So, I thought, he's charmed another member of his harem, which would probably free him up for the next one in line.

It was all I could do to be civil to him, but Hazel Marie asked one question after another about the babies so I was never put on the spot. She hurried up the stairs to the nursery to be sure they were unharmed and still breathing, while I hoped to goodness she wouldn't wake them.

Sam turned from speaking with Mr. Pickens and said, "Julia, we better be going so these folks can get to bed."

It was not too soon for me, but as I started for the hall closet to get my coat, Brother Vern—loud and expansive—abandoned the housewives and came into the living room.

"I'm here to tell you," he said, as if we'd all been waiting to hear from him, "my soup kitchen is comin' along like a house afire. Y'all ought to come see it. I had them two workers scrubbin' and moppin' and cleanin' every nook and cranny all day long. It don't look like the same place, an' you gotta come see that apartment. I tell you, when Miz Allen decides to do something, she goes whole hog. No halfway measures for her, no sirree."

"So when're you moving?" This from Mr. Pickens in a tone that would've brought the conversation to an end if it'd been addressed to anyone but Brother Vern.

"Oh, we got loads to do yet, Brother Pickens. Tables an' chairs'll be delivered tomorrow, an' the 'lectrician's comin' to hook up the sound system. Got to have a good sound system, you know. I'm tryin' to decide what I want—a handheld microphone or one of them little ones that hooks over your ear an' runs around to your mouth. Pro'bly just get both—be cheaper in the long run.

"Anyway," he went on when no one offered an opinion, "I been thinkin' I ought to have like a Gratitude Dinner for all the folks that's helped get me started. You know, to honor Miz Allen, first and foremost, but you, too, Miz Murdoch, an' you, Brother Pickens, for puttin' me up in my hour of need, an' anybody else I can think of who might like to contribute to the Lord's work." He suddenly turned to me. "I'd sure like a list of the finer people in an' around town, Miz Murdoch, soon as you can get it to me. I want to invite 'em to come see what we got goin', an' give 'em the opportunity to be sponsors, which would help me an' them both."

"So," I said, thinking to myself that he'd never get such a list from me, "you mean to have a fund-raiser."

"Oh, that's all part of it," he said knowingly. "How to raise funds is the first thing you learn whenever you strike out for the Lord. Else you wouldn't get nowhere. They ought to teach it in the seminaries, but they don't."

I wondered how he knew, since he had never darkened the door of a seminary. I knew that some churches didn't require formal training for their preachers—whoever felt a call to preach could preach, if a congregation could be found that would have them.

"Anyway," Brother Vern went on, having silenced me, "I'm thinkin' we'll be ready pretty soon, so I'll be invitin' you all over for barbecue, some good gospel music, an' a short program. You won't want to miss it."

Mr. Pickens had been listening to all this, his dark eyes never leaving Brother Vern. "I may be working," he said.

"Well, I hope not, Brother Pickens, but if you are, we'll miss you. Now that cook I hired is good, but she's a little tetchy. I'm countin' on Hazel Marie to help her out. With all her cookin' lessons, she can finally be of some use."

My top was just about to blow, but Sam quickly put his arm around me and changed the subject. "What're you calling your soup kitchen, Vern? You thought of a good name for it?"

Turning to Sam, Brother Vern said, "I'm glad you asked, Brother Sam. I been goin' back an' forth on this for days. My first thought was to call it Mary an' Martha's Place. You know, 'cause we'll be servin' up real food an' spiritual food, just like they did at their house in the Book of Luke, Chapter Ten. But I got to thinkin' that people might think it was for women only, an' that won't do."

"With a name like that," Mr. Pickens interrupted, a hard smile on his face, "you'd get more men than you wanted."

Brother Vern ignored him, something that I'd be hesitant to do. "Anyway, I've about decided on the Soup Spoon Mission, but I'm on the lookout for something better. 'Cause, see, I told Miz

Allen that we need a nice neon sign with a catchy name so the down-an'-out can see us from afar and come on in. You can't have a soup kitchen without nobody to eat in it, can you?"

No one answered, for Hazel Marie came down the stairs, her high heels exchanged for bedroom slippers. She came right up to me and threw her arms around me, something that I am usually quick enough to avoid, not being a hugging kind of person. But not this time. She hugged me and hugged me.

"Oh, Miss Julia, thank you for this wonderful day! I feel like a new woman, and it's all because of you. And the babies, you've taken such good care of them. They look like little angels, all tucked in and asleep."

I patted her shoulder and untangled myself, telling her that I was happy to do it, then looked at Sam to indicate I was ready to leave. So was he, and we soon left for home.

Almost too tired to talk as Sam drove my car toward the house, I wasn't too tired to think. And what I was thinking was how much I hoped that the night was not yet over for Hazel Marie and Mr. Pickens. And how bereft I would feel if I learned later that all my efforts to set his sights firmly on his wife had been for naught.

Chapter 37

"I hope James isn't getting sick," I said, as Sam turned onto Polk Street. "The last thing we need is a case of flu infecting everybody in the house. A cold would be about as bad."

"He didn't have any obvious symptoms when I looked in on him," Sam said, heading into the driveway. "I was going to check on him again before we left, but his lights were out. I figured it was best to let him sleep."

"Sleep is what I'm planning to do. I told Lillian to take her time coming in tomorrow. Do you know that she fried some bacon and put it in the refrigerator for their breakfast in the morning? She showed Lloyd how to unwrap the tinfoil and put it in the oven for a few minutes while those frozen biscuits that Hazel Marie buys are baking. That will be a help to Hazel Marie and may even be an example to Mr. Pickens to do more than open a box of cereal." I sniffed. "I just have no patience for a man who can't feed himself."

Sam grinned at me as he unlocked the front door. "Are you referring to Pickens or Brother Vern? Or to me?"

I smiled back, although I was almost too tired to do it. "Not you. But if the shoe fits . . ."

By this time we were in the house, and while Sam checked around, I made my way toward the stairs. Following me up, he said, "Don't be too hard on Pickens, Julia. He has his hands full."

Preparing to undress, I just nodded, not wanting to disabuse my kind husband of his good opinion of a friend. So I kept my suspicions to myself, but from what Lillian and I had witnessed, I pretty well knew just how full Mr. Pickens's hands were.

⟨∼⟩

The phone rang as I stepped into the kitchen Tuesday morning. Smiling a greeting to Lillian, I answered it on my way to the coffeepot.

"Julia," Emma Sue Ledbetter said in a rush, "I only have a minute, but this is my day to go to Hazel Marie's. Are you planning to be there?"

"Yes, I go whenever there's a demonstration to help with the babies. Why? You need me to do something?"

"Well, yes, I do. I need you to stay home." Emma Sue was nothing if not blunt. "I've already talked to Hazel Marie and she has that granny woman coming for the babies, so I'd just as soon you not be there."

"All right," I said slowly, wondering why I wasn't wanted while at the same time relishing the thought of a day at home. "May I ask why?"

"Well, you know I have to put my recipe together in between committee meetings, the first of which I'm almost late for already. So I'll have to run in, get everything out, and throw it all together. I'm not going to be able to visit. And if you're there, I know you'll want to talk and I won't have time for it."

I declare, I couldn't come up with a response to that to save my life, because *I* wasn't the one who liked to talk.

At my silence, Emma Sue hurried on. "Oh, I might as well be honest with you, Julia. I can't stand to have somebody watching me in the kitchen. I get so flustered that I mess up whatever I'm doing. I don't know how I'm going to handle having Hazel Marie standing over me watching every move I make. So you can come on if you'll keep her in the living room."

"Emma Sue," I said, drawing a deep breath, "that would defeat the whole purpose. I will stay home, but Hazel Marie has to be in the kitchen watching you. But don't be bothered by that. If you mess up, she won't know the difference."

After a few more words of encouragement in spite of my urge to cut her down to size, I was able to end the call without returning tit for tat—and felt quite virtuous for it, too.

"Sound like you need some breakfast, " Lillian said, putting a plate on the table.

"I certainly need something, or my eyes will be rolling so far back in my head they'll get stuck there." I started toward the table, then had a thought. "I'll be right back. I need to look at something."

"These eggs gonna be cold."

"I won't be but a minute." And off I hurried to retrieve the recipe that Emma Sue had given me with the promise that she would prepare it with Hazel Marie.

Returning to the kitchen, I thrust the recipe into Lillian's hands. "Look at this, Lillian. Emma Sue said she didn't want me watching her because I'd talk too much and make her mess up. Now tell me, how can she mess up when all she has to do is open half a dozen cans?"

Lillian studied the recipe, then said, "Well, I guess some people could. But this look pretty good, so I might try it myself. Now set down an' eat your eggs."

So I did, then went into our new library to finish copying the recipes into the book that I would give to Hazel Marie. I was quite pleased with the book. It had an attractive cover with plastic rings on one side that allowed the book to lie flat. I thought that would be most convenient for a cook who needed to constantly refer to the instructions.

But I didn't do more than look at it, deciding instead to read the newspaper and fiddle with the crossword puzzle first. By the time an hour or so had passed, I sighed, then spread the recipes out on the desk to begin copying, having convinced myself that I hadn't wanted to go to Hazel Marie's anyway. It was quite pleasant to have a whole day empty of chores and demands stretching out before me.

After lunch, I went back to the recipe book and began copying one of Binkie's mother's recipes. Then the thought of Mr. Pickens flashed in my mind—probably because I recalled Binkie or Coleman saying something about Mr. Pickens using a grill, assuming that he would be the one to do that kind of cooking. That's the way one thought leads to another, none of which has anything to do with what you're doing.

Mr. Pickens, I thought, and laid down my freshly sharpened pencil. *Wonder where he is and what he's doing?* As I leaned back in my chair, the wondering kept on flashing in my mind. I wondered how Hazel Marie looked this morning—was her hair still halfway styled or was it tangled all over her head? Had she had time to put on makeup? Was she in one of those sloppy running suits again? Had Mr. Pickens taken one look in the light of day and galloped off to work? Or to pick up one of those women he liked to ride around with?

I couldn't stand it. I got up and went to the kitchen. "Lillian," I said, "stop what you're doing and talk to me. I'm about to lose my mind worrying about those two."

"Who? Miz Ledbetter an' Miss Hazel Marie?" She turned from the sink and dried her hands. "They be all right without you."

"No, no. I'm not talking about them. I'm talking about Mr. Pickens and Hazel Marie. I haven't had a chance to tell you that I saw him again yesterday afternoon, and this time he was with a black-headed woman—the one, I expect, that you saw him with." I stopped as a sudden thought struck me. "Unless he's found a second brunette, and now has *three* girlfriends."

"Set down," Lillian ordered as she took two cups from a cupboard. "You gettin' upset when you don't really know what he doin'. Now listen," she went on, putting a cup of coffee before me, "I been knowin' men for a long time, an' some of 'em—none of 'em worth a lick—think they can handle two or three women at a time. But they can't, 'cause I don't care how much of a man he think he is, one or two of them women start feelin' like they bein' left out an' they don't like it. That's when trouble start boilin' up. An' another place trouble gonna start is when a man try to handle *three* women *and* a wife. Mark my words, the fur start to fly then."

"That's exactly what I'm worried about! I've only seen Hazel Marie really mad one time and, believe me, the fur was flying then. There's no telling what she'd do if she caught him with one of those women. Oh, Lillian, *what* is he doing?"

"Well," Lillian said, much too calmly, "irregardless of what I just said about high-struttin' men, I jus' don't b'lieve Mr. Pickens doin' any of that. He into something we don't know nothin' about, jus' like we don't know nothin' about them women. So, if it keep troublin' you, which, knowin' you, I 'spect it will, why don't you find out what he doin', an' when you find out it's not what you think he doin', you can put it to rest."

"That's exactly what I plan to do," I snapped, vexed that she was not being completely sympathetic to my concerns. I picked up my coffee cup, noticed it was empty, and set it back down. "How would you suggest I go about it?"

Lillian rose from the table, picked up our empty cups, and walked toward the sink, indicating that she had other things to do. "They's not much you can do," she said, "'cept keep your eyes open an' try to keep track of how many women get in his car. An' I'd be prayin' about it, too, if I was you. 'Less you want to straight out ask him what he doin'.'"

Knowing I didn't have the courage for that, I wandered back to the library, wishing I had something to do to fill the day. Leaning back in a leather wingchair, I slipped into a light nap, wakening only when I heard Lloyd come in from school. Feeling too drowsy to get up, I smiled at the thought of the little silver bell Mildred used to summon Ida Lee. How nice, I thought, if I had one to tinkle for Lillian to bring a cup of coffee. Except she'd probably take it away from me if I had one.

"Miss Julia?" Lloyd whispered from the door. "Are you asleep?"

"Not at all," I said, sitting up and trying to get my eyes open. "Come on in, Lloyd. I was just resting."

He edged into the room, then sat on the edge of a footstool. "Miss Julia?"

"Yes, honey. What is it?"

"I'm real worried about James."

I was fully awake by then, realizing how distressed the boy looked. "How sick is he? Does he need a doctor? I'll call Dr. Hargrove right away."

"No'm, don't do that. It's not that kinda sick." Lloyd sat with his back slumped over, his hands dangling between his knees. Then clasping his hands tightly together, he glanced up at me, then back down. "He just looks so pitiful and I feel so bad. He's already talked to the bank and there's nothing left. And it's . . ." He ducked his head as his voice suddenly broke, startling me because I couldn't tell if it was caused by emotion or by puberty. ". . . it's all my fault."

Chapter 38

"What? What's all your fault?" It was the best I could do because I didn't know which question to ask first. Had the bank failed? Had James spent all his money? Did James have any money to spend?

Lloyd straightened his shoulders and lifted his head. "I guess I should've known better, but I didn't, and you know how James believes anything anybody tells him, and I guess I do, too, but, Miss Julia, I promise I thought it was real. I mean, it *looked* real and the phone calls were real, and he was so happy. I wish I'd told somebody. Well, I wanted to, but they told James that he had to keep it confidential or he'd be disqualified, so I couldn't. And now it's too late."

"Lloyd," I said, "start at the beginning, honey, and tell me what happened."

"Well, you know those forms James has been sending in?"

"Oh, yes," I said with a bite of sarcasm, recalling my effort to caution James. "But he told me he'd stopped doing that."

"He did. He stopped, but that was because he got an e-mail all the way from Spain . . ."

"How could he get an e-mail? He doesn't have a computer."

"We used my address, so it came to me and I was so excited when it came that I couldn't wait to show it to him. I'm sorry for doing this, Miss Julia, but that was when I slipped out of the house and took it to him—you know, the night that something scared the fire out of us. But it came so late, because Spain is in a different time zone. Anyway, the e-mail notified him that he'd won their lottery and all he had to do was call the number they sent to confirm who he was."

"My word," I murmured, putting together a number of occurrences, chiefly the real reason for Lloyd's night flight to visit James. "Tell me this, then—how did James go about buying a lottery ticket in *Spain* of all places?"

"Well, he didn't! That's what was so great about it. The news just came out of the blue, like—well, like James said, it was like it came straight from above."

I tried not to moan aloud, but it was hard not to. "So what happened then?"

"Well, when he called the number, the man he talked to—a Mr. Stearnes—was real nice, and he didn't even speak in Spanish, which I was afraid he would do. But he told James that the taxes had to be paid and put in a separate account before the money could be sent. But when James told him that he'd had an accident and couldn't get to the bank, the man felt sorry for him and told him not to worry. All he had to do was fill out an official form stating his full name and account number and mail it in. Then they'd go ahead and take the taxes out and deposit his winnings in the same account."

"Wait à minute, Lloyd. Just how much did they say he'd won?"

"You won't believe this, Miss Julia, but it was one million, nine hundred and fifty thousand dollars, so, see, with that kind of money coming in, neither one of us thought a thing about going ahead and paying the taxes."

"Good land!" I exclaimed, doing some fast arithmetic in my head. "Where did James get the money to pay taxes on *that*?"

"Well, that's why we thought Mr. Stearnes was so nice. He said a lot of people had that problem when they won big, so not to worry about it. He said they'd match whatever James had and he wouldn't owe anything after that."

"So," I said, closing my eyes in near despair at this tale of innocence or ignorance, I couldn't decide which, "James gave him his account number."

"Yes'm, he did and mailed in the official form, and now his account's empty, and James can't pay his bills. And the worst of it all is the big prize didn't come when they said it would and Mr. Stearnes's phone is disconnected and we can't reach anybody. And I don't know what to think except I guess they were just after James's money."

I nodded agreement, knowing that I had failed by not teaching Lloyd how to avoid people who would rob him blind. Of course he would learn from this experience, but that was of little help to James.

"How much did James lose?" I asked.

"Every last cent."

"No, I mean how much in all."

"He had sixteen hundred dollars and forty-eight cents saved up, and it's all gone and his bank account is closed. That's all he had to his name, Miss Julia, and I feel so bad because I didn't see what they were doing." Lloyd rubbed his eyes and sniffed. "I wish I'd talked to you or Mr. Sam, but James was so happy and he was already planning what to do with all that money. He was going to buy Mama a pretty necklace and buy J.D. a new car and get some toys for my sisters. And a big new fishing boat for Mr. Sam and he was going to put some money away for Latisha to go to college because he knew Miss Lillian would like that. And he was going to get you a fur coat because you're always so cold, and he said, he said . . ." The words choked in his throat as he began wiping away the tears. In a strangled voice, Lloyd went on, "He was going to take me to Disney World, just me and him, and we'd go to the wax museum and ride in a glass-bottom boat and I don't know what all. But I don't care about any of that. All I care about is his life savings are all gone and I should've known better, and I kinda did. I started worrying about it after a while, but he was just so happy, I couldn't . . ."

"Lloyd," I said, putting my hand on his heaving shoulder, "listen to me, honey. You mustn't take all the responsibility on yourself. James is a grown man and you're only a boy. Both of you were too trusting and unaware that there are crooks who prey on honest people like you. They go after the elderly, too, and they've taken advantage of better-informed people than you and James. We'll report this to, well, whoever we're supposed to tell—Sam will know—and maybe they can be tracked down. But I'm afraid that James's savings are gone for good. You've had a hard lesson, but both of you will be the better for it."

"I guess," he said, wiping his face with his sleeve. "Anyway, James is going to start sending in those entry forms again, along with a donation—well, as soon as he gets a paycheck—because he thinks that gives him a better chance to win. He said he wouldn't turn up his nose at a measly ten thousand dollars now."

I really did moan then. "Has he not learned anything?"

"I don't know, but I think I ought to do something to help him because he's lost so much. I hate to tell Mama and J.D., 'cause I feel so bad about it, but do you think I could take some of my inheritance and give it to James?"

They Lord, I thought, the child could reimburse James many times over from the estate that Wesley Lloyd Springer left, but what good would that do when James was bound and determined to keep on throwing money away?

"You have a good heart, Lloyd, but your inheritance is invested for your future and can't be touched." That wasn't entirely true, but I'd just thought of something more commensurate with Lloyd's feelings of liability. "Why don't you tell James that you feel responsible for, let's say, half his loss, but only half because he has to take some responsibility, too. Tell him that you'll work and do chores and maybe contribute some from your allowance to make up your half. It'll take a long time, maybe months or a couple of years, but if he sees you adding a little here and a little there to his bank account, it might make him think twice about how he uses it."

For the first time Lloyd saw a glimmer of hope. "I can do that," he said, looking up with determination. "I can bring in firewood and cut grass next summer and babysit and help Mama around the house." Then he smiled, his tear-streaked face lighting up. "I better figure out how much I owe and how long it'll take me to get it. I may be working for James the rest of my life."

Lloyd stood up then, saying he was going to his mother's to see if she had any jobs for him. "I'll tell everybody I'm open for business," he said. "Thanks, Miss Julia. I feel a whole lot better now that I can help get James back on his feet."

I couldn't help but smile to myself, pleased first of all that I'd made the right suggestion and amused as I thought of Lloyd and Granny Wiggins both helping James get back on his feet—one with payments and one with Epsom salts.

I could hardly wait to tell Sam about the afternoon's revelations, but he hadn't yet come in. So I went to the kitchen to tell Lillian.

"Can you believe that, Lillian?" I said after telling her all the ins and outs of James's forms, donations, and lottery winnings. "You would think that he—and Lloyd, too, I admit—would know not to be taken in by something so outlandish."

"Yes'm," Lillian said, frowning, "but how you *know* it wasn't real? It coulda been."

I gave her a sharp look. "Don't tell me that you would've been taken in."

"I think it might be hard to tell. If it look real an' act real an' somebody nice say it real, then how you gonna know?"

"Lillian, you don't really think a complete stranger would just up and give you almost two million dollars, do you?"

She laughed. "If they did, they wouldn't be a stranger long." She leaned over and put a pan of cornbread in the oven. After giving a pot of beans a good stir, she said, "But it could happen. 'Member that man on TV long time ago? He went 'round handin' out a million dollars here an' a million dollars there. For all we know, he could still be at it."

"I wouldn't hold my breath waiting for him," I said. "And let me know if he knocks on your door, but with federal taxes and state taxes and health-care taxes, take it from me, Lillian, a million dollars is not what it used to be."

Chapter 39

"There's another thing I want to know," I said to Sam that evening after I'd told him of James's loss and Lloyd's determination to help rebuild his savings. When I described how the both of them had been taken in by a worldwide lottery scam, it was the first time I'd ever seen Sam's eyes roll back in his head. Since then, we'd been sitting in a dazed silence, thinking over how easily unconscionable people—not a scruple among them—could take advantage of the unsuspecting.

At my continued silence, Sam said, "What is it you want to know?"

"Just this: *Why* hasn't Brother Vern moved into that apartment he was bragging about? The whole purpose of helping him with the soup kitchen was to get him out of the house. There's no telling how much Mildred has spent on fixing that place up, and what's he doing? Showing up night after night at Hazel Marie's like he still lives there."

"Good question," Sam said, laying aside the book he was reading—one of those books on the Roman Empire he was so fond of. I'd once picked up a book about the rising and falling of same and couldn't get past the first two pages. It was full of long, involved, and convoluted sentences, plus footnotes that took up half of every page. "I'm surprised that Pickens hasn't bodily removed him. I've sensed a whole lot of tension there. Have you noticed it?"

"Oh, yes. Sometimes you could cut it with a knife, yet Brother

Vern acts as if he belongs in their house. And all the while Mr. Pickens is just smoldering. Of course Hazel Marie is so taken up with those children that she doesn't notice a thing. I sometimes think I should say something to her, but," I said somewhat primly, "it's not my place to interfere."

"Right," Sam agreed. "We'll help when we can and stand by to pick up the pieces if it comes to that."

"Of course," I went on, ignoring Sam's stand-by-and-wait suggestion, "even if I said something to her, what could she do? She'd never turn Brother Vern out and, as far as keeping Mr. Pickens happy, I've done my best by arranging cooking lessons and getting her made over. I don't know what else I can to do."

It was true that I didn't know what else I could do, but that didn't mean I wasn't giving the matter a lot of thought. There was always the possibility of simply confronting Mr. Pickens and demanding an explanation for all that consorting with strange women he was doing. But because I couldn't foresee what his reaction would be—I mean, there was no telling *what* he would do—I was leaving that as a last resort.

"Oh, by the way," Sam said, his eyes sparkling, "are you going trick-or-treating tomorrow night?"

"Tomorrow night? Is it Halloween already? I haven't bought a thing to hand out, and Poppy will be at Hazel Marie's in the morning, so that'll take up half the day. I declare, there's always so much to do. And no, Sam," I said, giving him a backhanded tap on his arm, "I'm not going trick-or-treating."

"What about Lloyd? Has he said anything about a costume? I can take him after school tomorrow if he wants to get one."

"You know," I said, frowning as I thought about it, "he hasn't said a word. He may think he's too old for that now, or maybe his mother has put something together for him."

"I doubt she's had time to think about it. You ought to say something to him, Julia. We can work up a costume if he wants to dress up."

The first thing I heard about when I got to the kitchen the next morning was Halloween. Lillian was full of it and, unbeknownst to me, had been making plans with Lloyd and Latisha. Obviously, I had been too taken up with Hazel Marie's problems to notice that life was proceeding along without my help. It seemed that Lloyd had agreed to take Latisha down to Main Street, where most of the shops would be open to hand out candy to all comers, and Latisha wanted to be first in line.

"That chile," Lillian said, "she already change her mind half a dozen times 'bout what she gonna be. First it was a princess and 'bout the time I figured out that costume, she say she gonna be a Indian, an' now all of a sudden it's a witch. I tol' her she couldn't change her mind another time, so she's goin' as a witch, 'less she want to put that tinfoil crown on her head, too."

Witch, I thought, wondering if Latisha had heard James and Lloyd talk about their night visitor. She certainly wouldn't have heard it from me.

"What about you, Lloyd?" I sat down across from him at the table, squeezed Sam's hand, and began to eat breakfast. "Have you decided on a costume?"

"No'm, I'll probably just put on last year's mask and not dress up. We're not going to really trick-or-treat anyway, just go up and down Main Street, then come home." If I wasn't mistaken, Lloyd didn't appear all that enthusiastic about Halloween. Maybe he was too old for it, or maybe having Latisha along was taking the fun out of it.

"Sooner the better," Lillian said, setting down a plate of hot toast. "That misty rain already set in for all day and Latisha gonna be so full of candy she can't walk nohow."

Sam laughed, then, looking at Lloyd, said, "I saw something the other day that would be perfect for you. You won't even have to dress up, just put it on and nobody'll recognize you. Why don't I pick it up for you today, then when you see it you can decide."

"Really? What is it?" Lloyd said, showing a little more interest.

"Well," Sam said, "it's just a bunch of hair all in one package. There's a black wig—not too long, but straggly—and thick black eyebrows that stick on and a huge black mustache. Oh, and a black eye patch. I figure your raincoat and my old fishing hat on top of that wig would make you look like a gunslinger out of the Old West."

Lloyd laughed. "That sounds easy. I'll see what the other kids are wearing first, though."

"Oh, I don't blame you," Sam agreed. "But I'll get it so you'll have it, just in case."

❦

I arrived at Hazel Marie's house just as Poppy was getting out of her car. We carried groceries through the drizzle and on into the house. Hazel Marie met us in the hall, still in her gown and robe, walking back and forth with a whiny, snuffling baby on each shoulder.

"Oh, I should've called you both," she said, her face drawn with fatigue. "I just haven't had time for anything. We've been up most of the night and . . ."

Granny Wiggins's rattly old truck drowned her out as it pulled into the driveway, but I didn't need to hear the rest of it. It was obvious that Hazel Marie was in no shape to have a cooking lesson.

"Let's just get these things to the kitchen," I said to Poppy, and led her on through the house. As we put the groceries on the counter, I went on. "We may not get much cooking done today. Those babies look sick to me."

"Me, too," Poppy said, "but I think I'll go ahead and get started. At least Hazel Marie will have supper done, even if she doesn't have a lesson."

Granny Wiggins popped through the back door and I introduced her to Poppy. "A preacher of the Gospel?" she said, squinching up her eyes at Poppy. "You're the best-lookin' one I ever seen, an' I've seen a bait of 'em. 'Specially Methodists—all of 'em men, though, an' ev'ry last one of 'em preachin' for sprinklin' an' against backslidin'."

"Well." Poppy laughed, not at all offended. "That's Methodists for you."

"Mrs. Wiggins," I said, lowering my voice, although I didn't need to because the babies were tuning up, "Poppy and I think the babies may be sick. Will you look at them?"

"Mighty right I will." And off came her coat and off she went, with me right behind her.

Granny went right up to Hazel Marie, took one of the babies from her, and put her hand on the baby's forehead. "Fever," she said. "I recognized the cryin' soon as I heard it. Let me feel the other'un." That forehead was tested, too, getting a nod from Granny. "Miz Pickens, these young'uns need a doctor. I 'spect it's nothing more'n a earache, but they's medicine that'll cure that right up. Give that other baby to Miz Murdoch an' get your clothes on. I'll go with you to the doctor's."

"I've already called him," Hazel Marie said, "but he hasn't called back."

"Typical," Granny said, shooing Hazel Marie up the stairs. "Get some clothes on. We'll go set in his office. That'll get him movin'."

Hazel Marie was back downstairs within minutes, barely put together and almost frantic. She had two heavy baby blankets, which she and Granny used to swaddle the babies against the cold rain. "Miss Julia," she said, taking the baby from me, "if J.D. calls, tell him I'll call him when we get back. He had to leave early this morning, and I couldn't reach him when I tried a little while ago. Brother Vern's still sleeping, so he won't be a problem. I hate to leave you and Poppy, but . . ."

"Don't worry about us. We'll take care of things here, but I can go with you if you need me."

"Thanks, Miss Julia," Hazel Marie said, opening the front door. Granny, with a swaddled baby held close, hurried out. "I think we can manage." Tears welled up in her eyes. "I'm so worried. They've never been sick before."

I tucked a flap of the blanket over the baby's head, patted Hazel Marie's shoulder, and told her that I was sure they'd be fine. As she scurried across the porch and out into the rain, I thanked the Lord that we were living in the age of antibiotics.

Chapter 40

◈

"I'm going to hurry with this," Poppy said when I returned to the kitchen. "I've already cooked and cut up a turkey breast, so it's just a matter of putting it together. Maybe when they get back, Hazel Marie and the babies can have a nap. She's not going to want to be fiddling around over a stove."

"You're very understanding, Poppy, but I'm sorry she won't have the benefit of your expertise." I checked the coffeepot and found it hot and full. "You have time for a cup?"

"Sure," Poppy said. "I've just put the water on for the spaghetti, so I have to wait for it to boil anyway. By the way I'm going to leave a note for Hazel Marie telling her to always put a nice pat of butter or some Wesson oil in the water when she cooks pasta. That'll keep it from boiling over."

I set two cups and saucers on the kitchen table, found the cream and sugar for Poppy, and pulled out a chair. She dried her hands and sat down as well. Poppy was a fine figure of a woman, luscious, even, with creamy skin and thick hair. She was just at that point before tipping over from full-bodied to overweight. I'd describe her as healthy-looking.

"So," she said, stirring her coffee, "how have you been doing, Miss Julia?"

"Oh, you know," I replied, wondering if I dared open myself up for some counseling, "staying busy with one thing and another. What about you?"

She looked down, a wry smile on her face. "Well, to tell the truth, I've been having a case of what-might-have-been, wondering if I've made the right choices. You see," she said, turning her cup around on the saucer, "my old boyfriend just got married, so I'm feeling a little blue. Not," she went on hurriedly, "that I want him back. It's just that I can't seem to help wondering what might have been if it had worked out."

"Perfectly understandable," I assured her, realizing that we were having a counseling session, but with the roles reversed. "I think it's normal to have some second thoughts when something like that happens. It's as if a door has closed forever."

"Yes, except I thought I'd closed that door years ago, but I guess I didn't lock it."

"You must've had a good reason for closing it."

"Oh, I did." Poppy looked up at me, then away. "He couldn't accept my going to seminary. His family was quite fundamental and the idea of a woman in the ministry was ludicrous, completely unscriptural, to them. And to him." Poppy attempted a laugh, but it came out wrong. "He quoted all kinds of Scripture at me, pointing out verse after verse that *proved* I was wrong to think I had a call to the ministry."

I knew what she was talking about because Pastor Ledbetter had made sure that his congregation realized the spiritual peril of having a female in the pulpit, in spite of what the General Assembly decreed. And, I admit, I'd pretty much agreed with him—until I met Poppy.

"Goodness," I said, "he had some powerful ammunition on his side. But if you were able to withstand that, I'd think it proves your call was a true one."

"Well," she said, smiling, "I couldn't match him verse for verse, but I had one he couldn't refute. Remember when Jesus had just risen from the dead and he told the two women who were at the tomb to go tell the disciples? Which means that the very first ones he sent with the good news were *women*. That, more than anything else, opened the way for me."

"That's a powerful testimony, Poppy, and the fact that your friend couldn't accept it just proves that he wasn't the right one for you. But the right one will come along sooner or later."

"You think?" Poppy didn't seem very sure about it. "They may all feel as he did. He said he didn't want people calling him the preacher's *wife*, of all things."

"That man had a lot of problems," I pronounced, "and you're better off without him. But, Poppy, I tell you, when I look around at some marriages, I wonder how any of them survive." I was hoping to ease into asking her professional opinion about a certain marriage that seemed headed for the rocks—without, of course, telling her which one it was—but the sound of flushing and footsteps in the house stopped me. Brother Vern was up and so was our counseling session.

"Uh-oh," I said. "That's Hazel Marie's uncle. Just overlook him, Poppy—there's no telling what he'll say."

She laughed. "I've had plenty of practice doing that. My water's about to boil away, so I'll finish up here." She went to the counter and began dumping spaghetti noodles into the pot.

"Well, well, well," Brother Vern said expansively as he stood in the doorway. "Another cook an' more cookin'. Any hope of breakfast around here?"

"I'm afraid not," I said, looking at my watch. "Since it's midmorning, the breakfast bar is closed." Then I introduced him to Poppy but neglected to tell him that she was a minister. He would have either gushed over her or insulted her, and I didn't care to find out which.

"Well, then, I guess I better get on to work." He rubbed his hands together as if preparing to pitch in. "Big day today. Yessir, a real big day. All my tables an' chairs're coming in, so maybe I better stop on my way an' pick up some breakfast. A man can't work on a empty stomach."

If that was meant to make me feel bad, it failed. "Good idea," I said. "But I'm surprised to find you still living here. I thought you told us that the apartment is all fixed up, and very nicely, too."

"Oh, it is. You wouldn't believe how nice it is. But," he said with a heaving of his shoulders, "we can't be selfish, now can we? My two workers—both of 'em slavin' away every minute of the day—didn't have a place to lay their head, so I give it up to them."

I couldn't help it. I gasped at the gall of him. "You mean, after Mrs. Allen fixed that place up for *you,* you've given it to someone else?"

He straightened himself and deigned to smile. "The Bible says, Mrs. Murdoch, that if a man asks for your coat, give him your cape, too, an' that's what I'm doin'. An' Miz Allen don't need to know about it till I'm ready to tell her. Besides I don't need that apartment, long as I got a bed here." Then, without a gracious word to Poppy or me, he said, "I got to get goin'," and left.

By that time I was beside myself, realizing that he had no intention of leaving Hazel Marie and Mr. Pickens in peace. Which meant that all my careful planning was tumbling down around me. The soup kitchen was supposed to have been the means of getting him out of their house, but now it seemed to be an excuse for him to become even more entrenched. Which meant that Mr. Pickens would stay away longer and more often, and Hazel Marie was in greater danger of seeing her marriage go up in smoke.

So, I told myself, Mildred certainly did need to know what he was doing, and I was the one to make sure she did. I could hardly wait to call her, but I had to wait for Poppy to finish her turkey tetrazzini and, even more important, wait to hear what the doctor said about the babies. After a little more desultory talk between us—Brother Vern had put a damper on our conversation—Poppy put the casserole into the refrigerator and wrote a note with heating directions.

I helped clean up the kitchen, then said, "Sit with me a while longer, Poppy, if you can. I want to wait for Hazel Marie, though I thought they'd be back by now. I'm getting a little worried, to tell the truth."

We went into the living room, where the easy chairs were,

although I kept getting up to look out the window, hoping to see them drive in.

"They probably had to get a prescription filled," Poppy said. "They may have to wait in line."

"Of course," I said. "I should've thought of that. But surely they'll be here before long." I tried to stop worrying, but too much was on my mind. Then I added something else: Mr. Pickens had not called. If he had left knowing his babies were sick and hadn't bothered to call, then what did that say about him? He was too busy? Doing what, I ask you, as if I didn't know.

When the car turned in to the drive, Poppy and I both jumped up and hurried to the door. We stood on the porch watching as Granny unbuckled one baby and Hazel Marie the other, then dashed through the drizzle to the house.

"How are they?" I asked. "What did the doctor say?"

"Bad colds and earaches, just as Granny said," Hazel Marie said as she and Granny headed upstairs with sleeping babies. "The doctor gave me prescriptions for antibiotics and something for the fever and for pain. Granny helped me dose them in the car, so I'm hoping they'll sleep for a while."

Her voice faded out as they reached the upstairs hall, but Granny's came through loud and clear. "Soon as we get them down, I want you in the bed, too. You can't look after sick babies when you're half sick yourself."

Poppy and I looked at each other, wondering whether to go or stay. Finally Poppy said, "I'll just get my things together and run on. Maybe Hazel Marie will lie down when the house is quiet."

"My thinking, too," I said, and went to the kitchen with her to gather her belongings.

In a few minutes, Granny and Hazel Marie came downstairs, with Granny still fussing because Hazel Marie hadn't taken to her bed. "I'll see to things down here. They's lots to be done, so you go on and lay down. You ought to get some rest while you can."

Hazel Marie nodded, studied the screen on her cell phone,

then said, "I will, Granny, I promise. I just need to ask Miss Julia something."

She came over to me, looking so tired and worn I wanted to hug her, even though I'm not a hugging kind of person. The dark circles under her eyes and lines on each side of her mouth made her look years older than she had the day before.

"Miss Julia, I just had a text from J.D. saying he'll be working late tonight, and Uncle Vern's handing out treats at his mission so he'll be late, too. But since it's Halloween, I wonder if you or Mr. Sam would mind coming over and answering the door for trick-or-treaters? With the babies so sick and fussy, I won't be able to do it, and James isn't feeling well so I can't ask him." She looked hopefully at me, then added, "I have plenty of candy I can put out and all you have to do is open the door and give it to them."

Before I could answer, Granny said, "I wisht I could do it, but if I'm not home them young'uns around there will toilet my house to a fare-thee-well."

"No, no, Mrs. Wiggins," I said, "there's no need for you to stay. I'll ask Sam to come—it's always good to have a man in the house on Halloween night. And he'd love to do it."

Which, of course, meant that there wouldn't be a man at my house, but I'd have Lillian, who'd be waiting for Latisha, so we would be fine. And with the rainy weather, I doubted there'd be all that many ghosts and goblins on the street anyway.

Chapter 41

After getting Poppy off, Hazel Marie dragged herself up the stairs to bed, leaving Granny and me to ourselves. I was ready to go home, but decided I should take lunch to James before leaving.

Putting on my coat, I said, "Mrs. Wiggins, there's no need for you to go out in this weather again. I'll take a couple of sandwiches to James on my way home, if you don't mind fixing something for yourself."

"Don't mind at all. I'll do it just as soon as I get some wax on this dining room table. It could stand a good polishin'. But," she went on, "you don't need to fix him anything. I took a whole mess of biscuits and country ham up to him yesterday. All he has to do is heat 'em up in the oven, an' he can do that left-handed or he can eat 'em cold."

"How thoughtful of you. I know he'd like that better than anything I could fix. I'll run up and be sure he's all right anyway. And Mrs. Wiggins," I said, "call me if the babies get sicker or if Hazel Marie needs anything."

I ran across the backyard and up the stairs to James's apartment, making as much noise as I could so I wouldn't startle him. It was Halloween, after all.

A man with defeat all over his face opened the door before I could tap on it. "Come on in, Miss Julia," James said. "I ain't feelin' much like comp'ny, but I 'preciate you droppin' by."

"I wanted to see how you were doing, James. Lloyd tells me that things haven't worked out as you hoped, and I want you to know how sorry I am."

Limping more noticeably than he had the last time I'd visited, James offered me his easy chair. Then, taking a straight chair from the table, he mournfully said, "That's real nice of you, Miss Julia, but you might as well say 'I tol' you so,' too."

"Not for the world, James." I started to add that I was sorry he'd been taken for a ride, then, thinking better of that, started to switch to being sorry that he'd lost all his savings, then switched again to being sorry he'd been so foolish—none of which was suitably sympathetic. So I settled for: "I am truly sorry for all you've been through. It might be helpful if you considered asking Mr. Pickens for a raise when you're able to go back to work."

He lifted his head. "You think I could?"

"I don't see why not. Call it extra pay for hazardous duty, maybe, or the cost of living upstairs." I had a tingle of pleasure in putting Mr. Pickens on the spot for a raise. If increasing James's salary made for more investigative work, maybe it would keep him out of parking lots.

"Lemme write that down." James got a pencil and paper, sat back down, and looked up expectantly. "Say that again, Miss Julia, so I can get it right."

So I did, then added, "And I don't mind if you tell Mr. Pickens that I suggested it." Reaching into my pocketbook for a notepad and pen, I went on. "Now, James, I know you're upset over the loss you've suffered and probably find it hard to think of anything else. But I wonder if you could see your way to sharing a recipe for the book I'm making for Hazel Marie."

"Yes, ma'am," he said, nodding, but with a lack of the enthusiasm I had expected. "I guess I can just about manage that. But I can't do no cookin'."

"Oh, I realize that. Later on you'll be able to show her how to make whatever you give me. We won't worry about a demonstration now, but, James, there has to be at least one recipe from you. The book wouldn't have the same value to her if you were left out."

He managed a weak smile at that, then seemed to think better of it. "You right, Miss Julia. If I don't put one in, she might think my cookin' not worth bein' in it."

"She would never think that, nor would I. You're an excellent cook, James, and I am so thankful that she—well, that the whole family—has you cooking for them."

He shook his head. "I ain't no good for 'em now, though, all broke up and cripplin' around. No use thinkin' 'bout no raise. I 'spect they fire me soon enough."

Lloyd had been right—James was certainly down on himself, deeply disappointed that his jackpot hadn't come through and probably scared because his savings were gone. It was up to me to encourage him and lift his spirits, so I set out to do just that.

"Fire you! I'd like to see them try. Why, James, you've been looking after Sam's house and doing his cooking for I don't know how long. Do you really think they'd fire you, knowing how much he thinks of you?"

"No'm, maybe not. But Miss Hazel Marie got that Miss Granny now, an' she cleanin' house like nobody's business, an' first thing you know, she gonna be in my kitchen, too. No'm, Miss Julia, I already give outta steam an' might as well move on, which I aim to do soon as this cask is off."

"James! You can't do that. What would we do without you? You've got to stop thinking that way and look on the bright side. You've almost recovered from your fall and Lloyd is going to help you replenish your bank account. You can't just give up."

"Might as well," he said, mournfully. "I knowed bad luck was comin' down on me soon as I saw that witch."

"What witch?"

"That witch that showed up at my door. I tol' Lloyd I thought it was something else, so he wouldn't be afraid. But I know a witch when I see a witch, an' I knowed it was a sign that bad times was comin'. I jus' hoped I'd get my jackpot before they got here. But it never come, an' here I am all stove up an' 'bout to get fired."

Well, they Lord, I thought, sprawling back in the easy chair. I never thought that I would be an omen of bad luck or evil times or anything of the like. I so wanted to tell James that he'd lost the jackpot because he'd been foolish enough to trust the wrong people and that he'd fallen down the stairs because he'd been clumsy. But I could do neither. He felt bad enough without my laying it on any thicker.

So there was nothing to do but tell him the truth, and the truth was that the witch had been neither the bearer of bad news nor the sign of worse to come. But, Lord, I hated to do it.

"James," I said, gathering my courage, "listen to me. That witch had no meaning at all. It wasn't even a witch—it was me, and I hope to goodness that I'm not an evil omen."

He lifted his eyes and stared at me. "What you mean?"

"I mean that I saw Lloyd slip out of the house on a dark and stormy night and I followed him because I was concerned for his safety. I came up those steps out yonder to see if he—and you—were all right, and he opened the door just as I got to the head of the stairs. He didn't recognize me because I'd been ravaged by the wind and we scared each other to death. So," I said, hoping I'd put his fears to rest even as I'd just given up my own dignity, "I hope that will reassure you about witches in general."

"That was you?" James was still staring at me.

"It was and, believe me, it taught me a lesson about running around in the middle of the night in a windstorm."

He leaned back in apparent relief. "Then they ain't no more bad luck comin'?"

"I wouldn't think so. Although you know that we all have our ups and downs. Nobody's immune. So you need to think more positively, and you can start by giving me a recipe so I can get this cookbook done."

"Yes, ma'am, I can do that." James had a brighter look on his face now that I'd laid his witch worries to rest. "But I don't have no recipe, jus' some d'rections, but I know Miss Hazel Marie like 'em both 'cause she told me so."

"That's just the kind I want," I said and prepared to take down directions.

"Well, both of 'em has to do with dippin', so they easy to do. Here's what you need for the first one." I wrote it down exactly as he dictated it.

James's Orange-Dipped-Rolls

"First, you take a package of plain ole brown-and-serve rolls an' 'bout a half a stick of butter, melted real good.

"Then you mix 2 tablespoons of grated orange peel with 1 cup of sugar in a little bowl, and add jus' enough orange juice to wet your sugar.

"Put your melted butter in a little bowl an' take an' dip the top of each roll in the butter, then you turn that top 'round and 'round in the sugar mixture till you get a lot on it. Then you put all the rolls on a buttered cookie sheet, so they won't stick, and bake 'em the way you us' ally do, an' that's it. Count two rolls for ev'ry one person eatin', an' that's how many it feed."

❦

"Well," I said, "that sounds easy enough."

"Yes'm, they tasty, too. An' if you got room in that book, I got another one jus' about as easy."

"I'd love to have two recipes from you. Let's have it."

That smug, pleased-with-himself smile bloomed on James's face as he crossed his legs and leaned back, readying himself to give dictation. I was fairly sure that the witch's spell had been thoroughly broken by then.

"If you ready, Miss Julia, here's what you need." Again, I copied it down.

James's Parmesan-Dipped-Chicken

"Have enough chicken breasts to go around, salt an' pepper 'em good. Then maybe 'bout one an' a half sticks of butter, melted, an' a pile of Pepperidge Farm cornbread or herb stuffin,' whichever one you want, crumbled up fine, an' some Parmesan cheese.

Then roll each piece around in the butter, then in the stuffin', so they covered all over. Then you lay 'em in a bakin' dish an' give 'em a right good sprinklin' of Parmesan cheese. You might oughta butter or spray your bakin' dish first. Then you bake 'em 'bout an hour with your oven on 350. They'll be nice an' crunchy an' real good eatin'. It'll feed however many chicken breasts you fix."

༄

"Goodness, James," I said, "that does sound good. And a nice change from fried chicken. Well," I went on, closing my pad and reaching for my pocketbook, "I should be on my way. Oh, before I forget, Lloyd and Latisha are going downtown tonight to trick-or-treat. But I expect they'll come by here, too, so be prepared if you hear little footsteps on your stairs. And just so you know, I think Latisha is going to be a witch."

"Law, that chile," James said, shaking his head. "I wisht she wouldn't do that. No tellin' what might get stirred up on a night like tonight."

"James, really now," I said reprovingly. "They're just children who'll do you no harm. And there're no such things as witches anyway."

"Uh-huh, I reckon. But if it was you that come that night it was stormin', then they was somebody else out there with you, 'cause I know what I saw an' Lloyd seen it, too."

I just shook my head and prepared to leave. You just can't talk some people out of anything once their minds are made up, and James was one of them. To his detriment, I might add.

Chapter 42

Supper was a hurried affair that Halloween evening, with Sam preparing to go to Hazel Marie's and Lloyd trying to glue on facial hair and Latisha so excited she couldn't sit still.

"I can't eat no more," she said when Lillian told her for the third time to sit down and eat her supper. "I got to save room for all that candy."

Lillian rolled her eyes, murmuring, "An' you gonna be throwin' up all night, too."

Sam pushed back from the table and helped Lloyd get his eyebrows and mustache pasted on. When he put the wig on Lloyd's head with the fishing hat on top of that, the boy looked almost like a Hollywood extra—a short one, but still.

"I need a better raincoat," Lloyd said. "Mine's yellow, so it won't work."

"Try mine," I said, and went to the pantry to get my old Burberry raincoat. It was perfect, reaching to his ankles and turning him into a Wild West gunslinger.

"Lloyd, you look real good," Latisha said, as she watched the transformation. "But I don't look like no witch I ever seen. I need something else 'sides this ole long black dress." Lillian had made her put two sweaters on under it, which helped with the fit and would keep her warm, but also turned her into an unusually chubby witch.

Then her face lit up. "I know what I can do. Great-Granny, le's undo all these pigtails so my hair'll stick out all over my head. That'll look real witchy."

"Law, chile," Lillian said, "you know how long it takes me to put your hair up like that? An' now you wanta take it all down? Well, I won't never hear the end of it, so come on over here." She did, and Latisha was correct—she was a scary sight with her un-plaited hair in stiff wavy strands.

"Now," Latisha said, as she admired herself in a mirror, "I need one of them eyebrow pencils like Miss Hazel Marie has to make me some wrinkles."

"You two come on with me," Sam said. "I'm going to Hazel Marie's. She'll make you some wrinkles and you can trick-or-treat her while you're there. Then I'll run you downtown. Julia," he went on, "you know how uneasy Hazel Marie can get, so I'll stay with her until Pickens or Brother Vern gets home. There're always some older boys who like to come around late, so somebody needs to be there."

"Good idea, Sam. If she's by herself, she won't go to the door, and no telling what kind of trick they'd pull. Lloyd," I cautioned as they began to troop out the door, "don't forget James. But, Latisha, be sure and tell him who you are. He'll be scared to death when he sees you."

She grinned with complete assurance that she would indeed give him a good scare.

Lillian and I looked at each other, relieved that the children were on their way and the house was now quiet. It was still early but already darkening outside. The rain had turned into a misty fog, making halos of the street lamps and turning the evening into a shadowy scene of ghostly possibilities.

"Le's have another piece of pie," Lillian said. "That doorbell gonna start ringin' any minute."

I had already placed a large bowl of wrapped candy on the hall table and had turned the porch light on, as well. We were ready for any trick-or-treaters who wanted to brave the night.

After a second piece of apple pie—mine with a slice of cheese and Lillian's with a scoop of ice cream—and some discussion of James's predicament, Lillian said, "I guess they down on Main

Street by now. If it wasn't so nasty outside, I'd like to go see all them dressed-up chil'ren goin' in an' out of the stores. But, tell you the truth, I'm jus' as glad to be settin' here warm an' dry."

"Me, too," I said, then, glancing at my watch, I went on, "I don't think we'll have many visitors, so what we'll do with all that candy, I don't know."

"We better hide it from Latisha," Lillian said, laughing, just as the doorbell rang.

We both went to the front door to see the costumes, most of which lacked any originality, having come out of a ready-made package from Wal-Mart or the like. Still, it was moderately entertaining to open the door to all the science-fiction and political masks and pretend to be frightened. There was a run of costumed children—with parents waiting in the shadows—for almost an hour, then it grew quiet. Lillian decided to sit with me in the living room, in case, she said, a real spook mixed in with the made-up ones. So we talked while I worked on my needlepoint and she read the paper, both of us yawning occasionally as we wondered when Lloyd and Latisha would tire of Main Street.

Looking at my watch, I wondered how long Sam would stay at Hazel Marie's. Obviously, since he was still there, Mr. Pickens hadn't come home, and that added another demerit to the Pickens account. I sighed at the thought, considered bringing up his failings to Lillian, but decided I didn't want to talk about him. So I changed the subject.

"Lillian, have you noticed how Hazel Marie has really taken to Granny Wiggins? As leery as she was at first about having her around the babies, she now seems to trust her completely."

"Yes'm, I seen that, too, an' I'm glad she fin'ly found some help. Though I notice Miss Granny don't do much cookin'. She do everything else, but she pretty much stay outta the kitchen."

"Well," I said, smiling, "we all have our likes and dislikes. So long as she's safe with the twins, I don't care. Besides, I'm hoping Hazel Marie will soon know how to cook and she should, what with all the demonstrations and my recipe book."

We both jumped when the doorbell rang, then hurried to fill the bag of a late caller. But when Lillian opened the door, Lloyd, his face free of extra hair, walked in without a word and headed straight for the staircase, my raincoat dragging along behind him.

Hauling her full Halloween bag with her, Latisha came in behind him. "Lloyd don't feel good," she announced. "He threw away his eyebrows an' mustache, but he give me his candy. See," she said, holding up the bag, "I got enough to last me awhile."

Looking toward the stairs, I said, "I'll go up and see about him. Don't leave yet, Lillian, if you don't mind."

"No'm, I got to wash them wrinkles off Latisha's face anyway. Let me know how he's feelin'."

I hurried up the stairs, went to Lloyd's closed door, and tapped softly. "Lloyd? Are you all right?"

Hearing a murmured response, I opened the door and hesitated. One lamp on the desk was on, leaving most of the room in shadows. The boy was sitting stiffly, his hands clasped between his knees, in the room's one easy chair.

"Honey, what's wrong?" I walked over to him, pulled out his desk chair, and sat beside him. "You have a stomachache? Your head hurts? Tell me, so I can give you something for it."

His shoulders slumped as he shook his head. "No'm, I'm all right. Just . . . just not feeling good."

"Maybe you caught something from the babies." I reached over and felt his forehead. "You don't feel hot. In fact, you may be chilled. Don't you want to get in bed and get warm?"

"No'm, not yet. I guess I'll just sit here for a while."

Not knowing what to do, I sat there for a while, too. Then I said, "Maybe a dose of Pepto-Bismol will help. I'll run down and get it."

As I moved toward the door, not only to get the medicine but to ask Lillian's advice, I heard Lloyd whisper, "Miss Julia?"

Turning back, I answered, "Yes? What do you need?"

"Can I ask you something?"

"Of course." Returning to the chair, I leaned toward him.

In a voice heavy with sadness and so low I could barely hear it, he asked, "Where would we live if Mama and J.D. got divorced?"

I opened my mouth to protest, then closed it to reconsider. Finally, I said, "Why, you'd live right here with Sam and me. But, Lloyd, that's so unlikely to happen that I've never even thought about it."

"I have. That's all I've been thinking about. But we couldn't live here. There's not enough room for me and Mama and my sisters. I don't know what we'd do."

"Well," I said decisively, "if it came to that, you could continue to live in Sam's house or we'd just build a bigger house for us all. Now, Lloyd, honey," I said, putting my hand on his arm, "that's the last thing you should be worrying about. So why are you? What's going on?"

I wasn't sure I wanted to hear his answer, because the fact of the matter was, I'd been worrying about a marriage breakup myself. Why else had I been harboring such enmity toward Mr. Pickens?

Lloyd sniffed and brushed his face with the back of his hand, almost breaking my heart. "I saw J.D. tonight and he . . . he was driving a lady around."

So, I thought, it's come to this—the very thing I didn't want it to come to. "Where did you see him?"

"He was crossing Main Street and we were waiting at the curb. He didn't see us, I don't think. He didn't wave or anything. Just drove by with . . . that lady."

"She could've been a client, Lloyd. Have you thought of that?"

"She didn't look like one. She was laughing real big, like she was having a good time."

I sat for a few minutes, running over in my mind what I could say to both relieve and reassure him. And me, as well.

"All right," I finally managed, "here's what we'll do. There's no need to worry yourself sick when there's very likely a simple explanation. We'll just ask him."

His head came up sharply. "Oh, no, I couldn't ask him. I don't want to know."

"Well, I do and I can." Standing, I went on, "You go on to bed, Lloyd, and leave this matter with me. I'll get to the bottom of it as soon as I can, and . . ." I stopped before I said too much. "And then we'll know that you've been worrying for nothing."

⟋⟍

Lord, I hoped that was true, but after I picked up my Burberry and casually left the room, I rushed down the stairs, anger toward Mr. Pickens almost blinding me. How could he drive around town with such impunity? Didn't he know he'd be seen? Well, he had been—by me, by Lillian, and now, worst of all, by Lloyd. And the child was sitting up there, mourning that cheating, unfaithful excuse of a husband who, I also realized, had the gall to set himself up as the boy's father.

Chapter 43

Hearing the television in the library, I reached the bottom step of the stairs and headed that way. I stopped at the door and looked in. "Lillian?"

But it was Latisha, sitting in a wingchair, eyes glued to the screen and mouth so full of chocolate she could barely speak. "She in the kitchen."

I hurried that way, calling again, "Lillian?"

"Yes'm, I'm over here," she said, closing the pantry door. "How's Lloyd feelin'? He need a doctor?"

"All he needs is for Mr. Pickens to start acting like a husband and a father. Oh, Lillian," I moaned, leaning against the counter, "Lloyd saw him tonight with one of those women. I knew, I just *knew* it would come to this."

She stopped short, her eyes wide. "Oh, Law, what was he doin' when he saw him?"

"Driving around looking for a parking lot, I guess. I don't know, Lillian. I just know my worst fears have come true, and Lloyd knows. He's sick about it, sitting up there worrying where they'll live after a divorce."

"*Divorce!* They not gettin' a divorce! Are they?"

"Not if I can help it, they're not. Can you stay awhile, Lillian? You and Latisha? I don't want to leave Lloyd by himself and there's no telling when Sam will be home. I guess," I added with a twist of my mouth, "he'll be at Hazel Marie's until Mr. Pickens decides to turn up."

"What you gonna be doin'?"

"I don't know, but this town's not that big and his car can hardly be missed. I'll check all the parking lots and just drive around until I find him."

"Then what you gonna do?"

"I don't know that, either, but *he* will most assuredly know when I get through doing it. I tell you, Lillian, it would be bad enough if Hazel Marie had seen him, but Lloyd? That child is just shattered, and I, for one, will not put up with it."

Shrugging on my raincoat and snatching up my pocketbook, I strode toward the back door. "I'll be back when I'm back."

"What I'm s'posed to tell Mr. Sam when he come home an' you not here?"

"He won't leave Hazel Marie until Mr. Pickens gets home, and it's fairly obvious that Mr. Pickens doesn't have going home in mind. Just tell him I had to go out." I opened the door and started out.

"Wait a minute," Lillian said, frowning. "You jus' be stirrin' up trouble, you don't watch out. I don't think you oughta . . ."

"I know," I said, pulling the door closed behind me, "but I'm doing it anyway."

❧

I backed the car out of the driveway, turned the wipers to intermittent, and mentally mapped the town by grids to cover all the church parking lots. Lillian had seen him in one, so it stood to reason that Mr. Pickens might be in another one. It shouldn't take long, I told myself, looking first at the Presbyterian lot across the street from my house. He surely wouldn't be so foolish as to park there, but then he'd already proven to have a fairly high level of foolishness. So I checked it.

Then I tooled through the First Baptist lot and, finding it empty, swept through the parking areas of the First United Methodist—Poppy's church. My search was going quickly enough: There was little traffic and all I had to slow me down was concern about bands of trick-or-treaters dashing across the streets.

Circling the town, going up one block and down another, I sought a black, low-slung two-seater car with a long antenna in the lots of the Lutheran church, the Assembly of God church, another Baptist church, a Seventh-Day Adventist church, an AME Zion church, a Catholic church, another Baptist church, an Episcopal church, a synagogue, and a Holy Word tabernacle. By that time, I was on the outskirts of town, convinced that not only was Mr. Pickens not parked in any of them, but also that, based on the number of its religious establishments, Abbotsville should've been the kindest, most generous, and least crime-ridden town in the country. It wasn't, but I had too much on my mind to wonder why.

The mall parking lot—where I'd first seen Mr. Pickens—was next on my mental list, so I headed there. Unfortunately, the lot was busy with trick-or-treaters going in and out, it not yet being the ten o'clock closing time. Nonetheless, I made a slow circuit, looking closely along the edges of the lot, where Mr. Pickens liked to park. Then I made another lap, thinking I might have missed him in my efforts to avoid hitting the stray bag-toting mummy or grinning Obama.

As I stopped for a family to cross in front of me, I glanced at the gas level, noting with a pang that I was almost on empty. I calmed myself by recalling that cars always have more gas than the needle indicates and, besides, I didn't want to stop at a filling station and have people wonder what I was doing out so late.

So, what next? Grocery stores, I decided, thinking that only a few would be open. That did not prove to be the case. More than one announced that it was open twenty-four hours, making me wonder when hours had changed so drastically. I could remember when groceries closed at six o'clock, and only the daring stayed open until eight.

Wal-Mart! That had a parking lot to rival the one at the mall, so I headed to the huge store that combined grocery, garden, drug, clothing, electronic, and toy stores into one.

When I turned off the highway onto the frontage road, I was doubly amazed at how busy the gigantic store was. Why did people shop—with school-age children and babies in strollers—in the middle of the night? I couldn't understand it but, with all the coming and going and stopping and waiting, it took me almost an hour to satisfy myself that Mr. Pickens was not there.

I sat for a few minutes, the car idling, waiting for traffic to clear enough for me to head back toward town. Having counted on Mr. Pickens's recent proclivity for parking lots, I couldn't think of any other obvious places for him to be. There were, of course, the fast-food drive-ins, but I doubted he'd stay long in one of those since they encouraged customers to drive up, through, and out. Then I thought of motel parking lots and wished I hadn't.

Pulling out when there was a gap in the traffic, I started home, disappointed that I hadn't been able to vent my outrage. Maybe it was for the best, though, that I be cool and collected when I faced Mr. Pickens with what he'd done to Lloyd, to say nothing of what he was doing—probably what he was in the process of doing at that very moment—to Hazel Marie.

At that thought, I determined to keep looking. He had to be *some*where. But first, I decided to check with Lillian. I'd be a laughingstock if I continued searching high and low, only to learn that Mr. Pickens was home and so was Sam. I turned in to the Burger King lot, parked, and started rummaging through my pocketbook for my cell phone. Then, with a groan, I recalled placing it in the charger on the kitchen counter and leaving it there.

Looking through the windows of the restaurant, I saw that it was crowded with tricked-out, costumed people eating hamburgers, and decided I couldn't call from there. Besides, I would have to turn off the ignition and then restart the car, and I'd heard that used more gas than letting it idle for a few minutes. I backed out and got on the street again. There were a couple of strip malls on the north edge of town that would bear looking into, so I headed that way.

Neither proved worth the time or the gas, consisting mostly of closed shops and offices—an insurance agency, a dentist, a surveyor, a pet shop, a storefront fitness center, and a computer repair shop. In between the two strips was a seafood restaurant that was doing a thriving business. I turned into that lot, almost getting hit by two SUVs, and thanking the Lord when I was able to get back onto the street unscathed.

Mr. Pickens, you scoundrel, where are you? I hated to give up and go home, letting all my righteous anger go to waste. At the thought of Lloyd, sitting pale and forlorn in his room grieving over what he'd seen, I determined to go on looking awhile longer.

Then I had a bright idea.

I was on the right side of town and I could be at Brother Vern's soup kitchen within five minutes. He was there—I assumed *still* there—handing out Halloween treats to hungry people expecting soup. I could use his phone to see if Sam had gotten home, which would, in turn, tell me if Mr. Pickens was home and not out in some parking lot I'd overlooked.

So I quickly turned onto a side street, getting a couple of horns blown at me because of it, and started toward the mission that I'd had a hand in founding. The street it was on had not looked the most prosperous in the daylight; on a wet October night it looked bedraggled and sad, with broken windows in padlocked buildings, sagging fences, peeling paint, and broken sidewalks. Only a few street lamps were on and they were far apart, and as I drove toward the mission, I wondered what in the world I was doing there. Slowing considerably—no cars were behind me—I scanned the street ahead, debating whether it was wise to get out of the car in such a place of destitution. Creeping along, I could see several blocks ahead some signs of life—meaning lighted windows and one or two people out front—in only two places. One such place was Miguel's Tacos, on the opposite side of the street more than a block ahead, and the other—the soup kitchen—was at the far end of that block on my side. A few cars, mostly old and listing to one side, were parked along the street, and shadows of slouching figures, hunched over against the rain, hurried toward the lighted windows. I noticed also a small cluster of men under a ragged awning directly across from Miguel's, a few going back and forth across the street.

The area was quiet—mine was the only car moving on the street and it was barely doing that. The neon signs advertising tacos and other eats and drinks at Miguel's place cast red and blue reflections on the cars parked in front and across the wet pavement.

Just as I eased into the next intersection, my car suddenly coughed, then lurched, and so did my heart. *Out of gas?* I couldn't be. There should've been enough to get me home, but the steering wheel turned stubborn and the gas pedal didn't respond and I was up a creek in the middle of the street. With both hands and a mighty effort, I turned the wheel toward the curb and pumped the gas pedal, and most reluctantly the car coasted off the street to a bus stop. And not only off the street but halfway up the curb, because the brakes didn't work, either.

Turning off the ignition—what use was it now?—I leaned my head against the steering wheel. Then, with a resigned sigh, I straightened up, gathered my pocketbook and umbrella, and stepped out of the car into the drizzle. There was nothing for it but to walk to the soup kitchen and throw myself on the mercy of Brother Vernon Puckett.

Chapter 44

But first I locked my car, although what good it would've done a thief in its present condition I didn't know. Then going around the car to the sidewalk, I opened my umbrella and prepared to walk the two blocks to Brother Vern's soup kitchen. It was a daunting prospect, considering what was between me and it, but I gained courage by recalling Mildred's advice about walking in a big city. Hold your purse tightly under your arm, she'd said, walk with purpose, and don't look anyone in the eye. If it worked in New York, it ought to work in Abbotsville.

As I started walking, although not quite as purposefully as Mildred had suggested, I could hear rain dripping from the bare branches of the trees that overhung the sidewalk. As I peered ahead toward the end of the block, I saw a dark figure slowly separate itself from a telephone pole and begin strolling toward me. I clamped down on my pocketbook and tightened my grip on the umbrella, keeping my eyes peeled on the ambling figure. He— and I was sure it *was* a he—didn't seem to be in a hurry, just purposeful.

Stepping on a rise in the sidewalk, I almost tripped, then, while regaining my footing, I caught a glimpse of another dark figure ambling up behind me. Oh, Lord, two of them! My first impulse was to run back to the car and lock myself in, but the one behind me was too close.

My heart pounding, I thought about screaming. I thought about running. I thought about dashing between the parked cars and running to Miguel's. I thought about dropping my pocketbook and running. I thought about *throwing* my pocketbook and running.

Scanning the street and the possibilities, my eyes happened to light on a familiar, low-slung car up ahead, snugged in among the few others parked along the street. Relief flooded my soul at the sight of the vague outline of a head and shoulders on the driver's side—Mr. Pickens, parked, but not in a lot! It had to be him—he wouldn't let anyone else drive his car.

Too scared to scream and barely able to breathe for fear I'd be grabbed before reaching his car, I kept walking, never breaking stride, even though I was almost petrified. Not wanting to give away my intentions, I stared straight ahead, letting them think that I hadn't noticed the trap I was in. If I could just get to Mr. Pickens's car before the two men met—with me in the middle—I would be safe.

It took only three of my most purposeful strides to get to the passenger door and, as I reached for the handle—almost dropping my pocketbook as I did—I heard running feet closing in on me from both directions.

Expecting an interior light to come on, which didn't, I slung open the door, jammed the open umbrella into the car, and followed it in headfirst, creating a bellow that almost broke my eardrums and a stream of ugly words like I'd never heard before. A plastic-foam coffee cup flew through the air as I crammed myself in behind the umbrella. I slammed the door and locked it, while Mr. Pickens, cursing and swearing, fought off my umbrella. Finally crushing it against the steering wheel, he swung open his door and scrambled out.

"Get back in, Mr. Pickens!" I screamed. "They're after me. Hurry. Let's go! Let's go!"

He stood in the open door, staring with unbelieving eyes at me, his shirt and pants dripping wet. "What in the . . ."

"Don't ask. I'll explain later. Now, come on—those men are after us."

"Oh, for god's sake," Mr. Pickens said as if he couldn't believe what was happening. Then he said something across the roof of the car to the two men and they began to slink away.

"Now," Mr. Pickens said through gritted teeth as he leaned in, "what are you doing here? Just tell me so I can understand. WHAT ARE YOU DOING HERE!"

"Well, it's like this," I began. "My car ran out of gas and . . . get in the car, Mr. Pickens. We can't have a decent conversation with you standing out there in the rain."

I think he took a deep breath, then another one—probably to calm himself after the fright I'd given him. Then he snatched my crumpled-up umbrella—now with a few broken ribs—jerked it out of the car, and slung it across the street. After that little display of peevishness, he took out his handkerchief and mopped up the coffee puddled on the driver's seat. He threw the sopping handkerchief onto the street, completely unmindful of a possible littering charge.

Then he crawled back in, slammed the door hard enough to rock the car, and folded his arms across the steering wheel. Leaning his head on his arms, he whispered, "Just tell me why."

"Oh, I will. But first, how did you get rid of those muggers? They were about to *accost* me, Mr. Pickens!"

He raised his head, stared out the windshield, and under his breath mumbled something about needing strength. Then, in a carefully controlled voice, he said, "They weren't muggers. They were undercover."

"Undercover! My goodness, why didn't they say so? I thought I was going to get robbed and beaten and left for dead."

He didn't respond, though I gave him plenty of time to do so. He just continued to sit there in that damp seat and stare through the windshield. I wondered what was going through his mind, but thought it best not to inquire.

"Well, anyway," I said, "like I said, I ran out of gas because I was looking for you. Mr. Pickens, I have been through every parking lot in this town looking for your car. You can't imagine what a blessing it was to find it here, right when I needed it. Ordinarily,

I wouldn't have expected it to be here—I mean, I wasn't *looking* for it here because I was going to the soup kitchen to use the phone. You can understand that, can't you?"

He glanced sideways at me, nodded, and said a little tightly, "Oh, yeah, perfectly clear. So far."

"All right. So I guess you want to know why I was looking for you."

"That would be nice."

I stared at the side of his face for a few seconds, wondering at his calm demeanor—so unlike him, but quite welcome under the circumstances.

Tapping into some of the outrage that had driven me out of my home and onto the streets on a cold, wet Halloween night, I went on the attack. "Aren't you concerned about your wife? Or your children? They could be sick and in fact they are. But as far as you know—because you're out rambling around all over the place—everything is just fine. You are a married man, Mr. Pickens, a fact that you seem to forget, and you have *responsibilities*."

Still in that deadly quiet voice, he said, "I just talked to Hazel Marie. Everything's fine."

"Well, from where I sit, everything is *not* fine." I drew in a deep breath and let him have what had been building up in me ever since that day in the mall parking lot. "You may think, Mr. Pickens, that what you do is your business and yours alone. You may think that you can do as you please, and no one will know or care. You may think that you are safe from prying eyes in a parking lot—be it church or mall—but you're in a small town now and, let me tell you, *you have been seen*. And not just you, but those women you've been driving around with and parking with have also been seen. What is the matter with you? Why are you jeopardizing what you have at home for some big-haired woman, or I should say *women*, because you've been seen with at least two and how many more there are, I'm sure I don't know. The only saving grace is that so far Hazel Marie hasn't seen you, so she doesn't know what you've been up to. But, believe me, sooner or later, someone will tell her and then where will you be? I'll tell you where you'll be, you'll be out on the street, that's where."

"She knows."

"What?" I stared at him. "She *knows*? She knows you're seeing other women? I don't believe it. She'd never put up with it."

"She knows I'm working."

"Well, *excuse* me. I've just never heard it called *working* before." I couldn't help giving the word a sarcastic twist, but that beat all I'd ever heard. "Well, I guess you've pulled the wool over her eyes. Bless her heart, she's so trusting she'd believe anything you told her. But what're you going to tell Lillian? Or me?" I paused, a catch in my throat. "Or Lloyd? We've all seen you, and working is not going to cut it."

"Lloyd?" That caught his attention, because he took his arms off the steering wheel and leaned back, staring at me.

"You shouldn't have gone through town tonight when children were all up and down the street. He saw you pass by with a laughing woman and, Mr. Pickens, I will tell you straight out, he is devastated. He thinks you're going to divorce his mother."

Mr. Pickens wiped his hand down his face, glanced out the window as if he might find an answer out there, then he turned back to me. In a defeated tone, he murmured, "This was not supposed to happen."

"Well, see, that's what does happen when you first start to deceive. You don't consider the consequences." I was ready to light into him again, but he suddenly sat up, stared intently out the windshield, opened the car door, and said, "Lock the doors and stay here."

And off he took, running up the street toward Miguel's or Brother Vern's soup kitchen, I didn't know which, leaving me with my mouth open and a lot more I wanted to say.

Chapter 45

So stunned by his sudden exit, I just sat there watching his shadowy figure race up the block, dodge between parked cars, bypass the loiterers on the sidewalk, and head for the soup kitchen. He didn't give Miguel's a glance, just plowed on toward Brother Vern's mission.

Except . . . I sat up straight to see over the parked cars, peering through the dark . . . he didn't go to Brother Vern's mission. I couldn't be sure, but he seemed to swerve off the sidewalk, then he was gone. I stared, not daring to blink, at the front door of the soup kitchen. There were lights on inside, as well as upstairs in the apartment, so I should've been able to see him go in. But I hadn't. He'd disappeared beside the building.

I knew from my earlier inspection of the building that there was an alley along the side, and I knew there was a back door for access to the Dumpster. But why would he be going to the back door? That didn't make sense. And, most important, what had he been doing, drinking coffee here in the dark, in the first place? Why would he do that, and what had he seen that was so urgent that he'd left me high and dry?

I vacillated between staying put and going to see what he was up to. My hand edged toward the door handle, then stopped. I'd get soaking wet, my poor bent and broken umbrella unusable and unavailable. And those muggers? Or rather, undercover agents— where were they? And what were they undercover for? I'd been so intent on venting my anger that I'd failed to get some basic answers.

There was only one way to get them, so I pulled on the door handle, unlatched the door, and had it snatched out of my hand. The door swung open and a sizable body crawled in on top of me. A rough, rasping voice said, "Get over! Get over and drive!"

The woman—for it was a woman and a hefty one at that—shoved and pushed as she squeezed herself in, ending up practically on my lap. I yelled, she yelled and kept on pushing. Not being able to sit on the console for long, I tumbled sideways into the driver's seat, my feet snared by the gear shift. I clawed for the door handle.

"No, you don't!" the woman screamed, pulling my shoulders around. "Crank this car and MOVE."

"Who are you? What do you want?" Trying to fight her off, I pushed her away but her fingers clamped down on my neck in a pinch so sharp that I screamed. "Stop, stop, let me out. You can have the car!"

"You're driving," she hissed right in my face, her breath reeking of onions, as her fingers clamped down tighter. "They're not looking for an old woman, so they won't stop you. Get me out of town, somewhere away from here, I don't care where."

Barely able to move, those pinching fingers biting into my skin, my eyes watering, taking note of a head of straggly hair—another of Mr. Pickens's girlfriends? She didn't look his type, but what did I know?

"Uh, miss," I said, "I think I'm a friend of a friend of yours. Mr. Pickens? J. D. Pickens? This is his car and . . ."

"I know whose car it is," she growled, breathing hard. "The low-down, lying, two-faced, under-handed . . ."

"Miscreant?" I supplied, wanting to be helpful before she pulled a plug from my neck.

The car's interior suddenly lit up, startling me and her, as four patrol cars with blue lights flickering swished swiftly and silently past like a ghostly convoy. Two of them slid to a stop in front of the soup kitchen, while the other two bounced into the alley beside it.

That did it. She gave my neck a vicious twist. I screamed and she shrieked, "Crank this car!"

I did, in wonderment that Mr. Pickens had left the key in the ignition. Of course he had expected it to be safe, locked in with me.

The car roared to life. I reached for the gear shift on the console and pulled at it, but it didn't move. I tried again and heard a grinding noise. "I can't find DRIVE," I said. "I can't find the lights, I can't find anything."

"The clutch!" she screamed.

"The what?" Oh, Lord, it had a straight-shift gear stick. No wonder Mr. Pickens wouldn't let anyone else drive it—no one could. But years before, I'd tried a straight-shift, so as my passenger reached for my neck again, I stomped on the clutch and rammed the shift stick into some kind of gear. The car shot forward and crashed into the back of the car in front. Glass tinkled onto the pavement.

The woman screamed in my face, calling me all kinds of outlandish and completely unearned—I was trying my best—names.

Stomping on the clutch again, I tried another gear, this time smashing into the car behind. A few more back-and-forth tries later, I was able to get the car out of the parking place.

We were out on the street, the car growling along in first gear because I couldn't find the next one, headed toward the soup kitchen and the brace of squad cars out front.

That woman started screaming again. "Turn on the lights, you fool! Turn around! Don't go past the cops! The other way, go the other way!"

I'd about had enough. "If you don't stop yelling in my ear," I said, "I'm going to run this car up a telephone pole. And if you pinch me again . . . well, you'll be sorry."

"Just get me out of here," she said, but she kept her hands to herself. "And shift gears! Don't you know anything?"

So I tried for the next gear but the car didn't like that one bit. *Find it or grind it,* I remembered, and I was not finding it.

"The clutch!" the woman screamed again, giving me a backhanded slap on the arm, which made me slam on the brakes. The motor died right there in the middle of the street.

"Don't you touch me," I said, as I quickly cranked the car, found first gear again, and revved the engine. "I'm doing the best I can."

Limping along in first gear, with the engine pulling hard and me searching for the light switch, I almost clipped a man running across the street from Miguel's. Dodging him, I sideswiped a pickup, then heard a chorus of yells from the loitering men watching the action at the soup kitchen. I wished they would stop me. I wished they'd call 911 and report me. I did not want to go off somewhere with this woman—no telling what she'd do.

At the thought of actually driving off into the night with this lunatic when Mr. Pickens and a whole bunch of police officers were right there in front of me, I knew what I had to do. So I did it.

It would've worked so much better if I'd been able to find third, or even second, gear to give me some speed, but that big engine growling along in first had the power of a truck. When I got abreast of the rear bumper of one of the parked cop cars, I turned the wheel, pressed the gas pedal to the floor, and sent Mr. Pickens's beloved car full on into WE PROTECT AND SERVE—and kept pressing the gas pedal. Metal squeaked and screamed as the squad car crumpled, and I kept pressing. The woman screamed bloody murder, slapping at me and trying to wrest away the steering wheel. I wanted to smack her good, but I had my hands full as I kept my foot on the gas pedal, that big engine groaning and growling as it pushed the squad car up onto the sidewalk and scraped it against Brother Vern's rented building. Flinching from the woman's slapping hands, I turned the wheel so that her side of Mr. Pickens's car scraped along the side of the squad car. She wouldn't be getting out that way.

Men—in uniform and out—poured from the door of the soup kitchen, Mr. Pickens leading the pack. I didn't wait for them. I was out of the car in a flash, tumbling out onto the pavement, unmindful of the drizzling rain and what it would do to my hair.

Screaming was all I heard—screaming and yelling and shriek-ing and some really bad words. The woman was crawling over the console, her mouth wide open and her face contorted, as she tried to follow me out.

Big hands helped me up as cops swarmed around the car and dragged out the woman, kicking and screaming and cursing. I think I was the object of her stream of profanity, but I just tuned her out. Mr. Pickens was there.

"Are you all right?" he yelled, his voice frantic with concern. "Are you hurt? Are you hurt?"

"Oh, Mr. Pickens, I've put a dent in your car, but I'll have it fixed. I didn't know what else to do—she made me do it. I wouldn't have driven it for the world, but she pinched me so hard I had to do it. I'm sorry, I'm sorry. I'll get it fixed." I looked over the scene of the accident. "And the police car, too."

Mr. Pickens took me by the shoulders and gave me a little shake. "Are you all right!"

"Why, yes, I think so. Maybe a little shaken, but, Mr. Pickens, I have to tell you, that woman is no friend of yours. You should've heard what she called you. Who is she anyway?"

"That's Trixie. She's the cook."

Trixie? She didn't look like a Trixie to me.

Pointing to the woman as an officer put her in the backseat of the undamaged squad car, Mr. Pickens said, "She'll have a few more names to call me before the night's over. She's going to jail."

"Well, no wonder she was in such a state."

Several police officers were standing around surveying the damage to their property and to Mr. Pickens's, some half grinning and others scratching their heads.

"Let's get out of the rain," Mr. Pickens said, taking my arm. "Then I want the whole story." As did I.

He walked me around the accident site and we edged in through the front door of the soup kitchen. Loud yells and crash-ing noises were coming from the apartment on the second floor, a few feminine shrieks and ugly words mixed in with them cascading down the stairs.

Mr. Pickens ignored the uproar but, as he led me into the main room, his face grew grim and tight. I'd realized by then that I might have stumbled into an official operation, but I intended to claim a familial interest in both Brother Vern and Mr. Pickens. I was, after all, almost their next of kin.

In the main room of the soup kitchen, fitted out now with tables and chairs, I saw Brother Vern seated at one of the tables, a police officer leaning over him. Open packages of tiny Hershey's candy bars, Reese's peanut butter cups, and Milky Way and Snickers bars were strewn across the table, waiting for trick-or-treaters who probably wouldn't be coming.

Brother Vern's normally florid face was so pallid it was almost gray, but when he saw me his eyes lit up. He tried to stand but the officer put a hand on his shoulder and kept him down.

"Mrs. Murdoch!" Brother Vern called. "Tell them. Tell them who I am. Tell them I don't have nothing to do with this, that I'm a minister of God and here only to minister to the needy. Oh, this is awful, jus' awful. All my good work gone right before my eyes." His voice breaking, he leaned his head on his hands in despair.

I thought he was going to cry, moving me to pity. But not a lot of it, for he had been so obnoxious to Hazel Marie.

Turning to Mr. Pickens, I asked, "What is going on? Is he in trouble?" Then flinched as something heavy fell or was thrown upstairs. Another shriek, followed by several masculine yells and the sound of thumping feet from upstairs. Mr. Pickens hadn't answered me—he was too busy running for the stairs while yelling back for me to sit down and stay there.

Those of us who were left looked up at the ceiling as something heavy fell again, then turned toward the door as the thumps and screams descended the stairs. Two officers were half-carrying, half-dragging a wild-haired, struggling, half-naked woman out the door. I stood watching in shock, my mouth open at the sight.

She was going neither gently nor quietly into the night, screaming abuse and insults specific enough to set my teeth on edge.

Brother Vern looked plaintively from the officer to me. "I don't understand," he said, plainly bewildered. "What's wrong? Why are they arresting her?"

The officer didn't respond and, heaven knew, I didn't know, so I couldn't. Nor did I know what happened next, for two more officers escorted a man in a raincoat—a Burberry, if I wasn't mistaken—down the stairs and out the door. He wasn't struggling, but he had his face half covered with the raincoat's collar. More thumps on the stairs followed as another man was quickly rushed through the door. Then Mr. Pickens and another officer led a sullen-faced woman with Texas-size blond hair past us. She was in handcuffs and didn't seem happy about it.

I was shocked. That could've been the woman I'd seen Mr. Pickens with at the mall and—of course! The first woman they'd led out, the brunette, was the one Lillian had seen. The *friends* of Mr. Pickens! And of Brother Vern? And who had been the woman forcing me to drive? Did that mean Mr. Pickens had been consorting with three of them?

I marched myself to the front door, watched as the two men and two women were put into squad cars, fully expecting Mr. Pickens to be shoved into the backseat with them. If they were involved in something illegal, he had to be up to his neck in it, too.

Instead, the officers shook his hand, got into the remaining drivable squad cars, and, making U-turns one after the other, left the premises. Mr. Pickens looked up from the sidewalk, tightened his mouth, and came toward me. His tie was crooked, a shirt button was missing, and his jacket pocket was hanging by a flap.

As he came fully into the light, I gasped and held out my hand. "Mr. Pickens, you . . ."

His hands on his hips, he addressed me coldly. "I thought I told you to stay inside."

"Oh, you did, but you've been injured. Your eye is swelling."

His hand flew to his right eye, covered it, then grimaced. "She's got a mean left. But you see what you stepped into. It could've been your eye."

He took my arm, swung me around, and marched me back into the main room. Brother Vern and the officer were still there, along with the leftover Halloween candy, which, from his quick swallow, I suspected the officer had been sampling.

"Oh, Brother Pickens," Brother Vern said, again attempting to rise and again being pushed down. "What is going on? I don't know anything—they just come bustin' in here, creatin' havoc an' not tellin' me anything an' takin' Junie an' Janie away an' all they was doin' was workin' for the Lord. Look at this place, just look at it. They did it, they cleaned it an' didn't charge me a cent. It was all done for the love of the Lord and for the love of mankind. An' I don't understand what y'all are doin' here."

He looked and sounded so pathetic that I was moved. It was a well-known fact that I didn't care for Hazel Marie's uncle and I would've been unperturbed if he'd been hustled into a squad car, too, but, clearly, he was out of whatever loop there was.

Mr. Pickens, his hands on his hips again, stood looking down at him. Well, looking as well as he could, for that eye was still swelling. Then he shook his head, gave a half-laugh, and said, "Yeah, Puckett, they were working for the love of mankind, all right. They had a prostitution ring right above your head. I don't wonder they worked for nothing during the day—they were making plenty at night."

Brother Vern's mouth gaped open. "Pros . . . no, oh no, that's not possible. Why, Brother Pickens, I gave them my bed, the one Mrs. Allen bought for me. I gave it up for them, so they'd have a place to lay their head."

"They laid more than that," Mr. Pickens said grimly. "Now, look, this all has to be straightened out, so Officer Winfield here will take you to the station and . . ."

"The *station*! But I didn't have anything to do with it. I don't know anything."

"There'll be questions," Mr. Pickens said with little sympathy. "It's your place and you're responsible."

"Oh, Lord," Brother Vern moaned. "My witness, my blessed witness will be ruined, tarnished forever. I don't know anything, I didn't know what they were doing, I just thanked the Lord for sending them to me. They worked hard, they did all this." He swept his arm around the room. "Every bit of it." He buried his face in his hands. "I can't believe it."

I could hardly believe it, either. Mildred Allen would have the shock of her life to learn that she'd sponsored Abbotsville's very own prostitution ring—and had decorated the bedroom for it, too.

Chapter 46

As Officer Winfield escorted Brother Vern out to the last squad car, Mr. Pickens turned to me. I almost smiled at his warped face, but decided against it. He wasn't in the mood.

"Why is it," he asked fairly calmly, but he gathered steam as he went, "that you stir up trouble wherever you go? You could've gotten hurt, you could've given it all away. The cops have been tracking those women all over town for weeks. You could've created a flat-out mess, and all because you can't stay out of trouble."

"I was looking for you," I said, determined to stand up to him. "I was looking for you to keep *you* out of trouble. To warn you about being seen with those women and to get you to turn your attention to your wife before she found out. And, while we're on the subject, just what were you doing with those women in the first place?" Let him see how it felt to be on the defensive end.

"I wasn't doing anything with them!" He yelled it so loudly I cringed. "I was working with the cops to find out who was running them. I was pumping them for information! And only somebody without a lick of trust in me would think any different. Right?" He leaned down in my face. "*Right?* The only thought in your head was that I was fooling around on Hazel Marie. Didn't give me the benefit of the doubt *at all*. Well, I hope you've learned your lesson."

"Oh, I have," I assured him, then hurried to clarify matters. "But you have to admit I had reason for being suspicious, and you have to admit that my concern was for your family—for Hazel Marie and Lloyd. Well, and your little girls, too. And for you as well, Mr. Pickens. But, really, what would you expect me to think when you were constantly seen in the company of strange women in parking lots all over town?"

He wiped his hand down his face, wincing when he touched his eye, He started to say something, but I got in first.

"And another thing," I went on. "You are completely unaware of what's going on with Hazel Marie. What with taking care of two babies, doing without James and having to nurse him, cooking and cleaning, *and* putting up with that uncle of hers who ought to be forcibly removed from your house, she is at the end of her rope. But what do you do? You go to work. You leave early and you come home late. And furthermore . . ."

He held up his hand. "Stop right there. I am not unaware of my own wife and what she's going through. For your information, I was trying to protect her."

"Hah!" I said, tossing my hair, wet ends flapping in my face. "Not when I saw you."

He rolled his eyes; at least he rolled the one I could see. "Listen to me. Just this once, listen to me. The cops thought Brother Vern brought the two women to town."

"Two? I counted three. What about Trixie, the one who almost pinched a plug out of my neck?" My hand rubbed the still-stinging place. "And I'll tell you, Mr. Pickens, from the little I saw of her in that dark car, she wasn't your usual type."

His good eye almost rolled out of its socket. "She came in later, and Puckett hired her to cook. But the three of them were in it together—either they'd been sent here or Puckett brought them here. So don't worry about her. She'll be charged with the other two. Plus charged with car theft, kidnapping, and assault and battery." He peered at my neck. "Better take a picture of that bruise. It's evidence."

I nodded, always willing to aid the court system. "You know I don't particularly like Vernon Puckett, but I can't believe he'd be involved in such debauchery as . . . what you said."

Mr. Pickens grimaced. "The cops thought this whole soup

kitchen idea was a cover for a prostitution ring he was running. I had to do some fast talking and arm twisting to get them to hold off until we could be sure. He's been under observation ever since he got to town, and I have been trying to get information from what's-their-names . . ."

"Janie and Junie."

"Right. Doing all that for the purpose of clearing Vernon Puckett—if he was clearable." He leaned over me as I leaned back. "For Hazel Marie's sake, so she wouldn't be embarrassed, humiliated, and hurt if he was involved."

I let that soak in for a minute. "Oh. Well, was he?"

"Was he what?"

"Involved."

"There's nothing to indicate he was." He turned and took a couple of steps. "The ladies came up from Florida, part of a larger ring that's targeting small towns, but so far we've found no connection to him before they showed up here. But I'll tell you this." He whirled and stepped back toward me. "The cops were ready to arrest 'em all, Brother Vern included, and play it up big all over the state. It took everything I had to talk 'em into waiting, into putting them under observation and giving me a chance to get information from the ladies, which," he suddenly bellowed, "WAS WHAT I WAS DOING IN THOSE PARKING LOTS!"

I flinched, but with a mighty effort he regained control and went on. "We wanted to be sure of who was doing what. And we got a couple of johns—'customers' to you—tonight as well, one big one, in fact, although I was hoping for more."

"Who?"

"Who what?"

"Who was the big one?"

He gave me a tight grin. "One of our commissioners. We knew he'd been visiting and, tonight, I saw him come in again. Caught him red-handed, you might say. Told us he was doing a survey on nonprofits in the county—in his underdrawers."

I could've done without the description, which put an unsavory image in my mind, but I let it go and instead asked, "And this has been going on ever since Brother Vern got here?"

"Janie and Junie had been here awhile, but Trixie came in on a Greyhound about the time Puckett rented the place. As far as we can determine, he met her at the bus station, where he was handing out flyers. But that put him under suspicion right then, because the cops had advance notice about all of them. I think, though, that Puckett's pretty much in the clear now. But let me tell you, there's been a steady stream in and out of here every night since he gave the ladies his bed."

"My goodness, *every* night? And they worked every day cleaning up this place? They must be healthy young women."

Mr. Pickens stared one-eyed at me, then he started laughing. It relieved me to see him so lighthearted, although I remained unamused. "You should go to the emergency room and have that eye looked at," I suggested. "I'll drive you in your car, if we can untangle it. Mine's out of gas."

He looked up at the sound of heavy motors outside, then started toward the door. "That'll be the wrecker. If it's drivable, I'll be the one doing it. Let's go."

"Wait. We should lock up first."

He looked around as if he'd just noticed where he was. "Okay, somebody might steal that candy. I sure haven't smelled any soup cooking."

Come to think of it, neither had I. The cook had been too busy wringing my neck.

❧

Announcing that he could drive better with one eye than I could with two, Mr. Pickens turned the car toward town. I was just relieved that anyone at all could drive it. We'd watched, along with the unhappy police chief, who was probably thinking of his budget, as the wrecker disentangled it from the city car.

I must say that even though Mr. Pickens's car had several

dents and dings, as well as a crushed grill and bumper, it still ran reasonably well, in spite of the strange knocks under the hood and the fact that the passenger door wouldn't open. He had examined it inside and out, opening the hood and crawling underneath, looking for leaks and other signs of damage. We were driving with one headlight, just to get it home.

Mr. Pickens didn't stop at the emergency room and he didn't stop at my house. He pulled into his own driveway, saying, "I've got a gas can in the garage. I'll fill it and take you back for your car."

"You're tired and injured, so let's put it off till tomorrow. It should be all right where it is."

"If you don't mind missing a few hubcaps and a couple of tires, it'll be fine."

"Oh, well, in that case . . ."

As we got out of the car, he said, "I'll let Hazel Marie know what we're doing, but don't tell her anything about tonight. After I get you on your way, I'll go to the police station for Puckett."

"And bring him here?"

"Nope." Mr. Pickens stopped at the porch steps, searching his key ring for the door key. "He's spent his last night here."

"Hearing that makes everything I've been through worth all the time and effort it took."

"Oh?" With a quizzical look aimed at me, Mr. Pickens cocked his head to one side. "What all have you done besides spy on me, interfere in an official investigation, ruin my car, and cost the town several thousand dollars?"

"Well," I said defensively, "all that's different. You don't know the effort I've put in, what with engaging Granny Wiggins and supervising cooking demonstrations and getting Hazel Marie made over and babysitting and collecting recipes and untangling James from a Spanish lottery he thought he'd won but hadn't— and, by the way, he's going to ask you for a raise—and comforting Lloyd when we both thought you were looking for greener pastures."

Before he could respond and as I saw in the glow from the porch lights that he'd raised his eyes heavenward, I went on, "But I acknowledge that I owe you a deep and abject apology, Mr. Pickens. You were acting with the best of intentions, protecting your wife, even as she was trying to learn to cook for you." I frowned. "I think I read a story about the same sort of thing sometime or another. But, never mind that—I do apologize for distrusting you and for interfering in your stalwart work and for hurting your car. You must, however, admit that if it hadn't been for me, that cook would've gotten away. I'm just sorry that stopping her caused so much damage to you and the city."

He stood looking at me for so long that I began to get fidgety. Finally he spread his hands and said, "What else can I do? Apology accepted. Now," he went on as he started up the steps to the porch, "not a word to Hazel Marie. All I want her to know is that Puckett is pulling up stakes on his own. Sponsors haven't been forthcoming and he's discovered several other nonprofits that are in competition with him—whatever she wants to think. It's going to be Puckett's idea to head out to look for greener pastures. Okay?"

"Absolutely," I agreed, then stopped on the bottom step with a sudden insight. "Why, Mr. Pickens, I've just realized that both of us had the same goal in mind—getting rid of Brother Vern. We'd have been better off if we'd worked together, don't you think?"

"Yeah, well, I'll remember that next time," he said.

Ignoring the wry twist he gave to his words, I asked, "And Lloyd? What're you going to tell him?"

"I'll talk to Lloyd tomorrow." He stopped on the top step and looked at his watch. "Almost today. I'll tell him a little more than I want Hazel Marie to know, because he'll understand." He paused as if deciding whether to say more, then he decided. "I've been meaning to talk to him for a while anyway. In fact, he'll probably say something to you about it, so I'll go ahead and tell you. If he's agreeable, I'm going to adopt him."

"Why, Mr. Pickens!" I exclaimed, surprised and delighted, but before I could say more, Sam opened the front door.

"More trick-or-treaters?" he called. "Good thing you got here—James and I are about to eat all the candy."

James came limping up behind him, grinning. "We had too good a supper to be eatin' much candy. Miss Hazel Marie, she cooked us up a feast, an' didn't burn anything. Come on in—we glad It's you an' not no witches or goblins."

Mr. Pickens walked in, asking, "Hazel Marie in bed?"

"Just went up," Sam said. "The babies are better and they're sleeping."

Mr. Pickens started up the stairs. "Sam, I didn't expect you to be here, but since you are, I need help with a little errand. I'll be back in a minute."

I stood by Sam and leaned my damp head on his chest. James took one look and went back to the television. "Oh, Sam, what a night." A lot of it poured out then—about running out of gas and about Trixie and about changing gears and about Brother Vern on his way out—all in no particular order, but he was accustomed to that. He kept patting my back and saying, "And I thought you were home all this time." Sort of in wonder or maybe disbelief. I had a little of both myself.

"Did Hazel Marie really cook supper?"

"She really did," he said. "She put turkey tetrazzini on the table and it was as good as anything Lillian could've fixed."

It had been a long day, but I seemed to recall that Pastor Poppy had left a turkey tetrazzini casserole in the refrigerator that morning. I smiled and didn't say anything. Hazel Marie had let Sam and James think whatever they wanted, just as I'd been known to do on occasion.

"Sam," I whispered, in case Mr. Pickens didn't want it known far and wide, "do you know what Mr. Pickens has in mind?"

"About Lloyd?"

I nodded against his chest. "What do you think about it?"

"I think it's the best thing that could happen," he said. "What about you?"

I thought about it for a minute, trying out my boy as Lloyd

Pickens. It was a stretch, though not all that far from Lloyd Puckett, so I could get used to it. "I think," I said, looking up at the face I loved, "that all is right with the world. At least for right now, right this minute, right at this moment in time, which is all we can count on anyway."

Lillian's Extras

꧁꧂

So the next morning I was back at it, determined to finish the recipe book, present it to Hazel Marie, and be done with it. With Brother Vernon Puckett soon to be out of the picture and Mr. Pickens safely within the fold—although Hazel Marie had never known my fear of his leaving it—and James the poorer but able to limp around, she should be able to get her house and herself in order. With the recipe book accomplished, I could turn my attention elsewhere.

But before turning anywhere, I had to add Lillian's recipes and—wouldn't you know it, because here she'd come with them—LuAnne's Helpful Household Hints, which I would have to add as well.

꧁꧂

As soon as I approached Lillian with my pad and pen and a glint in my eye, she put her hands on her hips and said, "I was 'bout to think you give up on me."

I smiled. "You couldn't possibly think that. I knew if I gave you a chance, you'd fill up an entire recipe book by yourself, so I had to let the others get theirs in first."

She liked that, a contented look settling on her face. As she brought the coffeepot to the kitchen table, I arranged cups and saucers and we sat down to fill up Hazel Marie's book with recipes that would complete a meal. I had earlier decided that I wouldn't push her to contribute a main dish recipe because I'd seen her fix too many chickens, fried, baked, and stewed, to say nothing of roasts, both pork and beef, and knew she didn't use recipes for them. In fact, she rarely used any recipes at all, but I also knew she occasionally consulted a loose-leaf notebook that she kept on a shelf on the pantry. It was aptly described as loose-leaf, for loose pages, index cards, and magazine clippings were stuffed into it.

"Now, Lillian," I said, "what I want from you are recipes that Hazel Marie can use to complete a meal. I don't care what they are—desserts, appetizers, side dishes—whatever you think she'd like and would be able to make."

"Well, I might have to help her with some of these, but I know what she like and that's what I'm gonna give her."

And did she ever. I copied recipe after recipe, all while Lillian entertained me with recollections of when she'd made each one, the guests we'd had for dinner the evening she'd served it, and which ones were favorites of Hazel Marie or Mr. Pickens.

"These here now," she said, pushing over several sheets of paper, "they mostly for appetizers an' odds 'n' ends. Mr. Pickens, he can eat a bait of toasted pecans, so she better do two batches of 'em when she start to do one."

Toasted Pecans

½ cup butter or margarine, melted
3 cups pecan halves
Salt, to taste

Preheat the oven to 275°F. In a bowl, pour the butter over the pecans, stirring to coat well. Arrange the pecans in a single layer on a baking sheet and sprinkle with salt. Bake for about 1 hour, stirring occasionally. Store in an airtight container.

Makes 3 cups.

Shrimp Cocktail Sauce

To ¾ cup of catsup, add 1½ tablespoons of lemon juice, 1 tablespoon of Worcestershire sauce, 1 tablespoon of horseradish, a few drops of Tabasco, and ½ teaspoon of salt. Stir well to combine. Chill thoroughly.

Gazpacho

½ cup diced celery
½ cup diced green pepper
½ cup diced onion
½ cup thinly sliced (or diced) cucumber
1 cup diced fresh tomatoes
10¾-ounce can tomato soup, undiluted
10¾ ounces water
1½ cups vegetable juice cocktail
1 tablespoon red wine vinegar
1 tablespoon commercial Italian dressing
Garlic salt, to taste
¼ teaspoon salt
⅛ teaspoon pepper
4 dashes hot sauce
Dash of Worcestershire sauce

Combine all the ingredients in a large bowl. Cover and refrigerate. Stir gently and serve in chilled bowls or mugs.

Makes 6 to 8 servings.

(Hazel Marie, Lillian says to go to a produce stand for the freshest vegetables in the summer. She also says that you need your vitamins and you can get them better with this recipe than with a pill.)

Lime-Ginger Ale Punch

Mix a 1-liter bottle of ginger ale with two 6-ounce cans of frozen limeade, undiluted. Stir well, pour over ice.

Serves 4.

Olive-Cheese Puffs

You can prepare this up to a week ahead, if desired.

Blend 1 cup of grated sharp Cheddar cheese with 3 tablespoons of soft butter or margarine. Stir in ½ cup of all-purpose flour, ¼ teaspoon of salt, and ½ teaspoon of paprika. Mix well.

Wrap 1 teaspoon of the cheese dough around each of 24 stuffed olives, completely covering the olive. Freezer-wrap, then freeze.

Makes 24 appetizers.

To serve:

Preheat the oven to 400°F. Unwrap the desired number of frozen puffs (do not thaw) and arrange them, without touching, on an ungreased cookie sheet. Bake for 10 to 15 minutes, or until golden. Serve warm.

(Lillian says that this is another recipe you should make two batches of, especially if you've invited Coleman.)

Now for a couple of congealed salads, which means you should make them ahead of time. If you wait too late in the day, you'll have to eat them with a spoon.

Good Salad

One 20-ounce can crushed pineapple and juice
Two 3-ounce packages cherry Jell-O
2 bananas, diced
Two 10-ounce packages thawed and sweetened raspberries
   and juice
2 cups sour cream

Add enough water to the pineapple mixture to make 3 cups of liquid. Heat the liquid and dissolve the Jell-O in it. Cool till syrupy. Add the rest of the ingredients except the sour cream.

Pour half of the mixture into a ring mold and let set. Spread the sour cream on top and spoon the rest of the Jell-O mixture over it.

You may use strawberry Jell-O and frozen strawberries instead of cherry Jell-O and raspberries.

Serves 6.

Christmas Cranberry Salad

3-ounce package cherry Jell-O
1 cup hot water
¾ cup sugar
1 tablespoon lemon juice
1 tablespoon plain gelatin dissolved in 1 cup pineapple juice,
    then melted over hot water
1 cup ground raw cranberries
1 orange and rind, ground fine
1 cup crushed pineapple, drained
1 cup chopped celery
½ cup chopped pecans

Dissolve the Jell-O in the hot water, then add the sugar, lemon juice, and pineapple juice–gelatin mixture, and stir until blended. Chill until partially set, then add the remaining ingredients and pour into a ring mold. To serve, unmold on lettuce leaves. Fill the ring with a small bowl of mayonnaise mixed with 1 or 2 tablespoons of orange juice for garnish.

Serves 8.

(Lillian says to tell you that both the above recipes make pretty Christmas salads, but I expect you already know that because she serves one or the other every year.)

Cottage Cheese Salad

3-ounce package lime Jell-O
1 envelope unflavored gelatin
½ cup hot water
½ cup chopped pecans
2 cups cottage cheese
½ cup mayonnaise
½ cup half-and-half
3-ounce bottle pimento-stuffed green olives, sliced

Dissolve the Jell-O and gelatin in the hot water, then stir in the rest of the ingredients. Pour into a ring mold and refrigerate until set.

Serves 4.

Pepperoni Quiche

Preheat the oven to 325°F. Sprinkle into a 9-inch unbaked pie shell:

¾ cup shredded Swiss cheese
¾ cup shredded mozzarella cheese
½ cup chopped pepperoni
1 tablespoon chopped green onion

In a bowl, mix together the following:

3 eggs, beaten
1 cup half-and-half
½ teaspoon salt
¼ teaspoon oregano
Parsley

Pour into the pie shell. Bake for about 45 minutes. Let stand 10 minutes before cutting.

Serves 6.

(Hazel Marie, this is good for a ladies' luncheon, but don't tell anybody what's in it–they may think it sounds too much like pizza.)

Salmon Croquettes

14¾-ounce can salmon, drained and picked over
1 egg, beaten
Handful crushed cornflakes
1 teaspoon grated onion
Cornmeal for coating

Mix together all the ingredients except the cornmeal. Form finger rolls and coat with the cornmeal. Fry quickly in hot oil.

(Lillian serves creamed corn, lima beans, and sliced tomatoes with this. It's one of my favorite family meals.)

Serves 4 to 6.

These next three recipes are for side dishes that go especially well with beef—steak or roast. They make tasty alternatives to fried, scalloped, or baked potatoes, although there's nothing wrong with potatoes any way you want to serve them. Lillian says that it's a marvel to her that women seem to prefer the rice casserole, while men rave over the cheese pudding and the company grits. Maybe it's the cheese that does it.)

Rice Casserole

½ stick margarine
10¾-ounce can beef consomme
10¾ ounces water
4-ounce can chopped mushrooms
1 cup white rice (not minute rice)
Dash of salt

Preheat the oven to 350°F. Cut up the margarine in the bottom of a casserole. Add the rest of the ingredients. Bake with the top on the casserole (or fasten foil tightly over the top) at least 1 hour.

Serves 6.

Company Grits

2 cups cooked grits
5-ounce can evaporated milk
Salt and pepper, to taste
2 tablespoons butter
4 eggs, beaten
½ pound sharp Cheddar cheese, grated

Preheat the oven to 350°F. Add all the ingredients to the cooked grits. Pour into a buttered baking dish. Bake until high and brown, about 30 minutes. Serve at once.

Serves 6.

(You've probably noticed that Lillian makes it a habit to serve Company Grits whenever we have a visitor from the North.)

Cheese Pudding

Butter, softened
10 slices loaf bread
½ pound sharp cheese, grated
2 cups milk
1 teaspoon salt
3 eggs, beaten

Butter one side of each slice of bread, then cut into cubes and put a layer into a casserole, lining the sides of the casserole. Then begin alternating grated cheese and more bread cubes until the dish is full, ending with cheese.

Mix together the rest of the ingredients and pour it over the bread and cheese. Let stand for several hours. Bake at 275°F for about 45 minutes, until high and brown. Wonderful with beef.

Serves 6.

Cornbread Dressing

Sauté 2 cups of finely chopped celery and 1 small finely chopped onion in ½ cup of butter until tender.
5 cups cornbread, crumbled (can make early and freeze)
2 cups herb-seasoned stuffing mix
2 teaspoons rubbed sage
½ teaspoon poultry seasoning
Salt and pepper, to taste
3 eggs, beaten
14½-ounce can ready-to-serve chicken broth

Preheat the oven to 350°F. Combine the cornbread, stuffing mix, sage, poultry seasoning, and salt and pepper in a large bowl. Add the celery mixture, eggs, and chicken broth. Stir until moist. Pour into a 13 × 9 × 2-inch baking dish. Bake for about 30 minutes.

(Lillian says that this looks complicated but it's not. She says you can cut down on preparation time, especially on a busy holiday, by chopping up your onions and celery the day before and storing them in Ziploc bags in the refrigerator till you're ready for them the next morning. And you really should make your cornbread about a week ahead of time and freeze it. That way, the dressing can be put together and ready for the oven in just a few minutes.)

These next four recipes are for vegetable casseroles. As you know, every meal (except breakfast) should have at least two vegetables, the fresher the better. If you ever want to do plain vegetables, like green beans, or collard, turnip, or mustard greens, plan to spend all day on them. Once you've shelled, snapped, picked over, and washed them, then run to the store for a streak-of-lean and let them cook for several hours, you'll probably decide to open cans the next time.

Sauce for Broccoli

10¾-ounce can cream of chicken soup
½ cup mayonnaise
Juice of ½ lemon
½ teaspoon curry powder

Mix all the ingredients together and stir well. No need to heat—
just pour over hot broccoli (fresh or frozen) and serve.

Makes about 3 cups.

Squash Casserole

1 stick margarine
8 ounce package Pepperldge Farm cornbread stuffing
2 pounds yellow squash, cooked, drained, and mashed
10 ¾-ounce can cream of celery soup
1 cup sour cream
2-ounce jar chopped pimento
5-ounce water chestnuts, drained and chopped fine
2 small onions, chopped

Preheat the oven to 350°F. Melt the margarine and, in a bowl, pour it over the stuffing. Line the bottom and sides of a 9 × 11-inch baking dish with half the stuffing.

Mix the remaining ingredients together and pour into the lined dish. Sprinkle the remaining stuffing on top. Bake for 30 minutes.

Serves 6 to 8.

Broccoli Casserole

Three 10-ounce packages frozen chopped broccoli, cooked
  and drained
½ cup mayonnaise
10¾-ounce can cream of mushroom soup
1 medium onion, chopped
1 egg, slightly beaten
Salt and pepper, to taste
1 cup Cheddar cheese, grated cracker crumbs for top

Preheat the oven to 350°F. Mix all the ingredients, except the
Cheddar cheese and cracker crumbs, and pour into a casserole.
Sprinkle the top with the grated Cheddar cheese and cracker
crumbs. Dot with butter. Bake for 35 to 45 minutes.

Serves 8.

Savory Succotash

One 16-ounce can French-style green beans, drained
16-ounce can whole kernel corn, drained
½ cup mayonnaise
½ cup shredded sharp Cheddar cheese
½ cup chopped green pepper
⅓ cup chopped celery
2 tablespoons chopped onion
1 cup soft bread crumbs
1 tablespoon butter, melted

Preheat the oven to 350°F. Combine all the above ingredients except the bread crumbs and butter. Place in a baking dish.

Combine the bread crumbs and the butter and sprinkle over the top. Bake for 30 minutes or until the crumbs are toasted.

Serves 6.

(Hazel Marie, I tried to get specific amounts for the following recipes, but Lillian said to just put in what looks right. Good luck with that.)

Here is a neat little trick that Lillian says she wouldn't recommend if you're cooking for a crowd. But for just one or two, you can take a sheet of tinfoil, put diced yellow summer squash on it, add a little cut-up onion, salt and pepper, and butter. Fold the tinfoil over it all and put it in the oven at 350°F until the squash is soft.

Do the same with potatoes, peeled and diced, instead of squash. And furthermore, Lillian says you can bake apples the same way, although you leave out the salt and pepper. Instead, you add a good bit of sugar and be generous with the butter, especially if you're using Granny Smith apples.

Lillian says she has so many dessert recipes, both in books and in her head, that if you want to try anything other than the ones here, just let her know. She recommends that you find (by trying several different ones) your favorite recipe for old stand-bys like apple pie and pecan pie. That way, she says, after you've made them half a dozen times, you can whip up either one blindfolded. I think I'd just keep the recipes close to hand.

My Dream Pie

Stir together:

14½-ounce can sour red cherries with juice

20-ounce can crushed pineapple with juice

1¼ cups sugar and 2 teaspoons all-purpose flour (combine before adding to fruit)

Mix the above and in a pot and bring to a boil. Remove from the heat and add two 3-ounce packages of orange Jell-O. Stir until dissolved and let cool at room temperature.

Add 1 cup of chopped pecans and 4 sliced bananas.

Pour into a baked 9-inch pie shell. Chill 2 to 3 hours.

Serve with whipped cream on top.

Serves 6 to 8.

Pineapple Upside-Down Cake

3 tablespoons butter or margarine
½ cup brown sugar, firmly packed
4 canned pineapple slices
At least 5 Maraschino cherries for garnish

Preheat the oven to 350°F. In a 9-inch heavy skillet, melt the butter with the brown sugar. Cool slightly and arrange the pineapple slices on the sugar mixture and garnish with the cherries.

Prepare the following:
⅓ cup butter
⅔ cup sugar
1 egg, beaten
1½ cups sifted cake flour
1½ teaspoons baking powder
⅛ teaspoon salt
½ cup milk
½ teaspoon vanilla

Cream the butter and sugar until light. Add the egg and mix well. Sift the flour, baking powder, and salt together into a separate bowl and add alternately with the milk to the butter mixture, mixing well after each addition. Add the vanilla. Pour this over the pineapple and cherry mixture.

Bake the cake 50 minutes. Turn the skillet upside down to turn out the cake. Serve warm.

Serves 6.

(Hazel Marie, the above recipe for Pineapple Upside-Down Cake is a very old one—you can tell by the instruction to sift the flour. Lillian says you don't have to do that now because flour is finer than it used to be. Anyway, she says her granny got the recipe from a lady she used to cook for in Georgia, and that lady got it from another lady, who saved it the time that Atlanta went up in flames. I'm not sure I believe all that, because in the case of a fire, a recipe would be the last thing I'd have on my mind.)

Best Chocolate Cake

Cake Batter

1 stick butter, softened
1 cup sugar
4 eggs
1 teaspoon vanilla
12-ounce can chocolate syrup
1 cup self-rising flour

Preheat the oven to 350°F. Cream the butter and sugar together in the bowl of an electric mixer (you may use a hand mixer). Add the eggs one at a time, mixing after each. Add the vanilla. Stir in the chocolate syrup and flour alternately. Beat only until the ingredients are just blended. Pour the batter into two well-greased and floured 8-inch cake pans. (You may also line the pans with wax paper cut to size to prevent sticking.) Bake for 25 minutes or until the cakes test done. Cool slightly and turn out the layers onto a rack. Cool completely before icing.

Icing

1 stick butter
½ cup heavy (whipping) cream
6-ounce package semisweet chocolate morsels
½ teaspoon instant coffee (optional)
1½ cups confectioner's sugar, sifted

Melt the butter, cream, and chocolate morsels in a double boiler or heavy-bottomed saucepan. Cool. Whisk in the confectioner's sugar until it reaches a desirable spreading consistency. Makes approximately 1½ cups.

Serves 8.

(Hazel Marie, the finished cake can be held in the refrigerator. When you're ready to serve it, warm each cake slice in the microwave just until the icing begins to melt. Serve with vanilla ice cream. If you like chocolate, and I know you do, you'll love this cake. Lillian just told me that it's the one she decided not to make while you were expecting. She was watching your weight and didn't want to tempt you.)

Well, that's it, and I say that with a great sigh of relief—not because it's been a burden but because there have been so many distractions to hinder me. But I hope that you will find these recipes helpful, and if you don't, that you will at least enjoy reading them and knowing that they were both given and collected with love.

Julia S. Murdoch

LuAnne's Helpful Household Hints

❧

LuAnne Conover showed up again at my house a week or so later, just when I thought my recipe project was over and done with. Having finished copying Lillian's recipes into the book, I was just about to wrap it for a formal presentation to Hazel Marie. To tell the truth, I was hoping that LuAnne had forgotten about her Helpful Household Hints, but she came bustling in, confident that Hazel Marie couldn't run a house without her help.

"Now, Julia," she said, "you don't need to rewrite any of this. You can copy it all into your book just as I have it, and I want Hazel Marie to know every word came from me."

I glanced at the notes, handwritten on her personal stationery, and assured her that I wouldn't dream of changing anything. "In fact," I said, "I'll put your name at the top of the page."

That was because I didn't want Hazel Marie to think they were my recommendations. Sometimes LuAnne gets carried away, and this was one of those times.

After looking over what she gave me, I said, "LuAnne, Hazel Marie doesn't play bridge. She doesn't know how, and, besides, bridge parties aren't as popular as they used to be."

"Oh, Julia, bridge is just an *example*. Now, listen," she went on, "I wrote these just as they occurred to me, so they're not in any particular order. But that just makes them more interesting, don't you think?"

Glancing farther down the list of Helpful Household Hints, I wondered if, in spite of my promise to keep them as written, I could safely omit a few that were over the top. Hazel Marie was so naïve about many things that she might take them to heart and try to follow them to the letter. Maybe I could get away with a little judicious editing.

⚬⚬⚬

Keep a guest book on a hall table, so you'll always have a record of who visits and who doesn't.

⚬⚬⚬

Always stay abreast of your social obligations. If someone asks you to a party, a dinner, or whatever, you must return the favor. It is not necessary, however, to return tit for tat. For instance, you may be invited to a dinner party, but that doesn't mean that you have to have your hosts for dinner as well. It is perfectly acceptable to invite them to a bridge party or something similar.

⚬⚬⚬

When you decide to have a dinner party, invite only as many people as your dining table will seat comfortably. You may think that is self-evident, but you'd be surprised at the hostesses who will seat eight in the dining room, then have a card table for four in the living room. That's like discrimination or something, and it's no fun to be cut off from the main party.

⚬⚬⚬

Anyway, when you plan a dinner party, you would be smart to plan some other event for the day after—like maybe an afternoon tea. And if you're really smart, you'll plan something else on the day following that, like maybe a small luncheon. That way, you only have to clean your house real good one time. You'll have your good china out and your silver polished, ready to use, and your flower arrangements should hold up for three days. You'll be killing three birds with one stone, and get a lot of paying back done in one fell swoop.

⌒⌒

Afternoon teas or morning coffees are excellent ways to fulfill your obligations. You can invite those people you owe, but who you don't feel especially close to or don't even like. It's easier to entertain them in a crowd of women who'll stand around and talk over each other than it is to have them at your table, where you actually have to make conversation with them.

⌒⌒

Remember that it is an honor to be asked to pour at a tea or coffee, so you should ask someone special to do it. It can be your closest friend or the minister's wife or anyone else except the honoree, if you have one. The honoree should be at the door with you to greet guests as they arrive.

⌒⌒

Whenever you use your good silver, be sure to count each piece as you wash it afterward. If you're missing a piece, look through the garbage before throwing it out. Chances are the missing spoon will be there, or else in the laundry, along with the table linens.

⌒⌒

You should hand-wash your good silver, especially the knives, because the heat in the dishwasher will loosen the silver handles from the blades.

⌒⌒

Whenever you receive a wedding invitation, it's a good idea to send the bride a piece of her silver or, if she's especially close, a place setting. As a general rule, if she doesn't get all her silver as wedding gifts, she may never get it.

It's also a good idea to select a silver pattern for each of your daughters while they're young. That way, you can add a piece over the years on their birthdays and at Christmas. By the time they're engaged to marry, they could have complete sets. I realize that many young women these days don't even list a silver pattern with department stores, preferring instead an everyday pattern in silver plate. They are making a bad mistake, especially if they marry well and are expected to entertain with some formality.

❧

Watch the January white sales. Neiman Marcus calls them "pink sales," so don't get confused. If you'll buy one sheet set every January or so, you'll always have decent linens and save yourself some money, too.

❧

Keep several cans of tuna in your pantry, and you will always have a meal in the making—tuna salad, tuna sandwiches, creamed tuna, or tuna casserole. If Mr. Pickens doesn't like tuna, don't tell him what it is.

❧

You should keep a shelf or drawer somewhere just for gifts to have on hand for somebody's birthday that sneaks up on you or a last-minute hostess gift or something like that. Keep wrapping paper, Scotch tape, and so forth with them, so you're always prepared. Get in the habit of watching for sales so you can buy items for your gift drawer ahead of time. I always start my Christmas shopping early—at least by the end of summer, when there are a lot of sales.

❧

Get your children on a schedule and keep them on it, especially at bedtime. Don't invite guests for an evening affair until your children know how to behave. There is nothing worse than to be invited to a home where the parents allow their children to run through the house, screaming like wild Indians so you can't hear yourself think.

❧

Keep a box of Arm & Hammer baking soda near your stove. If you ever have a grease fire, throw some on it and it will put out the fire. Throw the baking soda, not the box.

❧

An open box of baking soda (not baking powder) should be kept in your refrigerator to take care of any odors.

❧

Keep extra candles and batteries of all sizes on hand and in a special place so you can find them in case of a power failure.

❧

Change the batteries in your smoke alarm and your carbon monoxide alarm when Daylight Savings Time switches back to regular time. That'll be sometime in October, I think.

❧

Which reminds me. Buy Halloween trick-or-treat candy a little at a time—every time you go to the grocery store for a few weeks beforehand. And, if I were you, I wouldn't go overboard in decorating the front of the house for Halloween. It just encourages children to ring your doorbell.

❧

Whenever you make a casserole or something like spaghetti sauce, double the recipe and put half in the freezer. There will be times you won't want to cook, so it's nice to have something already made. Of course, you will have James cooking for you, so tell him to keep the freezer stocked. He might not always be there.

❧

Never go to the grocery store hungry—you'll buy too much. On the other hand, if you go right after you've eaten, you won't buy enough and you'll be going back several times a week. The best thing to do is make a list of what you need and stick to it.

❧

I know Julia has told you this, but it's worth repeating. Always have two CCC suits—one for summer and one for winter—cleaned and ready to wear with all their accessories. A CCC suit is one that is appropriate for Church, Country Club, and Cemetery, so that you're prepared for any church service, dinner party, or funeral. Black is the best color for meeting the requirements of each of the Cs—with, of course, suitable changes of shoes, jewelry, and tops for the occasion or the season. Décolletage is hardly appropriate for Sunday morning, much less for a funeral at any time.

❧

Whatever you do, don't get slack about your dinner table. Once you permit your children to eat by the television, they'll never learn any manners. They'll ruin your rugs and carpets, too. Teach them table manners early by setting a proper table and expecting them to learn which fork to use and to chew with their mouths closed. Use your good china, sterling, and crystal at least on holidays, until they're old enough to appreciate everyday use.

❧

Teach them also the correct way to cut meat with a knife and fork. Nothing says poor raising like clasping a fork upright in your fist and holding the meat like it's trying to get away from you.

And speaking of training children in the way they should go, little rhymes help to remind them. For instance, my children were trained to sit up straight and keep one hand in their laps by saying,

Mabel, Mabel, strong and able.
Get your elbows off the table.

There is also not one thing wrong with teaching children to say grace before they eat. A moment of prayer settles them down and makes for good digestion, besides teaching them to be thankful for what they have and especially for the hands that prepared it.

(Hazel Marie, this is a warning–LuAnne says she has a lot more helpful hints and will pass them along as soon as she thinks of them. So just thank her for her help, then do as you please. You know as much about gracious living as she does and probably more.)

List of Recipes

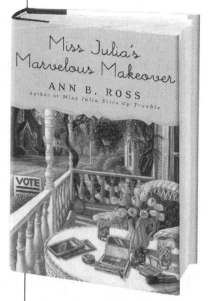

AVAILABLE FROM PENGUIN

Miss Julia to the Rescue
978-0-14-312281-4

Miss Julia Rocks the Cradle
978-0-14-312043-8

Miss Julia Renews Her Vows
978-0-14-311856-5

Miss Julia Delivers the Goods
978-0-14-311649-3

Miss Julia Paints the Town
978-0-14-311463-5

Miss Julia Strikes Back
978-0-14-311330-0

Miss Julia Stands Her Ground
978-0-14-303855-9

Miss Julia's School of Beauty
978-0-14-303670-8

Miss Julia Meets Her Match
978-0-14-303485-8

Miss Julia Hits the Road
978-0-14-200404-3

Miss Julia Throws a Wedding
978-0-14-200271-1

Miss Julia Takes Over
978-0-14-200089-2

PENGUIN BOOKS